Golden Prose
in the Age of Augustus

THE FOCUS CLASSICAL LIBRARY
Series Editors • James Clauss and Stephen Esposito

Golden Prose
in the Age of Augustus

PAUL T. ALESSI

ISBN 1-58510-125-7

10 9 8 7 6 5 4 3 2 1

CONTENTS

PREFACE

As in the case of my previous volume, *Golden Verses*, this book is designed for the general reading public and for students and teachers in courses on the literature of the Augustan Age. Although many anthologies exist that include one or two of the prose authors of the Augustan period, I do not know of any collection that concentrates solely on the writers in prose who belong strictly to the age. It is my hope that this volume, as the first, will fill a void and be useful in the classroom and be appealing to the public in its own right.

I have tried to offer translations that are accurate, idiomatic, and readable. They are for the most part literal, but not so literal as to be stilted or dry nor too free to frustrate the reader of Latin. I have felt that it is more important to keep the phraseology and metaphors—where possible—of the ancient author than to soar off into a faddish colloquial style filled with slangy expressions. I believe that readers want to feel as if they are encountering the words of the writer rather than the quirks and idiosyncrasies in phraseology of Alessi. Since it is impossible to reproduce the sounds of the original Latin in the English, in these translations I have striven to capture the tone of the original. I offer complete sections, books, or individual works, believing that a snippet here and there does not provide enough context and the proper "feel" of the author. Notes have been kept to a minimum. For the most significant names, places, and terms the reader is advised to consult the glossary. I hope that the modern readers of this volume can identify with the works and authors here presented and can feel for themselves the passions and emotions evoked by the words.

I would like to thank my colleague John Rundin and Ms. Linda Frausto for their assistance and Ms. Thu V. Cox for her patience. This book is dedicated to the memory of Theresa Lu Koch, devoted friend and helper.

INTRODUCTION

On 1 January, 42 BCE, the Senate of Rome voted divine honors to Gaius Iulius Caesar and vowed a temple to be built in the forum and dedicated to the new god, Divine Julius. His adopted grand-nephew Gaius Octavius, as recent triumvir, was instrumental in procuring and effecting these distinctions. This young man, now Caesar,[1] was not slow to claim that he was the son of a god. The coinage that he had minted and numerous inscriptions attest to the propagandistic value of Julius Caesar's deification. This young man had come a long way since the assassination of Julius Caesar on 15 March, 44 BCE. Indeed, barely twenty years old, he had achieved much and was an important political and military figure. He promoted his name and his background, two features that saved his life and helped win him allegiance and protection. His father, Gaius Octavius from Velitrae, a town about twenty-five miles southeast of Rome, had entered politics at Rome and achieved senatorial rank. He had married a certain Atia, the daughter of Marcus Atius Balbus and Julia, youngest sister of Gaius Iulius Caesar. For some reason Julius Caesar liked the young Octavius and showed to him a marked preference, introducing him to political and military life. At the time of Caesar's assassination Octavius was stationed in Apollonia, sent there by his great-uncle, to be trained in military tactics and strategy, and to complete his literary education. Caesar had chosen to include the young Octavius in his expected campaign against the Dacians and Parthia. But, March 44 changed all that and propelled Octavius on a course that was

---

1 Born Gaius Octavius, he became Gaius Iulius Caesar as soon as he was adopted. Writers of the period usually refer to him as Caesar or Octavius; modern scholars designate him as Octavian after his adoption. The honorific name Augustus was not bestowed upon him until January of 27 BCE.

to bring him to the pinnacle of power, to bring the Roman Republic to a close, and to make him a monarch overseeing the Roman Empire.

Although no one calculated the sudden arrival of Octavius into the political arena nor could have predicted the success that he was to enjoy, Cicero (*ad Att.* 14.12.2) notes his presence and is somewhat disquieted about the potential effect his entry could make. But, outside of Cicero, it is difficult to assess or to draw any conclusions about the kind and degree of Octavius' impact upon the politics of Rome. Our contemporary sources are few and scattered, and it is not until the late forties, as the *Eclogues* of Vergil abundantly show, that the literati begin to mention him. However, we do have the letters and orations of Cicero to consult; they provide much valuable information about Octavius' early period before he became a triumvir in November of 43 BCE and their presence helps make up the corpus of prose that punctuates the age of Augustus. Although it would be desirable to have more direct literary testimony and treatment of Octavius' (Augustus') history and life from contemporary witnesses, the age, nevertheless, does provide a wealth of material from a wide range of prose authors of varied political and literary tastes and diverse treatments of several genres. There are treatises on agriculture and architecture, biographies, histories, orations, letters, and an autobiography.

In general the works of the prose writers reflect two separate societal forces that shaped their themes and treatments: the turmoil of the late Republic that included the death of Julius Caesar with the resultant military and political struggle, and, secondly, the peace won and established by Octavian soon to be Augustus. In the former, civil war punctuated Roman life; a fierce rivalry between dynasts that seemed to repeat the partisan battles of Marius and Sulla, Pompey and Caesar, that engulfed citizens to fight against citizens, that rendered the rule of law and order virtually impossible, straining not only the Republican constitution but the nerves and will of the ruling class.[2] In the latter case, writers note and reflect upon the sense of relief from the wars, the constant recruiting, and the war-time demands upon the economy and psyche that depleted life and soul. In this arena the writers, like the winning survivor of the military and political battles, could turn attention back to ancestral mores and customs, re-instill a sense of purpose modeled upon the character and forms of the past, and herald ideals and values that resided deep

---

2 Since the expulsion of Lucius Tarquinius Superbus, the last king of Rome, in 509 BCE, Rome had been governed by elected magistrates. The highest office was the consulship shared by two men. Because it became the prerogative of leading members of the senatorial order, very few equestrians ever obtained this highest magistracy. The struggle for power by strong dynasts and generals in the Late Republic of the first century BCE weakened the control that the senatorial order had over the body politic.

in the Roman psyche. In this sense, Varro's treatise on agriculture and Livy's and Sallust's histories fit appropriately the Augustan program of renewal in the continuing values of the Republic, values and ideals heralded and observed as inherent in the yeoman farmer, in the pious man of manly courage, and in citizens willing to sacrifice on behalf of an idea larger than their individual selves.

AUGUSTUS

When Julius Caesar was assassinated on 15 March, 44 BCE, Gaius Octavius was not yet nineteen years old. No one could have predicted that he would eventually lend his name to a great era of military expansion, political success, and creative energy in the areas of art, architecture, and literature. And, it seems ironic that 2,000 years after his death we would be reading his own words as part of the literary scene of his age. But, that is exactly what chance has provided us. It has saved the autobiographical catalogue of his achievements which he had set up on bronze tablets in front of his mausoleum and had copies inscribed in stone in capitals of the Empire. As a literary form Augustus' *Res Gestae*, the usual title given to the document, has its antecedents in *elogia*, the inscriptional memorials that record the careers and achievements of famous men. Augustus had seen to the erection of such memorials in his Forum Augustum. In his own case he elaborated upon the genre with a grandiose and highly selective presentation of his virtues, achievements, and honors. The genre did not permit any outright falsification of fact, but in an autobiographical form such as this the author could present himself in the most favorable light, shape the account of events, and color the presentation and treatment. Much could be and was omitted. Octavius/Augustus did not provide the names of his political and military enemies: thus, Antony, for example, appears as a "faction." No mention is made of the Perusine War and its aftermath, nor is anything said about Octavian's role in the Battle of Mutina except that he became consul after it. The modern reader may be disappointed that Augustus did not present a comprehensive outline of his political positions and policies. However, the work was designed to show the people of Rome and to validate to them his preeminent status and merit. Little is stated or implied about his administrative reforms, his legislation, social or political, or his conscious attempts to revive traditional religious worship. Instead, there is an emphasis on his triumphs and successes in foreign policy that underscore the many honors which a grateful senate and Roman people bestowed upon him. Thus, Augustus included much routine matter, particularly covering the enormous expenditures that he made and incurred on behalf of the army and the people of the city. The work shows an accounting, a balancing of the books, as it were, of achievements and merited honors.

The style of the prose is not ornate. There are few rhetorical em-
bellishments in the relatively short sentences. Clarity dominates over
syntactical sophistication and complexity to such a degree that the style
often seems uninspired. Augustus does, however, emphasize himself
and the distinctive honors that he makes clear that he justly deserved.
Yet, the repetition of 'I' is never unreasonable—one would expect some
braggadocio in a genre of this type—and Augustus observes a sense of
propriety in his fluent and economic presentation. On the whole, the
simple and direct language leaves a positive feel and underscores Augustus' main purpose: to address the Roman people in a lucid apologia
consistent with his political, military, and social goals, messages, and
achievements.

CICERO

The details of Cicero's career are well-known. Born of the equestrian
class in 106 BCE at Arpinum, some ninety miles from Rome, he studied
law, literature, philosophy, and rhetoric in the capital city. His early career showed a distrust of the narrow social and political policies of the
senatorial order. In this regard he was not much different from other
equestrians who came from the Italian communities. In his first major
court case, the defense of Sextus Roscius, (80 BCE), he confronted Sulla's
freedman Chrysogonus and therein allusively censured Sulla's despotic
autocracy. In the following year Cicero expressed sympathy for many
Italian municipalities, such as Arezzo, which had been disenfranchised
so harshly by Sulla. In fact, most of Cicero's early political career consisted in opposing and protesting against senatorial irresponsibility and
corruption. The cases against Gnaeus Cornelius Dolabella and Gaius
Verres attest to the rampant abuse and oppression of the provinces. Yet,
Cicero could never openly support the political program of the *populares*,
the democratic faction that also promoted most of the interests of the
equestrian class. At the end of the 70s it seems that he refrained from
any active advocacy of Pompey's, Crassus', and Lucullus' positions and
measures that weakened the Sullan stranglehold on political reform.
Cicero did, however, endorse the change in the composition of the
criminal courts to include equestrians and wealthy plebeians along with
senators. He was lukewarm to reestablishing the powers of tribunes.
But he became enthusiastic in his advocacy of granting special powers
to Pompey for his campaigns against pirates in the Mediterranean and
for his command in the war against Mithradates and Tigranes. Cicero
saw Pompey as a champion of the cause of the equestrians and the best
possible choice to face the intransigence and narrow interests of the most
conservative elements of the senatorial order. He hoped for a coalition,
a union of equestrians and leading senators, and believed that despite

his inadequacies and egotism, Pompey should guide the coalition which he, Cicero, wanted fervently to help lead.

Cicero's own political career advanced after his successful prosecution of the corrupt senator Verres. A number of factors conspired to bring Cicero to the pinnacle of his political ambition, the election to the consulship for 63 BCE: the success of Pompey who was backed by equestrians and *populares* at the expense of the conservatives; the political vacuum created by Pompey's absence; some high-profile court cases involving extortion and consular misconduct; and the entry of Lucius Sergius Catiline, a bankrupt noble, into the political arena to vie for the consulship. Cicero's competition for the office was weak, and nasty rumors of extreme political activity and corruption concerning Catiline and Gaius Antonius, who were obviously being supported by the *populares*, turned even the most conservative wing of the senatorial class to support Cicero. Although he lacked the high birth and usual connections of the nobles, Cicero won on his personal popularity and merit, coupled with the outside factors mentioned above.

The year 63 BCE, the year of Cicero's consulship, marked a watershed in his public career. His quashing and adroit handling of Catiline's conspiracy won him fame and respect. His ideal of the "agreement of orders" (*concordia ordinum*) seemed to have come to fruition during his political watch. He was appreciated—but not beloved—by most of the nobles. The fear of revolution and violent extremism created a backlash and drove many to back senatorial government. To Cicero good politics meant not the trust directed to the masses with their popular demands and egalitarian policies nor the reliance on the narrow interests of a clique of powerful senators. He wanted a middle course, a policy that protected the rights and interests of the equestrians throughout Italy, a person or persons able to control the growing power of the army and to provide proper checks upon both revolutionary activity and reactionary designs. It was an ideal that was impossible to achieve and eventually marginalized Cicero's political influence.

When extremists in the senate frustrated Pompey after his return to Rome from his Eastern campaigns, Pompey was willing to join in political alliance with the *populares*. A loose coalition of Julius Caesar, Pompey, and Marcus Crassus managed to wrest control of the state from the dominance of senatorial conservatives. Although courted and flattered, Cicero refused to join this new union. His decision, made on principle, was to affect the course of the rest of his life. He could not in all good conscience abandon his cherished ideal of the independent moderate, nor, in his mind, stoop to support the causes, sometimes unscrupulous, of the *populares*, even if his political champion Pompey had joined them. And, when he was exiled from the city, Cicero saw that his banishment was the direct result of decisions and policies of the 'popular' faction of government. Thus, it was going to be difficult for him to trust ever again those politicians whom he perceived to be supporters and promoters of the cause and politics of a Caesar. It is no surprise then that Cicero was cool to the machinations of the so-called First Triumvirate and that he tried to disrupt and weaken its powers by actively supporting the conservatives in the senate, the most potent opposition to the programs and designs of the *populares*. Nor is it surprising that Cicero would lend his effort to dissolving the political union of Caesar and Pompey. When the split finally materialized, Cicero joined the Pompeians and looked upon Caesar as a criminal despot. He could never reconcile himself again to the popular cause even though he feared violence and tyranny from Pompey and the nobles. He also often disagreed with their tactics and their designs.

After the victory of Caesar over the Pompeians Cicero played only a small role in the public life of Rome. Marcus Antonius (Antony) had become Caesar's assistant and his powerful organizer and enforcer. Cicero had hoped that after the period of clemency Caesar would return the state to its traditional republican norms. He was disappointed that Caesar had maintained the office of dictator and for several years ahead had appointed consuls. Antony had been selected for 44 BCE. The Ides of March of that year briefly gave Cicero hope that the conspirators who had assassinated Caesar on that date could reestablish the Republic under control of the senate. But events and individuals conspired to frustrate Cicero's hope and expectations, primarily Antony's quick action to defuse the volatile atmosphere and his energetic exercise of his office. Then entered Gaius Octavius, who had been adopted and named heir in Caesar's will. When Octavius visited Cicero in Campania in April on his way to Rome to claim his inheritance, Cicero reacted with lukewarm congeniality. His early exultation over Caesar's assassination soon turned sour; he thought that Octavius could be used to counterbalance the power of Antony and Dolabella, the two consuls, and of Marcus Aemilius Lepidus, and that he could be manipulated in service of *some* of his and the senate's political maneuvers.

In the meanwhile, Cicero devoted himself to his studies and writing. He found it difficult to exercise any power or persuasion to influence deeply the twists and vicissitudes of the politics in Rome. The cause espoused by the conspirators was going nowhere and supporters of it lacked sufficient troops to make an impact, much less a strong statement, upon the numerous political factions with military backing. In this vacuum Octavius' popularity was growing. He had gained support among many veterans of Caesar's legions and in July he celebrated games in honor Caesar's victories. During that summer of 44 BCE Cicero spent most of his time in Campania. He entertained friends and political allies, including Brutus. After deciding to leave for Athens to visit his son and after receiving a privileged commission to leave Italy, he set out. He made it to Syracuse, but was forced to return to Italy. A second meeting with Brutus provided him with the latest political news and from it he learned the designs of the various political parties concerned. Cicero then decided to return to Rome. Although he arrived on 31 August, he skipped the meeting of the senate convened by Antony on the next day. On the following day, 2 September, Cicero addressed the senate in Antony's absence, delivering the so-called first *Philippic* in which he severely indicted Antony's recent political maneuvering and policy. Thus began the feud that was to lead ultimately to Cicero's death in December of 43, a victim of the proscriptions perpetrated by the triumvirs,[3] and was to draw Cicero nearer to the designs and position of Octavian. Cicero's intense dislike and fear of Antony prompted him first to advocate and then to support the claims of Octavian, even though some were unprecedented or illegal. Some scholars (e.g., Syme) have maintained that Cicero's actions and energetic support of Octavian in order to nullify Antony's power helped bring down his beloved Republican constitution that he professed to be preserving. Cicero's many letters sent to friends, foes, and acquaintances, from his gloating over the assassination of Julius Caesar to the final attested one to Plancus (*ad Fam.* 10.24) of late July, 43, affirm Cicero's growing reliance and hope that he (mis)placed upon Octavian. Marcus Brutus was not deceived and he complained that Cicero was being hoodwinked into thinking that Octavian would save the Republic (*ad Brutum* 1.16 and 17) and would restore the senate to political prominence and control over the state. The *Philippics* and the letters not only provide details of the historical record of that transitional period from 15 March, 44 to the creation of Octavian as consul, before he was twenty years old, but also illuminate the personalities, feelings, and motives of the participants involved in Octavian's rise to power.

SALLUST

We have little reliable information about the life and career of Gaius Sallustius Crispus. Born at Amiternum about fifty miles northeast of Rome in Sabine territory, Sallust died in 35 or 34 BCE a few years before war was declared against Cleopatra, the war that settled the political and military issue between Mark Antony and Octavian. This conflict between the two dynasts had been simmering and had been close to open hostilities for some time. Sallust's personal involvement in one civil war, that of Pompey and Julius Caesar, and his presence at the formation of the Second Triumvirate gave him a special vantage point to reflect upon the state of Roman politics and history.

---

3 Cicero's head and hands were cut off and were displayed on the rostra in the forum.

Sallust first comes to our notice as a tribune of 52. It is probable that a few years before that time he was a quaestor. Sallust attempted to bring about the condemnation of Titus Annius Milo who was being defended by Cicero on a charge of murdering Publius Clodius. It is most likely that Sallust's political actions led to his censure and expulsion from the senate in 50. Shortly afterward Sallust transferred to Caesar's camp and became an officer in Caesar's legions in Illyria. After serving in various campaigns—not all of them successfully—he was elected praetor in 46 and capably performed his duties during Caesar's African campaign. He was rewarded for his services by being appointed the first governor of Africa Nova with the rank of proconsul. Tradition relates that Sallust so misgoverned and plundered the province that he was charged with malfeasance and that only lavish bribery caused the charge to be dropped. There is no doubt that he amassed a huge fortune, enough to buy and maintain the extensive gardens that bear his name (*Horti Sallustiani*) and which later passed into the hands of Roman emperors. Somehow he survived the turmoil of the months following the assassination of Julius Caesar and the proscriptions. He then devoted himself to his writings, producing three historical works: two monographs, *The Conspiracy of Catiline (Bellum Catilinae)* and *The War with Jugurtha (Bellum Iugurthinum)*, and a history *(Historiae)* of which only fragments remain extant and which was left incomplete.

Published sometime between 43 and 40, the two monographs are not presented in an annalistic form but focus on analysis of character, on motive, and on lively description. These emphases frame a moral outlook of the events and characters presented. With powerful and highly polished speeches cast in the style of Thucydides, the works take on vivid dramatic features which are enhanced by Sallust's own terse style, a penchant for obscure words, sometimes poetical or archaic, a deliberate and compressed inconcinnity, a choice of variation in grammatical expression, and a love of antithesis. Sallust seems to make every effort to avoid the periodic structure that one finds in oratory. His terseness and lack of syntactical symmetry contrast sharply with the copious and graceful expressions of Cicero and Livy. He was well appreciated in antiquity, for Tacitus later successfully adapted Sallust's style.

Sallust had a rather bleak view of Roman history. He believed that foreign conquest and empire had introduced corrupting influences and changes into the political and social fabric of Rome. He particularly concerned himself with the decline of the ruling elite. He often railed against incompetent, venal aristocrats whose misuse of power prevents capable men from forwarding and assisting the state and the people. Within the moralizing of the two proemia of the two works is embedded Sallust's view on the destructive result of the power wielded by a few. His sentiments could not have escaped the notice of the triumvirs; nor could a reader have failed to draw the parallel of Catiline, of the pusillanimous and venal nobles of the earlier period, with the contemporary dynasts vying for power. It is a wonder that the outspoken Sallust was allowed to voice his strong opinions about the Roman ruling class and its ambitious politicians.

CORNELIUS NEPOS

Born in Cisalpine Gaul around 110 BCE, Cornelius Nepos took up residence in Rome and circulated among the intelligentsia of his day. He was a witness to Rome's numerous civil wars of the first century, its two proscriptions, and the rise of dynasts that culminated in the principate of Octavian Augustus. He knew Catullus, Cicero, and Titus Pomponius Atticus well. He devoted his life to literary pursuits undisturbed by political ambitions and the turmoil of the times. Although he was prolific in writing, producing a universal history (*Chronica*) in three books—which Catullus alludes to—and five books of moral anecdotes, and a work on geography, only a few biographical sketches remain of sixteen books entitled *On Famous Men*. The extant biographies include nineteen of famous Greeks, one of the Persian Datames, a sketch from Hamilcar Barca, a portrait of Hannibal, and only two lives of Romans: a very brief—and disappointing—presentation of Cato, supposedly drawn from a fuller treatment, and his best writing on Atticus; he also produced a short treatise *On Kings*.

As an historical source Nepos shows major deficiencies; he sometimes misuses his sources and is uncritical; he is lacking in intellectual depth. Yet, as a biographer he has some merit despite the shallow and undiscriminating treatment of individual lives. He enthusiastically looks for traits of character, incidents, and mannerisms. He sympathizes with the historical figures and customs of foreigners. For example, his *Hannibal* and *Alcibiades* humanize two men demonized as villains in the eyes of the Romans. Although his intellectual shortcomings are obvious, occasionally he shows sound judgment and perspicuity. He notes, for example, the historical and social value of Cicero's *Letters* (*Att.* 16.3).

In style Nepos is terse. His simple sentences often appear jerky and lead to some obscurities. His common and colloquial diction crowds upon some archaic language. He is fond of alliteration and antitheses.

MARCUS TERENTIUS VARRO

The sources of Varro's life provide evidence that he was born at or near Reate in Sabine country in 116 BCE. He had a distinguished political and military career, winning the office of praetor and serving under Pompey first in Spain during the war against Sertorius and again in Pompey's operations of 67 against the pirates harassing the Mediterranean. In the civil war between Caesar and Pompey he joined Pompey.

After Pharsalus, the site of Pompey's defeat, he received pardon from Caesar. Although he was proscribed in 43 by the Second Triumvirate, he escaped with his life but lost much of his property and his library at Casinum (Cassino). For the rest of his life he devoted himself to his studies and prolific writing. Much like Nepos he had lived through the turbulent period of the late Republic to see the ascendance of Octavian/Augustus. For a man of action who had a significant and continuing role in the political and military life of the city, it is truly remarkable to have completed over 600 books on a vast range of subjects. He was the leading scholar of his day and his literary achievement astounded his contemporaries. Only six books of twenty-five survive from his work *On the Latin Language (De Lingua Latina)*; his treatise on agriculture (*De Re Rustica*) in three books has come down virtually intact, and we have some 600 fragments of 150 books of humorous Menippean satire, a form that mixed prose and poetry. For the rest of his *oeuvre* we possess only tantalizing fragments from later writers that attest to Varro's great learning, varied interests, and his appreciation of antiquarian lore and cultural histories.

His treatise on agriculture is set in dialogue form. Each book is addressed to a different person with a different dramatic setting, and different sets of speakers and participants. For example, Book I is addressed to his wife Fundania and involves some pleasant banter between characters whose suggestive names relate them to the country and farm. In the third book the speakers are awaiting returns for the elections of aediles. In their conversation they treat, among other topics, game and fish preserves, nurseries, plantations, and aviaries, a topic which leads naturally to a discourse on bees. Within the treatise Varro invokes native gods (*Di Consentes*), praises Italy and the life of the farmer which he sees as honorable and admirable, the backbone of Roman and Italian life and patriotism. He sometimes overly analyzes his subjects; for example, he breaks down agriculture into four main categories, each with two subcategories; unfortunately this methodology is not always synthesized. Nor does Varro's style help clear away ambiguities and complexities. Sometimes the systematic scholarship produces a pedantic and wearisome taste. His dialogues are ponderous and mannered in comparison with the penetrating characterization of Cicero's mature work. Despite the enormous scholarship and erudition the style fails to inspire and elevate the thinking beyond compilation. Although Varro attempts to alleviate technical matters with dialogue, moral comment, or fanciful derivations, almost always incorrect, the style remains somewhat cumbersome. Yet the treatise on agriculture became an influential work. Vergil learned from it and in the next century Columella depended upon it. It would be difficult to imagine advancement in so many scholarly areas during and after the Augustan age without the enormous contributions and achievements of the "most erudite of Romans" as Quintilian characterized him.

VITRUVIUS POLLIO

Most of what we know of Vitruvius is gleaned from his surviving work, a treatise in ten books, *On Architecture*. He was an architect who served under Julius Caesar and became Octavian's/Augustus' chief military engineer. His work deals with both architecture and engineering and contains treatments of various branches of science and philosophy. It has been stated that the treatise is a book designed for people who want or need to understand architecture and its related fields. The first seven books deal with architectural building, the nature of architecture, materials, temple construction and form, fora, theaters, baths, houses, basilicas, and decoration. The last three concentrate on water supply, geometry, the science of sundials, and lastly, military machinery. The sections on materials (Book II) and methods of construction (Book VII) are very valuable. Vitruvius is enthusiastic in his presentation of a technical subject. He wanted to anchor his subject and its art on its philosophy and history. The amount and breadth of training that he maintains necessary for understanding and practicing the art and science of architecture are formidable and mind-boggling. It is difficult to ascertain to what depth he understood the many Greek authors whom he acknowledges, but it is clear that his knowledge of the subject—which is considerable—did not solely depend upon synthesizing Latin authors like Varro and Publius Septimius. His work, coupled with the early output of Celsus in medicine, Varro in numerous fields of scholarship, and the treatises of those productive in the area of grammar, signals a desire to challenge and match the vast encyclopedic scholarship of Greece. The prolific efforts of Varro and Cicero had begun the trend toward technical subjects that the age of Augustus fostered and welcomed.

Vitruvius, however, does not allow the technical aspects of his work to dominate so entirely as to bore his general readers. Much incidental information and absorbing sketches pepper the oeuvre, such as his treatment on the origin of building by primitive peoples, his critical remarks on current styles of painting, and his criticisms of gaudy excess observable in the decoration of fashionable houses. His prefaces, too, although somewhat talkative, display some personal touches and warm, human sentiment. His style is imperfect. He himself admits to the difficulty that he had in writing. He shows a tendency to use Grecisms and makes some mistakes in the use of moods. Sometimes it seems that the demands of the technical subject matter overwhelms clarity of expression.

LIVY

Tradition posits that Titus Livius (Livy) lived from 59 BCE to 17 CE, roughly the same years and span of Octavian Augustus himself. He was a native of Patavium (the modern Padua) which may have affected his views on the political state and social fabric of Rome and, especially, of Italy. There is some evidence that Patavium was anti-Caesarean and acted against Antony during the late forties. Livy was acquainted with Augustus who later teased him with the epithet "Pompeyite." Exactly when he began his great work on Roman history [the traditional title is *Ab Urbe Condita*] is not certain. It is now generally thought that the vast project was begun not too long after Actium (31 BCE) and that because of the direct reference to Caesar Augustus (1.19), the title conferred upon Octavian by the senate in January of 27, the first installments were produced in that year. The history comprised 142 books of which only books 1-10 and 21-45 survive. Only a couple of the books in the oeuvre lack epitomies, synopses that serve as guides to the proportion of the events. It may have been a calculated and prudent act of Livy to have suppressed the publication of the last twenty-two books, which treated the Augustan period from 43 to 9 BCE, until after the death of Augustus in 14 CE. In that way Livy could have expressed some criticism and treated areas that Augustus would have gladly wished away.

But the guiding ideas of Livy's voluminous subject converge with many of the Augustan themes and values. For example, Augustus' cardinal virtues such as *auctoritas* (honored prestige), *pietas* (familial and religious devotion), *iustitia* (sense of justice), and *virtus* (manly courage) are evident in the characters drawn and treated by Livy. The traditional morals and values that Augustus sought to restore resonate in the author's moral outlook. In Livy's view the past was, indeed, different from the present. A simple solution to regeneration and moral change was not easy but the events and characters embedded in the memory of the Roman people and in their history provided paradigms to emulate and to avoid. In tracing the rise of Rome to its mastery of the Mediterranean litoral Livy emphasizes the moral qualities of a people and of extraordinary individuals who brought military success against strong foes and who oversaw unprecedented expansion of Rome. Although to his way of thinking his day was in moral decline, yet he believed it was possible to regenerate, if not the same avatars of virtue, then at least the spirit of virtuous action and character that resided in the heroes of old.

Livy's approach to history and his personal beliefs in Roman virtues have produced a curious work. His methodology was to follow one historian for a particular period, theme, or event. After he completed his presentation of that section, another source was taken up for another theme and treatment. Sometimes Livy failed to account for the personal biases of the sources, which produce a coloring of events and personality in his own work. Livy's own bias toward the senate prejudiced him against the tribunes and their aims. His patriotism limited and rendered him less than kind toward Rome's enemies. He stereotyped foreigners and displayed an open distrust of foreign culture and ideas. In fact, his interest in foreign cultures was slight at best. We regret that Livy did not quote directly from documents and that he did not discuss constitutional problems nor delve very deeply into domestic issues and conflicts. To Livy Roman history served a didactic purpose; human behavior and conduct, noble or ignoble, provided instructive models.

The first book of the corpus shows a very poetic style and coloring. Archaisms abound. There is a lively narrative punctuated by dramatic speeches of central characters who are often depicted in a tragic way. The diction of the speeches is far ranging and varied. The work as a whole progresses to a more rhetorical and periodic style that approaches the abundant sweep of Cicero, although differing in syntax. Subordinate clauses skillfully woven together, intricate variety in construction, and a rich vocabulary attest to Quintilian's assessment of his "milky richness" and "indescribable eloquence." And throughout the corpus Livy sustains a certain dignity and energy. This energy produced a monumental achievement in the prose of the era and marks a remarkable talent in historical narrative, vivid character-drawing, and intricate phrasing and structure.

CHRONOLOGY

753 BCE	Traditional date of the founding of Rome
753-509	Monarchy; the seven kings of Rome
509	Expulsion of Tarquin the Proud; Lucius Iunius Brutus and Lucius Tarquinius Collatinus first elected consuls
509-27	Republic of Rome
451-449	The Twelve Tables, Rome's first law code
396-394	Veii besieged, captured, and destroyed by Marcus Furius Camillus
390 or 387	Sack of Rome by Gauls
343-341	First War with Samnites
327-304	Second War with Samnites
298-290	Third War with Samnites
280-275	War with Pyrrhus of Epirus who invaded Italy
264-241	First Punic War with Carthage
240-207	Livius Andronicus, founder of Latin Literature, active
218-201	Second Punic War with Carthage
213-211	Roman siege of Syracuse; victories of Marcus Claudius Marcellus
212-205	First Macedonian War with Philip V
202	Publius Cornelius Scipio defeats Hannibal at Zama
200-197	Second Macedonian War with Philip V
191-188	War with Antiochus III, Hellenistic king of Syria
188-183	War between Prusias I of Bithynia and Eumenes II of Pergamum
184	Cato the Elder is censor
183/182	Death of Hannibal
171-167	Third Macedonian War with Perses
149-146	Third Punic War with Carthage; Publius Cornelius Scipio (Aemilianus) destroys Carthage

148-146	Fourth Macedonian War; Corinth destroyed; Macedonia becomes a Roman province
133-121	The Gracchi brothers active in Rome
116	Birth of Marcus Terentius Varro
112-105	War with Jugurtha of Numidia
110	Birth of Cornelius Nepos; birth of Titus Pomponius Atticus
107-100	Gaius Marius consul six times
106	Birth of Cicero
91-88	War with Italian allies
88-82	Rome's first Civil War between "Marians" and "Sullans"
82-80	Dictatorship of Sulla
78	Death of Sulla
73-71	Slave revolt of Spartacus
70	Consulship of Marcus Licinius Crassus and Gnaeus Pompeius (Pompey)
63	Consulship of Marcus Tullius Cicero; the conspiracy of Catiline; Julius Caesar elected pontifex maximus; birth of Gaius Octavius (Augustus)
60	Formation of the First Triumvirate of Caesar, Pompey, and Crassus
59	Consulship of Julius Caesar; birth of Livy
49	Caesar crosses Rubicon; Civil War between Pompey and Caesar begins
48	Pompey defeated at Pharsalus and killed in Egypt
48-44	Caesar victorious over remaining opponents; dictatorship of Caesar
44	Assassination of Caesar on 15 March; Gaius Octavius designated Caesar's heir; *Philippic* I delivered 2 September; publication of *Philippic* II in October
43	Battle of Mutina and the deaths of the consuls Hirtius and Pansa; Mark Antony, Gaius Octavius, and Marcus Aemilius Lepidus form the Second Triumvirate; death of Cicero on 7 December
43/42	Publication of Sallust's *Conspiracy of Catiline*
42	Brutus and Cassius defeated at Philippi; the settlement of soldiers on confiscated land
41	The siege of Perugia by Octavius
41/40	Publication of Sallust's *War with Jugurtha*
41-30	Mark Antony's relationship with Cleopatra
40	Mark Antony marries Octavia, sister of Octavian
38	Octavian marries Livia
38/37	Triumvirate renewed at Tarentum
37	Publication of Varro's *De Re Rustica* (*On Agriculture*)

35/34	Death of Sallust
34	Cornelius Nepos' *On Famous Men* published
32	Death of Atticus
31	Battle of Actium
31-23	Consecutive consulships of Octavian/Augustus
30	Mark Antony and Cleopatra commit suicide
29	Octavian celebrates a triple triumph
28	Dedication of the Temple of Apollo on the Palatine
27	Octavius receives the name of Augustus; beginning of the Empire; Agrippa builds the first Pantheon; death of Varro; second edition of Nepos' "life of Atticus"
27-25	First decade of Livy's *History of Rome* published
27-20	Vitruvius publishes *On Architecture*
26	Disgrace and suicide of Gaius Cornelius Gallus
24	Death of Cornelius Nepos
23	Augustus given renewable "tribunician power"
20	The return of Roman standards by the Parthians lost by Crassus in 53 and Antony in 36
12	Death of Agrippa
8	Deaths of Maecenas and Horace
2	Exiling of Julia, Augustus' daughter; dedication of the Temple of Mars Ultor
4 CE	Augustus adopts Tiberius Claudius Nero , the son of Livia
14	Death of Augustus; Tiberius becomes the second Emperor of Rome
17	Death of Livy

Central Italy

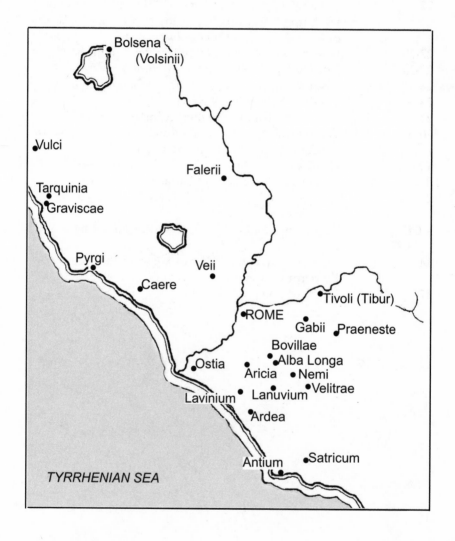

Bolsena (Volsinii)

Vulci

Falerii

Tarquinia
Graviscae

Pyrgi

Veii

Caere

Tivoli (Tibur)

ROME

Gabii Praeneste

Bovillae

Ostia

Alba Longa

Aricia Nemi

Lavinium

Lanuvium

Velitrae

Ardea

Antium

Satricum

TYRRHENIAN SEA

Italy

Greece
and Aegean Sea

MACEDONIA

Philippi

SAMOTHRACE

HELLESPONT

Apollonia

CHALCIDICE

Abytus

Acroceraunia

Mount
Olympus

Troy

Oricos

EPIRUS

LEMNOS

Dodona

LESBOS

AEGEAN SEA

THESSALY

EUBOEA

Actium

CHIOS

AETOLIA

BOEOTIA

Chalcis

Delphi

Thebes

Eretria

Eleusis

SAMOS

Megara

ACHAEA

Sicyon

Athens

Corinth

ARCADIA

Argos

DELOS

Olympia

CYCLADES

NAXOS

PELOPONNESUS

Sparta

IONIAN SEA

LACONIA

MELOS

THERA

Asia Minor during the Roman Empire

SCYTHIA

SARMATIA

GETAE

BLACK SEA

Danube R.

ARMENIA

THRACE   Byzantium

BITHYNIA   PONTUS

MACEDONIA

GALATIA

PARTHIAN
EMPIRE

COMMAGENE

PHRYGIA

Tigris R.

ACHAEA

Pergamum

LYCAONIA

LYDIA
Ephesus

Euphrates R.

LYCIA   CILICIA

Athens

SYRIA

Sparta

CYPRUS

Damascus

CRETE

MEDITERRANEAN SEA

JUDAEA

Jerusalem

Cyrene

Pelusium

Alexandria

ARABIA

PTOLEMAIC
KINGDOM

RES GESTAE

The so-called *monumentum Ancyranum* is without doubt one of the most important epigraphical documents that has survived classical antiquity. In his own words Augustus sets down and justifies what he believes to be the most significant of his political and military achievements. He glosses over the political machinations and brutal means by which he came to power in order to stress that it was by his *auctoritas* (authority, prestige) that the senate and people of Rome invested in him so much power and that allowed him to dominate and govern the Roman world. The style is deliberately unadorned and direct, as befits a document intended for the peoples of Rome, Italy, and the Empire.

Below is a copy of the achievements of the divine Augustus by which he subjected the world to the empire of the Roman people, and the expenses he incurred for the state and the Roman people as inscribed on two bronze pillars set up in Rome.[1]

(1) At the age of nineteen,[2] on my own initiative and at my own expense, I raised an army with which I championed the liberty of the state that had been oppressed by the tyranny of a faction.[3] For this rea-

---

1: Suetonius (*Aug.* 101.4) tells us that the document was set up in front of his mausoleum in Rome. Copies were also erected in provincial capitals, three of which exist in Asia Minor at Ancyra (modern Ankara), Antioch, and Apollonia in Pisidia

2: Octavius/Augustus proudly and emphatically heralds the age at which he led his first army. It is thought to intimate that he, Octavius, outdid Alexander the Great, whose first command was at twenty. The army to which he alludes came from some of Julius Caesar's veterans and those soldiers enticed from two of Antony's legions.

3: the reference is to Antony who was then consul, and to his supporters.

son the senate decreed me honors and co-opted me into its order, in the consulship of Gaius Pansa and Aulus Hirtius [43 BCE], according me the status of a consul with the right to give my opinion, and it granted me *imperium*.[4] It ordered me, together with the consuls, in the rank of a propraetor, to provide measures to protect the state from harm.[5] In the same year, when both consuls had died in war, the people appointed me consul and triumvir for regulating the government.[6]

(2) The assassins of my father[7] I drove into exile, avenging their crime at lawful trials with due process; and later I defeated them twice on the battle field,[8] when they brought war against the country.

(3) I waged many wars on land and sea, civil and foreign, all over the world, and as victor I spared all citizens who asked for pardon. The foreign peoples who could safely be pardoned I preferred to preserve rather then to extirpate. Roman citizens under military oath to me numbered about 500,000. Somewhat more than 300,000 of these I settled in colonies or sent back to their towns after they were honorably discharged. To all of them I assigned lands or bestowed money to reward their military service. I captured six hundred ships, excluding those smaller than triremes.[9]

(4) I twice celebrated an ovation and I was honored with three curule triumphs[10] and twenty-one times I was hailed *imperator*. All of the many more triumphs which the senate decreed to me, I refused. I deposited the laurels adorning my *fasces* in the Capitol, after fulfilling the vows I had publicly pronounced in each war. For the successful exploits accomplished by me or through my legates acting under my auspices, fifty-five times the senate decreed thanksgivings to the immortal gods. The days on which thanksgivings were given by decree of the senate numbered 890. In my triumphs nine kings or children of kings were paraded before my chariot.[11] At this writing I have been consul thirteen

---

4: on the motion of Cicero on 1 January, 43 Octavius' position was legalized.

5: this formula refers to the so-called "ultimate decree of the senate" that, in effect, proclaimed martial law, also passed on 1 January, 43.

6: the triumvirate of Octavius, Antony, and Marcus Aemilius Lepidus was legalized by the *lex Titia*, passed in November of 43.

7: an allusion to Julius Caesar, Octavius' adoptive father. In this document Augustus neither names nor mentions his natural father or mother.

8: the two battles of Philippi in 42 against the forces of Brutus and Cassius.

9: the 600 war ships captured in naval victories over Sextus Pompey off the coast of Sicily and over Antony and Cleopatra at Actium in 31.

10: the triple triumph of 13-15 August, 29 celebrated victories in Dalmatia, at Actium, and in Egypt.

11: included in this number were the two small children of Antony and Cleopatra, Alexander Helios (Sun) and Cleopatra Selene (Moon).

times and I am in the thirty-seventh year of tribunician power.[12]

(5) The dictatorship offered to me both in my absence and in my presence, both by the people and the senate, in the consulship of Marcus Marcellus and Lucius Arruntius [22 BCE], I did not accept. However, I did not decline, during an acute shortage of grain, the administration of the grain supply which I directed in such a manner that within a few days I freed the entire citizenry from fear and immediate danger at my own expense and by my own attention. The consulship also offered to me at that time to be held annually and in perpetuity, I refused.

(6) In the consulship of Marcus Vinicius and Quintus Lucretius [19 BCE], and later of Publius Lentulus and Gnaeus Lentulus [18 BCE], and a third time of Paullus Fabius Maximus and Quintus Tubero [11 BCE], the senate and Roman people agreed that I be appointed the sole supervisor of the laws and morals with supreme power,[13] but I did not accept any office offered to me contrary to the custom of our ancestors. The programs the senate proposed me to undertake, I carried out through the tribunician power. To share that power five times I voluntarily requested and received from the senate a colleague.[14]

(7) I was triumvir for regulation of the state for ten consecutive years.[15] Up to the day of this writing I have been the president of the senate for forty years.[16] I have been *Pontifex Maximus*, augur, member of the Board of Fifteen for Conducting Sacrifices, member of the Board of Seven in charge of Public Feasts, Arval brother, *Sodalis Titius*, and Fetial.[17]

(8) When I was the consul for the fifth time [29 BCE], by order of the people and the senate, I increased the number of patricians. I revised the roster of the senate three times, and in my sixth consulship [28 BCE] I conducted with my colleague Marcus Agrippa a census of the people

---

12: Augustus assumed this annual power in 23 from which he often dates his term of power. He was consul in the following years: 43, 33, 31, 30, 29, 28, 27, 26, 25, 24, 23, 5, and 2. He held the office in 5 and 2 in order to introduce his grandsons by Agrippa, Gaius and Lucius, to public life.

13: in some capacity Augustus was granted or exercised the power of the censor.

14: he refers first to Marcus Vipsanius Agrippa, his son-in-law and presumed successor, two times a colleague, and then to Tiberius, his heir, three times a colleague.

15: the triumvirate was legalized as a five-year term; it was renewed for a second five-year period in 38.

16: a Republican title given to a distinguished member who was the first to be asked his opinion in the deliberations of the senate.

17: subsequent Roman emperors held the first four of these seven priestly offices listed here. Augustus is proud, boasting of serving in these 'colleges' of which, in Republican times, a pre-eminent person normally held only one or, possibly, two.

and I performed a *lustrum* after a lapse of forty-two years. At that *lustrum* 4,063,000 Roman citizens were assessed. Then a second time with consular power I performed the *lustrum* alone, in the consulship of Gaius Censorinus and Gaius Asinius [8 BCE]; at that *lustrum* 4,233,000 citizens were registered. And a third time, with consular power and with my son Tiberius Caesar as colleague, in the consulship of Sextus Pompeius and Sextus Appuleius [14 CE], I performed the *lustrum* at which were assessed 4,937,000 Roman citizens. I sponsored and promulgated new laws to restore many traditions of our ancestors which were becoming obsolete in our generation, and I myself handed down traditions exemplary in many areas for imitation by future generations.

(9) The senate decreed that vows for my good health be undertaken every five years by the consuls and priests. To fulfill these vows games frequently were held in my lifetime, sometimes by the four most prestigious colleges of priests, sometimes by the consuls. Moreover, the entire body of the citizens, individually and by towns, has unanimously and continuously prayed at all the *pulvinaria* for my good health.

(10) By decree of the senate my name was included in the hymn of the *Salii*, and it was sanctioned by law that my person be sacrosanct in perpetuity, and that I possess the tribunician power for as long as I lived. I refused to be made *Pontifex Maximus* in the place of a colleague while he was still alive,[18] although the people offered me that priesthood which my father had held. This priesthood some years later, when he died who had used the opportunity of civil disturbance to seize it, I accepted in the consulship of Publius Sulpicius and Gaius Valgius [12 BCE]. In order to elect me, a multitude poured in from all of Italy such as had never before been recorded at Rome.

(11) The senate consecrated an Altar of Fortune the Home-bringer before the temples of Honor and Virtue at the Capena Gate in honor of my safe return, and ordered the priests and Vestal virgins to perform an annual sacrifice there on the anniversary of my return into the city from Syria in the consulship of Quintus Lucretius and Marcus Vinicius [19 BCE], and it named the day 'Augustalia' from my name.

(12) By authority of the senate, some of the praetors and tribunes of the plebs along with the consul Quintus Lucretius and prominent leaders were sent to meet me in Campania, an honor which up to that time had been decreed to no one except myself. Upon my return to Rome from Spain and Gaul, after I had successfully arranged affairs in those provinces, in the consulship of Tiberius Nero and Publius Quintilius [13 BCE] the senate voted to consecrate in honor of my return the Altar

---

18: the reference is to Lepidus who, although he had been deposed from the triumvirate in 36, technically still held the office of Pontifex Maximus which he had assumed after the death of Julius Caesar in 44.

of Augustan Peace[19] in the Campus Martius, on which it ordered the magistrates, priests, and Vestal virgins to perform an annual anniversary sacrifice.

(13) Our ancestors resolved that the temple of Janus Quirinus be shut, when victories had established peace on land and sea throughout the whole empire of the Roman people; from the foundation of the city to my day of birth tradition records that it was closed only twice, but the senate during my tenure as *princeps* three times decreed that it be shut.

(14) My sons, Gaius and Lucius Caesar,[20] whom fortune stole from me when they were youths, the senate and the Roman people, as an honor to me, designated as consuls when they were in their fifteenth year, providing that they would enter upon the office five years later. And from the very day on which they were conducted into the forum, the senate decreed that they were to participate in discussions of public policy. Moreover, the entire body of Roman equestrians presented them with silver shields and spears and hailed them as 'leaders of the youth.'[21]

(15)[22] To each man of the Roman plebs I paid 300 sesterces under the terms of my father's will, and in my own name during my fifth consulship [29 BCE], I gave them 400 sesterces from the spoils of war. Again in my tenth consulship [24 BCE], I paid out a largess from my own patrimony of 400 sesterces per man, and when I was the consul for the eleventh time [23 BCE], I bought grain from my personal funds and made twelve distributions; and in the twelfth year of my tribunician power [11 BCE] I gave each man 400 sesterces for the third time. These donatives of mine never reached fewer that 250,000 individuals. In the eighteenth year of my tribunician power, when I was consul for the twelfth time [5 BCE], I gave sixty *denarii* apiece to 320,000 men of the urban plebs. As consul for the fifth time [29 BCE], I gave to each of the colonists from my soldiers 1,000 sesterces out of booty; about 120,000 men in the colonies received this largess at my triumph. When I was the consul the thirteenth time [2 BCE], I gave sixty *denarii* apiece to the

---

19: in the significant remains of this altar the iconography shows the ideals and aspirations of the Augustan program.

20: the sons of Agrippa and Julia, Augustus' only child; they were both given extraordinary honors but they died very young, Lucius in 2 CE and Gaius in 4 CE.

21: an honorific title for the two young boys; they nominally headed organized clubs of equestrian youths who yearly paraded in elaborate exercise on horseback before the emperor.

22: chapters 15-24 treat and record the expenditures spent by Augustus. The list shows that public revenues were sometime insufficient to cover the expenses of empire.

plebs who were receiving public grain; these numbered a little more than 200,000 persons.

(16) In my fourth consulship [30 BCE] and later in the consulship of Marcus Crassus and Gnaeus Lentulus Augur [14 BCE], I paid cash to the towns for the lands which I assigned to soldiers. This sum amounted to about 600,000,000 sesterces which I paid out for Italian lands, and about 260,000,000 for lands in the provinces. Of all those who founded colonies of soldiers in Italy or in the provinces I was the first and only one to have done it in the memory of my generation. Later, in the consulships of Tiberius Nero and Gnaeus Piso [7 BCE], and of Gaius Antistius and Decimus Laelius [6 BCE], and of Gaius Calvisius and Lucius Pasienus [4 BCE], and of Lucius Lentulus and Marcus Messalla [3 BCE], and of Lucius Caninius and Quintus Fabricius [2 BCE], to soldiers who were honorably discharged I paid cash bonuses and settled them in their own towns; for this I spent about 400,000,000 sesterces.

(17) Four times I bolstered the treasury with my own money, transferring to those in charge of the treasury 150,000,000 sesterces. And in the consulship of Marcus Lepidus and Lucius Arruntius [6 CE] I transferred from my own patrimony 170,000,000 sesterces to the military treasury which was constituted from my idea for the purpose of providing bonuses to soldiers who had completed twenty years of service.

(18) From the year when Gnaeus and Publius Lentulus were consuls [18 BCE], if public monies were insufficient, I contributed outlays of grain from my granary and money from my patrimony, sometimes to 100,000 persons, sometimes to many more.

(19)[23] I built the senate house and the Chalcidicum right next to it, and the temple of Apollo on the Palatine with its porticoes, the temple of the Divine Julius, the Lupercal, the portico at the Circus Flaminius, which I allowed to be named Octavia after the name of the person who had built the previous construction on the same site, the *pulvinar* at the Circus Maximus, the temple of Jupiter the Striker and Jupiter the Thunderer on the Capitoline, the temples of Minerva, of Juno the Queen, and of Jupiter Freedom on the Aventine, the temple of Lares at the top of the Sacred Way, the temple of the Penates Gods on the Velia, the temple of Youth, and the temple of the Great Mother on the Palatine.

(20) I restored the Capitol and Pompey's theater, both operations at great expense and without inscribing my own name. I restored the channels of the aqueducts which in numerous places were falling into disrepair because of age.[24] I channeled water from a new spring into the

---

23: this chapter and the next two detail Augustus' building and restoration program. He is most proud of his building of temples and shrines throughout the city.

24: as aedile in 33, Agrippa built the Julian Aqueduct, and later in 19 the Virgo one.

aqueduct called the Marcia, doubling the amount. The Forum Iulium and the basilica located between the temple of Castor and the temple of Saturn, works begun and nearly finished by my father, I completed; and when that same basilica was gutted by fire [12 CE], I began rebuilding it on an enlarged site, inscribed in the name of my sons,[25] and in case I fail to complete it in my lifetime, I have ordered it be finished by my heirs. As consul for the sixth time [28 BCE], I restored eighty-two temples of the gods in the city on the authority of the senate, overlooking none which required repair at that time. In my seventh consulship I resurfaced the Flaminian Way from the city to Rimini; I also repaired all the bridges except the Mulvian and Minucian.

(21) On a private site I built from booty the temple of Mars the Avenger[26] and the Forum of Augustus. I constructed the theater near the temple of Apollo[27] on ground for the most part bought from private individuals to be named after Marcus Marcellus, my son-in-law.[28] From money deriving from spoils I dedicated gifts in the Capitol and in the temple of Mars the Avenger with a cost to me of about 100,000,000 sesterces. When I was consul for the fifth time [29 BCE], I remitted to the communities and colonies of Italy 35,000 pounds of crown gold which they were contributing to my triumphs; and later, whenever I was hailed as emperor, I refused the crown gold[29] which the communities and colonies kept voting as graciously and with the same good will as before.

(22) Three times I presented gladiatorial games in my own name, and five times in the name of my sons or grandsons. About 10,000 men fought at these games. Twice in my name and three times in the name of a grandson I gave a display for the people of athletes summoned from all parts. Four times I produced spectacles in my own name and twenty-three times in place of other magistrates. On behalf of the College of Fifteen as its sponsor with Marcus Agrippa as colleague, I produced the Secular Games in the consulship of Gaius Furnius and Gaius Silanus [17 BCE].[30] When I was consul for the thirteenth time [2 CE], I was the first to put on the Games of Mars which after that time in each subsequent year the consuls have produced in accordance with a decree of the sen-

25: Augustus refers to his adopted grandsons Gaius and Lucius Caesar.

26: Augustus had vowed the temple of Mars the Avenger in 42 with the defeat of Brutus and Cassius. It opened in 2 in the Forum Augustum where it stood.

27: this temple is Apollo Medicus or Sossianus, so-named from a consul who restored it during the Augustan Age. It was near the Tiber.

28: the theater of Marcellus was opened in 11.

29: originally an offering of crowns composed of gold made by communities to rulers and generals; during the Empire it became a tax imposed annually or on special occasions.

30: as chairman of the *quindecemviri* [Board of Fifteen] Augustus, along with his son-in-law Agrippa who shared tribunician power, sponsored these centennial games that by strict calculation should not have been put on until 47 CE.

ate and a law. I presented to the people hunts of beasts from Africa in my name and those of my sons and grandsons in the circus or forum or amphitheaters on twenty-six occasions during which about 3,500 beasts were killed.

(23) I produced for the people a display of a naval battle[31] across the Tiber in the place where there is now the grove of the Caesars, after excavating a site 1,800 feet in length and 1,200 feet in width. Here thirty beaked ships, triremes, or biremes, and very many smaller boats engaged in combat. In these fleets there fought, besides the rowers, about 3,000 men.

(24) Victorious in Asia, I replaced in the temples of all the city-states of the province of Asia the adornments which the person with whom I had been waging war[32] had taken into his private collection after he looted the temples. The eighty or so statues of me on foot, horse, and in chariot that stood in the city I removed, and from the money I set up golden gifts in the temple of Apollo under my own name and the names of those who had honored me with the statues.

(25) I swept the sea of pirates. In that war I captured about 30,000 slaves who had run away from their masters and taken up arms against the state; these I handed over to their masters for punishment. All of Italy voluntarily swore an oath of allegiance to me[33] and demanded that I be the leader of the war in which I was victorious at Actium. The same oath in the same wording was sworn by the provinces of the Gauls, Spains, Africa, Sicily, and Sardinia. Among those who campaigned under my standards at that time were more than 700 senators, including eighty-three who previously or afterwards up to the day of this writing were selected consuls, and about one hundred and seventy were priests.

(26) I enlarged the territory of all of the provinces of the Roman people that bordered peoples who were not subject to our empire. The provinces of Gaul and Spain, and Germany, too, the territory which the Ocean bounds from Gades to the mouth of the Elbe river I pacified. The Alps from the district bordering the Adriatic to the Tuscan Sea I pacified without bringing an unjust war against any people. My fleet sailed over the Ocean from the mouth of the Rhine to the far eastern territory of the Cimbri, where no Roman, either by land or by sea, had ever gone before. And the Cimbri, Charydes, and Semnones, and other German peoples of that area sent diplomats to seek alliances of friendship with me and the Roman people. Under my order and my auspices two armies at about the same time were led into Ethiopia and that Arabia called the Fortunate,

31: the mock sea battle to which Augustus refers took place in 2.
32: Augustus alludes to his opponent Antony.
33: an extra-constitutional oath that did not invest Octavian with legal power but did provide a basis for political and moral support and propaganda.

and numerous forces of the enemy of both peoples were killed in battle, and many towns were captured. In Ethiopia the army advanced as far as Napata, a town very close to Meroe; in Arabia the army penetrated into the territory of the Sabaeans to the town of Mariba.[34]

(27) I annexed Egypt to the empire of the Roman people. When the king of Greater Armenia, Artaxes, was killed, I could have made it a province, but I preferred to follow the example of our ancestors; I handed over this kingdom to Tigranes, the son of king Artavasdes, and grandson of king Tigranes, through Tiberius Nero who at that time was my stepson. And the same people, who later revolted and rebelled, I subdued through my son Gaius, and handed over to the rule of king Ariobarzanes, the son of Artabazus, king of the Medes; after he was killed, I sent to that kingdom Tigranes, who was a descendant of the royal family of Armenians. All the provinces which from beyond the Adriatic sea verge upon the East, and Cyrene, too, most of them already the possession of kings, as well as Sicily and Sardinia, which had been seized in the slave war, I recovered.

(28) I established colonies of soldiers in Africa, Sicily, Macedonia, both Spains, Achaea, Asia, Syria, Narbonese Gaul, and Pisidia. Italy, moreover, contains twenty-eight colonies that I founded under my authority; today they have become in my lifetime famous and densely populated.

(29) After defeating the enemy, I recovered from Spain and Gaul, and from the Dalmatians, a great number of standards lost by other generals.[35] I compelled the Parthians to restore to me the spoils and the standards of three Roman armies and, as suppliants, to petition for an alliance of friendship with the Roman people. Those standards I deposited in the inner shrine of the temple of Mars.[36]

(30) The Pannonian peoples, whom before my principate the army of the Roman people had never approached, were conquered through Tiberius Nero, who then was my stepson and legate. I subjected them to the empire of the Roman people and I extended the frontier of Illyricum to the banks of the Danube river. When an army of Dacians crossed this river, it was routed and overwhelmed under my auspices, and later my army crossed the Danube and forced the Dacian peoples to submit to the power of the Roman people.

34: in addition to campaigns in Gaul (27-25) and Spain (27-19), much fighting took place in German territory until the defeat of Publius Quinctilius Varus in 9 CE. The expeditions into Arabia and Ethiopia took place from 25-24 and 24-22 respectively. They met with little success.
35: in the Illyrian campaign of 35/34 Octavian recovered Roman standards which had been lost in Dalmatia in 48.
36: Augustus negotiated the return of the standards lost to Parthia by Crassus in 53 at Carrhae and those lost by Antony in 36. This diplomatic success was heralded as a great triumph. It is depicted upon the breastplate of the "Prima Porta" statue.

(31) Royal embassies from India were frequently sent to me, previously unseen in the presence of any Roman general.[37] The Bastarnes, Scythians, and the kings of the Sarmatians, who dwelled on both sides of the river Don, and the king of the Albanians, of the Hiberians, and of the Medes sent envoys to seek an alliance of friendship with me.

(32) Numerous kings fled to me seeking my protection: of the Parthians, Tiridates, and later, Phraates, the son of king Phraates, of the Medes, Artavasdes, Artaxares of the Adiabenians, Dumnobellaunus and Tincommius of the Britons, Maelo of the Sugambrians and...king of the Marcomanian Suebians. Phraates, son of Orodes, king of the Parthians, sent me in Italy all of his sons and grandsons, not because he had been bested in war, but because he sought friendship with us through his pledging of his children. Many other peoples, with whom previously there had been no exchange of embassies and friendship, experienced the good faith of the Roman people in my tenure as *princeps*.

(33) The Parthian and Median peoples, through ambassadors who were eminent leaders of those peoples, sought and received kings from us. The Parthians received Vonones, son of king Phraates, grandson of king Orodes; the Medes Ariobarzanes, son of king Artavasdes, grandson of king Ariobarzanes.

(34) In my sixth and seventh consulships [28-27 BCE], after I had extinguished the civil wars and by universal consent had complete control of political affairs, I transferred the state from my power to the will of the senate and the Roman people.[38] For this service, by decree of the senate I was awarded the name Augustus, and the doorposts of my house were publicly decorated with laurels, and a civic crown was attached above my doorway, and a golden shield was placed in the Julian senate house whose inscription attested that it was given to me by the senate and the Roman people for my manly courage, clemency, justice and piety. After this time I surpassed all in authority, yet I had no more power than others who were also my colleagues in office.[39]

(35) When I was holding the consulship for the thirteenth time[2 BCE], the senate, the equestrian order, and the Roman people unanimously called me "Father of the Country," and decreed that this title be inscribed in the vestibule of my house, in the Julian senate house, and in the Forum of Augustus on the pedestal of the four-horse chariot which had been dedicated to me by a decree of the senate. At this writing I was in my seventy-sixth year.

37: sections 31 and 32 provide a list of peoples and client kings who entered into treaties with Rome and with whom a détente was reached.

38: Augustus refers to his formal "handing over" of power in the senate in January of 27 at which time he was re-invested with proconsular power.

39: Augustus saved the honors bestowed by a grateful people and senate for the last. He was especially proud of the title "Father of the Country" mentioned in the next section.

CICERO

LETTERS

That the numerous letters written by and to Cicero from 15 March, 44 to 28 July, 43 serve as an important source of history would be a gross understatement. These letters also provide and detail the genuine and sometimes disingenuous emotions of their author(s) and reactions to the political and military events of those days and months surrounding the death of Julius Caesar, and to the machinations of principal players in the public arena of Rome. In this selection are letters relating to these major participants, including Cicero himself, as they grapple with the fluctuating currents of politics and personality. Italicized words are translations from Greek.

1 *Ad. Fam.* 12.1
Pompeii, 3 May, 44

Cicero to Cassius, greetings:

(1) Believe me, Cassius,[1] I cannot stop thinking about you and our friend Brutus, that is, about the entire country whose every hope resides in you two and in Decimus Brutus. After the most illustrious exploits of

---

1: Cassius was with Iunius Brutus at Lanuvium, a town about twenty miles south of Rome.

my good Dolabella,[2] I myself have much greater confidence concerning
the state. The contagion in the city was spreading, growing more powerful every day, so that I was pessimistic about the city and its general
peace. It seems to me, however, that the disease has been arrested to
such a degree that we may consider ourselves safe for all time, at least
from that most squalid condition.

Much remains to do and some are very important matters, but
everything depends on you. However, let us disentangle each strand
one by one. As the matter now stands, we appear to have been freed
from the tyrant but not from the tyranny. We have killed the king, yet
we serve the king's every nod. Not only that, we approve the projects
which he himself, even if he were alive, would not be undertaking as if
he had thought them through.[3] I see no end at all to the matter. Laws are
posted on tablets, exemptions given, huge sums allotted, exiles recalled,[4]
and decrees of the senate forged. It seems that we have removed only
that hatred of ours for a despicable person and the pain of enslavement,
whereas the country lies mired in the chaos into which he threw it.

(2) You must solve all the problems; don't think that you have
already done enough for the country. It has never entered my mind to
hope for as much as the state has received from you, but it is not satisfied; it desires from you mighty things, proportionate to the magnitude
of your soul and service. Up to this point it has avenged injustices by
the death of the tyrant through your actions, nothing more. But what
distinctions from its number has it recovered? To obey a dead man whom
it could not suffer alive? Do we defend the handwritten notes of one
whose bronze tablets we ought to remove? That is exactly what we have
decreed. We did that when we yielded to the circumstances,[5] which in
the political arena have a significant value. Some, however, are abusing
our good nature excessively and without gratitude; but very soon we'll
discuss these things and many others together. In the meantime, I hope
you will be assured that I care very deeply for your reputation, both for
the sake of the country, which I have always held most dear, and for our
affection. Pay attention to your health. Good-bye.

2: Dolabella was serving as consul after the death of Julius Caesar with Antony
as his colleague. Cicero alludes to Dolabella's handling of rioters and a pro-
Caesarian memorial erected in the forum. See *Phil.* 1.2.4.
3: Cicero frequently complains that projects and laws are brought forward which
cannot be substantiated. See the next letter, *ad Att.* 14.10.1.
4: the only exile recalled was Sextus Cloelius whose case is outlined in letters
#4 and #5, *ad Att.* 14.13 and *ad Att.* 14.13a respectively.
5: on 17 March during the meeting of the senate in the Temple of Tellus (Mother
Earth).

2 *Ad. Att.* 14.10
   Puteoli, 19 April, 44

Cicero to Atticus, greetings.

(1) So it has come to this?[6] This is the result that Brutus, my and your good friend, has accomplished? To hole up in Lanuvium? To send Trebonius off to his province by out-of-the-way routes? To have all the acts, writings, words, promises, and schemes of Caesar validated more than if he were alive? Do you remember how loudly I proclaimed on the first day on the Capitoline that the senate should be convened there by the praetors?[7] O immortal gods, what measures we could have achieved then when all the conservatives were celebrating, and even the moderates, while the criminals had been routed! You blame the Liberalia. What could have been done then? We had already had it by then. Do you remember claiming that our cause was lost, if he was carried out to his funeral. But he was even cremated in the forum and praised in a sorrowful eulogy, and slaves and poor were provoked to attack our houses with torches. So, then, what does it mean? That they dare to say: "Are you against Caesar's nod?" These things and others like them I cannot stomach. Therefore, I'm thinking of going from *land to land*[8]; your territory is too wide open.[9]

(2) Have you finished vomiting? From your letter I infer that you have. I return to the Tebassi, Scaevae, and Frangones.[10] Do you think that they are confident of keeping those lands while we are in power? They reckoned that we had more guts than they anticipated. But, of course, they must be lovers of peace and not criminal activists. When I wrote to you about Curtilius and Sextilianus' estate, I was writing of Censorinus, Messalla, Plancus, Postumus, and of that whole lot. It would have been better to have perished after he was killed, which would have never happened, than to see this turn of events. (3) Octavius came to Naples on the 18th.[11] There Balbus met him on the next morning and with me on the same day at Cumae he said that Octavius would enter on that

---

6: Cicero begins his complaint that the assassins of Caesar and their political supporters missed opportunities to take control of the state. They were outmaneuvered by the adroit manipulation of Antony.
7: the conspirators and supporters took refuge on the Capitoline, protected by a gang of gladiators.
8. I have italicized all translations of phrases and clauses in Greek.
9: Cicero means Greece where Atticus had spent many years of his life.
10: these names refer to veterans of Caesar's army who had been granted confiscated lands.
11: soon after he had heard of Julius Caesar's death, Octavius landed near Brundisium sometime early in the month (April). This letter attests to his presence in Campania and his desire to accept the legacy of Caesar.

inheritance. But, as you write, there will be a *brouhaha* with Antony. I am taking care of your affairs at Buthrotum, as is proper, and will continue doing so. It seems that Cluvius' account that you ask about is approaching 100,000 sesterces; in the first year we wiped up to the tune of 80,000.

(4) Quintus, the father[12], is complaining heavily to me about his son, mainly because he is now honoring his mother to whom, despite her services to him, he previously was hostile. The letter he sent me was burning with rage against Junior. If you know what he is up to, and, if you haven't left Rome, please write me, and include anything else of interest, damn it, for I am utterly addicted to your letters.

3   *Ad Att.* 14.12
    Puteoli, 22 April, 44

Cicero to Atticus, greetings.

(1) O my dear Atticus, I fear that the Ides of March have brought us no profit except the pleasure and revenge of our hatred and pain.[13] What news has come to me from Rome! What things I see now from here! *O what a splendid deed! Unfortunately only half-done.* You are aware how much I adore the Sicilians and what an honor I deem it to be their patron. Caesar granted them many benefits, and I wasn't displeased, although the grant of Latin rights was intolerable. Oh, well—now along comes Antony who received a large sum of money to post a law, supposedly promulgated by the dictator in the assembly, which made the Sicilians Roman citizens; no mention was made of the matter when he was alive. And what's this? Isn't the case of our friend Deiotarus much the same?[14] He deserves any kingdom but not through the agency of Fulvia.[15] There are countless similar cases, but I return to my previous point. Will we not maintain in some measure the case of Buthrotum, so clear, so well attested, and so just? Especially since Antony has made more grants?

12: i.e. Cicero's brother
13: as in letter #2 Cicero laments that the assassination of Caesar accomplished little because of the political success of Antony and the Caesarians.
14: King Deiotarus had been rewarded with the kingdom of Lesser Armenia by Pompey, but deprived of it by Caesar. After Caesar's death Deiotarus seized Galatia and paid Fulvia ten million sesterces to procure the recognition of this take-over. Cicero had defended him before Caesar in 45.
15: the remarkable widow in turn of Publius Clodius and Gaius Scribonius Curio and wife of Antony. Cicero detested her.

(2) Octavius has conducted himself honorably and in a friendly way with me. His own friends greet him as Caesar, but Philippus certainly does not nor do I. I claim he cannot be a good citizen. Many surround us, who threaten our friends with death and declare that they cannot bear the existing situation. What do you suppose will happen when the boy arrives in Rome where our liberators cannot be safe? They will always be renowned, even happy in the knowledge of their deed. But our party, unless I am mistaken, will be flattened. So, I wish to go 'where there will be no offspring of Pelops,'[16] as the poet says. I am not very fond of those consuls-elect[17] who have forced me into orating again so that even here at the waters I'm not allowed my rest; but this comes from my excessive good nature. In fact, it used to be almost obligatory; but now, whatever the situation, it just isn't the same.

For a long time now I have had nothing to write about, yet I write, not to provide you entertainment by my letters, but to get a reply from you. Whatever information you've got, and particularly any news about Brutus, send me. I write this letter on 22 April, while dining with Vestorius, a man quite distant from philosophical argument but happily enough engrossed in bean counting.[18]

4

Ad Att. 14.13
Puteoli, 26 April, 44

Cicero to Atticus, greetings.

(1) It took seven days for your letter dated the 19th to reach me. In it you ask—and you seem to think that I myself don't have a clue—whether I am charmed by the hilly mounds and the view or by walking along the *beach.* Damn it! Both are delightful, as you say, so that I hesitate to say which I prefer:

> But we are not concerned with matters of a pleasant dinner,
> No, seeing the great suffering, heaven-sent,
> We shudder, in doubt whether we will be saved or will perish.[19]

(2) You have written important and very pleasing information about Decimus Brutus' hookup with his legions and in that I see our greatest

---

16: this quote derives from Accius' *Atreus.* The 'Pelopidae' refers to the family of Pelops, namely Thyestes, Atreus, and Atreus' sons Agamemnon and Menelaus.

17: the consuls-elect are Aulus Hirtius and Gaius Vibius Pansa, whom Cicero later will praise.

18: Vestorius was a successful banker at Puteoli.

19: the quotation comes from *Iliad* 10.228-230.

hope. Yet, if there is going to be a civil war—and it is inevitable—and if Sextus[20] remains in arms as I am quite sure that he will, then I am at a loss what we should do. For it will not be possible, as it was in Caesar's war, to be wishy-washy. If this gang of desperados thinks anyone has exulted in Caesar's death (and we all, right out in the open, did our share of happy celebrating), they will chalk him up as an enemy; and that situation portends a slaughter-house. The only choice remaining is to go join Sextus' camp, or, if we can, Brutus'. The whole affair is distasteful and unsuitable at our age and risky because of the uncertain outcome of war; in some way or other I am able to say to you and to me:

> My son, the works of war are not your gifts,
> Instead employ the charming arts of speech.[21]

(3) Yet chance, a matter which can have more power in such affairs than reason, will see to the outcome. But for us, let us recognize that which should be within our scope, that whatever happens, we bear it with courage and like a wise man; that we also remember the accident of being human and we take as much solace in literature as in the Ides of March. (4) Now help me out with a dilemma that is bothering me: I set out for Greece, as I had decided, as a free legate;[22] thus, I appear to avoid altogether the danger of impending slaughter. I will, nonetheless, come under some criticism that I have failed the state in a serious crisis. On the other hand, if I stay, I see that I would be in critical danger, but I suspect that there is a distinct possibility that I could help the country. There are private factors too; namely, I feel it would be extremely useful to travel there in order to facilitate young Cicero's stay; and there was no other reason for my going when I seized the plan of being Caesar's legate. Therefore, if you think anything pertains to me, you will, as usual, consider all the ramifications of this affair.

(5) I return now to your letter. You write that there are rumors that I am on the point of selling my property on the lake and of handing over my small villa to Quintus at a big price. Quintus Jr. says that he intends to bring the wealthy heiress Aquilia there. But I have not a single thought of selling it, unless I find something which more meets my fancy. As for Quintus, he is not interested one whit in buying. He is already tormented with the debt he owes for the dowry, a matter for which he expresses extraordinary thanks to Quintus Egnatius. He absolutely shudders at the thought of remarrying, stating that, as nothing else, the couch of a "free man" is most appealing. (6) But enough of these matters.

I return now to the sorry state of the republic, or rather non-republic. Mark Antony has written to me about the recall of Sextus

---

20: Sextus Pompeius is meant.
21: the quotation is from *Iliad* 5.428-429; Cicero changes the last word from *gamoio* ('marriage') to *logoio* ('speech').
22: see the glossary under LEGATE, FREE.

Cloelius; you will see from his letter—I have sent along a copy for you—how honorably he deals with me; but you will easily judge how unrestrainedly, how disgracefully, and how destructively he otherwise conducts himself to the point that Caesar would seem to be someone desired. Certainly measures that Caesar would have never enacted nor allowed to be passed are now being promulgated from his forged notes. I, however, have shown myself most affable to Antony. When once it has penetrated his mind that he has the license to do what he wants, even if I opposed it, he would certainly do it. So, I have sent you a copy of my letter too.

5 *Ad Att.* 14.13a
   Rome, 22-25 April, 44

Antony the consul greets Marcus Cicero.

(1) My busy schedule and your sudden departure have been responsible for my not meeting with you personally about this issue. For that reason I fear my absence will cause me to have less influence with you. But if your good nature corresponds to my judgment that I have always had of you, then I will be very pleased. (2) I petitioned Caesar to recall Sextus Cloelius, and obtained his approval. Even then it was my intent to take advantage of his favor only if you approved. So I extend every effort to gain your permission to do it. But if you prove to be adamant to his wretched fortune and affliction, I will not oppose you, although I believe that I have an obligation to observe Caesar's written instructions. But, by heaven, if you are willing to consider me in a kind, discreet, and amiable manner, you will definitely prove yourself gracious and will wish Publius Clodius, a boy of highest promise, to think that you did not persecute his father's friends, when you had the chance. (3) Allow it, I beg you, to appear that you engaged in the rivalry with his father on behalf of the republic, not because you hated his family. We put aside our enmities sustained in the name of the country with more honor and willingness than those incurred from abusive insults. So permit me to train the boy in this belief and to persuade his young tractable mind that animosities should not be handed down to successive generations. I am sure that your fate, Cicero, is far removed from any danger; nevertheless, I believe that you would prefer spending your old age in peace and honor rather than in anxiety.[23] Finally, I have a right to

23: in this sentence there is a veiled threat. Because both this letter and Cicero's reply are so insincere, it is difficult to get below the sarcasm.

ask you this kind favor; I have left nothing undone on your behalf. But if I fail to gain it, I will not by any action of my own grant Cloelius his request, so you may know how much your authority counts with me, and so you may prove to be more appeasable.

6 *Ad Att.* 14.13b
Puteoli, 26 April, 44

Cicero to the consul Antony, greetings.

(1) I would have preferred that you had dealt with me face to face in the matter which you treat in your letter. You could have perceived my devotion to you not just from my words, but, as they say, from my expression and eyes and brow. Certainly I have always had an affection for you, influenced first by your partisanship, and then by your kind protection; now in recent times your public conduct has recommended you to me so that I hold no one in greater esteem. (2) The letter that you wrote to me in such a cordial and respectful tone has touched me; I seem not to be granting a favor to you but receiving one from you since you qualify your request by your refusal to reinstate without my consent an opponent who is related to you, although you could with no difficulty do so. (3) Yes, my dear Antony, I defer to you in that matter and believe that I have been treated most courteously and respectfully by you in the words that you wrote. I would have thought to grant your request without reservations, whatever the situation; and I am simply indulging my human nature. I was never really vindictive or too stern or more austere than the imperative of the state demanded. As it is, I never had any demonstrable hatred of Cloelius himself,[24] and I always followed the principle that the friends of enemies should not be assailed, especially those of the lower class, and that we should not be stripped of the aid of our dependents. (4) As for the young Clodius, I think it is your role to imbue his "young tractable mind" with those beliefs so that he will not think there remain any ill feelings among our families. I contended with Publius Clodius because I was defending the republic, whereas he defended his cause. The state decided upon the issue in dispute; if he were alive today, no quarrel with him would exist on my part. (5) Therefore, since you are petitioning me, and you claim that you will not use the power which you enjoy against my will, let my concession be in part a gift to the boy, if it seems best to you; not that one of my age should fear any danger from a child like him, or one of my rank to recoil

24: as other letters indicate (*ad Att.* 5.13 and 6.1) Cicero is being very insincere.

from any dispute, but that we, you and I, may be closer than we have
been up to this point. Because of the interference of these animosities,
your heart has been more open to me than your home.[25] But enough.

One final matter: whatever I think you want and judge to be in
your interest, I will not hesitate to do with the utmost enthusiasm. I'd
like to think that you are completely persuaded of this.

7   *Ad Att.* 14.17
    Pompeii, 4 May, 44

Cicero to Atticus, greetings.

(1) I arrived in Pompeii on 3 May after I had gotten, as I wrote you,
Pilia located at my place in Cumae on the day before. The letter which
you had given to the freedman Demetrius on 30 April was delivered to
me as I was dining there. It contained a good deal of wise advice, yet,
as you yourself say, every scheme seems to be placed in the hands of
fortune. (2) About the business of Buthrotum, I wish I could meet with
Antony; I'd surely accomplish much. Everyone believes, however, that he
will not deviate from Capua, so I fear his arrival there will cause much
trouble for the country. Lucius Caesar thinks the same. When I saw him
yesterday at Naples, he was seriously ill. Therefore, I'll have to handle
and take care of this matter on the first of June. But enough.

(3) Quintus Jr. has sent his father an utterly scathing letter, which
was delivered after we arrived in Pompeii. The thrust of it was that he
would not suffer Aquilia as a step-mother. Now that is perhaps tolerable,
but he also maintains that he owes everything that he has to Caesar,
nothing to his father, and he puts his hopes for the future on Antony,
that damn reprobate! *But we will take care of that.*

(4) I have written letters respectively to Brutus, Cassius, and Dolabella. I have sent you copies, although not in doubt whether I should
mail them. Indeed, clearly I have decided that they should be sent on
to you, because I don't doubt that you'll make the same judgment as I.

(5) For my boy Cicero, my dear Atticus, provide as much as you
think is best and respect me enough to allow this imposition upon you.
I am most grateful for all you have already done. (6) That *unpublished*
book of mine I have yet to polish;[26] those revisions that you want to be
included await a second volume. I think, however,—and I'd like you to
believe me—that one could have spoken out against that criminal party
with less risk while the tyrant was alive than after he died. He, in fact,

---

25: because Antony had married Fulvia, the widow of Publius Clodius.
26: it is not certain which book is intended.

in some manner put up with me to a remarkable degree; but now, wherever we shake ourselves, we are reminded not only of Caesar's acts but also of his intentions. See about Montanus, since Flamma has arrived. I think the situation ought to be on firmer ground.

——

8 *Ad Fam.* 11.27
Tusculum, last week of August, 44[27]

Marcus Cicero to Matius, greetings.

(1) I have not yet decided whether our Trebatius, a man who is not only conscientious but also a dear friend of us both, has brought me more annoyance or pleasure. Although his health was still weak, he came to visit me on the morning after my evening arrival in Tusculum. When I scolded him for neglecting his health, he then exclaimed that there was nothing more intolerable than his wait to see me. "Well," I asked, "What's new?" He then informed me of your complaint. Before responding to that, I will make a few remarks.

(2) As far back into the past as I can stretch my memory, there is no friend of mine older than you. The length of our friendship we have in common with many, not so its depth of affection. I liked you on the very day I met you and I thought you liked me too. But then your departure that extended for a very long time, my political career, and our different life styles[28] did not allow our feelings to bond by habitual association; yet, I was aware of your feelings towards me for many years before the civil war, when Caesar was in Gaul. What you deemed to be extremely useful to me and not disadvantageous to Caesar himself, you brought about so that Caesar took a liking to me and counted and held me among his circle of friends. I pass over the many intimacies that were spoken, written and exchanged between us in those days, for more serious matters ensued at the outbreak of the civil war. (3) When you were traveling on your way to Brundisium to join up with Caesar, you came to visit me in Formiae. First of all, it meant a great deal, especially in those times. Secondly, do you think that I have forgotten your advice, your talk, and your kindness? I recall that Trebatius was involved in this situation. Nor have I forgotten the letters that you sent me, when you left to meet Caesar in the territory, I believe, of the Trebula. (4) Then followed the time when either my regard for public opinion, or my sense of obliga-

——

27: the traditional dating of this letter is contested. Some put the date in mid-October just before Cicero was to leave for Puteoli.

28: Matius, like Cicero, was a Roman equestrian; like Atticus he did not pursue a political career.

tion, or fortune compelled me to set out to join Pompey. What service, what devoted interest was lacking in you toward me in my absence or toward my family who were at home? I came to Brundisium. Can you really believe that I have forgotten with what incredible speed, as soon as you heard, you flew off to meet me in Tarentum, how you sat by my side, the long talks, how you cheered up my mind depressed and in fear of our shared misfortunes? (5) At long last we began our stay in Rome. What did our intimate bond lack? In the most serious issues of our day I followed your advice about my conduct toward Caesar, in other matters I was directed by duty. With the exception of Caesar who, besides me, gained your concession to come to his home and often to while away the many hours in most sweet conversation? Even at that time, if you remember, you pushed me to write these *"philosophical treatises."*[29] After Caesar's return you had no greater concern than that I become quite intimate with him. In this you succeeded.

(6) You'd like to know where this speech—longer than I imagined it to be—is heading. I am surprised that you who ought to know better would believe that I would commit any offense that would endanger our friendship. Besides the matters I have mentioned above, which are well attested and conspicuous, there are many other more concealed which I find it difficult to express in words. I like all your traits, especially your loyalty in friendship, your judgment, your gravity, and your consistency, as well as your wit, refinement, and learning.

(7) So then, I now return to your complaint.[30] First I never for a moment believed that you voted for that law;[31] secondly, even if I had believed it, I would have never thought that you did so without a legitimate reason. Your sense of dignity brings whatever you do to notice, while the malice of men sometimes publishes a harsher picture of you than the facts attest. If you do not heed this, I don't know what to say; for my part, if I hear anything, I defend you as I know that you defend me again and again against my detractors. There are, however, two points in my defense: some things I flatly deny, such as the business about the vote, while in other cases I maintain that you do things out of a devout and kind nature, for example, in the supervision of the games.[32] (8) But it does not escape you, a most erudite man, that if Caesar was a king—which to me seems so—two opposing views may be taken

---

29: the philosophical work alluded to is the *Disputationes Tusculanae* ("Tusculan Disputations").

30: Matius has found out that Cicero directed some criticism against him for his political conduct contrary to the perceived interests of the 'conservative party,' the *optimates*.

31: most likely the law referred to is a recent one promulgated by Antony.

32: the games were paid for by Octavian; they lasted from 20 to 30 July and marked, among other things, funeral celebrations in honor of Julius Caesar.

of your conduct. One view, the one I usually hold, is that your loyalty and humane feeling must be commended, because you have remained true to a friend even though he is dead; or the other view, which some affirm, that the liberty of the country must take precedent over the life of a friend. I wish my arguments during such conversations had been reported to you. But who would recall either more willingly or more often than I the two characteristics that best attest to your honor: that you were the most prominent spokesman against initiating the civil war and for moderation in victory? On this point I have found no one who would disagree with me. Therefore, I am very grateful to Trebatius, our good friend, who provided me a reason for this letter; to disbelieve its contents is to deem me lacking in every sense of obligation and humane feeling. Nothing could be more grievous to me nor more alien to your character.

9 *Ad Fam.* 11.28
  Rome, end of August, 44

Matius to Cicero, greetings.

(1) I received great pleasure from your letter because I recognized from it that you hold the opinion about me that I had expected and desired; although I had no doubt about it, yet, because I prized your opinion highly, I labored to keep it unimpaired. In my conscience I knew that I had committed no act that would offend the feelings of any honorable person. I was, therefore, even less willing to believe that someone as endowed with so many and such excellent qualities as you could be persuaded so hastily, especially since I have felt toward you, and continue to do so, a good will which is both spontaneous and abiding. Since I know it is as I hoped, I will respond to the charge which you, as was befitting your exceptional fondness and our friendship, often refuted on my behalf.

(2) Yes, I am aware of the slurs cast against me after Caesar's death. They discredit me because I take the death of a close friend hard and am indignant that the man I cherish has perished. They assert that the country must take precedent over friendship, as if they have proven that his demise was beneficial to the state. I, however, will not play the clever speaker; I acknowledge that I have not soared to that level of philosophy. I did not follow Caesar in the civil conflict, but I followed a friend; although I disapproved of his program, I did not desert him; nor did I ever approve of the civil war or even the cause of the conflict which I strove most eagerly to extinguish as it began to ignite. So, in the victory of my close friend I was not ensnared by the sweet allure

of political office or money, the prizes which the others, although they had less influence with him than I, greedily appropriated. And even my estate suffered under one of Caesar's laws;[33] many who celebrated the death of Caesar with joy remained among the citizenry because of his kindness. I labored as hard for the pardon of defeated citizens as I would have for my own salvation.

(3) Tell me, how can I, who wanted everyone's safety, not be indignant that the man who granted it met his death? Especially since the very same men were responsible both for his unpopularity and his assassination? "OK," they say, "You'll be punished because you dare to oppose our deed." What unheard-of arrogance! That some may boast of a crime which others may not even deplore with impunity! Even slaves have always had the freedom to fear, to feel joy, and to grieve at their choosing, and not at someone else's option. Now "the authors of liberty," as they profess themselves, try to wrest that freedom from us by intimidation. (4) But they accomplish nothing. I will never shrink from my sense of duty and humane feeling because of threats of some danger; I have never thought an honorable death was something to run away from, but something to welcome. But why are they incensed at me for hoping that they should regret what they have done? I want Caesar's death to be a bitter pill for everyone.

"But it is my duty as a loyal citizen to wish for a safe republic," they say. That is what I long for, but, if neither my past life nor my hopes for the future prove it when I remain silent, then I do not try to prove it just by asserting it. (5) Therefore, I solemnly ask you to regard actions as more powerful than words; if you perceive that it is an advantage to be moral, you would believe that it is impossible for me to have any association with evil subversives. Or am I in my declining years to change the character which I showed as a young man, when I could have had an excuse to stray and to unravel my life? I will not do that nor will I do anything to displease anyone, except that I grieve the tragic fall of a man who was the closest of friends and a pre-eminent statesman. But even if I were otherwise disposed, I would never deny what I was doing to prevent being judged an unprincipled reprobate for my misconduct and being thought a coward and hypocrite for concealing it.

(6) "Well, I supervised the games put on by the young Caesar in honor of Caesar's victory." But that involved a private duty and did not pertain to the status of the republic. I was duty bound to fulfill that service to the memory and distinction of the dearest friend, even now that he is dead; and I could not refuse the request of a young man of the highest promise and most worthy of Caesar. (7) I often made courtesy visits to the consul Antony. You will find that those who judge that I am

---

33: the precise law is unknown, but it clearly dealt with debtors and targeted creditors like Matius.

lacking love for my country frequent his house to seek or curry some favor. But what arrogance this is! Caesar never prevented me from associating freely with whomever I chose, even if he personally disliked some of them. Yet those who have robbed me of my friend are trying by their carping to keep me from liking whomever I want.

(8) But I do not fear that my moderate life style will be insufficient strength in the future against false rumors, and that even those who do not love me because of my loyalty to Caesar would not prefer to have friends more like me than themselves. If my hopes are realized, I will spend the rest of my life in peace in Rhodes; but if some chance intervenes, I will stay in Rome to desire things rightly done. I give many thanks to our friend Trebatius because he revealed to me your frank and friendly feelings towards me and because he has provided even greater cause for me to cultivate and respect him whom I have always with pleasure cherished[34]. Good-bye, and remain in close affection.

10 *Ad Att.* 16.8
Puteoli, 2 November, 44

Cicero to Atticus, greetings.

(1) As soon as I know what day I will arrive, I'll let you know. I must wait for my baggage which is coming from Anagnia[35] and in my household there is some illness. On the evening of the first a letter came to me from Octavian. He's got big ideas. The veterans now settled at Casilinum and Calatia[36] he has enticed over to his side. No wonder! He gave them 500 denarii each. He is thinking of approaching the other colonies. Clearly he expects to lead and wage a war against Antony. So, I foresee that within a few days we will be in arms. But whom are we to follow? Look at his name, look at his age.[37] And the first thing that he asks of me is to have a secret parley either at Capua or some other place not far from there. It is really naïve, if he thinks that that can happen in secret. I have informed him by letter that it is quite unnecessary and cannot be done. (2) He sent to me Caecina, an intimate of his from Volterra, who reported that Antony was on his way to the city (Rome) with the legion Alauda, levying monies from the independent towns,

---

34: Matius is referring to Cicero.
35: Cicero had a house in this city about forty miles southeast of Rome.
36: Caesar had settled veterans in these two towns in ancient Capua of Campania.
37: Cicero is not inclined to trust the young Octavius, legally adopted or not. See the next letter where he is more explicit about his distrust.

and leading his legion in a march under banners. We had a discussion and he asked my counsel, if he should march on Rome with his 3,000 veterans, or take hold of Capua to cut off Antony's advance, or go to the Macedonian legions which were on the march along the upper Adriatic. These troops he hopes are behind him. They refused to accept the "gift" offered by Antony, and, as Octavian tells the story, they reviled him with insults and left him in the middle of his harangue. Now what's that you're asking? In a word, he announces himself as the candidate for general and thinks that we should not fail him. I advised him to proceed to Rome because it seems to me that he will gain the "little people" of the city and, if he wins their confidence, he'll also have the backing of the conservatives. O Brutus, what a *grand opportunity* you are missing! I really did not foresee this, but I thought something like it would happen. I now require your advice: do I go to Rome or stay put here or should I flee to Arpinum?—the place is a *safe haven*.[38] To Rome, in case I'd be missed, if it appears something good has been accomplished. So unravel this for me. I have never been at a greater *impasse*.

---

11 *Ad Att.* 16.9
Puteoli, 4 November, 44

Cicero to Atticus, greetings.[39]

Two letters for me from Octavian on the same day urgently requesting me to come to Rome at once. He wishes the senate to sanction his program. I responded that the senate could not meet before the first of January—which I truly believe is the case. He then added: "with your advice." In a word, he is pressing the issue, while *I am looking about for excuses*. I don't trust his age and I don't know his intentions. In any case, I do not want to do a single thing without your friend Pansa. I fear Antony will prevail and I'm not eager to go away from the sea, and I'm afraid that in my absence *heroic deeds* may be performed. For his part, Varro dislikes the boy's plan and so do I. If he has loyal troops, he can have Brutus, and he is conducting his affairs in the open. At Capua he is organizing his men into companies and paying them. I see war sooner than later. Write back. I am surprised that my messenger left on the first from Rome without a letter from you.

38: although Cicero had intended to go to Rome, he went to his home town Arpinum, when he had heard of Antony's possible march to Rome.
39: Cicero's distrust of Octavian is turning into suspicion of ulterior motives.

12 *Ad Att.* 16.11
Puteoli 5 November, 44

Cicero to Atticus greetings.

On the fifth I received two letters from you, one dated the first, the other the day before. I turn first to the former. I am happy that my volume from which you have quoted the *flowers* meets your approval, for they seem to me the more blossoming after your judgment. Well, I was afraid of those famous red pencil marks of yours. You are quite right in what you say about Sicca. I barely contain myself about that prick.[40] So I'll reproach him without insulting Sicca or Septimius so that our *children's children*, without recourse to Lucilius' *scurrility*, may know that Antony had children by the daughter of Gaius Fadius. I hope to see the day when that speech may be published widely and so freely as to enter even Sicca's house. But we need now that time when the triumvirs were around. I'm a dead man, if that's not neat! Now you, read the book to Sextus[41] and write me about his judgment of it. *With me his one opinion is worth ten thousand.* Watch out for the sudden coming of Calenus and Calvena.[42]

(2) You fear that you may seem to be a *wind-bag*. Who is less of one? As Archilochus' iambic verse seemed to Aristophanes,[43] so to me your longest letter seems to be the best. As for your lecturing me, if you too were to find fault with me, not only would I bear it with ease, but I would be glad about it, inasmuch as in your criticism there is wisdom and *kindness*. So, I will willingly correct those passages which you noted;[44] I'll write, "by the same right in the case of Rubrius," instead of, "in the case of Scipio," and I'll unpile the mound of my praises of Dolabella. And yet, as it seems to me, there is in that passage some neat *irony* in which I state that three times he was in the front ranks against fellow citizens. I also prefer your suggestion: "it is most shameful that he still lives" over "what is more shameful." (3) I am not upset that you approve of Varro's *Peplographia*,[45] from whom I have not yet extracted his *Like Heraclides*. You gently encourage me to write; well, I want you to know that I do nothing else. I'm sorry about your case of the flu. Do

40: the reference is to Antony.
41: this Sextus is Pedacaeus whose judgment Cicero trusted.
42: Calvena is a nickname for Matius. Despite the sentiment expressed in letter #8, Cicero did not trust him.
43: the literary critic and grammarian of Byzantium of the third century BCE.
44: Cicero refers to various passages in the *Second Philippic*.
45: this title is uncertain; most attribute it to Varro's *De Imaginibus*, a catalogue of 700 portraits, each with a biographical sketch in verse. Cicero's designation of it comes from the sacred robe of Athena in Athens (*peplos*) embroidered with mythological and historical scenes.

me a favor, take care of it, as you usually do. I am happy you found my "O Titus" a benefit to you. The "men of Anagnia" refers to Mustela, the NCO, and Laco, the sot. I will polish and send the book you request.

(4) Now to the second letter. My *On Duties*, so far as Panaetius goes, I have finished in two books. His are three; but at the beginning he divided his treatise so that there were three lines of inquiry about moral obligations; one, when we discuss the issue of right or wrong; the second, the question of what is expedient or inexpedient, and the third, how one can judge when these two issues, duty and expediency, seem to conflict: for example, in the case of Regulus, to return would be honorable, but to stay expedient. He analyzed the first two in brilliant fashion; he promised a third treatment, but he did not write it, Posidonius next treated the subject. I, in fact, have ordered his book and I have written to Athenodorus Calvus to send me his *critiques*, which I am awaiting. I'd like you to nudge and request of him to send it as soon as possible. Included in it is his handling of *situational duties*. You ask about the title; I have no doubt that *kathekon* means 'duty,' unless you have some other idea; but the extended title is: "On Moral Obligations." *I dedicate* it to my son, Cicero. It seemed not *inappropriate*.

(5) You are right about Myrtilus. What a gang you have there. So? Blame Decimus Brutus?[46] God help them. (6) I did not hide myself in Pompeii, as I wrote you; first because of the weather—there was nothing more foul—and then because I received a letter every day from Octavian urging me to engage myself, to come to Capua, to save the republic again, and, finally, to go to Rome at once,

Ashamed to refuse and afraid to accept.

Yet, he has been conducting himself and is still conducting himself with vigor. He will come with a large force, but he is a mere boy. He thinks to convene the senate immediately. Who will attend? If anyone comes, who will offend Antony in these uncertain times? On the first of January perhaps he will be able to protect the senate or the battle will be fought before then. The independent towns wildly support the boy. Making his way to Samnium, he came to Cales and stopped at Teanum. There took place there a wonderful greeting and encouragement of him. Who would have thought it? For that reason I'll go to Rome more quickly than I had intended.[47] As soon as I have made my plans, I'll write.

(7) Although I have not yet read the agreements—for Eros has not arrived—nevertheless, I'd like you to take care of the matter on the 12th. I'll be able to send letters more conveniently to Catania, Taurominium, and Syracuse, if Valerius, the interpreter, will communicate to me the names of the VIPs. They are different at different times and almost all

---

46: it is thought that Myrtilus was executed by Antony who alleged that Myrtilus had been paid by Decimus Brutus to plot against him.
47: see letter #10, footnote #37.

of my old friends are dead and gone. Yet I have written some official letters, if Valerius wishes to use them; or else he should send me the names.

(8) About the holidays set by Lepidus, Balbus has informed me that they will last until the 30th. I will await your letter and expect to find out about Torquatus' little affair. I have sent Quintus' letter to you so you may know how strongly he loves the person whom you do not, which causes him some grief. I'd like you to give Attica a kiss in my name for being such a spunky girl—which is the best thing in children.

---

13 Ad Fam. 10.28
Rome, 2/3 February, 43

Cicero to Trebonius, greetings.[48]

(1) How I wish you had invited me to that most sumptuous feast on the Ides of March. We would have had no leftovers. But now we have such trouble with these people that that divine service you and yours performed for the country occasions some complaint. When it occurs to me that you, a most excellent man, lured away that plague and because of your kindness he lives to this day,[49] I occasionally get a little perturbed with you, hardly right for me to do. You have left to me, myself, more trouble than to everybody else. As soon as it was possible to hold a free meeting of the senate after Antony's disgusting departure, I returned to that spirit which I had in the old days, the spirit which you and that fierce patriot, your father,[50] always had on the lips and in the heart. (2) For, when the tribunes of the plebeians had summoned the senate on 20 December and sought discussion on another issue,[51] I embraced the status of the entire body politic; I presented the case most passionately, and more by the power of my will than by my genius I reclaimed a senate, languishing and weary, to its traditional energy and courage. That day, my combative effort and my spirited delivery brought to the Roman people the first hope of recovering freedom. And ever since I have

---

48: this letter was written shortly after the return of two ambassadors (Lucius Marcius Philippus and Lucius Calpurnius Piso Caesonius) who had been sent to demand Antony's evacuation from Cisalpine Gaul. These ambassadors returned on 1 February, having failed to accomplish any diplomatic task. Trebonius never received this letter. He had been killed by Dolabella before the end of January.

49: on 15 March, 44 Trebonius deliberately detained Antony when Caesar entered the senate meeting in the portico of Pompey's Theater.

50: Antony referred to Trebonius' father as a buffoon.

51: the other issue involved providing an armed guard for the new consuls.

missed no opportunity either of reflecting or acting upon the welfare of the state.

(3) Now if I did not believe that you were kept abreast of the affairs in the city and all the public proceedings, I would outline them in detail myself, although I have been tied up in extremely important transactions. But you will find out about that from others; from me just a few items and those in summary. We have a courageous senate, some of those of consular rank are timid, others disinclined towards us. We have suffered a great loss in Servius.[52] Lucius Caesar is well disposed, but, as Antony's uncle, does not offer very strong opinions; the consuls are outstanding, Decimus Brutus is remarkable, and outstanding is the boy, Caesar,[53] from whom I hope there is more to come. But note this for certain: if he had not promptly enrolled the veterans and if the two legions from Antony's army had not gone over to his authority,[54] and if this menacing terror had not confronted Antony, then Antony would have omitted no crime, no cruelty. Although I reckon that you have heard all of this, I wanted you better informed. I will write in greater detail if I can find more leisure.

14 *Ad Fam.* 12.5
   Rome, ca. 5 February, 43

Cicero to Cassius, greetings.[55]

(1) I think that the winter weather has so far prevented us from being informed about you, what you have been doing, and, particularly, where you are. Everybody has been saying that you are in Syria (a case of wishful thinking, I believe) and that you have troops at your disposal. That belief is more easily credited because it seems closer to the truth. Our man Brutus has won illustrious distinction. Indeed, his achievements have been tremendous and so unexpected that they are as welcome in themselves as they are brilliant for their speed of execution. But if you hold the regions that we imagine you do, the state has been strengthened by mighty props; from the end of the Greek shoreline all the way to

---

52: joining Marcius and Piso, Servius Sulpicius Rufus was the third ambassador sent to deal with Antony in Cisalpine Gaul. He died on the journey.

53: earlier (letter #3) Cicero had been reluctant to address the young Octavius as Caesar. At this point, however, Cicero considers him to be on the "right side."

54: the allusion is to the Fourth and Marcian Legions that had switched their allegiance to Octavius by November of the previous year.

55: this letter shows Cicero's optimistic portrayal of the military situation in Cisalpine Gaul.

Egypt we will have the protections of the commands and forces of the conservative party. (2) But, unless I am mistaken, the situation is such that the critical outcome of the entire war seems to be placed totally in the hands of Decimus Brutus, and if, as we expect, he breaks out of Mutina, it appears that there will be no war left to fight. At the moment, in fact, he is under siege by a small contingency of troops because Antony keeps Bologna under a massive guard. Our man Hirtius is at Claterna, Caesar near Forum Cornelii,[56] each with a loyal and strong army; Pansa has amassed a huge number of troops at Rome from a levy throughout Italy. Up to this point the winter has prevented any engagement. Hirtius seems to take no action without careful deliberations, as he indicates to me in his frequent letters. Except for Bologna, Regium Lepidum, and Parma, we hold all of Cisalpine Gaul, which is most enthusiastic in its support of the republic. Even your clients across the Po we have amazingly allied with our cause. The senate is exceptionally firm, excluding the ex-consuls of whom only Lucius Caesar remains loyal and steadfast. (3) With the death of Servius Sulpicius[57] we have lost a mighty bulwark. As for the rest, some lack energy, some are downright unpatriotic; also, there are some who envy the distinction earned by those whom they see winning approval in the body politic. But the consensus of the Roman people and all of Italy is indeed a remarkable phenomenon. This is about all I wanted to inform you about. I earnestly hope now that the light of your excellence will shine from those lands of the rising sun. Good-bye.

15   *Ad Fam.* 10.30
Camp at Mutina, 15 April, 43

Galba to Cicero, greetings.[58]

(1) On 14 April I was with Pansa who was supposed to be in Hirtius' camp on that day. I had advanced one hundred miles to meet him and to hasten his arrival. Antony led out two legions, the Second and Thirty-fifth, and two cohorts of personal guards, one his own, the other Silanus'; he also commanded some of his reserves. He advanced to encounter us with this force because he thought that we had only four legions of raw recruits. But the night before Hirtius had sent to us

---

56: both Claterna and Forum Cornelii were near Bologna on the Via Aemilia.
57: see letter #13 and footnote #51.
58: an "eyewitness" account of the Battle of Forum Gallorum at which Antony was bested. A week later Antony suffered another defeat that forced him to raise the siege of Mutina.

the Martian legion, which I usually commanded, and two praetorian cohorts to facilitate our movement to the camp. (2) When Antony's cavalry appeared, neither the Martian legion nor the praetorian cohorts could be held in check. We began to follow them from the rear, since we could not restrain them. Antony kept his forces near Forum Gallorum and did not want it known that he had the legions; he only showed the cavalry and light-armed companies. When Pansa noticed that a legion was advancing without an order from him, he ordered two legions of recruits to follow him. After we crossed a narrow strip formed between the marsh and woods, we drew up the twelve cohorts in battle formation. The two legions of recruits had not yet come up. (3) Suddenly Antony was there, having led his troops from the village and without delay he drew them into ranks and immediately engaged ours. The battle was hotly contested; each side fought as fiercely as it could. The right wing, where I was stationed with eight cohorts of the Martian legion, routed Antony's Thirty-fifth legion with the first attack; it pushed forward about a half-mile beyond the main line and original position. Next, as the cavalry was attempting to surround our flank, I began to retreat and to send the light-armed troops against the cavalry of the Moors to keep them from attacking our rear guard. Meanwhile, I was myself among Antony's men and saw that Antony was somewhat behind me. At once I flung my shield back and drove the horse to that legion of recruits who were coming up from the camp. The Antonians were hot on my heels while our soldiers were aiming their spears. By some stroke of luck I was saved and quickly recognized by our men. (4) On the Aemilian Way itself where Caesar's praetorian cohort was posted, a long battle took place. The left flank, where the two cohorts of the Martian legion and the praetorian cohort had been stationed, was weaker and began to fall back, because they were being surrounded by cavalry, Antony's strongest element. When all our ranks had moved back, I started to retreat—I was the last one—toward the camp. Antony acted the victor supposing that he could capture the camp. When he arrived, he lost many men there and accomplished nothing.

After Hirtius heard the report of the situation, with twenty cohorts he attacked Antony on his way back to his own camp, totally destroyed his forces, and routed them at the very spot where the battle had been fought near Forum Gallorum. About four hours after nightfall Antony retreated with his cavalry to his camp near Mutina. (5) Hirtius returned to the camp from which Pansa had set out and where he had left two legions,[59] which had been under attack by Antony. So Antony has lost the majority of his veteran forces; yet this operation could not escape

---

59: Pansa, in fact, had been fatally wounded and taken to Bologna.

heavy losses among our praetorian cohorts and Martian legion.[60] Two "eagles" and sixty standards of Antony were brought back;[61] the result: success. 15 April, from camp.

///

16 *Ad Fam.* 10.11
      Country of the Allobroges, ca. 30 April, 43

Plancus to Cicero.

(1) I give you undying thanks and I will thank you as long as I live. How to repay you I cannot state.[62] I don't think I can ever match your tremendous services, unless by chance, as you have so pointedly and articulately written, you deem my remembrance to be repayment in kind. If it had been an issue about your own son's status, you could not in any way have displayed more loving kindness. Your first proposals in the senate of unlimited honors for me, and subsequent ones accommodated to the occasion and to the preference of my friends, your constant and unending speeches on my behalf, your quarrels with detractors, sticking up for me, all these are well known by me. I must concentrate my attention, and not in a moderate way, to show myself a citizen loyal to the state and worthy of your praises, and one mindful and grateful for your friendship. As for the rest, preserve the reputation of your service, and if in outcome and existing circumstances you find in me the person you wished me to be, protect and support me.

(2) When I had crossed the Rhone with all my forces,[63] I sent my brother ahead with 3,000 cavalry and I myself made my way toward Mutina. During the march I heard about the battle, about Brutus, and about Mutina's liberation from siege. I noted that Antony and the remnants who were with him had no other refuge except in these regions; also, that in his mind he had two hopes, one in Lepidus himself, the other in Lepidus' army. Since part of that army is no less deranged than the men who accompanied Antony, I have recalled the cavalry; I have stopped among the Allobroges to prepare myself for any eventuality as

---

60: Galba tends to exaggerate Antony's losses and to minimize the losses of his own recruits. He was unaware of Pansa's wound and Octavian's difficult success in holding his camp.

61: most maintain that the loss of all of Antony's standards of his two legions is an exaggeration.

62: Plancus is responding to a letter from Cicero that indicated a senatorial decree honoring him.

63: Plancus was proconsul of Gallia Comata, i.e. across the Alps, having three veteran legions and at least a legion of recruits.

the circumstances may dictate. If Antony comes here without support, I am confident that I can easily hold him off on my own and serve the state to your pleasure, even though he may hook up with Lepidus' army. But if he brings additional troops and if the Tenth legion of veterans, which by my efforts was restored along with the others, returns to his treasonous madness, I'll take pains—and I hope to prevail—to see that no harm is done until forces from Italy are sent and that, united with us, they easily smash the desperate renegades.

(3) I promise you this, Cicero; neither my spirit nor diligence will ever fail. By heaven I want no residual anxiety; but in case there should be, on your behalf I will yield to no man in spirit, good will, or endurance. I am giving my every effort to influence Lepidus, too, over to our alliance. I am promising complete deference to him, if only he would think of the republic. In this situation I am using deputies and agents, my brother, Laterensis, our man Furnius. Personal insults will not stop me from compromising with my worst enemy on behalf of the safety of the country.[64] If I fail in these negotiations, nonetheless I am in very good spirits and perhaps I will satisfy you enough with greater glory for me. Take care and may you esteem me as I do you.

17
Ad Fam 11.20
Eporedia, 24 May, 43

Decimus Brutus to Marcus Cicero, greetings.

(1) My feelings for you and for the services you did for me compel me to experience on your behalf what I do not experience for myself: fear. I have often been told and I have not taken any item lightly; a recent case in point is Segulius Labeo, a man always himself, who tells me that, while he was with Caesar, much conversation centered on you; he claims that Caesar expressed no resentment whatsoever against you except for that quip which he ascribed to you: "the young man should be praised, honored, and *elevated*." He maintained that he would not allow being *"elevated."*[65] I believe that Labeo reported the quip to him or made it up. I doubt the youth had originated it. About the veterans Labeo wants me to believe that they are muttering and complaining and

---

64: despite his enmity with Lepidus, Plancus eventually sided with Antony and Lepidus.

65: in the Latin there is a double entendre with *tollendum* which normally means 'to raise, to lift.' Frequently used to mean 'to get rid of,' it can also mean 'to exalt' as in the expression *ad caelum tollere* ('to raise to the sky'). In any event, Octavian took offense.

that danger threatens you from their hands. He claims they are most resentful that neither Caesar nor I have been appointed to the Committee of Ten[66] and all business has been transferred to your authority. (2) When I heard this, I was already on the march, but I thought that I should not commit myself to a passage across the Alps before I knew what was going on there in Rome. Now, as for the danger, believe me, by their boasting and intimidating threats they hope to terrify you and to incite the young man in order to obtain large rewards. The entire song and dance derives from this purpose: for them to make as much profit as possible. Most of all I want you to be cautious and wary of plots. (3) To me nothing is sweeter or dearer than your life. Watch out; don't let fear force you to fear even more. However, you should meet the veterans half way. First, do what they want regarding the Board of Ten; then, regarding the bonuses, if it seems right to you, propose the lands of those veterans who were with Antony be granted to them by both of us; about the money the senate will deliberate and make an accounting of the finances to decide the issue. As for those four legions for whom the senate voted the land grants, I see their feasible distribution from Sullan[67] and Campanian lands. I think the lands should be distributed to the legions equally and by lot.

(4) My soundness of judgment does not urge me to write you this, but rather my warm feelings for you and my desire for leisure which cannot exist without you. As for me, unless it is truly necessary, I will not depart from Italy. I am arming and preparing the legions. I hope I will not end up with an incompetent army for all the eventualities and attacks. Caesar is not sending the legions from Pansa's army back to me.

Respond to this letter immediately and send one of your own men, if there is anything of a confidential nature and if you think I need to know. 24 May, Eporedia.

66: this board was established to review the acts of Antony, but Decimus Brutus thinks that it was appointed to look into land grants and payments to veterans.

67: presumably land that had been confiscated by Sulla and was occupied illegally or land that had been purchased from veterans who were not entitled to it.

18 *Ad Fam.* 10.23
Cularo, 6 June, 43

Plancus to Cicero.[68]

I will never, by god! ever regret, my Cicero, the extreme risks I am undertaking on behalf of the country as long as I am free from criticism of rashness, if anything should accidentally befall me. I would admit a mistake of imprudence if ever I had genuinely trusted Lepidus. Credulity is, after all, more an error than a fault that easily snakes its way into the mind of an outstanding person. But it was not the case that I was almost deluded by such a defect, no, not I, for I knew Lepidus quite well. So what's the reason? It was my sensitivity, a fault that is most dangerous in war, that drove me to risk this chance. I am very afraid that, if I remain in one place, it may seem to a detractor that I am too stubborn in my grudge match against Lepidus and that my inertia is feeding the appetite for war. (2) So, I led my troops almost in sight of Lepidus and Antony, and stationed them at a distance of about forty miles with the idea that I could either advance rapidly or retreat successfully. In choosing the spot, I kept the river[69] in my front to delay the crossing and to have the Vocontii[70] close at hand, whose territory afforded me free passage. After he tried, and not with a moderate effort, to bait me, Lepidus gave up hope of my arrival and joined with Antony on 29 May; on the same day they struck camp near me. From an intelligence report I learned that they were twenty miles away. (3) With the kind help of the gods I took measures, careful to retreat quickly, but to prevent this movement from seeming to be a retreat so that not a single soldier, not a cavalryman, nor a single piece of luggage was lost or intercepted by those fiery renegades. Therefore, on 4 June I sent all my troops across the Isara and demolished the bridges that I had built, so people could have time to compose themselves and I could, in the meantime, join up with my colleague. After I mail this letter, I expect him within three days.

(4) I will always attest to the singular spirit and loyalty to the republic of our friend Laterensis. His liberal treatment, excessively kind to be sure, of Lepidus caused him to be less wary in perceiving the dangers involved. When he saw that he had been hoodwinked, he tried to kill himself with hands that he could have better armed to bring down Lepidus. Pure chance interceded, and at this point he is alive and it is

---

68: Plancus has become cautious and suspects that Lepidus is intending to trap him and his army. He has crossed the Isara and made his way toward Lepidus' and Antony's camp.

69: the river is, most likely, the Verdon, a tributary of the Durance.

70: the Vocontii occupied much of the territory between the Rhone and Alps.

said that he will survive[71]. But I have little reliable information about that point.

(5) My escape brought much pain to those treasonous parricides. They came after me with the same fury that incited them against the country; and they expressed recent angers over these events: that I had not ceased from reproaching Lepidus to extinguish the war, that I disapproved of the current talks, that I refused the ambassadors, sent to me under Lepidus' promise of safe-conduct, to come into my sight, that I intercepted Gaius Catius Vestinus, a military tribune sent by Antony with a letter to me, and counted him as a member of the enemy. I take some pleasure in the fact that the more they have assailed me, so their frustration has proportionately brought them greater annoyance. (6) Now, my dear Cicero, guarantee to show the same support as you have done up to now in vigilantly and vigorously protecting us as we stand in the front lines. Let Caesar come with the most loyal troops that he has, or, if something prevents him, let his army be sent. He himself is involved in much danger. Every renegade in camp who has intended to go against the fatherland is gathered here. Why wouldn't we use all the resources at our disposal for the salvation of the city? But if you do not fail me there in Rome, as for me, I will support the state in all exigencies.[72]

(7) As for you, my Cicero, day by day, by heaven, I hold you dearer; your good qualities daily sharpen my concern not to lose any of your affection or respect. I pray that by my devotion and charitable gifts I may in person make your services more pleasurable. 6 June, from Cularo on the Allobrogian border.

---

19 *Ad Fam.* 11.14
Rome, 7 June, 43

Marcus Cicero to Decimus Brutus, consul-elect, greetings.

(1) It's wonderful! I am so happy that my policies and my proposals about the Board of Ten, and about the honoring of the young man,[73] meet with your approval. But what does it matter? Believe me, my Brutus, that I, a person not boastful, have cooled off. The senate was my *work*; and now it has lost its energy. Your illustrious breakout from Mutina and Antony's flight with his army cut to pieces have produced such high hopes of a confirmed victory that everyone's mind has relaxed and those fervid tirades of mine seem like *shadow boxing*. (2) But I return to

---

71: Laterensis died of his wound.
72. a very telling statement that turns out to be false because Plancus later reconciled with Antony. See letter #21.
73: Cicero alludes to Octavian. For the Committee of Ten see letter #17.

the point: those who know well the Martian and Fourth legions say that under no circumstance can they be induced to your side.[74] An accounting of the money that you need can be made, and will be. As for sending for Brutus and retaining Caesar to protect Italy, I wholeheartedly agree with you. But, as you write, you have your detractors whom I easily put up with, yet they are an obstruction. The legions from Africa are expected.[75]

(3) People, however, are amazed at the renewal of war there. Nothing was more unexpected. When the victory was announced on your birthday, we saw that the republic was freed for many centuries to come. These recent fears unravel our earlier accomplishments.[76] In a letter dated on the Ides of May you wrote me, however, that you had just received a communication from Plancus that Antony is not being sheltered by Lepidus. If that is the case, everything will be easier; but if not, then a major task is at hand. I'm not, however, afraid of the outcome. You have your part; for me I can do no more that what I have already done. Still I am eager to see you as the greatest and most famous of all, which I expect.

20 *Ad Fam.* 12.10
Rome, ca. 1 July, 43

Cicero to Cassius, greetings.

(1) Lepidus, your relative,[77] and my friend, was declared a public enemy by the senate in an unanimous judgment on the last day of June, and others who also together with him defected from the republic. Yet, they have extended the opportunity of returning to sanity until the first of September. The senate is clearly courageous, especially since they expect your aid. As I write this, we are engaged in a serious war because of Lepidus' crimes and fickle nature.

(2) We hear daily the expected reports about Dolabella, but up to now without any authoritative corroboration, just reported rumor. Since this is so, we received your letter, dated 9 May and sent from camp, which convinced the entire citizenry to believe that he has already been crushed, and that you, however, are coming to Italy with an army. So, we may then rely upon your advice in policy and your prestige, if mat-

---

74: these two legions, bitterly resentful of Antony, remained under Octavian.
75: the two legions mentioned here arrived in Rome but subsequently joined Octavian.
76: Cicero sees that Antony's unexpected escape and his alliance with Lepidus produce a problem for the senatorial cause.
77: Lepidus' and Cassius' wives were sisters.

ters here have been cleared up to our liking, and upon your army, if we meet some stumbling block, as it happens in war. I will equip that army with whatever provisions I can. The time for that operation will take place as soon as it begins to be known what aid that army will bring or has already brought to the country. Up to this point we only hear of undertakings, beyond question valiant and most splendid, but we expect results; some I trust have already been accomplished or are in the making. (3) Nothing is more noble than your manliness and your excellence. Therefore, we pray that we may see you in Italy as soon as possible. If we have you both, we think that we have a republic.[78]

We had a smashing victory in our hands, if Lepidus had not sheltered Antony who had been stripped bare, was unarmed, and on the run. Thus, Lepidus has engendered more hatred among the citizenry than Antony ever had. For Antony fomented war during a turbulent period of the republic; Lepidus, on the other hand, stirred it up in a time of peace and of victory. We have consul-elects[79] standing against him and we place great hope in them; but we also have suspenseful anxiety because the results of battle are not certain.

(4) Be convinced, therefore, that all is in your hands and Brutus', and that expectations are high for you—particularly for Brutus. If, as I hope, you arrive after the defeat of our enemies, the republic will rise again under your authority and will stand in some tolerable condition.[80] Very many diseases will need cures, even if the state seems sufficiently liberated from the crimes of its enemies. Good-bye.

21 *Ad Fam.* 10.24
Camp in Gaul, 28 July, 43

Plancus, supreme commander, consul-elect, to Cicero, greetings.[81]

I cannot do otherwise than to thank you for your services in individual matters, but, by god, I'm embarrassed to do so. For the intimate relationship which you chose for me to share with you does not seem to

---

78: Cicero's appeal that Brutus and Cassius and other commanders in the East come to the aid of Italy and of the senatorial cause weakened by Antony's and Lepidus' alliance and by the demands of Octavian seems almost desperate.

79: the consuls-elect were Decimus Brutus and Plancus.

80: Cicero acknowledges the political necessity of the presence of Brutus and Cassius.

81: chronologically, the last datable letter in the collection. That it survived is a wonder because the four months of letters before Cicero's death were suppressed by order of Octavian. Shortly after this letter was written, Octavian marched on Rome.

need the outward manifestation of gratitude; and in exchange for your splendid favors I am unwilling to employ the cheap tribute of words. I prefer to prove myself grateful to you in person by constant observance and kindness. And if life is granted me, I will succeed in transcending all the gratitude of friendship and all the devotion of kinship by my constant observance of you. I cannot easily say whether your feelings and regard for me will bring me more esteem forever or more daily pleasure.

(2) You have made my soldiers' interests your concern.[82] I wanted them honored by the senate, not for the sake of my own personal power (I know that I am thinking only of the general welfare), but first because I thought that they earned it, and secondly because I wanted them more connected to the interests of the republic in all circumstances, and lastly, so that I may pledge to you that they will turn from every attempt of tampering by any one, conducting themselves as they have up to this point.

(3) We have maintained our position unimpaired. Nevertheless, I hope that our policy meets the approval of all of you, although I am aware of the natural and reasonable desire for victory. If these armies encounter a setback, the republic lacks an available supply of reserves ready to withstand any sudden attack and raid by those murderous traitors. But I think you know our troops well. In my camp are three legions of veterans, one of recruits, the most conspicuous of that group; Brutus has in his camp one legion of veterans, one with two years of experience, but eight of raw recruits. So together the army is impressive from their number but meager in reliable strength. Too often we have seen how much we can trust recruits in battle. (4) If we could add the veteran African army to that of Caesar's to the might of our forces, we would with confidence risk the fate of the state on a decisive engagement. We observe in Caesar's situation how close he actually is. I have not failed to urge him in letter after letter and he has not ceased stating and restating that he is coming without delay; yet, in the meantime, I see him diverted from that idea and to have turned to other designs. Nevertheless, for my part I have sent our friend Furnius to him with a letter and instructions; perhaps he can accomplish something.

(5) You know quite well, my dear Cicero, as far as the affection for Caesar is concerned, you and I have a partnership; and, as an intimate friend of [Julius] Caesar, while he was alive, I was duty-bound to value and cherish the young Caesar. As far as I was able to know, he had a most moderate and kind nature; in view of Caesar's and my remarkable friendship and his decision, as well as that of all of you, that he be adopted as a son of Caesar, I think that it would be a disgrace for me not

---

82: as a member of the Board of Ten Cicero could influence the grants of land to Plancus' and Decimus Brutus' veterans.

to consider him as such.[83] (6) But, whatever I write to you, damn it, I do more in grief than from enmity. The fact that Antony lives today, that Lepidus is with him, that they have an army not to be sneered at, that they have hopes and daring, all this they can attribute to Caesar.[84] I will not repeat his earlier actions, but go back to the time when he asserted to me that he was coming; if he had decided to come, the war would have already been suppressed or pushed back into Spain, a province most hostile to them, and with heavy casualties to boot. What is in his mind and whose counsels have turned him away from a glorious distinction, so necessary as well as favorable to him, and have changed his thinking to pursue a consulship of several months duration which has produced a general terror with his most offensive demands, I cannot comprehend. In this situation his relatives,[85] so it seems to me, can do much to benefit the state and him; you, too, I think, can do the most, as he has enjoyed your many services as no one else except me. In fact, I'll never forget the extensive and numerous debts I owe. I have commissioned Furnius to delve into these matters with him. If I receive some recognition from him, as I ought, I will have done him the greatest service.

(8) Meanwhile we sustain the war under ever more harsh conditions. We do not think a military engagement is free from risk nor are about to put our trust in flight that could bring a greater disaster to the state. But if either Caesar takes stock of himself and his interests or if the African legions come promptly, we will make you safe and secure in this quarter.

Please show me your affection, as you have in the past, and be convinced that I am exclusively yours. From camp, 28 July, 43.

83: strictly, Octavian's adoption was not sanctioned by the Comitia Curiata until August.

84: this section of the letter details Plancus' growing resentment and disgust with Octavian's failure to help the cause. Octavian's independent military and political moves may have pushed Plancus into reconciling with Antony.

85: namely his mother Atia, his brother-in-law, the noble Gaius Claudius Marcellus, and his stepfather Lucius Marcius Philippus.

CICERO

PHILIPPIC I

As letters *ad Att.* 14.13a and *ad Att.* 14.13b (#4 and #5 in this collection) of April 44 attest, the relationship between Antony and Cicero was formal and cool. The two men had reached an insincere détente. When Cicero arrived in Rome on 31 August of that year after spending most of the summer in Campania, he was faced with a summons from Antony to attend a meeting of the senate the next day, 1 September. Cicero refused the summons. In his absence Antony assailed Cicero for his failure to attend; on the following day Cicero addressed the senate in Antony's absence. The following speech is that address. Although he spared him any personal abuse, Cicero harshly indicted Antony's policies. Thus began a series of speeches directed against Antony that were called the *Philippics* after the celebrated speeches of Demosthenes attacking Philip II of Macedon. On 19 September Antony responded with a virulent attack on Cicero's career and character, which led to Cicero's vituperative and bitter *Second Philippic*, the most famous of the series and which incurred Antony's lasting hatred.

1. (1) Before I speak out, conscript fathers, on the things that I think ought to be said about the state of the republic, I will briefly explain to you the rationale for both my departure from Rome and my return. As long as I possessed the hope that you had reclaimed the direction of policy and your authority over the body politic, I was determined, as an ex-consul and senator, to stay here, as it were, on watch. In fact, from the very day when we convened in the temple of Tellus,[1] I have

---

1: on 17 March, 44 the senate met in the temple of Tellus (Mother Earth) located on the Esquiline Hill.

41

never left nor shifted my eyes away from the political arena. In that temple I strove to the best of my ability to lay the foundations of peace and I adopted an old precedent from the Athenians. I even appropriated the Greek term which that city-state had used in conciliating civil discord and I formally proposed that every memory of civic strife be expunged in oblivion—forever.[2] (2) Mark Antony's speech on that day was outstanding; his intentions also were admirable; in fact, he and his children were the ones to establish firmly the peace with our most pre-eminent citizens.[3] And with these beginnings the ensuing events corresponded. He held deliberations about the political state of affairs in his house and invited the leading men of the state there; and to the rank and file of this body he brought the best recommendations. At that particular period nothing was discovered among Caesar's notes that was not generally known. (3) He showed remarkable control in his replies to questions asked: Were any exiles recalled? "One," he said, "and no one else."[4] Were exemptions from taxes granted? "None," he replied. He even wanted us to approve the motion of that most distinguished Servius Sulpicius that no notice of any decree or favor of Caesar's after the Ides of March would be posted. I pass over his many other exceptional actions to mention promptly one particular measure directly attributable to Antony. The dictatorship, which had already appropriated the violence of monarchial power, he exterminated from the state. That issue we did not even debate. He produced a written draft of a decree which he wanted the senate to enact.[5] After it was read, we deferred to his authority and with great enthusiasm supported it, and in most gracious words we decreed him heartfelt thanks.

2. (4) A light seemed to have flashed before us: not only tyrannical power, which we had endured, but the fear of dictatorship was eliminated. Because of the recent memory of that perpetual dictatorship he made an important pledge to the republic, that he wanted the state free: he utterly abolished the office of the dictator, although it had often been justified in the past. (5) A few days later the senate was rescued from the peril of a massacre when a fugitive slave who had usurped the name of Marius was impaled on a hook of execution.[6] Antony performed these actions jointly with his colleague; other acts, later, Dolabella did on his

---

2: Cicero alludes to the granting of amnesty in 403 to the supporters of the so-called "thirty tyrants" who ruled Athens after its defeat at the hands of the Spartans in 404.

3: Mark Antony had sent his son Marcus Antonius, usually called Antylus, to the Capitoline as a hostage.

4: Cicero refers to the case of Sextus Cloelius whose recall Antony had supported. See letters #4, 5, and 6.

5: later on Cicero will criticize Antony's haste in drafting this decree.

6: after a criminal was executed, his body was dragged by a hook to the top of the Capitoline, tossed from the hill, and then dumped into the Tiber river.

own, although I believe that they would have collaborated, if his colleague had not been away. Indeed, during this period an insidious evil was slithering in the city and spreading day by day. The same men who had executed the ersatz burial were constructing a monument in the forum; desperate men, their number growing daily, as well as slaves very much like them, were threatening buildings and temples of the city; but Dolabella's punishment of the renegade and criminal slaves, as well as of the vile and impious freemen, his yanking down that damned column were exemplary.[7] It seems amazing to me the difference between that single day and the time that followed.

(6) But look! By the first of June, the day on which they fixed for us to convene, matters had changed. Nothing went through the senate; many significant issues were handled in the popular assembly, regardless of the people's absence or reluctant attitude. Consuls-elect[8] said that they did not dare to come to the senate; the liberators of the fatherland were without a country,[9] the very city from whose neck they had slipped the yoke of slavery; yet the consuls all the while were praising them in public meetings and in every private conversation. Those who had earned the name of "veteran" and to whose interests this very order had shown the most attentive concern, were being incited not to preserve those possessions that they had but to hope for new plunder. Since I had more of a mind to hear rather than to see such goings-on and I had the right of "free legation,"[10] I decided to depart, thinking that I would be present on the first of January, the date that seemed the first possible for convening the senate.

3. (7) I have explained, conscript fathers, the rationale for my departure; now I will briefly set forth the reasons for my return, which brings more surprise. I had good reason to avoid Brundisium and the well-traveled route to Greece.[11] I arrived at Syracuse on the first of August, hearing that the passage over to Greece from that city was recommended. Despite the fact that I had the closest ties with that city,[12] it could not detain me for more than one night, although it desired to do

7: in early April after several days of rioting, Antony had the ringleader arrested and executed without a trial. His name was Hierophilus. He had erected an altar and column to Julius Caesar.
8: the consuls-elect were Gaius Vibius Pansa and Aulus Hirtius.
9: the liberators are Brutus and Cassius; they had departed from the city by mid-April.
10: the "free legation" refers to an honorary commission that allowed individuals (senators) to travel at public expense. See letter #4 and consult the glossary under LEGATE, FREE OR VOTIVE.
11: Antony had instructed four legions from Macedonia to disembark at Brundisium.
12: Cicero's contacts in Sicily date from the time he was a quaestor at Liybaeum (75) and his prosecution of Verres on charges of provincial corruption (70).

so. I feared that, if I tarried there, my sudden arrival would bring some suspicions among my intimate friends. Favorable winds carried me from Sicily to Leucopetra, the promontory in the area around Rhegium, where I embarked to make the passage over. But I had not traveled very far when a gale from the south drove me back to the very place where I had embarked. (8) It was the dark of night and I stopped to stay at the villa of Publius Valerius, an associate and friend of mine. On the next day, while I waited for a favorable wind at the same place, a good number of townsmen from Rhegium came to visit me, several of them just recently arrived from Rome. It was from them that I heard about Mark Antony's speech before the people. I was so very pleased that, after I read it, I began to think of returning to Rome. Not much later I received a copy of Brutus' and Cassius' public declaration.[13] Perhaps because I esteem them more for their political contributions to the country than for their personal friendship, their document seemed to me to be overflowing with compromise and fairness. But as it often happens, bearers of some good news invent additional favorable items to make their message even more welcome, so messengers added for me that an agreement was in the making: on the first of the month a meeting of the senate with a full house was likely; at that time Antony would get rid of his bad advisers, resign his command over the Gallic provinces, and return to the authority of the senate.

4. (9) At that point I was fired with a passion so enthusiastic to return that no oars, no winds were fast enough for me; I didn't really believe that I would arrive on time, but I fervently desired to offer my belated—but not too belated—congratulations to the state. So, I quickly sailed to Velia where I saw Brutus—I do not comment on this painful experience.[14] It just seemed a disgrace for me to return to the city which Brutus was leaving and to settle myself to living in safety whereas he could not. It was from him that I first learned of the speech delivered by Lucius Piso in the senate on the first of August. As I got it from Brutus, Piso garnered very little support from those who ought to have provided it. (10) Yet from Brutus' evidence—and what could be more authoritative than that—and the comments of all those whom I saw later, Piso seemed to me to have won great distinction. So I hurried to lend my support to him whom those present on that day in the senate did not. I did not expect to do much good—I could not accomplish that in any event—but, whereas many things against nature and even against fate seem to be looming over us, and, should that lot that befalls all humanity happen to me, I wanted to bequeath the voice of this day to the republic as a witness of my constant good will toward it.

13: in a communique Brutus and Cassius requested Antony to release them from
    their commission to supervise the grain supply of the city.
14: Brutus had criticized Cicero for his absence from Rome.

(11) I trust that I have adequately demonstrated to you, conscript fathers, the rationale for my two decisions. Now, before I begin my speech about the political issues of the state, I'll express a brief complaint of the wrong done me yesterday by Antony. I am his friend and I owe him for a particular service rendered on my behalf;[15] for that I have always felt to maintain good relations. 5. But why on earth did he resort to such unpleasant tactics to force me to yesterday's meeting of the senate? Was I the only one absent? Surely you have had less in attendance. Or was the issue so important that even sick men had to be carried in to the meeting? Hannibal, I suppose, was at the city-gates or a peace with Pyrrhus was under consideration, to which debate tradition relates that even Appius, blind and old, was carted in.[16] (12) *Au contraire*, the issue involved public thanksgiving, a kind of proceeding for which senators are usually not lacking. For they are compelled to attend, not by securities, but out of respect for those whose honor is under discussion; the same thing happens when a motion is made for a triumph. Under these circumstances the consuls are so nonchalant that a senator is almost free not to attend.[17] This practice I know perfectly well; and besides, I was tired from my trip and I was not feeling well. Out of my sense of friendship I sent him a message to tell him this. But he said, and you heard him say it, that he would come to my house with a wrecking crew. This was truly an angry and very intemperate reaction. What offense deserved a punishment so severe that he would dare to say in this august order that he would employ public workers to raze a house constructed at public expense by a decree of the senate?[18] Who has ever coerced a senator with such a sanction? A security bond or fine is the maximum penalty. But if he had known what opinion I was going to express, he would have relaxed the rigor of his coercion.

6. (13) Surely you cannot suppose, conscript fathers, that I would support the decree which you yourselves passed against your will: that sacrifices in honor of the dead be confused with thanksgivings, that sacrilegious rituals be introduced into the republic, that thanksgivings be decreed in honor of a man who is dead—I say nothing. Were he

---

15: Cicero alludes to Antony's intervention to spare his life at Brundisium in 48 after the battle of Pharsalia.

16: Cicero sarcastically provides two examples of a meeting of the senate summoned to address a crisis. After Pyrrhus' victory over the Romans at Heraclea in 280 Appius Claudius Caecus argued against accepting peace terms with Pyrrhus.

17: Cicero attempts to rationalize his absence from the senate meeting on 1 September. Senators were expected to attend a convening of the senate by a consul. For his failure to be present a senator could face a fine.

18: after his return from exile in 57 Cicero's house on the Palatine that had been burned down by political opponents was rebuilt at public expense.

that Brutus[19] who both freed the state of the tyranny of monarchy and fathered offspring possessing similar valor and accomplishing similar feats for almost five hundred years, I could not be influenced to couple the worship of a dead man with that of the immortal gods and to accept that he who has a ready tomb for rites honoring the dead be awarded public thanksgiving.[20] On the contrary, for my part I would have cast my vote to enable me to defend myself before the Roman people, if some more catastrophic disaster, such as war, disease, or famine, befell the country; some of these catastrophes already exist, some, I fear, are impending. But my hope is that the immortal gods pardon the Roman people who disapprove of the decree and pardon this order of the senate that passed it against its will.

(14) Very well then, concerning the rest of the problems afflicting the state, am I permitted to speak? Certainly I am allowed and will always be allowed to defend my honor, to despise death. If I have the power of entering this place, I do not shrink from the risk involved in speaking. How I wish, conscript fathers, I had been able to attend the meeting on the first of August. Not that anything could have been accomplished, but my presence would have shown at least one ex-consul, as it happened, to be worthy of his rank and worthy of the republic. It was painful for me to think that men who enjoyed the greatest rewards from the Roman people did not rally to support Lucius Piso, the sponsor of an excellent motion. Did the Roman people make us consuls with that in mind? That elevated to the highest level of honor we would take no account of the state of the republic? No ex-consul seconded Lucius Piso either by word or by the expression on his face. (15) Damn! Why this voluntary slavery? I grant it may once have been necessary; and I do not criticize every person in the rank of ex-consul who speaks his opinion. The case of those whose silence I pardon[21] differs from those whose voice I consider imperative; I am pained that the Roman people have come to suspect them, believing that not only are they are afraid, which in itself would be disgraceful, but also that, for various and sundry reasons, they have failed the requirements of their rank and position.

7. To begin with, I thank Piso profusely and hold the deepest gratitude for him. He did not consider how he could benefit in the body politic, but he weighed what was his duty to do. Next, conscript fathers, although I am aware you will not dare to support my schemes

---

19: the reference is to Lucius Iunius Brutus who expelled the Tarquins from Rome, thereby bringing an end to the Monarchy (509). See Livy, 1. 56-60.
20: Cicero is decrying that the rites of the Parentalia, a festival honoring the spirits of dead relatives, were being misused to support the deification of Julius Caesar, a move that Cicero opposed.
21: Cicero alludes to Lucius Iulius Caesar, Antony's uncle.

and proposals, nevertheless, please hear me out with the respect that you have granted me so far.

(16) First of all, I vote that Caesar's acts should be accepted, not that I approve of them—for who in good conscience can do that?—but I argue the position because I believe that we should maintain the highest regard for peace and tranquility. I wish Mark Antony were present now—but without his "advisers."[22] Yet, I guess he is allowed to be indisposed, a condition which he did not concede me yesterday. Were he present, he would stress to me, or rather to you, conscript fathers, in what way he defended Caesar's acts. The question is: are the acts which are to be ratified those contained in the memoranda, hand-written notes, and notebooks produced solely on the authority of Antony, not, you understand, actually produced, but merely quoted by him? Or, conversely, are those acts which Caesar inscribed on bronze that he intended to be the directives and authoritative laws of the people to be summarily disregarded? (17) For my part, I think that nothing in Caesar's acts has the force of the laws passed under Caesar's name. And another case: what if he promised someone something? Is that promise binding, even if he is not around to fulfill it? In his life he made many commitments to many people which he did not execute; but those promises that have been discovered after his death exceed the number of the benefits he dispensed and granted throughout all the years he was alive.

But I am not tampering with any of these, not out to disturb them. No! Rather with utmost enthusiasm I defend those illustrious acts of his. I wish that the monies in the temple of Ops were still there;[23] they were definitely blood-stained, but, as they cannot be returned to their rightful owners, they would be extremely useful today. Yet, if it was noted in his acts, then let's accept the dispersal of those funds. (18) And what about this? No act can be truly said to belong to him who, as a public figure is invested with civil power and military command, except that law enacted by him. Consider Gracchus' acts,[24] then the Sempronian laws will be produced; look for Sulla's, and the Cornelian laws are the ones available; and what about Pompey's third consulship, what acts came of it?[25] Just his laws, naturally. Now if you could ask Caesar what were his contributions to the political and civic life of the city, he would respond that he authored many outstanding laws; however, his hand-written notes he would either amend or suppress; even if he produced them, he would not regard their contents among his acts. But, I concede these points, and in some cases I give a big wink of the eye; yet in issues of

22: a snide reference to Antony's bodyguard.
23: Antony had taken the money placed by Julius Caesar in the temple of Ops (goddess of Plenty) on the Capitoline.
24: Gaius Sempronius Gracchus, tribune of 123, is meant.
25: Pompey was consul for the third time in 52.

the utmost importance, that is in his laws, I think it would be intolerable to rescind Caesar's acts.

8. (19) What law was better, more valuable, more often longed for in the best years of the republic than the one that stipulated that ex-praetors should not obtain the governance of a province for more than one year or that ex-consuls not govern them for more than two. If this law were abolished, do you suppose you could keep Caesar's acts in force? And this too: rescind the law that was passed concerning the third judicial panel, then surely do not all of the judicial laws of Caesar fade away?[26] And if you abolish Caesar's laws, how can you defend his acts? It is inconsistent to regard as his acts anything he chanced to scribble down in a notebook to jog his memory, however unfair and useless it may be; whereas, that which he carried before the people in the centuriate assembly will not be counted as one of Caesar's acts.

(20) But to return to the third judicial panel: what's its nature? It is made up of centurions, so Antony says.[27] What? Was not the office of judge open to that class under a Julian law, and before that a Pompeian, and previously an Aurelian one? A property qualification was prescribed, he says; but, I may add, not just for a centurion but also for a Roman equestrian. Therefore, men of the outstanding courage and integrity who have commanded the rank and file serve as judges and have served as such in the past. "I don't mean those men," he replies, "I mean whoever has commanded a century. I propose him to serve as judge." But if you proposed that everyone be put on the bench who has served as equestrian, which is a more elevated rank, you convince absolutely no one; for in the appointment of a judge property and rank are proper guidelines. "I'm not looking for those qualifications," he continues; "In fact, I want to add privates from the Alauda legion to serve as judges; otherwise, our followers maintain that they cannot be safe." What an insult to the honor of those whom to their surprise you are marshalling to be judges. In fact, the import of this law is this: that those who dare not make an impartial judgment are to be judges of the third judicial panel. Immortal gods! What an error on the part of those who devised that law. The more sordid his reputation, the more he will be most willing to wipe the dirt of his infamy by issuing strict decisions and will strive to seem worthy of his promotion to more noble judicial panels rather than wallow in a disgraceful one into which he was hurled by law.

9. (21) Another law has been promulgated that those convicted of violence and treason have a right of appeal to the people. Mind you, is

---

26: Julius Caesar did away with the jury-panel made up of the tribunes of the treasury.

27: Cicero alludes to Caesar's and then Antony's proposal to establish a third judicial panel composed of centurions drawn from the Alauda Legion, so-called because of the lark-like plume on the helmet's crest.

this a law or the annulment of all laws? Who is there today who cares if that law endures? Not one person has been charged under those laws, and we think that in the future not a single person will likely be indicted, since deeds carried out under arms never will be brought into court. "But the measure is a popular one." I wish you *had* intended something popular![28] As a matter of fact, all the citizens are of one mind and voice regarding the political health of the country. Why do you so desire to propose a law which in itself contains the worst shame and no gratitude? What can be more disgraceful than this: that a person who committed violence, and betrayed the Roman people and was convicted at trial returned to that very violence that was responsible for his conviction in the first place? (22) But I have no reason to keep on arguing about the law. Its object is phony: ostensibly about a person's right of appeal, but its real purpose, as is the proposal you offered, is to prevent anyone ever being prosecuted under these laws. Who could ever find a prosecutor so mentally deficient as to convict a defendant and expose himself to hired riffraff, or find a judge who would dare sentence an accused, and risk being dragged before a gang of thugs?

No, an appeal is not guaranteed by that law, but, instead, two very beneficial laws and courts are abolished. In short, it encourages young men to riot, to become treasonous, and to be pernicious citizens. I wonder what ruin the madness of tribunes will bring when those two courts for violence and treason are abolished. (23) And what of this? The bill will supersede the laws of Caesar which require that he who is convicted of violence as well as he who is condemned for treason will be banned from water and fire. If the right of appeal is granted to them, then surely the acts of Caesar are voided.[29] Although I have never personally approved of those acts, conscript fathers, nevertheless, I have thought that for the sake of unity that they should be preserved. For that reason I disagreed that the laws should be annulled which Caesar carried while he was alive as well as those that you have seen brought forward and posted after his death.

10. (24) Exiles have been recalled by a dead man; citizenship has been conferred not only upon individuals but upon whole tribes and provinces by a dead man;[30] and a dead man has eliminated tax revenues by an unlimited number of exemptions. Yet we defend these measures produced from Antony's house on the authority of one person—an ex-

---

28: Cicero facetiously puns on the word *'popularis'* referring to something of the people (popular), but also to the technical political term that means a politician who directs policy through the Assembly of the People rather than through the senate.

29: one declared an outlaw of the state had no right of appeal.

30: Cicero alludes to Antony's support of a proposal by Julius Caesar to enfranchise Sicily.

cellent one at that. Those laws which Caesar himself read to us as we looked on, which he published and proposed, those very laws which he was proud to have sponsored, and upon which he thought the republic depended, the laws about provinces, and about courts—I ask you now, are those the laws of Caesar, I say, that we who defend his acts now claim should be abolished? (25) Yet, we can at least complain about those laws which have been publicly announced; but when we hear of those that have already been passed, we don't even have a chance to complain. And then there were those laws passed without any public announcement before a first draft of them was even written.

But I ask: why should I or any of you, conscript fathers, fear bad laws being passed when we have some honest tribunes of the people? And we have such tribunes, ready to cast their veto and prepared to avail themselves of their religious office to defend the state. We ought to be free of fear. "What vetoes are you talking about?" he asks,[31] "What religious offices do you mean?" Naturally, I mean those which upon which the security of the state depend. Antony then adds: "We disregard all of those because we consider them antiquated and foolish; we will barricade the forum, close off all the exits and entrances, and station armed guards at several strategic points." (26) So, I suppose then that whatever is transacted in this way will be law and you will order it inscribed on bronze tablets in proper legalese: "The consuls by right of law put the question before the people." Now I ask you, is this the lawful right of putting the question that our ancestors handed down to us? And then: "The people by lawful right have passed the proposal." What people? The ones excluded? By what right of law? The one that armed violence has completely demolished? I am expressing these comments with an eye toward the future—which is the proper role of friends, to speak out beforehand on things that can be avoided. If my misgivings turn out to be misguided, then my speech will be refuted. I am speaking about those promulgated laws with which you are at liberty to deal. For my part, I point out their flaws: your duty, remove them. I denounce violence: your duty, eliminate it.[32]

11. (27) When I speak on behalf of the country, you consuls, Dolabella, should not become angry at me. I do not believe that you, however, would ever do so—for I know that easy-going nature of yours—but I hear that some are saying that your colleague, basking in the position which he believes to be so special and good (I would think he would be counted more successful, to say the least, if he emulated the consulship

---

31: this section of the speech imagines an argument between Antony and opposing senators. Tribunes had the right to veto the actions of any magistrate.
32: Cicero addresses Antony and Dolabella, the two consuls.

of his grandfathers or his uncle), has felt offended.[33] In fact, I see how disagreeable it is to have the same person angry and armed, especially since swords these days go without punishment. But I will propose a fair and just arrangement, so I think; I do not believe Mark Antony will reject it out of hand. For my part, if I say anything that insults his life or character, I will make no objection whatsoever against him if he considers me a most bitter enemy. If, on the other hand, I persist in the practice of my entire political life, that is, frankly proclaiming my sentiments about the political issues of the country, first of all I implore him not to rage against me; and secondly, if I fail to gain that concession, I beg him personally to vent his anger against me as a fellow-citizen. Let him use an armed guard, if it is as vital for self-defense as he contends; but do not let those armed men retaliate against those who express their opinions on the political issues of the day. (28) Now what could be a fairer proposition than that? But if, as some of his intimate friends have told me, every speech which counters his wishes offends him deeply, even though it contains no insult whatsoever, then we will just suffer the sensitive nature of a friend. But those same partisans of his will say to me: "As an adversary of Caesar you will not be afforded the same treatment as his father-in-law Piso;" and at the same time they throw in a mild warning for me to keep an alert guard: obviously, the excuse of illness for missing a senate meeting will have no more legitimate standing than death.

12. (29) But by the immortal gods! As I look at you, my good friend Dollabella, I cannot keep silent about the mistake that both of you are making. I believe that you both are noble gentlemen, men who aspire to greatness; I reject the rumor perpetrated by overly suspicious and overly gullible skeptics who claim that you crave money which every man of the highest rank and integrity has always despised, or that you covet wealth won by violence and the power that is intolerable to the Roman people. On the contrary, I am sure that you want the good will of your fellow-citizens and glory. Yes, glory, the distinction won by honorable deeds and eminent services performed for the country, confirmed and approved by the testimony of every aristocrat and the general population. (30) I would tell you, Dolabella, what was the reward of honorable action, if I did not see that you in the current atmosphere have passed the test of honor beyond anyone else.

There is no day in your life, I imagine, that you can remember shining more brightly for you than that day when you cleaned out the forum, scattered that gang of impious misfits, punished ringleaders of crime, and saved the city from burning and the terror of murder, and

---

33: Antony's grandfathers, Marcus Antonius (called Orator) and Lucius Iulius Caesar (consul of 90), were distinguished. His uncle was the aforementioned Lucius Iulius Caesar. See note #21.

then went home—mission accomplished. Members of what rank, of what class, and of what economic station gathered to praise and congratulate you? In fact, good men everywhere offered me thanks and congratulated me in your name because they believed that in these affairs I sponsored the deeds that you performed. I ask you, Dolabella, recall the consensus expressed in the theater when the entire audience, forgetting those matters that made them so hostile to you, signified by their applause that because of your recent service they had dismissed the memory of their old pain.[34] (31) That you, Dolabella, yes, you, I claim—and I speak with great pain—were prepared to toss aside with such nonchalance this honor, this esteem, hurts me deeply.

13. And you, Mark Antony—I appeal to you even in your absence—certainly you set that one day on which the senate met in the temple of Tellus above all these recent months when some—in sharp disagreement with me—think that you are just damn lucky. What an outstanding speech you made on unity! You freed the senate from terror and rescued the state from deep anxiety when you put aside animosity toward your colleague, when you overlooked the unfavorable auspices which you yourself announced in your capacity as augur of the Roman people, when on that day you consented for the first time to accept him as your colleague, and when you sent your young son to the Capitol to be a hostage for peace. (32) No day was happier for the senate, no day happier for the Roman people, who never packed a public assembly with a bigger crowd. At last it seemed then that the men who freed us were most valiant because the peace that followed the liberation of the country happened by their design. And then again on the next day, the second, and the third, and finally on all the following days you did not let pass conferring upon the country a steady stream of gifts, as it were, and the most significant, of course, was your abolishing of the title of dictator. You, yes, you I say, branded that mark upon the name of the dead Caesar to his eternal infamy. For as the Manlian clan once decreed that because of the crime of one Marcus Manlius[35] that no patrician Manlius would ever again be named Marcus, thus, because of the hatred associated with one dictator you eliminated once and for all the name of dictator. (33) After you had contributed so much for the security of the republic, did you have misgivings about your good fortune, your eminence, your renown, your glory? Where did this sudden change come from? I cannot bring myself to suspect that you were corrupted by greed. Let everyone say what they want, I don't have to believe them. I have perceived nothing in your character that is sordid

34: as tribune in 47 Dolabella proposed a cancellation of debt. When riots erupted soon afterwards, they had to be quelled by Antony.
35: Marcus Manlius (Capitolinus), hero of Roman effort against the invading Gauls of 390, was executed in 384 for treason.

or base. Sometimes those in the household may pervert a person, but in your case I know the strength of your character. And how I wish you could avoid the suspicion as you have avoided the guilt.

14. But I am frightened more by this: you may mistake the true path of glory and, instead, think that it is glorious to have more power than all others and to be feared by your fellow-citizens. But if you believe that, then you are truly misguided about the road to glory. To be regarded as a dear citizen, to earn the country's commitment, to be praised, respected, and loved—that is glorious; but, on the contrary, to be feared and loathed brings resentment and hate, and is a mark of weakness and instability. (34) We can see this easily from the scene of that play in which a character asserted: "Let them hate as long as they fear."[36] For him the sentiment turned out to be fatal. I wish, Mark Antony, that you had remembered your grandfather; you have heard me speak of him again and again. Do you think he would have wanted the immortality that he won to have been based on the exercise of terror by armed gangs? To share liberty with others, to become the first man in honor, *that* was his life, *that* his favorable fortune. His accomplishments I pass over; but, I'd like to state that his last and bitterest day was to be preferred over the despotism of Lucius Cinna who so brutally killed him.[37]

(35) But how can I persuade you to change by what I say? For if the demise of Gaius Caesar does not convince you that it is preferable to be loved than feared, then no speech of any man will do any good and prevail upon you. Those who think that Caesar was successful, are themselves deluded. No man is a success who lives a life under a contract that he can be murdered with impunity as well as with the utmost glory to his killers. So then, amend your ways, I beg you, and look back at your ancestors and govern our country in such a manner that your fellow-citizens will celebrate that you were born; without that no one can be either successful and happy, or illustrious, or secure.

15. (36) Both of you consuls have the benefit of the many judgments of the Roman people and I am extremely bothered that they have not sufficiently swayed you. What's the meaning of this: the shouts of innumerable citizens at the gladiatorial games? And this: the popular ditties? The endless applause to Pompey's statue?[38] And this: the opposition of two tribunes of the people against you? These actions surely attest in no small way to the incredible unity and political will of the entire Roman people. And again: did the applause at the games honoring Apollo, or

---

36: the line belongs to Atreus, the titled character of the playwright Accius. Atreus was killed by his nephew Aegisthus to avenge wrongs committed by Atreus against his father Thyestes.
37: Lucius Cornelius Cinna was consul four consecutive times from 87-84.
38: Julius Caesar fell at the base of Pompey's statue in the portico of Pompey's Theater.

should I say the testimony and mighty judgments of the Roman people, mean so little to you? Honored indeed are those who, although barred by armed violence from being there in person, yet were present, sticking and lingering in the marrow and innards of the Roman people.[39] Surely you could not have imagined that Accius was being applauded and his play was being awarded a prize after some sixty years.[40] No! It was for Brutus who was absent from the very games he was to sponsor. Yes, at that sumptuous spectacle the Roman people were bestowing their enthusiastic tribute upon him in his absence, and their incessant applause and cheering soothed their heartache over the loss of their liberator.

(37) Now, personally, I am one who have always despised applause of that sort when it is directed to citizens seeking popularity. And likewise, when the acclaim comes from the highest, the middle, and the lowest classes, and from all unanimously, and when those, who habitually submitted to popular sentiment before, now turn tail, then I judge that to be not applause of approval but a verdict. But if you regard this to be a trifling matter, whereas it is most important, do you also dismiss it with a sneer when you perceive how cherished to the Roman people is the life of Aulus Hirtius?[41] It was already enough for him to meet the approval of the people of Rome, as he has, and to have the affection of friends which surpasses all others, and to love his family as dearly as they love him. Tell me, can we remember a man arousing so much anxiety among the good citizens and such universal apprehension? Certainly we recall no such person. (38) Now what about it? Don't you understand, by the immortal gods, the meaning of this? And again: do you think they do not take stake of your lives, when they hold the lives of those whom they hope will contribute to the country so dear?

(39) I have plucked the fruit, conscript fathers, of my return. I have said the things that, no matter what fate befalls, are a living testimony of my determination, and I have received a kind and attentive hearing from you. If an opportunity to address you again will be afforded me without risk to myself or to you, I will use it; if not, then I will reserve my powers and to the best of my ability strive to benefit not just myself but the state as well. For me, long enough I have lived, calculated by the number of years and by my fame. If an extra span be granted to me, it will be placed in service not so much to myself but to you and the citizenry of Rome.

39: Cicero refers to Cassius and Brutus. Brutus, as the "urban" praetor should have presided at the games, but Antony and his brother Gaius sponsored them with the financial support of Atticus.
40: the play was the *Tereus*.
41: Aulus Hirtius, the consul-elect for 43, was ill.

SALLUST

The following selections from Sallust contain the entire "prefaces" from the two monographs, the *Catiline* and the *Jugurtha*, and the speech of Marius delivered before the people's assembly after he was elected consul and voted the governorship of Numidia and the command of the army in North Africa. The two prefaces well illustrate Sallust's views on the moral decline of Roman society, on political corruption, and on senatorial venality. Sallust also presents his thoughts on historiography and offers up some political theory. The speech of Marius shows in dramatic fashion the author's ability to integrate within his narrative a speech, powerful in its characterization and rhetorical impact. The reader is left to decide whether Marius is to be viewed as a statesman-like hero whose achievements and abilities had been blunted by the political actions of nobles, or to be judged a conceited demagogue.

THE CONSPIRACY OF CATILINE

(1) [1]All men who desire to excel the other animals should strive with their every fiber not to wallow in a life, unnoticed, like cattle, which nature has created groveling and obedient to their belly. But all our power resides in the mind and in the body; we use the mind chiefly to command us, the body to serve us; the one, i.e. mental faculties, we share with the gods, the other, i.e. bodily functions, we have in common with the brutes. So I think it more virtuous for us to seek fame using the resources of innate intelligence rather than the power of brute strength, and, since this very life which we enjoy is so brief, for us to prolong the memory of our lives as long as possible. For the glory which riches and

---

1: chapters 1-4 comprise a prologue in which Sallust justifies his decision to write history.

beauty bring is fleeting and perishable, whereas intellectual excellence is a splendid and everlasting possession.[2]

Yet for a long time humans have disputed this very point: whether military success proceeds from physical prowess or mental excellence. Before beginning, deliberation is necessary, but then after planning, there is need of quick action. Thus, each of these, mind and body, lacking in itself, requires the other's aid. (2) Consequently, in the beginning kings[3]—for that was the first title of government in the world—had two different approaches, some trained their intellects, others their bodies. Even at that time men led lives without greed. Each person was content with what he had. But when Cyrus[4] in Asia and the Spartans and Athenians in Greece began to subdue cities and tribes, to consider the lust for rule a pretext for war, and to find the greatest glory was constituted in the greatest empire, then at last it was discovered from experience and risky ventures that mental qualities availed most in war. But if the mental endowments of kings and rulers were as powerful in peace as in war, human affairs would maintain a more consistent and stable course, and one would not see power changing hands from one to another nor all kinds of political shifts and social disorder. For empire is easily retained by those very qualities by which it was first acquired. When laziness, however, has supplanted hard work, and lust and arrogance have displaced self-restraint and fairness, the fortune of leaders changes with their morality. Thus power always devolves from the inferior to the best man.

All the activities in which men engage—farming, sailing, building—depend upon excellence. Yet many people, once they have surrendered to their belly and to sleep, pass through life, ignorant and uneducated, like gypsies; clearly in these men, contrary to nature's ideal, the body is meant for pleasure, the soul is a burden. In my view, I judge their lives and deaths about the same, since silence records neither. For the truth is that only he, as it seems to me, really lives and enjoys life who devotes himself to some enterprise and pursues the renown of a famous deed or honorable occupation. As the opportunities are abundant, nature provides one path for one person and another way for someone else.

(3) To serve the country by action is glorious; even to glorify it in words is no mean thing; one may become famous in peace or in war.[5] Both those who have themselves performed great deeds and those who

---

2: in this first paragraph Sallust has outlined the qualities necessary for glory and fame. There is a contrast in his concept of mental excellence and of physical strength.

3: that monarchy was the first form of government occurs in several ancient writers, both Greek and Latin.

4: the military conquests of Cyrus the Great of Persia provided the formation of a mighty empire that encompassed much of the Middle East.

5: this chapter begins with Sallust's comment on two forms of glory: active performance and the recording of history.

have chronicled the accomplishments of others are often applauded. Now as for me, although it is very evident that equal repute in no way follows the writer as it does the maker of history, it seems particularly arduous to compose history, mainly because the text must match the historical facts, and, secondly, because many believe that whatever faults you criticize in others are attributable to malice and envy.[6] Also, when you recall the distinguished excellence and renown of good men, every person readily accepts those things which he thinks that he himself could easily do, but everything beyond that he regards as fiction or fabrication.

When I was a young man, I, like so many others, at first was passionately drawn to pursue a public career;[7] in it I met many obstacles. Instead of propriety, instead of uncorrupted behavior, and instead of virtuous living, there thrived incontinence, bribery, and rapacious greed. Although my mind, a stranger to evil practices, rejected such wrongs, nevertheless, amid so many vices, young and weak, it became corrupted and was embraced by ambition. While I distanced myself from the immoral behavior of others, the lust for political office, nonetheless, seduced me, bringing upon me a censure and envy equal to theirs.[8] (4) So, when my mind found rest from numerous troubles and dangers, and after I pledged to myself to spend the rest of my life far from politics, I decided not to fritter away my precious leisure in sloth and indolence or to indulge myself in farming some land or to devote my life to hunting, both slavish pursuits.[9] No, instead, I resolved to return to that very undertaking and study from which base ambition had impeded me: to write a history of the Roman people, selecting that which seemed worthy of recording, all the more confirmed in my mind because I was free from hope, fear, and partisan politics. I shall, therefore, briefly treat, as truthfully as I can, the conspiracy of Catiline; for I think that event worthy of special notice because of the revolutionary nature of the crime and the danger associated with it. Before I begin the narrative, however, I believe a few words about that man's character are in order.

(5) Lucius Catiline[10] was born of a noble family and possessed great vigor both of mind and body, but had a vicious and depraved nature.

6: in his Preface Livy shares similar sentiments concerning the difficulty in composing history.

7: Sallust begins to establish a proper arena for the exercise of "excellence" in writing history.

8: this self-portrait corresponds to Sallust's own life. He was expelled from the senate in 50 for political reasons.

9: Sallust's rejection of farming and hunting as worthy pursuits in the exercise of "leisure" contrasts sharply with the image depicted by Vergil and Varro and must have seemed "un-Roman" to many aristocrats.

10: the subject of the monograph is briefly introduced. This sketch provides a summary reference to the Sullan period and an extreme example of the potential of the age.

From his youth he found to his liking the civil wars, murder, looting, and political dissension, matters that also occupied his early manhood. To an incredible extent his body could endure hunger, cold, and lack of sleep; his mind was reckless, cunning, and shifty, available for any pretense and dissimulation. He was acquisitive of other people's goods, prodigal of his own, and was a man of flaming passions. He possessed a modicum of eloquence, but little discretion; his insatiable mind always lusted after the shameless, the incredible, the ever lofty. After the autocracy of Lucius Sulla, a most passionate desire for seizing control of the government overwhelmed him and it concerned him not a whit by what means he would acquire sole power as long as he acquired it. Day by day his vicious spirit increased his resentment over his poverty and his guilty conscience, both factors exacerbated by those qualities which I have already mentioned. Moreover, the corrupted morals of the body politic incited him; they were degenerating under the influence of two vices of different character: extravagance and greed.

Since I have had occasion to mention public morals, my theme seems to demand that I delve further back and briefly sketch the institutions of our ancestors in domestic and military affairs, how they governed the state, its status when they bequeathed it to us, and how little by little it changed from the noblest and most beautiful to become the vilest and most profligate.

(6) The city of Rome,[11] as I have it on good authority, was founded and held early on by Trojans,[12] who under the leadership of Aeneas wandered in exile keeping no fixed homes; they were joined by natives, the so-called Aboriginals, a rustic people without laws, without government, free and unrestrained. After these two peoples of different races, unlike in language and way of life, united within the same walls, they merged and coalesced with incredible ease; so very quickly did a diverse and roving mob metamorphose into a harmonious community. But after their state expanded in population, in culture, and in territory, and seemed rich enough and powerful enough, then, as is usual in mortal endeavors, affluence engendered envy. Thus, neighboring kings and peoples tested them in war, and only a few of their friends provided aid;[13] the rest, impaled by fear, shrank from the dangers involved. But the Romans, deeply committed at home and in the field, hurried, made preparations, encouraged one another, went to confront their enemies, and defended by arms their liberty, their country, and their parents. Later, when their military prowess pushed aside their perils, they furnished aid to allies

---

11: Sallust expands and analyzes his moral concepts in the framework of Catiline's conspiracy.

12: for a contrasting view on the foundation of Rome and its conflicting origins, Trojan and native, see Livy 1.1-2.

13: for example, Lars Porsenna, the Latins, Aequians, Volscians, and Sabines.

and friends, and established pacts of friendship by rendering services rather than by accepting favors. They had a government regulated by law, in name a monarchy; a select few whose bodies were weak because of years, yet whose mental faculties were strong in wisdom, advised in council the state; either because of their age or because of similarity in their attention, these men were called "Fathers."[14] Afterwards, when kingly power, which at the outset had been wielded to preserve liberty and to expand the state had degenerated into arrogant tyranny, they changed the character of government by selecting two rulers with annual power; for they believed it to be most unlikely that human nature would accept unbridled authority.

(7) Now in that period every person began to elevate himself and to display his talents. For good men more than depraved men draw the suspicions of kings, who always fear the excellence of others. But once liberty was won, the state grew incredibly strong in a very short time, such a passion for glory had permeated it. As soon as the young men could endure the rigor of war, they learned the vigorous discipline of military life in the camp, and took greater delight in seemly arms and horses fitted for war than in whores and dinner-parties. To such men no labor of the camp was unfamiliar, no terrain too rugged or steep, no armed enemy terrifying; manly valor mastered everything. Their most competitive struggle for renown was with one another; each person eagerly sought to be the first to strike the enemy, to scale a wall, to be conspicuous while he was performing such a deed. These actions they believed were riches, a good reputation, a mighty nobility. Eager for praise, they were generous with money; they craved great glory, riches earned by honor. I could relate the battle sites where the outnumbered Romans with a small force routed the mightiest armies of their enemies, the cities fortified by nature they stormed and captured, were it not that such a theme would pull us too far from the subject.

(8) In my opinion, fortune is master in every affair, illuminating and obscuring all enterprises according to caprice rather than truth. The accomplishments of the Athenians, as I think, were extensive and very glorious, but yet are somewhat less significant than their reputation records them. But because Athens produced a copious crop of brilliant writers, the exploits of the Athenians are celebrated throughout the world as the most distinguished. Thus the merit of those who made history is regarded only as highly as pre-eminent intellects have been able to glorify it in treatises.[15] The Roman people, however, never had that opportunity because all the most capable were always occupied in one venture or

---

14: compare Livy 1.8.7

15: Sallust is probably thinking of Herodotus, Thucydides, and Xenophon and others like Isocrates and Demosthenes. The point is that the Greeks had great historians in contrast with Romans who had men of affairs.

another; no one exercised his mental faculties apart from his body; their most prominent citizens preferred action to words, thinking that their own exploits were to be praised by others rather than that they narrate others' deeds.

(9) Consequently, an ethic of right conduct was celebrated at home and in the field; there was the greatest harmony, the minimum amount of greed; justice and goodness won out among them not primarily because of laws but rather because of natural disposition. The quarrels, disputes, and rivalries that they engaged in were with enemies; citizens vied with citizens over honor. In their votives to the gods they were unstinting, in the home frugal, to their friends loyal. By cultivating these two qualities, undaunted aggressiveness in war and justice in peace time, they protected themselves and their state. As proof of these assertions I present the following evidence: that in war punishment was more often imposed upon those who against orders had attacked the enemy[16] and who had withdrawn from battle too late when ordered back than upon those who had abandoned the standards or had ventured to retreat though pressed hard; secondly, in time of peace they governed from kindness more than from intimidation and preferred to forgive an injustice rather than to avenge it.

(10) But when the state expanded through hard work and just rule, when mighty kings had been defeated in war, when savage tribes and powerful peoples were subdued by force, when Carthage, the rival of Rome's power, had perished utterly, and all the seas and lands lay open, then fortune began to rage and revolutionize everything.[17] Those who had endured toils, dangers, anxiety, and adversity with ease found leisure and affluence, desirable in other venues, to be a burden or misery. Thus, lust first for money, then for power, grew. These were, in a word, the source of all evils. For avarice subverted good faith, integrity, and all other virtues; in their place it taught arrogance, cruelty, neglect of the gods, and total venality. Ambition compelled many men to play false, to have one sentiment locked in the heart, another ready on the tongue, to value friendships and enmities not in accordance with their intrinsic worth but on the basis of self-interest, and to present a good face rather than noble character. At first these vices grew gradually, sometimes even were punished; but later, after the disease had invaded society like a plague, the state was changed and the government, once the finest and most just, came to be cruel and intolerable.

(11) At first it was ambition rather than greed that plied men's minds, a fault somewhat akin to virtue; for the virtuous and base alike crave

16: most likely Sallust refers to Titus Manlius Torquatus who executed his own son for fighting a duel against his orders.
17: Sallust's excursus on the moral decline of Rome. He attributes the turning point to the defeat of Carthage in 146.

glory, honor, and power, but the former strive for them by the true path, whereas the latter, lacking noble traits, vie by treacherous intrigue and deception. Greed means the zealous pursuit of money which no wise man has ever coveted; imbued, so to speak, with harmful poisons, it renders effeminate the manly body and mind. Always limitless and insatiable, it never diminishes either from plenty or from want. But after Lucius Sulla had recovered the government by arms, he was responsible for the ugly consequences after his initial success: all men began to rob and loot; one longed for another's house, another wanted lands; the victors displayed neither moderation nor restraint; they committed foul and cruel crimes against fellow citizens. Moreover, in order to win the loyalty of the army which he had led into Asia, Lucius Sulla contrary to the practice of our ancestors permitted too much indulgence and license. During their periods of leisure the attractive and voluptuous regions easily softened the warlike spirit of his soldiers. There for the first time an army of the Roman people indulged in extremes: making love, drinking to excess, admiring statues, paintings, and sculpted vases, then stealing them from private homes and public buildings, looting shrines, and desecrating all things sacred and profane. These soldiers, therefore, left nothing to the conquered after they had won the victory. For as is well known, prosperous conditions try the spirit of wise men, so, still less would those men of corrupt character moderate their victory.

(12) As soon as wealth began to be upheld as an honor, and glory, military command, and political power ensued, virtue started to rust away, poverty to be considered a disgrace, integrity to pass for mean-spiritedness. As a result of wealth, luxury and greed combined with arrogance to overwhelm the youth; they looted, they squandered, they set little value on their own goods, coveting those of others; they took no stock in self-respect or in chastity, things human or divine—in short, they had no values, they had no restraint. It is worth your attention, when you have seen the homes and villas constructed like cities, to visit the temples of the gods which our ancestors, that most religious people, built. They embellished the shrines of the gods with piety, and their own homes with glory; yet not a single thing did they steal from the defeated except the power to do harm. But these Romans of today, on the contrary, these basest of humans, with supreme criminality are robbing the allies of those things which those victorious heroes had left them, just as if doing wrong were the only way to use power.

(13) Why should I relate those enterprises which are incredible except to those who have witnessed them, that gangs of private individuals have leveled mountains and paved the seas? These men seem to me to have handled their riches as a derisive sport. Whereas they could have employed them honorably, instead they rushed to squander them disgracefully. A lust for lewdness, gluttony, and for other self-indulgences equally overpowered them; men experienced the role of women, women

prostituted their chastity; to gorge themselves they ransacked land and sea for everything; they slept before they needed sleep; they did not await hunger or thirst, cold or weariness, forestalling instead all these things by their self-indulgent appetites. Such were the abuses that incited the young men to crime, as soon as they had used up the family's resources. Their minds, imbued with evil qualities, were never free from libidinous vices, so they devoted themselves all the more recklessly to every profit and extravagance.

(14) Among a citizenry so great and so corrupt, it was a very easy thing for Catiline to surround himself with gangs of criminals and scoundrels, as it were, a retinue; every kind of reprobate, adulterer, and profligate who had squandered his ancestral estate on his gaming hand, on his gullet, on his crotch; whoever had contracted an enormous debt to pay off his debauchery and crime, all those who had been convicted, from wherever, of murder or sacrilege, or who feared indictment for their crimes; moreover, those who lived by the hand and tongue, nourished by perjury and the blood of fellow citizens, in short, all those who were disgraced, pinched by poverty or troubled by a bad conscience—these were Catiline's associates and intimates.[18] But if someone, who was free of guilt, chanced to enter upon friendship with Catiline, daily association and temptations easily converted him to a thug equal or similar to the others. But he especially courted the intimacy of young men; because their minds were still impressionable and tractable, he had no difficulty in captivating them by his guile. To satisfy the burning passion of each one according to his time of life, he furnished whores to some, bought dogs and horses for others, sparing no expense nor his own self-respect until he could render them submissive and make them loyal to himself.

THE WAR WITH JUGURTHA

(1) [19]Erroneously does humankind complain about its nature, namely that it is feeble and short-lived, and is governed by chance rather then merit. On the contrary, upon reflection you would discover that nothing is greater or more pre-eminent and that human energy, not its rigor or length of duration, fails mortals. But the ruler and director of human life is the soul; when it aspires to glory by the path of virtue,[20] it becomes mighty and powerful and very illustrious; it has no need of fortune which can neither bestow nor take away virtue, diligence, and other excellent

---

18: Sallust firmly places the conspiracy within the framework of moral degenera- tion that he sketched in chapters 12 and 13.

19: like the introduction of the *Catiline* these first four chapters serve as a prelude to the work.

20: one should compare *Cat.* 1.2 for an expression of a similar idea that the spirit (mind) governs life.

qualities. But if the mind is debauched by depraved desires and has been degraded to sloth and sensual pleasures, and has indulged even for a short period in ruinous sexuality, then strength, time, and natural endowments vanish in indolence, and nature gets the blame for its weakness; the guilt that is his own, each transfers to independent circumstances. But if men had as deep concern for virtuous qualities as they have passion in their pursuit of unsuitable and unprofitable—sometimes very dangerous and pernicious—interests, they would be in control of events rather than be controlled by them, and they would progress to such a greatness that their glory would make mere mortals immortal.

(2) As the human race is composed of body and soul, so all our possessions and all our pursuits partake of the nature of the body or of the spirit.[21] Therefore, conspicuous beauty, enormous wealth, as well as physical power and other temporal qualities of this kind fade away in all too brief of time. But the distinguished achievements of the intellect, like the soul, are deathless. In a word, the gifts of the body and of fortune have both a beginning and an end, all things rise only to set, grow only to become old. But the soul, incorruptible and eternal, the ruler of the human race, drives and controls all things as it itself is controlled by none. All the more astonishing is the depravity of those who surrender themselves to carnal pleasures and pass their lives in excess and in indolence, but allow the intellect, which is finer and greater than any other quality in the nature of mortal beings, to grow dull from neglect and inactivity, especially since so numerous and varied are the intellectual capabilities that acquire splendor.

(3) I believe that of these pursuits, political offices and military commands, and, in fact, all political activity are the least desirable in this day and age, since neither honor is granted for merit nor are those who have obtained power illegally protected and any more honored. For to rule the country and parents by force, even though one may have the power and may correct abuses, yet it is not fitting, especially since all political change portends bloodshed, exile, and other acts of violence.[22] On the other hand, to strive in vain and exert oneself in weary labors that win nothing but hatred is the utmost madness,[23] unless someone just happens to be possessed by a dishonorable and pernicious lust to sacrifice his personal integrity and freedom to the power of a few.

21: again, similar contrasts in similar language are developed in *Cat.* 1.2-4.
22: the sentiment expressed in this section reflects the rampant fears after the death of Julius Caesar. Many were weary of the power struggle between dynasts and the political instability of the times, and were fearful of what the triumvirs would do.
23: the word employed for 'madness' is *dementia* which connotes a personal folly. Sallust usually uses *furor* to denote 'madness' in the political arena, i.e. the policies of political extremism.

(4)   But in the other pursuits which are plied by the intellect, the recording of history is very useful.[24] Because many have spoken of its value, I think I should let it be to prevent anyone believing that I am arrogant to extol my vocation in praise. Yet I believe, because I have decided to live my life far from political affairs, there will be some who will lay the charge of indolence against my laborious and useful efforts. I am sure it will seem so to those whose greatest industry is devoted to soliciting the people and currying favor by banquets. But if they would take into account the character of the times in which I won office and the character of the men who failed to obtain the same distinction,[25] and finally, what sorts of men reached the senate, they will surely come to believe that I changed my mind from just motives rather than from laziness and they will come to think that greater benefit will accrue to the state from my leisure than from the activities of others. I have often heard that Quintus Maximus, Publius Scipio,[26] and other prominent men used to declare that, when they gazed upon the portrait busts of their ancestors, their minds were inflamed with the hottest fire to pursue excellence. Of course, the waxen images did not possess that inherent power, but the remembrance of their forefathers' achievements enkindled the growth of this flame in the hearts of eminent men and was not quenched before their valor equaled the fame and glory of their ancestors. In these immoral times, however, there is no one at all who does not compete with ancestors in wealth and excessive living rather than in honesty and diligence. Even the "new men," who in earlier days surpassed the nobles by merit, now by intrigue and villainy rather than by honorable qualities compete for military power and political offices; just as if a praetorship, consulship, and all other honors of this kind were in themselves illustrious and magnificent and were not valued in accordance with the excellence of those who uphold them. But I have proceeded too far and conveyed too freely the disgust and indignation I have for the standard of morality in this country. I return now to my main theme.

(84) As I stated above, Marius was elected consul by the most enthusiastic support of the plebeians.[27] After the people then voted the province of Numidia to him, his hostility to the party of the nobles turned to an open attack, pervasive and scathing, sometimes denouncing individuals, other times the entire group; he declared over and over that he had won

---

24: as in the proemium of the *Catiline* Sallust defends and justifies his undertaking of writing history.

25: in 52 Sallust was the tribune of the people; in that same year Marcus Porcius Cato failed to win election to the consulship.

26: Quintus Fabius Maximus Aemilianus and Publius Cornelius Scipio Aemilianus, two sons of Lucius Aemilius Paulus, who ended the Third Macedonian War by his victory at Pydna (168), were adopted respectively into the Fabian and Scipionic families.

27: the year is 107.

the consulship as the spoils of his victory over them, boasting of other accomplishments designed to exalt himself at the painful expense of those men. In the meantime, he gave priority to what was needed for the war: he demanded reinforcements for the legions, called auxiliary troops from various peoples and client kings, and in particular, he summoned the bravest men from the Latin and Italian Allies; the majority of them he knew from their military service under him, but a few by reputation only. He made personal appeals to veterans and summoned them to re-enlist in his campaign. The senate, although it was completely against him, did not dare to deny any of his program. As for the reinforcements, the senators were happy to vote them, because they believed that military service was distasteful to the plebeians and Marius would thereby lose either the requisites of war or the enthusiastic support of the common people. But events were to frustrate their hopes: an incredible desire to follow Marius stirred the men; each one cherished the dream of becoming wealthy from the plunder, of returning home a victorious hero, or had other dreams of this kind.[28] And Marius also provoked them considerably in a speech. For, after all the measures which he had demanded were decreed, and it was the time that he wanted to enlist the soldiers, he convened an assembly of the people to urge them to sign up and to attack the nobles as he liked to do. He then delivered the following address:

(85)[29] "I know very well, fellow citizens,[30] that the majority of men seek power from you with a set of morals unlike those they actually employ in fulfilling the offices that they have won. At first they are diligent, humble, and moderate, but afterwards they lead lives of laziness and arrogance. But to me the converse seems to be the right course. For whereas the state as a whole has more value than a consulship or praetorship, so greater attention should be directed to its governance than in the quest for its offices. The size of the undertaking to which I commit myself because of this great kindness of yours does not escape me. To prepare for war without exhausting the treasury, to force into military service those whom you do not want to offend, to manage affairs at home and abroad, and to do all of these things amid envy, opposition, and factional intrigue, is much more difficult, my fellow citizens, than one might think. Moreover, if the others fail, they have these supports: their long-standing nobility, the brave exploits of their ancestors, the resources of relations, by both blood and by marriage, and many clients.[31] For me, all my hopes which

---

28: Marius opened enlistment into the army to the proletariat.

29: Marius sketches his life and character, contrasting himself and his achievements with the debauched, decadent, and corrupt nobles.

30: 'fellow citizens' translates 'Quirites,' a term used ten times in the speech. The name designates 'offspring of Quirinus,' the deified Romulus, and it adds a certain solemnity to the address.

31: in this section Marius details the political difficulties of a "new man" in the arena of Roman politics.

I must secure by merit and integrity reside in myself; all other supports are insubstantial. And I understand that, my fellow citizens; the eyes of all are turned upon me; the just and honorable favor me because my services go to benefit the state, but the nobility look for an opportunity to assail me. So I must strive all the more fiercely in order to frustrate them and to prevent your being misled. From my boyhood up to this very day I have been the sort of person familiar with all kinds of labor and all types of risks. It is not my policy, my fellow citizens, now that I have received recompense, to abandon those services which I performed for you at no cost. For those who during their quest for votes have pretended to be upright it is difficult to be moderate in the exercise of power; for me, who have conducted all my life in the best pursuits, public service has become second nature.[32]

You have voted me the command in the war against Jugurtha, a commission which has annoyed the party of the nobles to distraction.[33] Now I ask you, mull it over in your minds whether it would be better to change your decision and send on this or on some other one equally important mission a member of that cabal of nobles, a man of ancient pedigree, a person who parades numerous portrait busts, but has no military experience: naturally, ignorant of all procedures in a crisis, he hurries and scurries about, and chooses a plebeian to advise him of his duty.[34] So it generally happens that your choice to command the army looks for another man to be the general. I also know, my fellow citizens, of some who, once they have been elected consuls, began to read of their ancestral exploits and the Greek military manuals. In this they put the cart before the horse; in their case administering the office comes after their election to it, whereas in importance and practical experience it *is* first. Compare, now, my fellow citizens, me, a "new man," with those arrogant nobles. What they have acquired from hearsay or reading, I have seen or done first hand; what they have learned from books, I have learned from military experience in the field. Now, consider whether deeds or words are of greater value to you. They despise my recent rank, I detest their indolence; they reproach me with my low birth, I censure their depraved acts. And yet for my part, I believe that all men share a single nature, but that the bravest are the noblest. Suppose that one could ask the fathers of Albinus and Bestia[35] whether they would prefer to have me or them for

---

32: this last sentence in the opening paragraph summarizes and provides a concrete example of the opening sentence of the chapter.

33. Marius supplanted the noble Quintus Caecilius Metellus as commander of the forces in North Africa.

34: Marius snidely alludes to Metellus.

35: Lucius Calpurnius Bestia had been the Roman commander in charge of the first year of campaigning against Jugurtha (111). His terms for peace were disavowed in Rome. Spurius and Aulus Albinus were the commanders in charge of the second year of the war against Jugurtha (110). The Albini and Bestia were losers in the campaign and corrupt.

sons, what other response do you think they would make other than that they would want the best possible children? But if they rightly disdain me, let them also scorn their ancestors whose nobility was founded on manliness like my own. They envy my elected office; let them, therefore, begrudge my hard work, my integrity, and all the risks I have assumed to attain it. In fact they are corrupt and arrogant, and spend their time as if they also despise the honors you bestow. They are completely deceived if they expect most disparate matters, the pleasure of idleness and the rewards of merit, to be considered equal. And even when they address you or the senate in the body of the speech, they praise their ancestors, thinking that by trumpeting their brave exploits they themselves become more illustrious. The converse, however, holds true. The more glorious was the life of the forefathers, the more shameful the indolence of those nowadays. Surely, the truth is that the glory of our ancestors serves as a torch for the lives of posterity, and does not allow either their virtues or their weaknesses to remain in the dark.[36] I confess my lack of such glory, fellow citizens, but I can claim deeds that are my own—which is much more illustrious. Now look how unfair they are. What they appropriate for themselves from the excellence of another, they deny me because of my merit, of course, because I lack their busts of pedigree and because my nobility is recent. But surely it is better to have merited a noble rank than to have inherited and then dishonored it.

I am not unaware, of course, that, if my adversaries wish to respond to me, they have abundant eloquence and elaborate skill in oratory. But since on every occasion of this illustrious distinction that you have bestowed, they have cursed and assailed both me and you, I decided not to keep quiet lest anyone should equate my self-restraint with a guilty conscience. For I am convinced that no speech can harm me; if they tell the truth, then they must speak well of me; if they lie, then my life and character will refute them. But since they impugn your decision to invest me with this highest honor and most distinguished commission, rethink and reconsider whether you should regret your choice. I cannot, to inspire your confidence in me, parade before you the portrait busts, the triumphs, and consulships of my ancestors, but, if circumstances require, I can display spears, ribbons, medals, and other military prizes, especially the scars on the front of my body. These are my busts, my nobility, not bequeathed as an inheritance, as they are for them, but won by my countless labors and risks to my person. My words are not well chosen; I consider that of little value. My worth speaks for itself; it doesn't need rhetorical artifice and a glib argument to whitewash shameful acts, as is the case with

---

36: Marius intimates that the disgrace is greater for contemporary aristocrats who do not have a torch or who have allowed the torch of glory to go out.

them. I have not learned Greek literature;[37] inasmuch as it did not confer manliness upon its teachers, I wasn't much concerned to study it. But I have earned an education in matters of the greatest value to the state: to strike the enemy, to stand guard, to fear nothing except a disgraceful reputation, to endure equally the cold of winter and the heat of summer, to bivouac on the ground, and to suffer at the same time hunger and hard work. These are the lessons that I teach to soldiers; I will see to this: they will not do without, while I live in opulence, nor will I claim all the glory when they do all the work. This is the proper way to command; this is the command befitting a citizen. For when an officer lives a life of ease, but forces upon his army a life of punishing discipline, that is the command of a martinet, not a general. By performing such deeds as these your forefathers made themselves and the country renowned. But the present nobility, relying upon these very ancestors, yet so incompatible with them in their character and morals, despise us who emulate their conduct, and again and again they court you for all political offices, not because they have deserved them, but, as it were, because they feel they are entitled to them. But these men are most arrogant and are greatly in error. Their ancestors bequeathed to them all that they could, wealth, pedigree, and the memory of their own glorious tradition; they failed, however, to leave them virtue, because they could not: it is the only thing that neither can be given nor be received as a gift. They claim that I am vulgar and lack good manners because I know not how to host a party with taste and elegance, and because I fail to keep an actor[38] or cook at greater cost than the ramrod of my farm. For from my father and other morally virtuous men I have learned that refined delicacies are for women, but toil befits men, and that all good men should possess a reputation greater than the sum of his riches, and that arms, not furniture, are the proper ornamentation of life. So, by all means, then, let them do what pleases them and what they cherish: making love, drinking; let them pass their old age in the pursuits in which they engaged in their youth: at parties in surrender to their belly and a slave to that most indecent body part. The sweat, the dust, and other such markers, let them leave to us who find them sweeter than banquets. But it is not to be the case; for when these most disgraceful men have dishonored themselves with depravity, they set out to steal the rewards of the honorable. So, their extravagance and sloth, the very worst vices, combine with their injustice to bring no detriment to those who cultivate them but to bring disaster to an innocent republic.

Now that I have responded to them as much as my character has demanded, but not as much as their crimes deserve, I will say a few words about the state. First, my fellow citizens, do not worry about Numidia. You

---

37: there is a certain irony in the statement because Sallust himself is very well-versed in Greek literature.

38: an actor was commonly kept at the banquets of the wealthy.

have removed all the obstacles which up to now have protected Jugurtha: greed, incompetence, and arrogance. Moreover, there is an army there that knows the terrain, but more courageous than successful, damn it all, because most of it was worn down by the venality and rashness of its generals.[39] Therefore, you, yes, those of you of military age, join with me in my struggle and serve your country! Do not allow fear to grip a single one of you because of the disastrous defeat of others or the haughty pride of generals. On the march and in the front ranks I will be your guide, I will share your every danger, and in all matters I will treat each of you exactly the same. Know full well that with the help of the gods all the fruits are ripe for us: victory, spoils, glory; even if these rewards were uncertain or remote, still all good men should come to the aid of their country.[40] Cowardice has surely made no man immortal, and no parent has ever hoped his children to live eternal, but rather that they live their lives as virtuous and honorable men. I could say much more, fellow citizens, if words could imbue cowards with courage; I think, however, I have said more than enough for the brave."

(86) Marius delivered an address of this kind. After he saw that the passions of the plebeians had been aroused, he quickly had ships loaded with supplies, money for the campaign, weapons, and other necessities. He gave orders to Aulus Manlius, his legate, to set out with them. In the meantime, he himself recruited soldiers, but not in the custom of our predecessors nor by the propertied classes, for he admitted volunteers, the majority of whom were the proletariat, those assessed by the head.[41] Some relate that he did that because there was a lack of qualified men, others maintain that because in his drive to be consul he curried support of the very class which had brought him fame and prominence.[42] For one in quest for power the most helpful person is the poorest, for he has no concern for his own goods, since he has none, and to him all things seem honorable if they command a price.

Therefore, Marius set sail for Africa with a force considerably larger than was decreed; after a few days he arrived at Utica where the army was handed over to him by the legate Publius Rutilius, since Metellus, of course, shunned the sight of Marius to avoid seeing what he could not tolerate even to hear.

39: a veiled reference not only to Bestia and the Albini but also to Metellus.

40: I have rendered this all-too-familiar line literally.

41: the admitting of volunteers from the proletariat signaled a break in tradition and set a precedent with grave consequences for the Republic.

42: Marius was forced to recruit from the proletariat because the senate refused to sanction and fund the recruitment.

CORNELIUS NEPOS

The impact of the Carthaginian Wars upon the Romans was enormous. Even in the Augustan Age writers alluded to the wars and some, like Sallust, attributed Rome's moral decline to Rome's conquest of Carthage and the Eastern Mediterranean. Thus, it is fitting that the brief biographical sketch of Hamilcar Barca, Hannibal's father, and the fuller and somewhat sympathetic treatment of Hannibal be included in this book. Perhaps because of Nepos' personal relationship with Atticus he decided to compose a biography of the "famous" man. Indeed, Atticus was a remarkable figure in his own right during the age and it is a wonder, despite his famed neutrality, that he escaped with his life from the turmoil of first century BCE. Nepos' life of Atticus is probably his best written and most poignant, although it is often too uncritical and too laudable of its subject. In the end a more penetrating analysis of why Atticus was able to maintain his connections with many different politicians of varied political persuasions and yet was able to survive would have been welcomed. But Nepos does present us a compelling look at a fascinating character who belongs to the political and social milieu of late Republican Rome, a look at the person behind the many letters sent by Cicero.

HAMILCAR BARCA

(1) When he was still a young man, Hamilcar Barca, the Carthaginian, son of Hannibal, was put in charge of the army in Sicily as the first Punic war was nearing its end [247 BCE]. Before his arrival the Carthaginian cause on land and sea was going badly, but, whenever he was present and personally in command, he never yielded to the enemy or gave them a chance to inflict much damage; on the contrary, when opportunity knocked, he often attacked and invariably left the field victorious. Moreover, whereas the Carthaginians had lost almost all their holdings in Sicily, he, on the other hand, defended Eryx so well

71

that one would have thought that no war had been fought in that area. In the meantime, the Carthaginians, after they were defeated at sea near the Aegates islands by a fleet under the command of the Roman consul, Gaius Lutatius [Catulus], decided to negotiate an end to the war and empowered Hamilcar to conduct the proceedings.

Although Hamilcar burned with the passion of making war, yet he thought that peace should be served; he understood that his country was exhausted from the financial burden of the war and could no longer bear the military disasters. Still he was planning in his mind, once the state made a little recovery, to renew the war and to pursue the Romans with armed forces until the Carthaginians either won by their valor or were defeated and surrendered. He negotiated the peace with this scheme in mind; so intense were his feelings that, when Catulus said he would not settle the war, unless Hamilcar and the defenders of Eryx lay down their arms and left Sicily, he swore that his fatherland would collapse and he himself would perish before he would return home in so much disgrace; his valor would not permit him to hand over to his adversaries the arms which he had received from his country to fight enemies. In the face of such stubborn resolve, Catulus yielded.

(2) But when he arrived at Carthage, he found that the status of the state was much worse than he had expected. The length of misfortune abroad had kindled a civil war, putting the city at an unparalleled risk, excepting that time when Carthage was destroyed. In the first place, the twenty thousand mercenaries employed against the Romans revolted. They alienated the whole of Africa against the city and assaulted Carthage itself. Distressed and alarmed by these troubles, the Carthaginians even petitioned the Romans for help, and received it. But in the end, almost reduced to despair, they made Hamilcar the commander-in-chief. He repelled the enemy from the walls of Carthage, although they were more than 100,000 armed men, and driving them to some narrows, he blocked their movements, where more perished from hunger than by the sword. All the estranged towns, including Utica and Hippo,[1] the most thriving of all in Africa, he restored to the country. Not content with that success, he also extended the frontiers under Carthaginian control. The peace he restored to the whole of Africa made it appear that for many years there had been no war at all.

(3) When he completed these operations to his satisfaction, harboring hatred toward the Romans, he was confident in his search of a ready pretext for making war. He devised to be sent to Spain with an army under his command and took with him his young son Hannibal, then nine years old. Also accompanying him was a distinguished and

---

1: Utica was only about twenty miles northwest of Carthage and from very early times had been under the control of Carthage. Hippo, on the other hand, was almost 100 miles west of Carthage.

handsome young man, Hasdrubal by name, whom some gossiped that Hamilcar loved in a way more improper than proper: even a man of his reputation could not escape slander. The gossip, however, did its work, for the official in charge of morals ordered Hasdrubal not to accompany him. Hamilcar, however, gave his daughter in marriage to him, since the customs of the Carthaginians prohibit the interdiction of a father-in-law from a son-in-law. I have mentioned Hasdrubal because, after Hamilcar was killed, he was put in charge of the army and succeeded in accomplishing a great many things. On the other hand he took the lead in largess and corrupted the pristine morals of the Carthaginians; after his death the army chose Hannibal to succeed to the command.

(4) Hamilcar, favored by fortune, after crossing the sea and coming to Spain, accomplished great feats. He subdued very powerful and warlike tribes and enriched all of Africa with horses, weapons, men, and money. As he was scheming to bring war into Italy, he was killed in battle, fighting against the Vettones,[2] in the ninth year after his arrival into Spain. His inexorable hatred toward the Romans, more than anything else, seems to have motivated the second Punic war; for his son, Hannibal, heard his father's constant execrations and was so convinced that he preferred death to failure against the Romans.

HANNIBAL

(1) Hannibal, the son of Hamilcar, Carthaginian. If it is true—and no one doubts it—that the Roman people have surpassed all others in manly courage, one cannot deny that Hannibal excelled all other generals in strategy as much as the Roman people transcend all nations in bravery. For as often as he contested with Romans on Italian soil, he invariably came away the victor, and, had he not been weakened at home by the spite of his own citizens, he might, it seems, have overcome the Romans. His many detractors, however, undermined his singular ability.[3] But the hatred of his father toward the Romans, left to him, as it were, as an inheritance, he sustained so intensely that he would have sooner surrendered his life than renounce it. In fact, even after he was driven from his fatherland and was reduced to begging for assistance from foreigners, it never entered his mind to cease warring with the Romans.

(2) With the exception of Philip, whom Hannibal during his absence from home rendered into an enemy to the Romans, the most powerful of all was king Antiochus. He inflamed Antiochus' mind with such a

---

2: he drowned in his retreat at the battle of Helice.

3: a reference primarily to Hanno who opposed many of Hannibal's policies and who argued for peace negotiations with the Romans throughout the Second Punic War.

passion for war that he prepared to bring it to Italy[4] all the way from the Red Sea.[5] When Roman ambassadors came to him to explore his intentions, they set their minds to intrigue, provoking suspicions of Hannibal in the king; they misrepresented that they had corrupted him and that he felt differently from the way he had earlier. And they were not unsuccessful in their intrigue. Indeed, Hannibal discovered it and saw that he was being excluded from the more intimate discussions of policy. He then approached the king at a suitable time and, after he related his many instances of good faith and his hatred of the Romans, he added: "My father, Hamilcar, when I was still a little boy, no more than nine years old, on his departure from Carthage to Spain as general, sacrificed victims to Jupiter Best and Greatest.[6] As he was performing these religious rites, he asked me if I wanted to accompany him on campaign. I eagerly accepted the proposal and began to press him not to hesitate to take me; he then said, 'I'll do it, if you promise me what I ask.' He led me at once to the altar at which he had begun his sacrifice; separated from the others, he ordered me to take hold of it and swear that I would never enter into friendship with the Romans. The oath which I swore to my father I have preserved to this very day, and no one should doubt that for the rest of time I will feel the same. Therefore, if you have any kind thought toward the Romans, you will not be acting unwisely to keep them hidden from me; you will disappoint yourself in your preparations for war, if you do not make me the leader in that operation."

(3) Accordingly, at the age previously mentioned he departed for Spain with his father, and after his father's passing, Hasdrubal assumed chief command, and Hannibal was put in charge of the cavalry. When Hasdrubal died, the supreme command of the army devolved to him. This news, reported to Carthage, won official approval. Thus Hannibal was made supreme commander at less than twenty-five years old.[7] Within the next three years he had subdued in war all the peoples of Spain; he had assaulted and stormed Saguntum, a city-state allied with Rome, and he had assembled three mighty armies. Of these he sent one to Africa, the second he left with his brother Hasdrubal in Spain, and the third he led with him into Italy. He crossed the chain of the Pyrenees. Wherever he marched, he had conflicts with all the natives; he defeated all and released none. When he came to the Alps that separate Italy from Gaul, and which no one before him except the Greek hero Hercules had ever crossed with an army—for which reason it is still called the Greek pass

---

4: Antiochus' military encounters with the Romans were defeats both on land and sea. He never invaded Italy.
5: the Persian Gulf is meant.
6: the god would be Baal.
7: the date is 221 and Hannibal was twenty-six at the time.

today—he cut to pieces the Alpine tribes who were trying to prevent his crossing. He lay open the districts, constructed roads, and provided a route for an equipped elephant to pass through; previously a single man without his pack was scarcely able to crawl through it. Via this pass he led his forces and came into Italy.

(4) He had already fought with the consul Publius Cornelius Scipio at the Rhone and had routed him; he engaged the same general at Clastidium on the Po and drove him into flight as a wounded man. A third time this same Scipio with his colleague Tiberius Longus met him at the Trebia. Hannibal joined battle and routed them both. Then through Ligurian territory he crossed the Apennines, making his way to Etruria. During this march he suffered an affliction of the eyes so serious that never again could he see as well from his right eye. While he was still distressed and ailing from this sickness, and was being carried about on a litter, at Lake Trasimene he surrounded and ambushed the consul Gaius Flaminius and his army and killed him. Not much later he killed Gaius Centenius, a praetor, who was holding a pass with a select company of men. He then arrived in Apulia. There, two consuls, Gaius Terentius and Lucius Aemilius [Paulus], engaged him. In a single battle he routed their armies and slew the consul Paulus and several ex-consuls, including Gnaeus Servilius Geminus who had been consul the year before.

(5) After this battle no one resisted Hannibal on his march toward Rome. In the mountains near the city he stopped. After he had held camp there for several days and was making his return to Capua, Quintus Fabius Maximus, dictator of Rome, blocked his way in the Falernian district. Although he was trapped in some narrows, at night he extricated himself without the loss of any in his army, thereby giving the slip to Fabius, himself a most crafty general. For under the cover of darkness he tied bundles of brushwood to the horns of cattle and set them afire, then scattered a great number of the animals to wander about here and there. This sudden sight before them threw the Roman army into such a panic that no one dared to go outside the rampart. Not so many days after this event he routed Marcus Minucius Rufus, master of the horse, and co-dictator with equal power.[8] Tiberius Sempronius Gracchus, two times a consul, he tricked into an ambush and eliminated him, although he was not there in person. In a similar fashion he killed Marcus Claudius Marcellus, a five-time consul, near Venusia. It would be tedious to list all of his battles. It will suffice to mention this one point, from which one can understand how great a general he was: as long as he was in Italy, no one stopped him on the battle field; no one after the battle of Cannae pitched camp to force him on the open plain.

8: after a minor victory Minucius considered himself a joint dictator, a constitutional anomaly.

(6) Undefeated, he was recalled to defend his country, where he waged a campaign against Publius Scipio, the son of that Scipio whom he had routed first at the Rhone, then at the Po, and lastly at the Trebia. Since the resources of his fatherland had by now been exhausted, he wanted to arrange with Scipio a respite from the war so that later with renewed strength he could reenter the fight. They held a parley but could not agree on the terms. A few days after the meeting he fought Scipio at Zama.[9] Routed—incredible to say—after two nights and a day he reached Hadrumetum, which is about 300 miles from Zama. During his retreat the Numidians, who had left the battlefield with him, ambushed him; he not only escaped their trap, but also crushed them. At Hadrumetum he gathered together the remnants from the retreat; within a few days he enlisted many new recruits.

(7) While he was intensely occupied in making preparations, the Carthaginians settled the war with the Romans; Hannibal, however, still commanded the army; he administered military affairs in Africa and, likewise, his brother Mago, up until the consulship of Publius Sulpicius and Gaius Aurelius [200 BCE]. While these men were in office, Carthaginian ambassadors arrived in Rome to thank the senate and Roman people for making peace with them; and in gratitude they presented them a golden crown, at the same time requesting that their hostages be allowed to stay in Fregellae, but that their captives be returned. In response to them the senate decreed that their gift was acceptable and they thanked them for it; the hostages could live where they had requested, but they would not send home the prisoners, since Hannibal, who initiated the war by his military action, was most hostile to the Roman people and was still in command of an army, as was his brother Mago. When the Carthaginians heard that reply, they recalled both Hannibal and Mago to Carthage. When he returned, Hannibal, after serving as general for twenty-two years, was made king[10]. For as is the case of consuls at Rome, in Carthage two kings annually were elected to serve one year. In this office Hannibal applied himself as diligently as he had in the war, for he made it possible not only to raise money by new taxes in order to pay to the Romans the indemnity specified in the treaty, but also to produce a surplus to be deposited in the treasury. Then, during the consulship of Marcus Claudius and Lucius Furius [196 BCE], ambassadors from Rome came to Carthage. Before the senate could give them a hearing, Hannibal, perceiving that their mission was to demand his surrender, secretly boarded a ship and fled to Antiochus in Syria. When the facts of this matter became known, the Carthaginians sent two ships to arrest

9: the battle was fought on the very next day after the meeting of Scipio and Hannibal.
10: the actual title was *sufete*, the chief magistrate who also had judicial powers.

him, if they could catch up to him; they then confiscated his property, razed his house, foundations and all, and proclaimed him an outlaw.

(8) But Hannibal, in the fourth year after his exile from home,[11] during the consulship of Lucius Cornelius and Quintus Minucius [193 BCE], landed five ships in Africa along the frontiers of Cyrene on the chance that the Carthaginians could be persuaded to go to war in the confident hope of support from Antiochus whom he had already convinced to advance upon Italy with his armies. There he quickly dispatched his brother Mago. When the Carthaginians found about it, they inflicted upon Mago in his absence the same penalty as that accorded his brother, Hannibal. Feeling that the situation was desperate, the two launched the ships and set sail. Hannibal then arrived to Antiochus. There are two accounts of the tradition about Mago's demise; some have written that he perished in a shipwreck, while others have claimed that he was killed by his own slaves. As for Antiochus, if he had been willing to follow Hannibal's strategy in conducting the war as he had been in undertaking it, he would have fought for supreme power nearer the banks of the Tiber rather than at Thermopylae.[12] Although he saw that many of Antiochus' enterprises were ill-conceived, nevertheless, in no instance did Hannibal desert him. For example, he was put in charge of a few ships which he was ordered to bring from Syria to Asia, and with them he engaged a Rhodian fleet in the Pamphylian Sea. Although in that encounter his fleet was defeated by the overwhelmingly superior number of its enemy, Hannibal himself was a winner on the wing where he commanded.

(9) After Antiochus was routed, Hannibal was afraid that he would be surrendered, which would have happened, if he had allowed the opportunity; he came to Gortyna in Crete to consider his next step. This man, shrewdest of all, perceived that he would face much danger unless he devised a plan against the greed of the Cretans. He was, in fact, carrying a large amount of money with him and was aware that its existence was common knowledge. He therefore seized upon the following plan: he filled numerous vessels with lead, topping them off with gold and silver. In the presence of the city's leaders he deposited them in the temple of Diana, pretending that he was entrusting his fortune to their safekeeping. After he misled them, he stuffed some bronze statues, which he was transporting with him, with all his money and threw them out in the courtyard of his house. The Gortynians guarded the temple with utmost care not to prevent theft by others but to keep Hannibal from taking the vessels without their knowledge, and from carrying his (wealth) away with him.

11: Romans normally counted "both ends" of a sequence; we would reckon it
    to be the third year.
12: the battle was fought in 191 and Antiochus suffered a defeat.

(10) After he had saved his property and had tricked all the Cretans, the wily Carthaginian made his way to king Prusias in Pontus. In his presence Hannibal showed the same old feelings toward Italy and directed all his energy to arming the king and training his troops to fight the Romans. When he saw that the king's personal resources were too little to make him strong, he won over the other kings and united with him the warlike nations. Prusias was on different sides from Eumenes, the king of Pergamum, who was a very faithful ally of Rome. They fought with each other on land and sea, but Eumenes was stronger in both areas—land or sea—because of his alliance with the Romans, which made Hannibal all the more eager to crush him. If Hannibal got rid of Eumenes, he thought that all his difficulties would disappear. In order to kill him he entered upon the following stratagem. In fact, in a few days they were intending to fight a naval battle. Since Hannibal was outnumbered in ships, and was also outmatched in arms, he had to do his fighting by trickery. He ordered his men to collect the largest possible number of poisonous snakes and to put them alive into clay jars. By the day they were to engage in the sea battle, he had gathered a large number of them. He summoned the sailors in the fleet and instructed them to head directly to one ship, that of king Eumenes, and to be content to defend themselves from the others that would be attacking. He assured them that they would easily succeed because of the great quantity of snakes; he would let them know which ship the king was sailing on, and promised them a bonus, if they either captured or killed him.

(11) After he exhorted the soldiers, both of the fleets sailed out to do battle. When they were drawn up in line, before the signal of battle was sounded, Hannibal sent a messenger in a boat with a herald's staff to make it clear to his men where Eumenes would be. When he came to the enemy's ships, this messenger waved a letter and stated that he was looking for the king. At once he was escorted to Eumenes because no one doubted that the letter communicated some peace offering. In this way the letter carrier's actions pinpointed the commander's ship for his men and he took himself off to the same place from where he had come. But after Eumenes opened the letter, he found nothing in it except what was intended to mock and insult him. Although he speculated over the letter, he discovered no reason for it. Yet, he did not hesitate to commit to do battle at once. The Bithynians followed Hannibal's order in the clash and launched their attack against Eumenes' ship in unison. Since the king could not sustain the force of the attack, he sought safety in flight, which he would not have attained, if he had not retreated to fortifications which he had constructed on the nearest shore. While the rest of the Pergamene ships were pressing hard upon their opponents, suddenly the Bithynians began to hurl onto the ships those clay vessels which I mentioned previously. At first those missiles evoked laughter from the fighters and they could not understand what it was all about. But when

they saw their ships filled with snakes, terrified by the strange sight, and not understanding how to avoid the worst, they turned the ships and retreated to their naval station. By this scheme Hannibal overcame the arms of the Pergamenes, and that was not the sole occasion; for with his infantry he quite frequently routed his adversaries by using a similar tactic.

(12) While this was happening in Asia, it chanced that ambassadors of Prusias were dining in Rome at the home of Titus Quinctius Flamininus, an ex-consul, and, when mention was made of Hannibal over dinner conversation, one of them said that he was in Prusias' kingdom.[13] On the next day Flamininus reported that information to the senate. The conscript fathers, thinking that they would never be safe from plots as long as Hannibal was alive, sent ambassadors to Bithynia, including Flamininus, to ask the king not to harbor their most bitter enemy, but to surrender him to them. Prusias did not dare to refuse; but he made an objection that they not ask him to do anything which would violate the rights of hospitality; if they could, then they should arrest Hannibal; they could easily find the place where he was. For Hannibal used to stay in one spot in a fortified castle which the king had presented to him for his service; Hannibal had it built so that he would have exits in every part of the building, apparently fearing that he would come to use it exactly as it occurred. When the Roman ambassadors arrived, they surrounded his house with a great number of men. A slave boy, looking out the door, told Hannibal that an unusual number of men were visible. Hannibal ordered him to inspect all the doors and report back to him promptly if he saw that the house was under siege on every side. The slave boy quickly reported what was happening and pointed out that all the exits were blocked. Hannibal perceived that this was not taking place by accident, that he was the quarry whom they were seeking, and that he could no longer hold on to life. To prevent losing it at the discretion of someone else, and remembering the glory of his past deeds of valor, he took the poison which he had always kept on his person.[14]

(13) Thus this bravest man, this man who had performed so many and varied labors, entered into rest in his seventieth year.[15] There is no agreement on who the consuls were when he died. For Atticus has recorded in his history that he died in the consulship of Marcus Claudius Marcellus and Quintus Fabius Labeo [183]; but Polybius has maintained the consulship of Lucius Aemilius Paulus and Gnaeus Baebius Tamphilus [182], and Sulpicius Blitho has assigned the consulship of Publius Cornelius Cethegus and Marcus Baebius Tamphilus [181]. Although seriously occupied with mighty wars, yet this giant of a man devoted some time

---

13: the year of this and the following events is 183.
14: Juvenal, *Sat.* 10.164 says that Hannibal kept the poison in a ring.
15: in fact, Hannibal was only sixty-three years old in 183.

to literature. Several of his books, written in a Greek dialect, exist; they include one addressed to the Rhodians concerning the exploits in Asia of Gnaeus Manlius Vulso. Many have recorded the traditions of Hannibal's military accomplishments; two of them, who lived at the same time and served with him in camp, were Silenus and Sosylus, the Spartan. This Sosylus Hannibal had hired as his teacher of Greek literature.

ATTICUS

(1) Titus Pomponius Atticus, born from the oldest stock of the Roman race, maintained his equestrian rank which he had inherited from his ancestors.[16] He had a father who, solicitous and rich for the times, was extremely interested in literature. Because of his love for literature the father educated his son in those studies which young boys ought to master. Moreover, besides a natural ability for intellectual pursuits the boy had a most pleasant pronunciation and diction so that he not only quickly learned traditional narratives, but also delivered them in public without flaw. So, even in childhood he had a noble reputation among his peers and distinguished himself far more than his fellow students of aristocratic birth could bear with equanimity. Therefore, he excited all with his passion; and in their number were included Lucius Torquatus, Gaius Marius, the son, and Marcus Cicero; he united them in such an intimate bond that no one was ever dearer to them.

(2) His father died prematurely. When he was a teen-ager, he himself was not immune from risk because of his relationship by marriage to Publius Sulpicius, who as tribune of the plebs was executed; for Anicia, Pomponius Atticus' cousin, had married Servius, the brother of Sulpicius. Therefore, after Sulpicius was killed, he observed that the state was in turmoil because of the agitation of Cinna, and that no means were offered to him of living in accordance with his rank without offending one or the other political faction. Feelings of the citizens were estranged, some favoring the party of Sulla, the others that of Cinna, and believing that it was the right time to indulge his own interests, he went to Athens.[17] Nevertheless, he aided from his own resources the young Marius after he had been proclaimed a public enemy, and alleviated his flight by grants of money. To prevent the loss of his personal property because of his travel abroad, he transferred a great part of his fortune to Athens.

His lifestyle in Athens endeared him to all its citizens. Besides his influence, which was considerable even in his youth, he often relieved

16: Atticus' family, the Pomponii, traced their lineage back to a certain Pompo, a son of Numa Pompilius, the second king of Rome.
17: Nepos puts a favorable "spin" on Atticus' lengthy sojourn in Athens. Most likely, Atticus feared that he might be drawn into the political turmoil of the period and be accused by the conservative party of Sulla.

their public debt from his supply of funds. For instance, whenever the state needed to secure a loan and the terms were unfair to them, he always intervened, never receiving an unethically high rate of interest, nor allowing the loan to remain outstanding any longer than what was agreed upon. Both practices were to the Athenians' advantage, because he did not permit their debt to lapse out of complacency nor to let it grow by compounding interest. He enriched this service by another act of generous largess, for he made a gift of grain to everyone, a distribution to each person of six bushels of wheat, by a measure which the Athenians call the *medimnus*.

(3) In his conduct at Athens he seemed to be accessible to the lowest class and on equal terms with the prominent. As a result, the people publicly bestowed upon him all the honors they could and were eager to make him a citizen. But he refused to entertain the kind offer because jurists interpreted that Roman citizenship was lost if another was obtained. As long as he was in Athens, he opposed any statue being erected in his honor; but when he was no longer there, he could not prevent it. So, they erected some to him and to Pilia[18] in the most sacred areas; for they considered him an initiator and sponsor in all the administration of the state. First of all fortune provided him a gift, that he was born in the most powerful city, the seat of a world empire, and the one that he regarded as his fatherland and home. It was an example of his acumen that, when he had immigrated to that city-state which surpassed all others in antiquity, refinement, and learning, he alone was its dearest member.

(4) After Sulla departed from Asia, he stopped in Athens.[19] As long as he stayed there, he entertained Pomponius, captivated by the young man's culture and learning. On the one hand, he spoke fluent Greek, so well that he seemed to be a native Athenian; while on the other, the gracefulness of the Latin language appeared in him to encompass an innate charm, not an acquired one. He also gave public readings of his poems, both in Greek and in Latin, to which nothing could be added. The result of all this was that Sulla would not let go of him and desired to take Atticus back home with him. But at his attempt to persuade him, Atticus said: "Don't, I beg you, think to lead me against those with whom I left Italy to avoid bearing arms against you." Sulla praised the young man for his sense of duty and ordered that the gifts which he had received in Athens be returned to him.

While he sojourned in Athens for many years, Atticus gave as much attention to his personal property as a diligent head of the household is obliged to, and, as he had devoted all the rest of his time either to

18: Pilia is Atticus' wife. See Cicero, letter #7 *ad Att.* 14.17.1.
19: Nepos is engaging in gross understatement. Sulla attacked the Piraeus and captured parts of Athens.

literature or to public issues of the Athenians, at the same time for his friends in the city he provided services. He was present at their canvassing for election and was not missing whenever some major issue was acted upon. Thus, to Cicero in all his trials he showed a unique loyalty. As he was setting out into exile from the country, Atticus gave him 250,000 sesterces. When the Roman state had been restored to tranquility, he returned to Rome during the consulship, I believe, of Lucius Cotta and Lucius Torquatus [65 BCE]. As he was departing, the whole citizenry escorted him; their tears revealed the pain that would come from missing him.

(5) He had an uncle, Quintus Caecilius who was a Roman equestrian and good friend of Lucius Lucullus; Caecilius was a rich man, but of a most difficult disposition. Atticus feared his grouchy nature. Yet, whereas no one else could stand him, he retained, without showing any offence, his uncle's good will right up to his extreme old age. In this way he reaped the fruit of his devotion, for Caecilius at his death adopted him in his will and made him heir to three quarters of the estate. From this legacy he received about ten million sesterces. Atticus' sister married Quintus Tullius Cicero; Marcus Cicero arranged this marriage; with him Atticus had lived as the dearest friend from their school days together, much more intimately than with Quintus—which demonstrates that similarity in character has more importance in matters of friendship than family connections. He had an intimate friendship with Quintus Hortensius who in that period claimed the first rank in oratory. One could not know which of the two, Cicero or Hortensius, loved him more. Atticus, at any rate, accomplished a most difficult task, that no rancor came between the rivals for glory, as he was the bond between those famous men.

(6) His conduct in public affairs showed that he was, or appeared to be, a partisan of the party of the "best men;"[20] yet, he did not commit himself to the tides of political life, for he believed that those who surrendered themselves to politics were no more under their own power than those who were tossed upon the sea. He did not seek political offices, although they were open to him because of his influence and status. Honest men could not seek them in the traditional manner, nor win them in an atmosphere of rampant bribery, nor preserve the laws, nor govern the state without personal risk when public morals were so corrupted. He never attended a public auction at the spear.[21] He never became a bondsman or public contractor.[22] He accused no one either under his

---

20: a reference to the 'optimates.' Consult the glossary.
21: a spear was set up in the forum to indicate a public auction; originally it heralded the sale of the booty taken in military campaigns.
22: Nepos means that Atticus was not engaged in the state contracting of taxes that went to bidding equestrians.

own name or in support of another. He never went to court concerning his own property, nor held trial. The subordinate commands offered by the many consuls and praetors he accepted only with the stipulation that he would accompany no one into his province,[23] being content with the honor because he scorned profiteering. He even refused to accompany Quintus Cicero into Asia,[24] although he could have held the post of his legate. He did not think it was becoming for him to be the assistant of the praetor, when he himself had refused to hold the office. Therefore, he not only accommodated his dignity but also his peace of mind in which case he also avoided the suspicion of a criminal act.[25] The result was that his scrupulous attention endeared him to all when they saw it was attributable to his sense of duty, not to fear or hope.

(7) When Atticus was about sixty years old, the civil war with Caesar erupted. He used the exemption of age and did not move from the city. Whatever his friends needed as they set out to Pompey, he provided from his personal funds, and he did not offend Pompey himself, since he was not receiving any reward from him as the rest were who had gained offices or wealth through him, some of whom joined his camp most reluctantly, while others offended him deeply by remaining at home. Moreover, the neutrality of Atticus pleased Caesar immensely; returning in victory, when in writing he ordered contributions from private citizens, he did not bother Atticus, but pardoned his sister's son and Quintus Cicero from Pompey's camp. Thus, by his rule of life, instituted long before, he escaped new dangers.

(8) Then followed that period, after the assassination of Caesar, when it appeared the government was in the control of the two Bruti[26] and Cassius, and it seemed that the entire citizenry had converted to them and their side. His association with Brutus developed to the point that that young man had no peer more intimate with the old man and that he kept Atticus as a chief planner as well as his close companion.[27] Certain men had devised a scheme to constitute a private fund for the murderers of Caesar from the Roman equestrians. They thought it would work easily, if the leaders of that order contributed money. So, Gaius Flavius, a friend of Brutus, asked Atticus if he were willing to be the initiator of this plan. But Atticus thought that his obligation was to provide services to his friends without factious partisanship, and, whereas he had always removed himself from such enterprises, he responded that,

---

23: these subordinate commands were under proconsular or propraetorian governors of provinces; they afforded abundant opportunities for profit.
24: Quintus was propraetorian governor of Asia from 61 to 57.
25: Nepos alludes to extortion, a common charge against crooked and unscrupulous governors of provinces.
26: the two Bruti are Marcus Iunius Brutus and Decimus Iunius Brutus Albinus.
27: Atticus was thirty-one years older than Brutus.

if Brutus wanted to use any of his resources, he could use the extent of his means, but that he would neither discuss the matter with anyone nor meet anyone to do so. Thus, by the dissent of this one person the unanimity of that cabal was broken up.

Not much later Antony began to become supreme and, as a result, Brutus and Cassius, abandoning their roles and official duties which the consul had assigned to them,[28] in despair of their position, went into exile.[29] But Atticus did not stoop to flatter the powerful Antony nor abandon those whose cause was desperate. Instead, Atticus, the man who had refused to join the others and contribute money to the party when it was thriving, sent to Brutus, after he had been ousted and was departing from Italy, the gift of 100,000 sesterces. And, although he was far away in Epirus,[30] to this same Brutus he ordered an additional 300,000 be given.

(9) There followed the war waged near Mutina.[31] If I were to claim that he was clairvoyant in it, I'd be saying much less than I ought, since he was truly a divine seer, if divination were the correct word to assign to a constant, innate goodness which no event shakes or diminishes. After Antony was judged an enemy and left Italy, there was no expectation of restoring him. Not only his personal enemies, who at that time were most powerful and numerous, but also those who had volunteered themselves to his opponents and who had hoped to win some advantage by injuring him, persecuted his friends; they desired to rob his wife Fulvia of all her property, and were even making preparations to kill his children.

Although he shared a most intimate relationship with Cicero and was a very close friend of Brutus, in no way whatsoever did he defer to them in their outrage against Antony; on the contrary, he protected Antony's friends, as well as he could, as they fled from the city, and he assisted them with whatever items they required. To Publius Volumnius he rendered more things than one could expect from a parent. However, to Fulvia herself, when she was distracted by lawsuits and beset by terrors, he displayed such diligent loyalty that she stood no bail without Atticus; Atticus was her guarantor in all cases. In fact, when she had

28: in 44 Brutus and Cassius were praetors. In fear of violence at the hands of Caesar's veterans they left Rome, although it was against the law for them to be absent more than ten days. Antony, as consul, arranged a special commission for them, putting them in charge of the grain supply from Sicily and Asia.

29: Nepos again is being generous, providing the stated reasons for Brutus' and Cassius' actions. They began preparing for war by taking possession of Macedonia and Syria, provinces that had been designated to them by Julius Caesar.

30: Atticus had an estate in Epirus.

31: see Cicero, letter #15 (ad Fam. 10.30)

bought an estate on time during her days of prosperity and then was unable to secure a loan after the disastrous setbacks, he intervened and lent her money without interest and without a written contract. And believing it was the greatest gain to be regarded as mindful and grateful, he openly proved that he made it a practice to be a friend to humanity and not to their fortune. While he was doing these things, no one could claim he was acting to temporize; for it never entered the mind of anyone that Antony would recover power. But little by little some members of the "best men" began to criticize Atticus because they thought that he insufficiently hated the "bad" citizens.[32] But, he was a man of independent judgment; he looked to what was right for him to do rather than what everybody else would praise.

(10) A sudden change of fortune happened. When Antony returned to Italy, everyone thought that Atticus was in great danger because of his intimate association with Cicero and Brutus. So, upon the arrival of the generals, he left the forum, fearing proscription, and hid in the home of Publius Volumnius to whom, as I have pointed out, he had brought assistance a little before—the vicissitudes of fortune in those times led now these, now those, to the summit of power or to the gravest danger—and had with him Quintus Gellius Canus, a contemporary and one very much like himself. This, too, is an example of Atticus' goodness: that he lived so closely associated with him whom he had known in their boyhood schooldays and that their friendship grew until extreme old age.

For Antony, however, so much hatred of Cicero swept him along that he was not only a personal enemy of him, but also all of his friends, and he wanted to proscribe them. Although many encouraged him to do it, yet he remained mindful of Atticus' service. When he found out where Atticus was, in his own hand he wrote to him stating that he had nothing to fear and for him to come; that he had removed him and, in deference to him, Canus from the list of the proscribed. To prevent any danger befalling him, because this was taking place at night, he sent him a guard. Thus Atticus in the time of acute anxiety protected himself as well as one he regarded as a very dear friend. For he did not seek aid on behalf of his own safety, which served to prove that he desired no fortune separate from his friend. But if the pilot wins the greatest praise for saving his ship in a winter storm upon a rocky sea, why would the opinion of him not be judged as unique who out of the frequent heavy storms of civil strife arrived to safety unharmed?

(11) When he emerged from these troubles, he did nothing else than provide assistance to as many as possible and by whatever means. While

32: so characterized by the conservatives, the "bad" citizens refer to the political faction opposite of the 'optimates'. They had political agenda based on the vote of the assembly of the people.

the mob was hunting down the proscribed for the bounty offered by the generals, no one came to Epirus who failed to obtain something; he turned down no one, extending the opportunity of staying there permanently. In fact, after the battle of Philippi and the death of Gaius Cassius and of Marcus Brutus, he set about to protect the ex-praetor Lucius Iulius Mocilla, his son, and Aulus Torquatus, and the others ruined by the same disaster, and ordered that everything from Epirus be transferred to Samothrace for them. It is difficult to detail everything, and it is unnecessary. This one thing I want understood: that his generosity was neither expedient nor calculated. One can judge it from the circumstances and from the times, because he did not sell himself to the powerful, but always helped the afflicted. For instance, he cultivated Servilia, the mother of Brutus, no less after her son's death than when he was prospering.

Using his generosity in that way, he incurred no enmities, because he did not wrong anyone, and, if he suffered an injustice, he preferred to forget it rather than to take revenge. Besides, he gathered and retained in his non-human memory the kindnesses that he received,[33] but those humane acts which he himself exhibited, he remembered them for only as long as he who had received them was grateful. He proved the truth of the dictum: *each man's character fashions his fortune.* Nevertheless, before he fashioned his fortune, Atticus fashioned himself to guard against ever being hurt justly.

(12) In these circumstances Atticus influenced Marcus Vipsanius Agrippa, who was bonded in intimate friendship with the young Caesar,[34] although he had the ability to make any match because of his influence and the power of Caesar behind him, to choose instead a marriage alliance with his family and to prefer the daughter of a Roman equestrian over noble women. And the arranger of this marriage (for I cannot conceal it) was Mark Antony, the triumvir for regulating the state.[35] Although Antony's influence could have augmented his own property, Atticus was so far from desiring money that in no circumstances did he ever use it except to entreat on behalf of friends to get them out of danger or trouble. This fact was most clearly seen during the proscriptions [43 BCE]. For example, there was the case of Lucius Saufeius, a contemporary of Atticus, who, drawn by his devotion to philosophy, lived for several years in Athens, and had valuable possessions in Italy. When the triumvirs sold his property, following the practice of the way things were done at that time, Atticus' effort and industry provided that

---

33: i.e. his memory was so sharp that it seemed divine rather than human.

34: this "young Caesar'" is Octavius, soon to be Augustus.

35: the triumvirate was formed and ratified for the legal purpose of regulating the state (*rei publicae constituendae*). At the time of Nepos' writing Antony and Octavian were at loggerheads.

the same messenger informed him of the loss of his property and its recovery. He likewise rescued Lucius Iulius Calidus, who, after the deaths of Lucretius and of Catullus, was arguably the most polished poet our generation has produced by far, and was also a good man and learned in the highest arts. After the proscriptions of the equestrians, this man, because of his extensive estates in Africa, was entered in absentia into the number of those proscribed by Publius Volumnius, Antony's official in charge of his engineers, was set free because of Atticus. Whether this activity earned him trouble at that time or earned him more glory, it is difficult to decide, since it was a known fact that Atticus' friends, absent or present, were his special care in times of dangers.

(13) And truly this man was regarded as good a father of the household as he was a citizen. For instance, although he was enormously rich, no one was less eager to buy property or be less of a builder. Yet, at the same time, he lived in a very fine house and enjoyed all the best things. He had a home on the Quirinal, the Tamphilia,[36] which was left him in his uncle's will; its charm consisted not in its construction, but in its wooded grounds—for the building itself was constructed in days long ago and it exuded taste rather than cost. He made no changes to it unless he was compelled by its age. In his household he owned a company of slaves who were excellent, if you judge them from the standpoint of their usefulness, but scarcely mediocre in their looks. They included young servants who were extremely well-educated, some excellent readers, and numerous copiers of texts; there was not even a valet who could not perform either of these skills. In the same way, the rest of the craftsmen who were required for the upkeep of the house were first-rate. Nevertheless, he kept none of these slaves who were not born on the estate or reared in the house, which is a clear sign not only of his self-control, but also of his thrifty habits. For not to desire immoderately that which you see craved by the many must be considered characteristic of moderation, and to purchase something by diligence rather than for its price is the mark of no mean frugality. In his person he was refined rather than magnificent, distinguished rather than ostentatious. All of his attentiveness directed him to refinement, not pompous extravagance. His furniture was modest, not excessive, so that it was not conspicuous in any area of the house.

And I will not pass over the fact that, although I reckon some will see it as a trivial matter, he, one of the most refined Roman equestrians, and with no mean generosity, invited men of all classes to his home; and this we know from his daily ledger. In his budget, as a rule, he allowed three thousand sesterces each month for total expenses. I publish this item of information not from hearsay, but from personal knowledge,

36: so-called because the house had belonged to a certain Tamphilus.

inasmuch as because of our intimate association I was often involved with his domestic agenda.

(14) At any of his dinner parties no one heard any entertainment other than a reader—which I think is the most pleasurable entertainment of all; at his house one did not ever dine without a reading of some kind. For this reason the mind as well as the appetite of the guests was indulged. He invited those whose tastes were not different from his own. When that huge increase was made to his bank account,[37] he changed nothing of his daily habits, made no change of lifestyle, but lived moderately so that he conducted himself in splendid style on the two million sesterces that he inherited from his father, and did not live more extravagantly on the ten million than he did before; instead, with both fortunes he lived the same high life. He had no gardens, no expensive suburban or coastal villa, no country estate in Italy except for one at Arezzo and Nomentum; his income derived from his holdings in Epirus and in the city. From all these practices one can readily discern that his habit was to manage his expenses not by the extent of his money but by reason.

(15) He neither lied nor tolerated lying. His good nature combined with a modicum of severity and his sense of seriousness with an affability so that it was difficult to know whether his friends more respected or loved him. For whatever he was asked, he promised with discretion because he thought to make a promise that one could not keep characterized weakness, not generosity. Once he assented to an endeavor, he also was extremely careful to exert himself so that he seemed to be acting not on a commission but in his own interests. He never became bored by any enterprise that he undertook; he thought that it concerned his reputation, and nothing he held dearer than that. Thus, he conducted and directed the business interests of the Ciceros, of Marcus Cato, Quintus Hortensius, Aulus Torquatus, and many Roman equestrian besides; and from this one can judge that it was not from laziness, but from solid judgment that he avoided participation in the governance of the state.

(16) I can offer no greater testimony of his humanity than this: as a young man, he was most congenial to an elderly Sulla, whereas as an old man to the young Marcus Brutus; and with his contemporaries, Quintus Hortensius and Marcus Cicero, he enjoyed a great life; it is difficult to decide to which generation he was most suited. And yet Cicero loved him so that not even his brother Quintus was dearer or more intimate. Proof of these matters resides in those widely published books in which he mentions Atticus, and in the sixteen volumes of letters sent to him, writ-

---

37: a reference to the legacy from his uncle, Quintus Caecilius, mentioned in chapter five.

ten during the time of his consulship until the end of his life.[38] In them have been recorded all the details about the partisanship of the foremost citizens, the faults of the leaders, and the changes of government so that there is nothing unclear, and one can easily understand that Cicero's clairvoyance was something like divination. He not only predicted what happened during his lifetime, but also, like a prophet, chanted his predictions of what now has come to pass in our experience.[39]

(17) What more should I say about Atticus' devotion? I myself heard him boasting at the funeral of his mother, whom he buried at the age of ninety when he was sixty-seven, that he never had to return to the good graces of his mother, nor entered into a feud with his sister who was about his age. Now that is either a sign that no dispute ever came between them or that he had so much indulgent fondness for them that he considered it a sin to become angry with those whom he was morally bound to love. And not his nature—we all obey nature—produced this attitude, but his upbringing. For he had thoroughly grasped the precepts of the most eminent philosophers which he used, not to show off, but in the very conduct of his life.

(18) He was the supreme avatar of the customs of our ancestors and a profound lover of the old days. His knowledge of them was deep and he revealed it all in that volume in which he chronologically systematized the magistrates.[40] There was no law, no peace treaty, no war, no illustrious exploit of the Roman people that he failed to include with chronological precision in that book. He also appended a genealogy of families—a most difficult undertaking—from which we can learn the descendants of famous heroes. This same subject he dealt with separately in other books.[41] For example, at the request of Marcus Brutus, he detailed in chronological order the Iunian family from its origin down to this day, noting the family roots of each member and the offices he won and the dates. Similarly, he handled the request of Claudius Marcellus regarding the Marcelli, and likewise Cornelius Scipio and Fabius Maximus considering the Fabian and Aemilian families. Those who yearn for accounts of famous men can find nothing sweeter than these books.

He also dabbled in poetry, I think, in order to experience its special charm. For he heralded in verse form those who, because they had gained some distinction or because of the grandeur of their achievements, surpassed the rest of the Roman people. Under their portrait busts he set forth their accomplishments and the political offices in no more then

---

38: the *Letters* date from as early as 68 BCE, five years before Cicero's consulship. The manuscripts read eleven books rather than sixteen.

39: Nepos' respect for his subject has led him into a gross exaggeration.

40: the work referred to is Atticus' *Liber Annalis* that treated a chronological history, organized under the names of magistrates.

41: these books were eulogistic histories of numerous noble families.

four or five lines.[42] It can hardly be believed that careers so illustrious could be outlined so briefly. He also completed a single book in Greek on the consulship of Cicero.

(19) Up to this point I have published this account of Atticus while he was alive; now, since fortune has willed that I would survive him, I will pursue the rest of his story, and, as much as I can, I will instruct my readers by examples of the facts that, as I pointed out above, character is the decisive factor in everyone's fortune. So he, content with the equestrian rank to which he was born, yet attained a relationship by marriage with the emperor, son of a deified man.[43] Atticus had previously earned his friendship by no other quality than the refinement of his life, by which he had influenced other leaders of the state of the same rank but of more humble means. Such prosperity accompanied Caesar that Fortune provided him everything that it had previously endowed upon another and won for him what no Roman citizen up to then had been able to achieve. He also had a granddaughter by Agrippa, with whom he had arranged a marriage of his virgin daughter. This granddaughter, barely a year old, Caesar pledged to his stepson Tiberius Claudius Nero, son of Drusilla;[44] this union confirmed the tight bond of Atticus and Caesar and rendered their association even closer.

(20) Before this formal engagement of marriage, when he was away from the city, Octavius never sent a letter to his intimates without writing Atticus what he was up to, where he was, and how long he was staying. And when he was in the city, he enjoyed Atticus' company less frequently than he wanted because of his endless engagements; almost no day went by that he did not write to Atticus, sometimes asking him some detail about ancient lore, sometimes proposing some question of poetic interpretation, and sometimes jokingly suggesting to him that he write newsier letters. This relationship caused Caesar, when the temple of Jupiter the Striker on the Capitoline was collapsing because of its age, neglect, and exposure—after all it had been constructed by Romulus—to follow Atticus' advice and to see to its restoration. He was equally cultivated by Mark Antony through correspondence and from afar, who from the ends of the earth took care to inform Atticus of the details of his activities. One will able to make up his mind and judge the nature and depth of his shrewdness by which he retained the enjoyment and goodwill of those who were rivals for the supremacy of the state

42: similar epitaphs are credited to Varro. The extant *elogiae* of several members of noble Roman families, like the Scipios, illustrate the possibilities in the form.

43: this relationship is detailed in the following sentences. The phrase "son of a deified man" was used by Octavian/Augustus in propaganda after the deification of Julius Caesar on the New Year of 42.

44: the granddaughter is Vipsania who married the future emperor Tiberius, the son of Livia Drusilla.

and who engaged in bitter insults. For by necessity came the enmity of Caesar and Antony, who both desired to be the leader not only of the city Rome but also of the world.

(21) In such a fashion Atticus completed seventy-seven years, and up to that extreme old age his dignity increased as much as his influence and fortune—for he acquired many inheritances by no other quality than his goodness. Because he also enjoyed such fine health that he required no medical treatment for thirty years, when he contracted a disease, at first he and his doctors minimized it. They thought it was a case of bowel difficulty for which quick and easy remedies were proposed. When this condition had consumed him for three months, though with no pain except what the treatment brought, suddenly the disease broke out violently, affecting his lower intestines; finally fistulas full of pus erupted throughout his lumbar region.

Before this happened, he felt pain that increased day by day and which was accompanied by fever. He ordered that his son-in-law Agrippa be summoned and with him Lucius Cornelius Balbus and Sextus Peducaeus. As soon as he saw that they had come, he leaned on his elbow and said, "The amount of care and attention I have devoted at this time to protecting my health, it is not necessary for me to relate to you in more detail, since you have been witnesses to it. I hope that these efforts of mine have satisfied you that I have left nothing to complete that would apply to my recovery. But it remains for me to consult my own well-being. I do not want you to be unaware: I have resolved to cease nourishing the disease. Whatever food I have consumed these days has prolonged my life and increased my pain without hope of recovery. Therefore, I beg you first that you approve my decision, and secondly that you do not try to impede it by bootless entreaties."

(22) At the close of the speech the firmness of his voice and expression seemed not to be leaving his life, but to be migrating from one home to another. Agrippa in tears kissed him and then begged and beseeched him not to accelerate nature's inexorable necessity on his own. He added that, since it was still possible for him to survive the crisis, he should save himself for his own sake and that of his family. But Atticus by his unyielding silence disparaged his entreaties. Accordingly, after he abstained from food for two days, the fever suddenly subsided and the disease began to go into remission. Nevertheless, he carried through his decision and died on the fifth day after he entered upon his resolution, and that was the day before the Kalends of April, i.e. the thirty-first of March, in the consulship of Gnaeus Domitius and Gaius Sosius [32 BCE]. He was carried out for burial on a small bier, as he himself had prescribed; there was no formal procession. But the funeral was attended by all the members of the "good party," and by a huge throng of plebeians. He was buried near the fifth milestone beside the Appian Way in the tomb of Quintus Caecilius, his uncle.

MARCUS TERENTIUS VARRO

ON AGRICULTURE

The fact that Vergil used the *De Re Rustica* of Varro makes it an important prose text of the Augustan period. But the work itself is of interest and deserves some scrutiny. Varro lends his scholarly temperament and attention to a subject dear to the hearts of many Romans. Octavian/ Augustus himself strove to renew the old Italian love for farming and the agricultural ethos that marked the lives of yeomen farmers, the heroes of early Roman history and lore. The systematic arrangement of the themes provides a storehouse of valuable information; occasional digressions and comments and some banter between the discussants lend a respectable literary bent and atmosphere to the work. The section on bees from Book III can stand on its own and should be closely compared with Vergil's superior poetic treatment.

BOOK I

1. (1) If I had acquired the leisure time, my Fundania,[1] I would be writing this treatise to you in a more appropriate style which I will now develop, as best I can, thinking that I must hurry because, as the saying goes, if a man is a mere bubble, doubly so is an old man. You see, my eightieth year now is warning me to pick up my bags before I depart this life. (2) So, since you have bought an estate and want to make it productive by sound cultivation, and you are asking me to make it my concern, I will try. I'll advise you what you must do not only as long

---

1: Fundania is Varro's wife.

as I live, but even after my death. (3) I will not allow the Sibyl[2] to have chanted prophecies, while she was alive, that helped mankind and, even after she died, benefited individuals unknown to her as well. Many years later we are accustomed publicly to consult her books when we desire to find out what we ought to do after some omen. (4) Nor, as long as I live, will I suffer myself not doing something to benefit my relatives and friends. For that reason I will compose for you these technical books to which you may refer in search of how you should go about the practice of farming. And since, as they say, the gods help those who act, I will involve them, not the muses as Homer and Ennius, but the twelve *Consentes* gods;[3] and I do not refer to those urban gods whose gilded images stand near the forum, six male and six female, but I mean those twelve gods who are the chief sponsors of farmers. (5) First, I call upon Jupiter and Tellus, who encompass all the fruits of agriculture by sky and earth. Since people say that they are the great parents, Jupiter is called "father" and Tellus "mother earth." Second, Sol (Sun) and Luna (Moon), whose seasons are carefully observed for planting and harvesting. Third, Ceres and Liber, because their fruits are absolutely indispensable to life; because of their bounty food and drink come from the farm. (6) Fourth, Robigus (Mold) and Flora; under their propitious gifts mold will not damage the grain or fruit trees, nor will they blossom out of season. Therefore, the holidays of the Robigalia[4] were established to honor Robigus, the Floralia[5] games to honor Flora. Similarly, I revere Minerva and Venus; the bailiwick of the former is the olive grove, of the latter the garden, to whom the rustic Vinalia[6] was established and whom the celebration honors. And I also pray to Lympha (Moisture) and Bonus Eventus (Good Result), since without water all cultivation of the land remains dry and barren, and without success and good result frustration supplants cultivation. (7) Therefore, since I have invoked the proper veneration of these gods, I will now relate the conversations which we recently had on the topic of agriculture, from which you will be able to discern what you ought to do. If you fail to find the topics that you are looking for, I will indicate the Greek, as well as our Roman writers, to whom you may have recourse.

2: the Sibyl is of Cumae who legendarily brought to Rome her books of prophecy which she sold to Tarquin the Proud, the last king of Rome.

3: the *Consentes* gods are twelve deities—six male and six female—worshipped at a public banquet whose images were placed on couches and whose gilded statues stood in the forum.

4: this festival was celebrated on 19 August and propitiated good weather for the vines.

5: this festival was celebrated on 25 April.

6: this Italic goddess of flowering plants and cereals was worshipped in a moveable festival.

(8) There are more than fifty separate treatises written in Greek on various aspects of the subject. The following are those which you will be able to consult whenever you want to delve into any topic: Hiero of Sicily[7] and Attalus Philometor;[8] of the philosophers note Democritus the physicist, Xenophon the Socratic, Aristotle and Theophrastus the peripatetics, Archytas the Pythagorean, and likewise, Amphilochus of Athens, Anaxipolis of Thasos, Apollodorus of Lemnos, Aristophanes from Mallos, Antigonus of Cyme, Agathocles of Chios, Apollonius of Pergamum, Aristandrus of Athens, Bacchius of Miletus, Bion of Soli, Chaeresteus and Chaereas of Athens, Diodorus of Priene, Dion of Colophon, Diophanes of Nicaea, Epigenes of Rhodes, Euagon of Thasos, two Euphronii, one from Athens, the other from Amphipolis, Hegesias of Maronea, two Menanders, one of Priene, the second of Heraclea, Nicesius of Maronea, and Pythion of Rhodes. (9) Among the rest of the authors whose home city or fatherland I have not ascertained are: Androtion, Aeschrion, Aristomenes, Athenagoras, Crates, Dadis, Dionysios, Euphiton, Euphorion, Eubulus, Lysimachus, Mnaseas, Menestratus, Plentiphanes, Persis, and Theophilus.[9] All of these whom I have listed have written in prose. But some, like Hesiod of Ascra and Menecrates of Ephesus, have written on the same topics in verse. (10) But surpassing all of these in renown was Mago of Carthage who in the Punic language compiled in twenty-eight books and treated separately the various subjects. These books, edited down to twenty volumes, Cassius Dionysius[10] translated into Greek and dedicated to the praetor Sextilius. For these volumes he added much material from the books of those Greek authors whom I have mentioned and from Mago's he adapted the equivalent of eight books. In Bithynia Diophanes of Nicaea condensed these volumes into a useful six books which he dedicated to King Deiotarus.[11] (11) I am attempting to set forth the subject in a briefer compass of three books, one on agriculture proper, the second on stock breeding, and the third on estate grazing and production, cutting out in this book topics which I do not think are pertinent to agriculture. So first I will show what matter should be excised, then I will discuss the subject following natural divisions. My ideas spring from three sources: the things I have observed

7: probably Hieron I, tyrant of Syracuse from 478-466 BCE is meant. He supported the arts and poets such as Pindar and Aeschylus.
8: the reference is to Attalus III (ca 170-133 BCE), the last king of Pergamum, who bequeathed his kingdom to Rome.
9: Varro's extensive list of authors who wrote on agricultural topics comprises many names unknown outside of this list.
10: in 88 Cassius Dionysius of Utica composed a Greek translation of the work on agriculture of Mago, the Carthaginian; his treatise became the standard of the subject.
11: a king of Galatia who skillfully maneuvered himself during the Roman Civil Wars between Pompey and Julius Caesar and then Antony and Octavius.

in cultivating my own estates, what I have read, and the things which I have heard from experts.

2. (1) During the festivities of the Sementivae[12] I had gone to the temple of Tellus,[13] invited by the *aeditumus* (keeper of the shrine) as we have learned from our fathers to call him, by the *aedituus*, as we are corrected to say by our modern wits. There I ran into Gaius Fundanius, my father-in-law, Gaius Agrius, a Roman equestrian and Socratic philosopher, and Publius Agrasius,[14] a tax-contractor; they were looking at a map of Italy painted on the wall. "What are you up to here?" I asked, "Has the celebration of the Sementivae brought you here to spend your leisure time as it used to attract our fathers and grandfathers?" (2) "I suppose," said Agrius, "the same reason brought us as it did you: the invitation of the temple keeper. If that is the case, as your nod indicates, you'll have to wait for his return like us. He has been summoned by the aedile who supervises this temple, and has yet to return, but has left a person to request us to wait for him. In the meantime do you want us to observe the old proverb: 'the Roman wins out by sitting,'[15] until he comes?" "Yes," said Agrius; and thinking that the longest leg of a trip is said to be reaching the gate, he proceeded to a bench as we followed along.

(3) When we sat down, Agrasius began: "You have traveled the world over; have you ever seen a country more cultivated than Italy?" he asked. "For my part," enjoined Agrius, "I don't think any land is as totally cultivated. First, Eratosthenes divided the earth into two parts, a very natural division, one to the south, the other to the north; (4) and since there is no doubt that the northern section is healthier than the southern, and the part that is more conducive to good health is also the more fruitful, then one must admit that Italy has been more suitable for cultivation than Asia, first, because it is in Europe, and secondly, because this region of Europe possesses a more temperate climate than is the case farther inland. For in the interior winters are almost continuous, and it is no surprise, since those regions are situated between the Arctic Circle and North Pole, where the sun is not seen for at least six months. Consequently, they tell us that in that part of the world it

12: the pontiffs set the precise date for this festival that followed the sowing of seeds.
13: this temple was on a spur of the Esquiline Hill. Tellus (Earth) was associated with the festival of the *Sementivae*.
14: these names, Fundanius, Agrius, and Agrasius are genuine Roman names, but they are puns deriving from *fundus*, 'estate,' and *ager*, 'field.' Their names are befitting the topic of agriculture.
15: the exact proverb is not known but Livy (22.39) has Quintus Fabius Maximus Verrucosus, called the "Delayer," saying to Lucius Aemilius Paullus: "do you doubt that we will win by sitting?" The idea is to begin to do something at once.

is impossible to sail because the sea is frozen solid with ice." (5) Then Fundanius rejoined, "OK, then, do you think anything there can sprout or be cultivated once it has sprouted? Surely Pacuvius' adage is true: that if sunshine or darkness of night is constant, then all fruits of the earth perish from steamy vapor or cold. As for me, I cannot even live here, where night and day come and go at moderate intervals, if I do not split up my days of summer with my usual midday siesta. (6) And there? How can any planting, growing, or harvesting take place, if day and night each last for six months? On the other hand, in Italy every beneficial product grows and not only that, it is of excellent quality. What spelt can I compare with that of Campania? No wheat compares with the Apulian, no wine matches Falernian,[16] and the olive oil of Venafrum[17] is unsurpassed. All of Italy is planted with so many trees that it seems to be one vast orchard. (7) Is Phrygia which Homer calls *teeming with vines* more covered in vines than this land? Or does Argos which the same poet says is *abounding in wheat* teem with more wheat fields? In what land, I ask, does one iugerum yield ten or fifteen large demijohns as do some regions in Italy? As our Marcus Cato says in one book of his *Origines*: 'The land on this side of Ariminium and beyond the region of Picentium,[18] which was distributed in individual lots to veterans, is known as Gallo-Roman territory. In several places of that land some iugera produce ten demijohns of wine each.' Is it not the same for the territory around Faventia?[19] There the vines are called 'three-hundred producers' because they yield three hundred amphorae per iugerum." He looked toward me and added: "Now your friend Marcius Libo, the prefect of engineers, often said that the vines on his estate yielded this same amount. (8) Italians seem to have considered two factors in farming: whether the crops could yield a return commensurate with the investment of money and labor, and whether the locale was conducive to good health or not. If either of these conditions is lacking, whoever wishes to farm in spite of it, is mentally deficient and should be turned over to his male relatives and family as insane. For no sane person would want to incur the cost and the expense of cultivation, if he sees that they cannot be recovered, or if he sees that whatever produce he can raise will be utterly ruined by some blight. (9) But, I think, there are some among us who can better attest to that. Yes, I see Gaius Licinius Stolo and Gnaeus

---

16: the very fertile agricultural area in northern Campania most famous for its wines.

17: Venafrum was a Samnite city on the border of Latium and Campania.

18: Ariminium, modern Rimini, lies on the Adriatic in the territory of Picenum, the large area in central-east Italy that bounds Cisalpine Gaul and the Apennines.

19: Faventia, modern Faenza, is a city in Cisalpine Gaul.

Tremelius Scrofa coming;[20] the ancestors of one of them carried the law to limit the amount of land—the law in question which forbids a Roman citizen possess more than 500 iugera was sponsored by a Stolo[21]—and he has confirmed the validity of his family's name through his attentive care to farming; on his farm no sucker could be found because he used to dig up around his trees the roots from which shoot up out of the soil those suckers called 'stolones;' of the same clan was Gaius Licinius. When he was tribune of the people, 365 years after the expulsion of the kings, he was the first to conduct a meeting of the people in the seven-iugera forum,[22] leading them there from the comitium to hear laws. (10) The other man whom I see approaching is your colleague who was a member of the Board of Twenty to allot lands in Campania, Gnaeus Tremelius Scrofa, a gentleman refined with all excellent qualities, and who is deemed to be the Roman expert on agriculture." "And that's right," I added. "Because of their refinements in cultivation his estates are a more delightful sight to many than the regally embellished villas of others. When people come to view his villas, they do not arrive to see a gallery of paintings as at Lucullus', but to see his *greenhouses*. The top of the Sacred Way," I said, "where fruits outsell gold, is a mere reflection of his orchard."

(11) In the meantime, they reached us, and Stolo asked, "We haven't come with dinner already eaten, no? We don't see Lucius Fundilius[23] who invited us." "Be calm," Agrius said, "as the egg which marks the end of the last lap at the chariot races during the games has not been removed, so then we have yet to catch sight of that egg which is usually served first at the dinner parade.[24] (12) And so, until you, along with us, see that egg and our temple keeper comes, instruct us, what purpose agriculture has, profit or pleasure, or perhaps both. The scuttlebutt is that you are the champion practitioner of agriculture, as once Stolo, now retired, was." "First," Scrofa enjoined, "we should decide whether only those things that are planted be considered 'agriculture,' or other operations such as the raising of sheep and cattle which are introduced into the farms. (13)

20: the names "Stolo" and "Scrofa" are true Roman names, but, as in the case of Fundanius, Agrius, and Agrasius above (note # 14), were chosen to reflect terms associated with the farm. Stolo means 'plant shoot' and Scrofa means 'sow.'

21: this law was passed in 367 and applied to 'public land' that had been taken in war.

22: after the expulsion of the kings (509) each citizen was assigned seven *iugera* for a farm.

23: again there is a pun on the name "Fundilius;" it is connected to *fundus*, 'estate.'

24: seven wooden-shaped "eggs" lined the center section of the race track; one by one they were removed with the completion of each lap. The Romans often began dinner with an egg.

I notice that those who have written on agriculture, in Punic, Greek, or Latin, have strayed farther than they ought from the topic." "But as for me," Stolo remarked, "I do not believe that they should be emulated completely, but that those who have prescribed smaller parameters by excising material that does not pertain to this subject have done a better job. Thus, the entire treatment of grazing which many authors combine with agriculture seems to me to relate more to the herder than the farmer. (14) For that reason different titles indicate the men who are set in charge of the two separate jobs; the one is called a ramrod, the other the master of the flock or herd. The ramrod is designated to work the land and his name (*vilicus*) is derived from *villa* because the produce is conveyed by him into and then out of it when it is put up for sale. Farmers even now call a road *veha* because of the transporting, and they call it a *vella*, not villa, to which and from which they transport goods. Similarly, those who make a living in transportation are said to be 'doing conveyance' (*facere velaturam*)." (15) "Certainly," Fundanius said, "grazing is different from agriculture, but somewhat related, as the right pipe of the double-flute is different from the left, but yet combined in a way, since the one is the treble, the other the bass accompanying the melody of the same song." (16) "And you may add this," I remarked, "that the shepherd's life is the treble, and the accompanying bass is performed by the life of farmers, according to that most learned authority Dicaearchus. Now he presented to us in his scholarly treatise the nature of early Greek life in primitive times when people led a pastoral life not even knowing how to plow the earth, plant trees, or prune them; it was at a later stage that they took up agriculture. In this way then, agriculture accompanies the subordinate pastoral existence as the bass, the left pipe, accords with the stops of the right."[25] (17) "Hey you," Agrius interrupted, "yes, you, the flute player, you are robbing the master of his flock as well as the slaves of their allowance which masters grant them as grazing rights;[26] and you are also abolishing the homestead acts in which we see written that a settler may not graze his flock of young goats on a plot planted with young trees, the genus of animal which astrology has also placed in the sky, not far from Taurus the Bull."[27] (18) In response to him Fundanius said, "Look here, Agrius, don't confuse the issue; it is also written in the laws: 'a certain kind of flock.' Some herding animals are natural enemies of cultivation and are poisonous, such as those goats you mentioned. When they crop, they destroy the young shoots, and in particular vines and

---

25: the melody was played on the right instrument, while the rhythm or accompaniment on the left.

26: a master could extend money to a slave, but by law these assets were administered by the master, since slaves could not legally own property.

27: the astrological allusion is to Capricorn, ascendant from 23 December to 22 January.

olives. (19) Therefore, a custom stemmed from different reasons whereby a member of the goat family as a sacrificial victim was brought to the altar of one god, but at the altar of another god it was not sacrificed; the same hatred produced the anomaly that one god did not want even to see the goat, whereas the other wanted it to die. Thus it was instituted that he-goats be sacrificed to father Liber, the discoverer of the vine, to pay, as it were, the ultimate penalty for their damage. On the other hand, no member of the goat family was to be slaughtered on behalf of Minerva over the olive, because it is reported that the olive sprout they crop becomes sterile, and their saliva is poisonous to the fruit. (20) This is the pretext given that they are not driven to the acropolis in Athens, except for once a year for a sacrifice necessary to prevent the olive tree, which is said to have originated on that hill, being touched by a goat." And then I added: "None of the herding animals are appropriate in our treatment of agriculture, except those which help by their work to make the land more productive, such as those that can plow the earth under yoke." (21) "If that is the case," interrupted Agrasius, "how can we keep the cattle off the land when the manure which the herds provide is so enriching of the soil?" "So, then," said Agrius, "we'll be able to say that trafficking in gangs of slaves belongs to agriculture, if we decide to keep them for that purpose. But there is an error in the reasoning that does not follow: by keeping a herd on the land, necessarily they bring profit to this farm. Similarly, we would have to accept other things alien to agriculture per se, such as keeping on the estate a host of weavers and loom workers, and other such artisans."

(22) "OK," Scrofa said, "then let us separate grazing from agriculture, and whatever else anyone wants." And then I asked: "Do I or do I not follow the books of Saserna Senior and Junior and consider how pottery shops are worked to be more relevant to agriculture than the mining of silver and other metals which without doubt take place on some estates? (23) But as neither stone quarries nor sand-pits are related to agriculture, so neither are pottery shops;[28] not that they should not be worked on a farm where they are suitable and from which some profit is recouped; and also, if a farm is adjacent to a road and the site is convenient for travelers where inns and bars could be constructed, yet, however lucrative the enterprise, they still have no part at all in agriculture. Also, if some success comes to an owner because of his land or on his land, he must not attribute it to agriculture, but accredit only that which comes from sowing and is born of the earth for our enjoyment." (24) Stolo then interrupted, "You are envious of that marvelous writer

---

28: strictly, Varro mentions pits from which clay was dug to make tiles, bricks, and vessels. The argument is that the working of stone quarries and the production of pottery are not properly a part of agriculture, although they may be profitable to the farmer.

and you are being mean to criticize his pottery workshops when you purposely pass over and fail to praise his many outstanding comments which strongly relate to agriculture." (25) Scrofa smiled; he knew the books in question and despised them, but Agrisius, who thought that he was the only one to know the works, asked Stolo to quote something. He then began: "He writes of the proper procedure for killing bugs in the following formula: 'Soak a snaky cucumber in water, and wherever you choose to sprinkle it; no bugs will appear.' And another: 'smear your bed with bull's bile mixed with vinegar.'" (26) Fundanius glared at Scrofa and said, "True enough, what he says, even though he wrote it in a book on agriculture." And then he responded, "As true, by god, as the one that bids: 'if you want to make some one bald, throw a pale and ghastly frog into some water, boil it down to a third, then smear on the body.'" "It would be better for you," I said, "to quote from that book something that relates more closely to Fundanius' ailment; his feet are always killing him and bringing wrinkles to his brow." (27) "Tell me, please!" Fundanius interjected. "I prefer hearing about my feet than how beet-plants should be planted." "I will tell you," Stolo replied with a smile, "in the very same words he wrote—I have heard Tarquenna[29] say that when a man's feet have begun to hurt, he can be healed, if he has concentrated his mind on you—'I now think of you, heal my feet; keep the disease in the ground; let my feet stay healthy.' He bids you chant this formula thrice nine times, touch the ground, spit, and observe a fast during the chant." (28) "Many other miracles," I said, "you will find in the volumes of the two Sasernas which all are equally foreign to agriculture, and for that reason should be rejected." "As if to say," he replied, "that such items are not found in other authors. In fact, are there not many similar details in the book of that famous Cato who published his treatise on agriculture, such as the directions for making cookies, the recipe for sacrificial cake or for prosciutto?" "You fail to mention," Agrius said, "his statement: 'If you wish to drink a lot and eat abundantly at a dinner party, then you should eat some raw cabbage—about five leaves—with vinegar ahead of time.'"

3. "OK, then," Agrasius said, "since we have determined what sorts of subjects are to be excluded from discussion on agriculture, instruct us whether the knowledge of those elements in agriculture is an art or some other thing, and what course it runs from starting gates to finish line." Stolo turned toward Scrofa and said, "Because you surpass us in age, esteem, and wisdom, you ought to speak." And he, not at all bothered, began: "First of all, agriculture is not only an art, but a necessary and important one; it is also a science, the knowledge of what should be

---

29: Tarquenna is not known; it has been suggested that the name refers to the eponymous founder of Tarquinia.

planted in each type of soil, and what work is to be performed to make the earth consistently produce the most abundant crops.

4. (1) The elements of this science are the same elements as those that Ennius writes comprise the universe: water, earth, air, and fire. You must know these before you sow seeds, the first stage of production. Undertaking their tasks with this in mind, farmers must take direct aim at two goals: profit and pleasure. Profit strives to obtain a return, pleasure seeks enjoyment; the profitable aspect plays a more significant role than the enjoyable. (2) The measures of cultivation that improve the value of the land, particularly when fruit and olive trees are planted in rows, not only make it more profitable but also more saleable, and add value to the estate. Any person would prefer to buy an attractive, profitable farm for a higher price than an ugly one, even though it is productive. (3) The most valuable land is that which is more healthy than the others, because the profit on it is certain; on the other hand, misfortune on a farm afflicted with blight, otherwise very fertile, does not allow the farmer to produce a profit. And where an accounting is made with death, there profit is uncertain as well as the life of the farmers. Therefore, where good health is lacking, agriculture is nothing other than a toss of the dice for the life and personal property of the owner. (4) But the odds can be reduced by science. The health of the farm is a correlative function of the climate and of the earth, which lie not in our power but in nature's; nevertheless, it is heavily incumbent upon us because by our diligence we can reduce serious troubles to minor ones. Indeed, if the farm experiences harmful disease because of the nature of the land or the poor quality of the water that belches a stench from some spots; or due to the climate the land becomes too hot and there blows an unhealthy wind, these faults are usually corrected by the know-how and the outlay of the owner. The placement of the estate houses, their size, and the orientation of their colonnades, the doors, and windows are of extreme importance. (5) Did not that famous physician Hippocrates during a plague save not just one farm but many towns by his expertise? But why do I bother to cite him as an authority? We have our good friend Varro here. When the army and fleet were stationed at Corcyra, and all the houses filled with the sick and dead, he made new windows to let in the northern breeze and to bar infecting winds; and he changed the door entries, and took other precautions of the same kind so that he brought back his comrades and personal staff safe and sound.[30]

5. (1) But now that I have presented the origin and parameters of agriculture, it remains to investigate the divisions that the science has." "I think," interrupted Agrius, "that surely they are endless, when I read the numerous books of Theophrastus, such as *The History of Plants* and

---

30: Varro served as an officer under Pompey the Great whose forces were stationed at Corcyra (Corfu) before Pharsalia.

The Causes of Plant Growth." (2) "Those books of his," Stolo replied, "are not so suitable to those who wish to cultivate the land as to those who cultivate the schools of philosophers. Now, I don't mean by that that they do not contain some useful and general information." (3) "OK, then explain to us the divisions of agriculture." Scrofa then began, "There are four main categories of agriculture. First, a knowledge of the farm, its soil, and the nature of its constituents; second, the necessary tools for the cultivation on the farm; third, the procedures needed on the estate for cultivating; and fourth, the proper season for each of these activities. (4) Each of these four major divisions is sub-divided into a minimum of two subcategories each; the first contains matters relating to the soil of the land, and matters pertaining to the houses and stables. The second category, which is made up of the moveable equipment needed for the cultivating of the farm, also has two subcategories: those who are to perform the farming and, secondly, the remaining tools; the third division which comprises the farm's operations is subdivided into the planned preparations for each activity and the location for each operation. The fourth category involves the seasons, subdivided into those activities to be renewed in the annual revolution of the sun and by the monthly circuit of the moon. I will treat the four main categories first, then delve into the eight subcategories in more detail.

6. (1) First, four features of the soil of the farm must be dealt with: the topography, the quality of the soil, the extent, and the means of its natural preservation. As there are two kinds of topographical structures, the one nature provides, and one that which cultivation affords, the former type shows one field well formed, another badly endowed; and the latter type manifests one estate well-planted, another badly; first, I shall treat natural topography. (2) There are, then, three simple kinds of land: the plain, the hilly, and the mountainous; a fourth kind consists of a combination of these three to form two or three other types on a farm, as one may see in many places. But of these three simple types without doubt a more suitable cultivation takes place in the lowlands than on the mountains because they are warmer than the heights; similarly, the hillsides because they are more temperate than the lowlands or the mountains. These features are more readily apparent in broad areas, when they are unvarying. (3) Thus the heat is more intense on sweeping plains such as in Apulia where areas are warmer and more humid, in contrast with mountainous territory such as Vesuvius[31] whose climate is lighter, and for that reason, healthier. Those who inhabit the plain suffer more in summer, whereas the inhabitants of the highlands suffer a harsher winter. The same crops are planted earlier in the spring in the lowlands than in the higher plateaus and are harvested sooner; in a word, both sowing and reaping take place later in the high country

---

31: Mount Vesuvius is the prominent peak dominating the Bay of Naples.

than down in the plain. (4) Certain trees, such as the firs and pines, grow more abundantly and become sturdier in the mountains because of the cold, while the poplars and willows flourish here on the plain, where the climate is warmer; the wild strawberry and oak are more prolific in higher elevations, whereas the almond and large fig thrive in the lowlands. In the foothills the yield parallels the produce on the plain rather than that of the mountains; high up, it is the converse. (5) Because of these three topographical differences a variety of crops is planted; grain crops are thought to do better in the plains, vines are best suited to the hills, and forests thrive in the mountains. The winter season is better for those who cultivate the plains, because the pastures are grassy and pruning of trees at that season is more tolerable; on the other hand, the summer months are more comfortable in the mountains because forage is plentiful then, whereas the plains are dry, and cultivation of trees is more suitable because of the cooler mountain air. (6) That plain is better which slopes evenly in one direction than one that is level as a ruler; the level plain does not have a discharge for water and, therefore, tends to become swampy. Even less suitable is an irregular plain because water forms into pools. These three types of topography have a disparate significance for agriculture."

7. (1) "In regard to natural topography," Stolo said, "Cato seems to be stating the proper case when he writes that the best farm was one that was located at the foot of a mountain facing toward the southern sky." (2) Scrofa then continued, "About the topography afforded by cultivation I assert that features more charming to view bring greater profit; as is the case, for example, of tree orchards that owners plant in the form of a quincunx in rows and at moderate intervals. Thus our ancestors from plots of equal size, but irregularly planted, produced much less wine and grain, and of poorer quality, than we do because trees which have been planted each in their proper spot occupy less space, and block each other less from the sun, moon, and wind. (3) It is possible to understand this from a reasonable inference of several factors; for example, the unshelled nuts that you can amass in one bushel because nature has encased them in shells with a specific volume, when you crack them, however, you can hardly stuff them into a bushel and a half. (4) Secondly, when the trees are planted in rows both the sun and the moon bathe them equally on all sides in light that causes the grapes and the olives to form and to ripen sooner. These two consequences bring in turn two other results: that the grapes produce more must and the olives more oil, and they both demand a higher price.

(5) Now follows the second category: the kind of soil on the farm, which mainly determines the farm's quality, good and bad. For it signals what crops and what varieties can be planted and raised in it, since not all of them can produce the same yield on the same land. One type of soil is appropriate for the vine, another for grain, so, in the other cases

the diversity of land suits diverse crops. (6) Thus near Cortynia in Crete they say that there is a sycamore tree that does not lose its leaves in winter; and likewise, as Theophrastus claims, one in Cyprus; and similarly in Sybaris, which is now called Thurii, there is an oak, in sight of the town, of similar nature; and contrary to what happens with us, near Elaphantine neither fig trees nor vines ever lose their leaves. For the same reason there are many trees that bear produce twice a year, such as the vine along the coast of Smyrna and the apple around the area of Consentia. (7) That trees produce more fruit in the wild, but better fruit in places that are cultivated, proves the same point. By the same reason some plants cannot survive except in a swampy environment or in actual water—and in that, too, there is a distinction—some survive in ponds, like the reeds around Reate, others in rivers, as the alders in Epirus, and others still, like the palms and sea onion, in the sea, so Theophrastus writes. (8) When I commanded an army deep in Transalpine Gaul near the Rhine, I visited several sites where neither vines, nor olives, nor fruit trees grew, where the people fertilized the fields with a white chalk that they dug up, where they had no salt, either extracted nor marine, but in place of it they used salty coals that came from the burning of certain kinds of wood." (9) "Now Cato," Stolo added, "arranged fields graded by excellence; he claims they consist of nine categories: first, the land where the vines can produce abundant, good wine; second, the land for an irrigated garden; third, that appropriate for osiers of willow, fourth, land for an olive grove, fifth, for a pasture, sixth, enough land for a grain field, seventh, a forest area for cutting firewood, eighth, land for an orchard, and ninth, for a forest producing acorns." (10) "I know," Scrofa said, "that he wrote that, but not everybody agrees with him on that point. Some designate, as I do, good pasturing land the prime objective from which the ancients called pastures (*prata*) as lands prepared (*parata*). Caesar Vopiscus, in a case he was pleading before the censors, as aedile, declared that the plains of Rosea[32] were the udders of Italy because, if a measuring rod were left there, the overgrowth of grass by the next morning would make it disappear.

8. (1) Those who argue against the vineyard think that the overhead devours the profits. It depends, I say, on the type of vineyard involved because there are many different kinds. Some are low on the ground and employ no props, as in Spain; others are constructed high up, called 'yoked,' as are most of the vineyards in Italy. Of this class belong two named types, the *pedamenta* (vinous stakes) and the *iuga* (yoking). They call the type *pedamenta* when the vines run vertically, *iuga* when the vines run horizontally; from this practice derives the phrase 'yoked vines.' (2) There are four kinds of the yoked variety employing respectively: poles, reeds, ropes, and vines. The pole type is used in Falernum, the reed in

32: Rosea is near Reate.

Arpi, the rope around Brundisium, and the vine in Milan. Two types
of trellising in 'yokes' exist: one in a straight line as in the territory of
Canusium;[33] the other is interlocked vertically and horizontally like a
sloping atrium roof, as is found in most of Italy.[34] When the materials
are grown locally, the vineyard need not fear a loss of profit; when most
of them come from a neighboring estate, there is a slight chance of loss.
(3) The first variety, which I mentioned, requires in the main a willow
thicket, the second, a large clump of reeds, the third, a bed of rushes
or some other material of that kind, and the fourth, an orchard where
trellises can form of vines, as the natives of Milan do with the trees that
they call *opuli*, a genus of maple, and as the people of Canusium erect on
fig trees with reinforcements of reeds. (4) Likewise, the wooden supports
for lattice work also come in four kinds: one is very stout and makes
the best pole to support the vines; it is called the *ridica* and is made of
oak or juniper. The second is the long pole, better hard to make it last
longer; when the bottom end has rotted away in the ground, the stake is
reversed, so that the bottom, rotted end becomes the top. The third type
is composed of reeds that help support gaps; these they bundle and tie
together with bark, and then set them in terracotta pipes with pierced
bottom—they call them *cuspides*, 'pointed pipes'—so that collected water
has an outlet. The fourth kind is the natural support where the vineyard is comprised of vines trained to cross from tree to tree; some call
this lattice work 'support runners' (*rumpi*). (5) The limit of a vineyard's
height is the average height of a man and the intervals between the
support stakes should be wide enough for a yoked team to be able to
plow. Those vineyards are less expensive to maintain which provide
wine to a demijohn without trellising. There are two of this type: one
in which the ground provides a bed for the grape clusters, as is found
in many locales in Asia, and is often shared by foxes and humans. Also,
if the ground breeds mice, the yield of the vintage is diminished unless
you fill the entire vineyard with mousetraps, as they do on the island
of Pandateria.[35]

(6) For the other type, only a vine which shows that it is producing
clusters if lifted off the ground and under it, when the grapes are forming, they place small supports made of fork-like sticks about two feet
long. In this way after the harvest the clusters do not learn to hang on a
tendril tied by a string or ribbon called a *cestus* by our ancestors. In this
type of vineyard, as soon as the owner sees the back of his vintager's
head, he removes the forks to store away in a shed for the winter to be
able to make use of them without additional cost in the next year. In

---

33: both Arpi and Canusium are in northern Apulia.
34: a rectangular opening in the center of the atrium (the *compluvium*) was cre-
    ated by a framework sloping inwards from the corners.
35: a small island in the Tyrrhenian Sea.

Italy this custom is observed by the people of Reate. (7) This variation in practice depends particularly on the nature of the soil. Where it is naturally moist, the vine must be elevated higher because in the process of forming and of maturing the grape does not need water, as the wine does in a cup, but requires sun. And for that reason I think that vines climb trees.

9. (1) The nature of the soil determines to what it is suitable or not. This word 'soil' (terra) has three senses, a general, a specific, and a figurative.[36] In the general sense we speak of the world, the land of Italy, or some other country; in that meaning both rock, and sand, and other things of this nature are encompassed by the term. In the second sense the word has a specific meaning used without any other attributive or modifier added. (2) The third sense of terra has a mixed semantic range: in it a seed can be planted and germinate, such as in clay soil, rocky soil, or other such; in this sense there are as numerous types of soil as of earth in the general sense because of the various possible combinations. Indeed, there are many constituents of the soil of varying density and strength, such as rock, marble, rubble, sand, gravel, clay, red ochre, dust, chalk, ash, or carbuncle; that is, the sun boils the ground so hot that it cooks the roots of the plants. (3) And the soil, the word used in its specific sense, is said to be chalky mixed with substances of those kinds...and other distinctions deriving from the various mixtures. The variety of these classes is so rich that some are more detailed, at least three subcategories for each; one soil is very rocky, another moderately so, and another almost totally free of rocks. The other varieties of mixed soil show the same three grades. (4) Besides, these very three grades each have three subcategories; they are: the very wet, the very dry, and the in-between. And these distinctions, too, have a strong connection to the crops. For that reason the experienced farmers plant spelt rather than wheat in a moist field; on the other hand, in a dry area they raise barley rather than spelt; but in the moderate climate they plant both. (5) In addition, there exist even more detailed distinctions in all these categories, such as in gravelly soil it matters whether it is white or reddish ground; for a whitish color of the ground is not suitable for planting young shoots, whereas the reddish colored soil is quite appropriate. Thus, there are three main distinctions in soil, and it depends whether it is poor, or rich, or of medium quality; the rich soil produces lush vegetation, the poor soil, the converse. In thin soil, as in Pupinia,[37] you cannot see tall trees, strong, clinging vines, tough straw, and the large variety of figs; in fact most of the trees and the parched pastures are covered with moss. (6) On the other hand, in rich ground, as in Etruria, you can see fertile crops, renewable land, tall trees, and no moss in sight.

36: the three meanings are respectively, 'land,' 'ground,' and 'soil.'
37: a sterile area near Rome.

In medium soil, however, as in the district of Tibur, it closer approaches to the not-thin variety rather than the sterile, and the more suited it is for all crops than if it inclines to the poorer quality." (7) At this point Stolo interrupted, "Diophanes of Bithynia does not put it badly, when he writes that the signs either from the soil itself or from the growth on it can affirm what land is suitable for cultivation or not; first, from the soil itself, if it is white or black, or if it is light and crumbles easily when dug up, or if it has a non-ashy and not exceedingly thick consistency; secondly, from the vegetation that grows wild on it, if it is lush and fertile, producing natural goods as it should. But continue, please, go on to your next subject on measurements."

10. (1) Scrofa continued: "All locales vary in the methods used to measure farmlands. In farther Spain they measure by the *iugum*, in Campania the unit of measure is the *versus*, but in Roman and Latin territory we use the *iugerum*. The *iugum* is so called because it indicates what a team of yoked oxen (*iugum*) can plow in a single day; the *versus* encompasses one hundred feet square; (2) the *iugerum* contains two square *actus*. Now the square *actus* is 120 feet wide by 120 feet long; this measure in Latin is called an *Acnua*. The smallest subdivision of the *iugerum*, which comprises ten feet square, is called a *scripulum*. From this foundation surveyors often name the remaining patch of land an 'ounce' (*uncia*) or a 'sixth of a pound' (*sextans*), or some such thing; as far as the *iugerum* goes, it has 288 *scripula*, one *scripulum* equaling the weight of our old *as* before the Punic War.[38] Two *iugera* make an 'heir's plot' (*heredium*), so called from the amount to have been first allotted by Romulus to each individual citizen, which could then be inherited. Later one hundred of these plots were called a *centuria* (i.e. a 'century'), which is a square area with each side having 2,400 feet in length. When four such 'centuries' are joined contiguously with two per side, in the distribution of public land to individuals they call them *saltus*.

11. (1) Many have made a mistake in their failure to take account of the dimensions of a farm; some have built a villa either too small or too large in proportion to the size of the estate; each size, too small or too large, is outside the property's requirement and is detrimental to the farm and its profit. Buildings which are too large cost more to build and the expense for their upkeep is considerably high; whereas when buildings are smaller than the estate requires, produce goes to waste. (2) There is no doubt at all that a larger wine cellar should be built on estates where there are vineyards, and more ample granaries constructed for grain farms.

Special attention should be given to the building of the villa so that it has a source of water within its confines, or at least very close by. Best is to have a source from a spring; second best is a constant stream. But

---

38: fractions of the pound were applied to the fractions of land measurement.

if there is no running water on the grounds, then cisterns have to be built with covers and reservoirs under the open sky; the one people can use, the other is for cattle.

12. (1) And special care ought to be taken to locate the villa at the foot of a wooded hill, where the pasture lands are broad and it is exposed to the most healthy prevailing winds that blow in the area. The orientation that is most suitable is facing the equator toward the east because in summer it has shade and in winter sun. But if you are forced to build along a river, make sure you do not orient the villa toward it, since in winter it becomes bitterly cold and in summer it is very unhealthy. (2) You must also take precautions in swampy areas both because of the same reasons just mentioned and because tiny beasties, bred and maturing there, and which the eyes cannot detect, fly through the air and penetrate the body through the mouth or nostrils and bring severe diseases." "What can I do," Fundanius asked, "if I chance to have inherited that kind of estate?" "Even I can respond to that question," Agrius said: "you sell for all the cash that you can get; or if you can't, then leave it." (3) Scrofa, however, continued: "You must avoid orienting the villa in that direction from which oppressive wind blows, and do not build in a depressed area or hollow, but rather on high ground; in a place that is well-ventilated, any foreign or harmful matter that has been introduced is more easily swept away. Also the estate that basks in the sun all day long is especially healthy because any tiny creatures bred or imported there are either blown away or quickly die from the dryness. (4) Sudden rainstorms and flooding streams are a danger to those who have built their houses in the low-lying and depressed areas; and the sudden attacks of gangs of looters can easily catch owners by surprise. Therefore, the higher sites are much safer from both these dangers.

13. (1) In constructing the villa, the stables should be set up so that the stalls receive as much heat as possible in winter. Produce like wine and olive oil should be stored in specially made rooms on level ground; and, likewise, the jars for the wine and oil; dry goods, on the other hand, like beans and hay, should be stocked in floored quarters. The staff should be provided with quarters, if they are tired from work or weary from cold or heat, where they can rest and recover in comfortable surroundings. (2) The ramrod's room should be next to the front door so he can know who enters and goes out at night and what he takes with him, especially if there is no butler. Special attention should be directed to placing the kitchen because in winter several operations take place in it before daylight, primarily the preparation and consumption of food. In every barnyard sufficiently large sheds should be built to store carts and other implements which rain and weather damage. If these items are enclosed in a pen under the open sky, they do not have to fear a thief, but will be unable to resist the harm from the weather. (3) On a large estate two farmyards are more appropriate: one to have a reservoir to

catch rain water, where water may burble to become, as it were, a colon-
naded fishpond. Here the cattle, driven back from the field, can drink
in summer, here they can bathe themselves, and the geese and the sows
and boars as well, once they have returned from pasture. In the outer
barnyard there should be a pool for soaking peas and other products
which, once soaked in water, become more fit for use. (4) This outer yard,
often covered with straw and chaff and trampled by the farm animals,
becomes the servant of the farm because of what is swept out of it. Near
the main house the estate should have two manure pits or one divided
into two distinct sections. One part should have fresh manure, the other,
a compost, should be hauled into the field because manure that has de-
composed is better than the fresh. That manure pit is best whose sides
and top are protected from the sun by branches and leaves. Indeed, the
sun should not suck out the sap which the land needs. Therefore, experienced farmers see to it, if they can, that water is kept flowing there
(in this way the pit best retains the strengthening moisture); and some
farmers place outhouse seats there for the servants. (5) You should build
a structure with a cover under which you can store the entire yield of
the farm. This storage barn some call a *nubilarium* (i.e. 'cloud cover').
This building should be constructed near the floor where you thresh
grain, and proportionate in size to the extent of the estate, with one side
open—the one by the threshing floor—so that you can easily throw the
grain on it and, if it begins to cloud over, quickly throw it back in the
building. On another side it should have windows to facilitate ventilation
for comfort." (6) "No doubt," said Fundanius, "an estate is more profitable, when it comes to building, if you direct your construction following
the economical approach of the ancients rather than the luxurious style
of our contemporaries. The former built motivated by their yields, the
latter are motivated by their unchecked pleasure. So, rustic villas of the
old-timers cost more than their urban houses, which nowadays is for the
most part the exact opposite. In earlier times the villa was praised if it
had a good country kitchen, spacious stables, a wine cellar, and oil storage proportionate to the size of the farm, and with a floor sloping to a
reservoir because, after the new wine is stored, the storage jars, like those
in Spain and the large ones employed in Italy, break from the fermenting gasses of the must. Similarly, they saw to it that the villa had all the
other things of this sort which cultivation requires; (7) but those today
strive to have the largest and most decorated urban villas possible, and
they compete with the villas of Metellus and Lucullus, built with great
detriment to the public. Today they work to orient their summer dining
rooms to the cool of the east, and their winter ones toward the setting sun
rather than, as the ancients did, paying attention on what side the wine
cellar and oil storage have their windows. In the cellar wine requires a
cooler temperature for the jars, while olive oil requires a warmer one.
Likewise, you should provide that, if there is a hill, the farm house be
placed specifically there, unless something impedes it.

14. (1) Now I will discuss fences which are constructed to protect the farm and its constituent parts. There are four kinds of these defenses: one, the natural, second, the rustic, third, the military, and fourth, the masonry. Each of these types has several sub-classes. The first of them, the natural type, is a hedge which is usually planted with brush or thorn thickets; it has roots and is alive, and has no fear of the blazing torch of a malicious passerby. (2) The second kind, the rustic, is a palisade made of wood, but is not alive; it is constructed of stakes packed close together and intertwined with brush or thick perforated poles that have rails—usually two or three—passed through the bored holes, or of tree trunks arranged successively and driven into the ground. The third type, the military, is a fence with a ditch and an earthen embankment; the ditch is suitable only if it can retain all the rain water or has a slope in order to drain it off the land. (3) The bank is reliable insomuch as the inside is linked with the ditch or is so steep that it is not easy to climb. This kind of fence is usually constructed along public roads and rivers. Along the Salt Road[39] in the district of Crustumeria at several spots it is possible to see embankments joined with ditches to prevent the river doing damage to the fields. Banks are also constructed without ditches such as those found in the territory of Reate: some call them walls. (4) The fourth and last type is the masonry fence, that is, a wall. Usually it comes in four categories: that built of stone as in the district of Tusculum, that made of fired bricks as in the "Gallic Land,"[40] that made of sun-dried bricks as in Sabine territory, and that made of earth and fine gravel in molds, as in Spain and the district of Tarentum.

15   And besides, without fences the boundaries of the estate are made more secure by planting trees; this keeps the servant staff from quarreling with neighbors and prevents a judge in a lawsuit from setting the boundary line. Some, for example, plant pines all around the borders, as my wife has done on her Sabine property; others cypresses, as I have planted on Mount Vesuvius; and others elms, as many have around Crustumeria. Where it is possible, as it is there in Crustumeria, because of the plain, no better tree than the elm exists for planting; it is very profitable because it both supports and harvests many baskets of grapes and provides most delightful foliage to sheep and cattle, and furnishes stakes for the fences and kindling for fireplace and furnace. These topics," Scrofa said, "which I have treated, are the four matters to which a farmer must direct his attention: the topography of the land, the nature of the soil, the extent of the farm, and the protection of the boundaries.

39: the Salt Road (*Via Salaria*) led north along the Tiber from Rome into Sabine country; it was so-called from the track followed by the Sabines to procure salt from the flats near the mouth of the Tiber.
40: a strip of coastal land in northeast Umbria that comprises a part of Cisalpine Gaul.

16. (1) There remains to deal with the second theme: the nature of matters outside the estate that are supplements to the farm and are extremely relevant and closely connected to agriculture. The categories are the same in number: four. The first is whether the neighboring territory is dangerous; second, whether its nature makes it inconvenient to export our products or import necessities; third, whether roads or rivers for transport either are non-existent or unsuitable; fourth, whether any condition exists on neighboring farms to benefit or harm our fields. (2) The first of the four deals with the question of the safety or the danger of the neighboring area. It is not prudent to cultivate many prime farms because of the presence of outlaws in neighboring territory, as is the case in Sardinia on certain farms near Oleis and in Spain near Lusitania. The estates that have suitable conveyances to transport goods to sell produced there in the vicinity, and convenient conveyances to import those things necessary for the farm, are thereby profitable. Many have estates to which grain or wine or some other commodity that they lack must be imported; on the other hand, several must export their surplus. (3) Therefore, it is profitable to cultivate extensive gardens on the outskirts of a city, such as violet and rose nurseries, and many other products that a city has a demand for; whereas it would not be profitable to cultivate the same goods on a farm far away where there is no market to transport items up for sale. Likewise, if those towns or villages in the neighborhood, or even the abundant farms and estates of the wealthy owners from whom you can buy at a price (not unreasonable) the necessities for your farm and to whom you can sell your surplus, such as support stakes, poles, or reeds, are accessible, then your farm can show a greater profit than if those goods had to be imported from far away, and would be even more profitable sometimes than if you have the capability to produce them for yourself on your own farm. (4) Therefore, under those conditions, farmers choose yearly to employ neighbors, such as doctors, laundrymen, and blacksmiths, to perform tasks that he orders rather then to keep them on their estate as their own; for the death of a single craftsman sometimes robs a farm of profit. Usually rich proprietors entrust this unit of a large farm to members of the household. If towns or villages are too far away, they train blacksmiths and all other necessary craftsmen in order to keep them on the estate to prevent their farm staff from leaving their work, and loitering about, and celebrating a holiday on working days, instead of doing their jobs to enrich the revenues of the farm. (5) For this reason, Saserna's book outlines the precept that no one is to leave the estate except the ramrod, the steward, and one designated by the ramrod; if one leaves against the rule, he does not go with impunity; and if he does leave, the punishment is directed to the foreman. The regulations should rather be stipulated in this way: no one will leave the farm without the permission of the ramrod; nor will the ramrod leave any longer than one day before his return without the permission of the owner; nor will

he be absent more frequently than is necessary for the work of the farm. (6) Transportation makes a farm more profitable, if there are roads on which carts can easily be driven, or rivers nearby which are navigable. In fact, we know that many farms use both methods to haul to and fro. Also important to the farm's profit is how a neighbor keeps the land planted on the boundary. If, for example, he has an oak thicket near the borderline, you cannot really plant olives alongside this grove because it is by nature so destructive that your trees not only will produce less, but also will wilt,[41] as the vine usually does planted near cabbage, turning and bending inward and low into the ground. Like oaks, so numerous large walnut trees also make the border of the farm sterile.

17. (1) I have treated the four categories of the estate which are connected with the soil, and the other set of four which lie outside of the farm proper but pertain to its cultivation. Now I will speak of the means by which the lands are worked. Some have divided them into two parts: the men who do the work and the auxiliaries without which they cannot cultivate; others make the division into three parts: the category of instruments either endowed with speech, or endowed with the ability to make sounds, or mute. The category of 'endowed with speech,' that is the articulate, comprises slaves, that of semi-articulate, that is, making sounds, designates the cattle, and that of the mute comprises the conveyances. (2) All crops are cultivated by slaves or by freemen or both; by freemen either when they cultivate the land themselves, as most poor people and their families do; or by hired laborers when they perform major operations such as the vintage and baling hay, as do those whom we call debtors (obaerarii),[42] many of whom are still to be found in Asia, in Egypt, and in Illyricum. (3) About these, the debtors, as a whole I claim the following: it is more profitable to use hired laborers rather than slaves to work the lands that are oppressive and unhealthy, and even in healthy locations it is better that they undertake the more laborious farm operations, such as storing the products of the vintage or harvest. Concerning what these men should be like, Cassius[43] writes this: such workers should be obtained who can endure the heavy labor, be no less than twenty-two years old, and have an aptitude for farm work. One can infer the truth of this from how they execute orders in other instances, and in the case of the new-hired help, by asking what they did for their former master.

(4) Purchased slaves should be neither timid nor spirited. Those in charge of them should be men who are literate and imbued with some liberal education, who are honest and older than the workers whom I

41: other authors, such as Pliny and Columella, comment on this phenomenon.

42: i.e. those who disengage a debt by labor.

43: i.e. Cassius Dionysius, one of Varro's major sources.

have mentioned above, because these slaves more readily listen to men who are older rather than to those who are younger. Besides, foremen particularly should be skilled in the methods and operations of farming; not only must the boss give orders, but he must do the work so that workers will emulate his performance and come to realize that he justifiably directs them because he excels them in expertise. (5) He must not be granted the license to command the workers, controlling them with whips rather than words, if you can bring about the same result. Nor should you acquire slaves of the same ethnicity because it is the leading contributor to frequent domestic squabbles. Foremen should be made more motivated by rewards; and special attention should be directed that they have some property of their own and that they enjoy mates from fellow-slaves to bear them children. In this way they become more reliable and connected to the estate. Thus, because of relationships like that, slave families of Epirus have gained high renown and command higher prices. (6) Foremen should be courted for their good will, by showing them some respect; and those workers who manage others should be consulted about the operations to be done. When this gesture is made, they think it less likely that they are despised, but reckon they are esteemed by their master. (7) They are enticed to be more enthusiastic toward their work by being treated like a freeman either by increasing food rations, or by providing more clothes, or by exempting them from work, or by granting permission to herd their own stock on the estate, or in other ways of this kind. Should they be ordered to perform some heavy job or inflicted with a severe punishment, their loyalty and good will toward the master may be restored by the consolation from these matters.

18. (1) Concerning the slaves Cato guides his thinking toward two goals: to measuring the size of the farm and to the nature of the crop. He provides two formulas in his writings on olive groves and vineyards: one in which he points out how one should staff an olive grove of 240 iugera. He says, in fact, for one of that size thirteen slaves should be kept: a foreman, a woman housekeeper, five workers, three teamsters, one mule driver, one swineherd, and one shepherd. In the second formula he provides a vineyard of 100 iugera saying that it should support fifteen slaves: a foreman, a woman housekeeper, ten laborers, a teamster, a mule driver, and a swineherd. (2) Saserna writes that a single person is enough for eight iugera and that by digging he ought to be able to prepare that amount of land in forty-five days, although he can dig up a single iugerum with four days work; but he leaves thirteen days in case of illness, bad weather, laziness, and slackness. (3) Neither of these authors has left us clear formulas. If Cato had decided to do it, he should have written it so that we might add or subtract the number in proportion to a larger farm or a smaller one. And besides, he ought to have designated the foreman and woman overseer outside of the number of slaves. In fact,

if you tend to less than 240 iugera of olive trees, you cannot have less than one ramrod, nor, if you cultivate an estate twice as large or more, will you need two or three foremen. (4) Only workers and teamsters should be added in proportion to the larger tracts of farmland, and those men only if the land is consistently the same. But if it is so varied that it cannot be plowed because it is rough or has steep slopes, then fewer bulls and teamsters are needed. I pass over the fact that the measure of 240 iugera mentioned is neither a unit nor a set (a set is defined as a century which is comprised of 200 iugera).[44] (5) When one-sixth, that is forty iugera, is subtracted from the 240, I do not see how, according to his formula, I can also subtract one-sixth of the thirteen slaves, much less, if I omit the foreman and the woman, how can I deduct one-sixth of the remaining eleven. And in regard to his statement that fifteen slaves are required for a vineyard of 100 iugera, if someone has a century, half of which is a vineyard, and the other half an olive grove, it follows that he should have two foremen and two women overseers, which is totally absurd. (6) Therefore, the configuration of the slaves must be determined by some other formula and in this matter Saserna is more to be trusted; he says that one worker is enough to complete each iugerum in four days of work. But if the period was enough for Saserna's farm in Gaul, the same may not hold true for a farm somewhere in the mountainous regions of Liguria. (7) You will know best the number of the slaves and the other apparatus which you should have ready, if you attend with care to these three factors: the nature and size of the farms in the vicinity, the number of men working on each, and how many workers are to be added or deducted for you to maintain cultivation in better or worse condition. Nature has provided us with two avenues to agriculture, experiment and imitation. The most ancient farmers instituted practices after some experimentation; their descendants imitated them for the most part. (8) We ought to use both: to imitate others and to attempt by experiment to do some things differently, following not the throw of the dice, but some rational system; for example, that we replow more or less deeper than others to find out what impact that has, as those men did in hoeing twice and three times and as those who transferred the grafting of fig trees from the spring to the summer time.

19. (1) Concerning the other division regarding auxiliaries, which I have called 'semi-articulate,' Saserna states two teams of oxen are sufficient for a farm of 200 iugera, while Cato says that three teams are needed for an olive grove of 240 iugera. Therefore, if Saserna is correct, then one team is needed for 100 iugera, whereas, if Cato has the right idea, one for every eighty iugera. But as for me, I do not think either of these formulas applies to every farm, but that each conforms to some particular property. One tract of farm land is easier to manage or more

44: see chapter 10.1-2 for Varro's units of land measurement.

difficult than another; (2) and oxen cannot split open some land without strenuous effort and often they leave a plow with a broken beam behind in the field. Thus, we must follow on each farm, as long as we are novices, three guidelines: the operations instituted by the former owner, the practice of owners in the neighborhood, and some experimentation. (3) He adds three donkeys to haul manure, and one to work the mill, and for a vineyard of one hundred iugera a team of oxen, a pair of donkeys, and a donkey for the mill; in this classification of semi-articulate animals must be added only those that are useful for agriculture and those few which are normally kept as the personal property of the slaves so they may be able to support themselves more easily and to keep themselves busier. In this number of animals those owners who have pastures take care to maintain sheep over pigs because of their manure, and some also keep animals not necessarily for the pastures. For example, dogs are beneficial because without them an estate is not very secure.

20. (1) The first factor to be examined concerning all the quadrupeds is what bulls are suitable to buy for plowing. They should be unbroken, not less than three years old but not more than four when you obtain them; they should have great strength and be of equal size so that the sturdier one does not exhaust the weaker during their work; their horns should be large and black instead of any other color; they should be wide across the face and have a flat nose, broad chest, and thick haunches. (2) You should not purchase mature bulls experienced in plowing level ground to be used for rugged mountainous regions, and you should avoid having the opposite happen.[45] When someone has bought young bullocks, if he loosely yokes their necks with a forked wooden bar and gives them food, within a few days they will become gentle and ready for taming. They should be broken in gradually, growing accustomed to work, and after yoking the inexperienced bullock with a mature broken bull—imitation makes for easier training—first you should work them on level ground without a plow, then with a light one in sand or somewhat soft soil. (3) The draft animals at first should be trained to pull empty carts, if you can manage it, through a village or town. A continual racket, a variety of sights, and frequent repetition of the same activity introduce them to useful service. The bull which you have yoked on the right should not constantly remain on that side because, if alternated with the left, it secures rest by laboring on alternate sides. (4) In soil that is light, as in Campania, heavy oxen do not do the plowing, but cows or donkeys, with the result that they can more easily adjust to the light plow, to the mill, and to those common operations that require hauling on the farm. In this situation some use small donkeys, others cows and mules, depending upon the source of fodder. It is less expensive to

---

45: i.e. do not buy bulls experienced in plowing mountainous terrain for work on the plain.

feed the donkey than the cow, but the cow brings in more profit. (5) In this general matter the farmer must take into account the nature of the land. In rugged and hard-to-work land he must obtain stronger animals, preferably those which can return a profit on their own, although they perform the same work as the others.

21. You should keep fierce and courageous dogs, just a few, not many, and train them to keep watch at night and sleep locked up inside during the day. Concerning unbroken quadrupeds and flocks the following should be done: if an owner has pasture lands and no herd on the farm, he should carry out this project, sell the forage, and feed and fold flocks and herds of others on his farm.

22. (1) I will now treat the last category of services to the farm, the 'mute' equipment that includes baskets, jars, and other such things. The guidelines consist of the following: nothing should be bought which can be produced on the farm and made by the staff; for instance, items made of wicker and timber of the farm, such as baskets, containers, threshing combs, winnowing fans, and rakes; also things made of hemp, flax, rushes, palm, and bulrushes, such as ropes, cords, and mats. (2) With items that cannot be garnered from the estate, if appropriate goods are purchased for their usefulness rather than for show, the expenditure for them will not thin out the profits, and especially if articles for the most part are bought from where they can be purchased at the cheapest price, have good quality, and be from the nearest outlet possible. The various types of equipment and their number are defined by the size of the farm; more items are needed, if the confines of the farm extend far." (3) "Therefore," Stolo added, "about this category, after he established the size of the estate, Cato writes that the owner who cultivates 240 iugera of olives should outfit it in this way: first, he should construct five sets of oil machinery and itemize them, piece by piece, such as the bronze vessels, jugs, pitchers, and the like; then the equipment made of wood or iron, such as three large carts, six complete plows, four manure baskets, and the like; he ought also to list the type and number of necessary iron tools, such as eight pitchforks, the same number of hoes, half as many shovels, and other things of the same kind. (4) He has also made another formula for the implements used in a vineyard; he writes that, if an owner has a vineyard of 100 iugera, he should possess three complete apparatus and machinery for pressing, vats with covers with a volume of 800 large demijohns, twenty grape baskets, twenty grain baskets, and similar items of this sort. Other authors maintain that much less equipment is needed, but I think that he prescribed so high a number of demijohns to prevent being forced to sell off the wine every year; when aged, wine demands a higher price at one time than another. (5) Likewise, he writes a lot about the variety of tools, the types and number necessary for the farm, such as pruning hooks, shovels, rakes, and the like; there are some categories that have many subdivisions, such as in the case of pruning

hooks. The same author argues that forty are needed for vines, five for rushes, three for shrubs, and ten for bushes." Stolo finished and Scrofa resumed: "The owner ought to maintain a complete written inventory of the equipment and tools of the farm both in the city and on the grounds; on the other hand, the foreman on the farm should have all equipment stored near the estate house in their respective places; those tools, which cannot be kept under lock and key, he should keep in sight to the best of his ability, and in particular, those that are infrequently used, such as the baskets employed at vintage and others of that sort. Items which are seen every day have less to fear from the thief."

23 (1) Agrasius then added: "And since we have now heard the first two categories of the quadripartite division, that is, about the farm and the equipment usually employed in cultivation, I am waiting for the treatment of the third topic." "As I think," Scrofa continued, "that the profit of a farm derives from the planting undertaken for a useful purpose, two matters must be addressed: what is particularly beneficial to plant and in what place. Some locales are suitable for hay, some for grain, some for grape vines, others for olive, and the same can be said of forage crops that include clover, mixed fodder, vetch, alfalfa, sweet clover, and the lupine. (2) It is not good to plant all the different crops on rich soil and to plant nothing on thin soil; but it is much better to plant in thinner soil those crops which need little moisture and nourishment, such as clover and legumes, except the chickpea, although it is properly a legume as are all the plants which are uprooted from the earth and not mowed, and are called legumes because they are 'gathered up' (*leguntur*). (3) In fat soil it is better to plant those that need more nutriments, such as cabbage, wheat, winter wheat, and flax. Some crops should be planted not for a quick profit but rather in expectation of bigger return a year later, for example, in the case of crops mowed and left on the ground that enrich the soil. Thus, if the soil is somewhat thin, it is customary to plow under, instead of manuring, a crop of lupines when they have taken on a pod, and the same for bean stalks before pods have started to take shape, when it is not yet profitable to harvest the beans. (4) In planting, also, attentive care should be shown in selecting profitable crops that bring pleasure, such as the so-called orchard and flower gardens, and likewise in those crops which do not provide sustenance to humans or appeal to the senses, but are not removed from useful applications to the farm. You ought to select a suitable spot for planting willow and reed beds, and other plants that require a humid location. (5) On the other hand, for grain crops and especially for beans and some other plants, you should select dry areas for planting. Similarly, plant in shady spots others, such as wild asparagus, because members of the asparagus family like that kind of environment; but set out gardens and plant violets, and others of that sort, in sunny locations because these are nourished by the sun. In another place you should plant thickets that you may have a

supply of osiers with which to weave together in order to make articles like flat beds of wagons, winnowing fans, and baskets; and in another location plant and cultivate a forest for supplying cut wood, and another grove for catching birds; (6) and then a section for hemp, flax, rushes, and broom from which you can fashion shoes for cattle,[46] threads, cords, and ropes. Some places are ideal for planting other crops. For example, in young fruit orchards, after the seedlings have been planted and the saplings have been set in rows, during the tender years before the roots can penetrate deep and spread wide, some owners plant gardens, others something else; but they do not do this planting after the trees have become strong and sturdy because they fear damaging the roots."

24. (1) Stolo then spoke: "Cato does not fail to be pertinent writing on this subject of planting: soil that is thick, rich, and without trees should be used for a grain field; and the same soil, if it is exposed to lots of fog, should raise mustard, turnips, millet, and panic grass; in thick and moist ground plant olives, those for curing, the long and large variety, the Sallentine, the oblong variety, the posea, the Sergian, the Colminian, and the waxy, light-colored variety.[47] Plant especially those kinds that are said to grow best in the local regions. The right land for planting an olive orchard is one that faces the prevailing westerly wind and is exposed to the sun. (2) Plant the Licinian variety in colder and thinner soil. If you plant it in thick or warm soil, the yield will be worthless, the tree will die from producing, and a reddish moss will damage it. (3) They call the return on one *factus* a *hostus*, and a *factus* (that is 'making') is what they produce at one time. Some say the amount is 160 bushels, others maintain it is less, reduced to 120 bushels, proportionate to the number and size of pressing machines with which they make the oil. Regarding Cato's statement that elms and poplars ought to be planted around the farm to afford leaves to sheep and cattle, and timber, although this planting is not necessary on all farms, nor on farms where it is necessary, is it mainly for the leaves. Because they do not block the sun, they are planted without causing damage on the northern side."

(4) Scrofa then added the following from the same author: "Wherever you find wet ground, you should plant saplings of poplars and a reed thicket. First, turn the soil with a hoe, then plant the eyes of the reeds three feet apart from each other…almost the same cultivation is adapted for both. Plant the Greek willow around the edge of the reed thicket so as to have osiers to tie up the vines.

25. One should observe the following guidelines of the soil for planting a vineyard: where the soil is best for grape vines and oriented to

---

46: various shrubs of broom made up the most common shoes for cattle and horses. The ancients did not use metal shoes nailed on the hoof.

47: these types and varieties of olives cannot be correlated to any variety known today.

the sun, plant the small Aminnian, the double 'noble' and the tiny Pinot Grigio. In soil that is thick or in foggy areas plant the large Aminnian, the Murgentine, the Apician, or the Lucanian;[48] the other varietals, and especially the hybrids, are suitable to every type of soil.

26. In every vineyard they diligently observe that a system of supports oriented to the north protects the vines; and if they plant live cypresses to act as supports, they place them in alternate rows, and they do not allow them to grow any higher than the supports; nor do they plant the vines near these trees because they are incompatible."

Agrius then commented to Fundanius, " I am afraid that the temple keeper will arrive here before he (Scrofa) reaches the fourth act. I am still waiting for the vintage." "Stay calm," Scrofa said, "and get the baskets and jar ready."

27. (1) "Now since we have two ways of observing time, one annual, which the circuit of the sun determines, the other monthly which the lunar cycle encompasses, I will deal with the sun first. Its annual circuit is divided into four periods of about three months each, and in more detail eight divisions of a month and a half. The four divisions are spring, summer, fall, and winter. (2) To plant in the spring you must split the unplowed earth so that the growth springing from it be uprooted before any seed falls from it. At the same time, when the clods have been baked by the sun, to make them more suitable for catching rain and easier to work once broken up, you should plow the land no less than two times, preferably three. (3) In summer harvest the grain crop, and in autumn during dry weather harvest the vintage; that is also the most proper time to clear the woods, and to cut the trees close to the ground; the roots, however, should be dug out at the earliest showers to prevent any re-growth from them. In winter trees should be pruned as long as it takes place when the bark is free from frost and ice, formed from the rain.

28. The first day of spring occurs when Aquarius is in ascendance, that of summer with Taurus, of fall with Leo, and of winter with Scorpio in ascendance. Since the twenty-third day of each one of these four zodiacal signs is the first day of one of the four seasons, spring, therefore, contains 91 days, summer 94, autumn 91, and winter 89, that rendered in terms of the days which our community now uses,[49] makes the first day of spring fall on 7 February; the beginning of summer commences on 9 May, of autumn on 11 August, and of winter on 10 November. In the more exact divisions of seasons certain matters must be observed, as they are divided into eight periods: first, from the onset of the prevailing

---

48: like the olives these types and varieties of grapes are unknown. 'Pinot Grigio' is my translation of *helvium* which literally means 'spotted.'

49: the Julian calendar had been in effect since 1 January, 45, eight years before the composing of this treatise.

westerlies to the vernal equinox are 45 days; from then to the rising of the Pleiades total 44 days, from that period to the solstice 48 days, from then to the ascendance of the Dog Star 67 days, from there to the setting of the Pleiades makes 32 days, from then to the winter solstice 57 days, and finally back to the onset of west winds 45 days.

29. (1) In that first interval between the onset of the west wind and the vernal equinox these are the operations that should be done: nurseries of all kinds should be planted, trees pruned, pastures manured, and channels dug around the vines; roots protruding along the ground should be cut back, meadows cleared, willow beds planted, and cropland weeded. The word *seges* means plowed land that has been sown; *arvum*, on the other hand, is plowed land that has not been sown, and *novalis* (fallow land) refers to land left after being planted before a second plowing 'renews' it. (2) When farmers plow the land the first time, they call it 'splitting,' the second time is called 'breaking apart' by cross plowing, because with the first plowing large clods are usually raised up; when it is repeated, they call the process 'breaking apart.' When they have scattered the seed and plow for the third time, the oxen are said to be 'furrowing,' that is to say, by attaching flaps to the plow blade they both cover the sown seeds of grain and cut furrows to allow the drainage of rain water. Some, who have field crops that do not extend far, as in Apulia and on farms of that kind, usually harrow and break up by hoeing whatever large clods were turned up and left on the ridges of the furrows. (3) Where the blade of the plow has made a hollow or channel, it is called a 'furrow.' Between two furrows where the earth is raised is called a 'ridge' (*porca*), because that cropland brings forth (*porricit*) the grain; thus, they used the word *porricere* ('bring forth'),[50] when they offered entrails to the gods.

30. In the second interval between the vernal equinox and the rising of the Pleiades the following should be done: crops weeded, that is, grass cleared from the crops, the earth split by oxen, willows cut, and pastures fenced. The jobs that should have been done but were left uncompleted, should be finished before plants form buds and begin to flower, because, if those trees which usually drop their leaves begin to sprout leaves, at that point they are not suitable for planting. Olives should be planted and pruned.

31. (1) In the third period between the rising of the Pleiades and the solstice these jobs must be done: dig or plow the young vines, and later break up and level the ground to get rid of the clods. They say *occare* because they smash (*occidunt*) the ground. Trim the vines—that is better than pruning—but do it by a professional, not in the orchard, but in the vineyard. (2) Trimming is leaving the stalks which shoot from the stock, the first and second, and sometimes even the third layer of the sturdiest

---

50: as in chapter 31, Varro engages in some fancy and fanciful etymologies.

shoots, and plucking off the rest to prevent the stock from being too weak to furnish sap to the stalks that are left. For that reason, in the nursery, when the vine first shoots out, it is usual to cut back all of it so that it may rise from the ground with a stronger stock and have greater energy in producing stalks. (3) A slender stock is sterile as a result of its weakness and because it cannot produce the vine which, when it is small, they call a young sprout (*flagellum*); but the larger form from which the grapes come is called a palm (*palma*). The previous word seems at first to have been called *parilema* deriving from *pariendo* ('giving birth') because the vine grows without restraint to produce grapes; (4) so, by changing letters, as is the case with many words, it began to be called *palma* ('palm'). On the other side of the vine it produces a tendril. This is a curled and twisted stem. With these tendrils the vine holds on and creeps along to grasp a place; from this grasping (*capiendo*) it is said to be a *capreolus*. All feed crops ought to be cut, first, clover, then mixed fodder, vetch, and last of all hay. The word for clover (*ocinum*) as well as the word for basil (*ocimum*), the common garden variety, derive from the Greek word *OKEOS*, which means 'quickly.' Further, clover is called *ocinum* because it hurries (*citat*) the bowels of cattle, and for that reason it is provided to them as a purgative. It is cut while it is green from the bean crop before it generates pods. (5) The mixed variety (*farrago*), on the other hand, derives from the crop of mixed seeds, barley, vetch, and legumes, all sown for green feed, either because it is cut with an iron blade (*ferro*) or because it was first sown in a crop of spelt (*far*). With this feed horses and other working animals are purged and fattened up in the spring. The vetch is so called from 'binding' (*vinciendo*) because it, too, has tendrils, like the vine, with which it creeps up to take hold of and cling to the lupine stalk or some other plant and normally 'binds' (*vincire*) it. If you have pastures to irrigate, then irrigate them as soon as you have baled the hay. During dry spells provide water every evening to the fruit trees that have been grafted. It is possible that people call them fruit trees (*poma*) because they need drink (*potus*).

32. (1) In the fourth interval between the summer solstice and the rising of the Dog Star the majority of farmers do the harvesting because they say that grain is in the sheath for fifteen days, blooms for fifteen days, and dries for fifteen days when it ripens. All plowings are to be completed and the warmer the soil in the plowing, so more productive are the crops. If you split up the ground, then you should crush it, that is, repeat the plowing to break up the clods; in the first plowing large clods are produced by the splitting of the earth. (2) You should sow vetch, lentils, small chickpeas, peas, and other vegetables which some call legumes, and others, like Gallic farmers, call *legarica*; both terms are derived from 'gathering' (*legendo*) because they are not reaped, but gathered (*leguntur*) by picking. Hoe old vines a second time, a third time for young ones, if there are clods still around.

33. In the fifth interval between the setting of the Dog Star and the

autumnal equinox, you should cut straw and stack it into piles, harrow plowed land, cut leafage, and mow irrigated pastures a second time.

34. (1) In the sixth interval from the autumnal equinox authors assert that you should begin to sow and continue this until the ninety-first day. After the winter solstice you should not sow, unless absolute necessity demands it; it is of great interest that seeds planted before the solstice emerge within seven days, but those planted after the solstice hardly sprout in forty. And they think that you should not begin the sowing before the equinox, because if inclement weather persists, the seeds usually rot. (2) It is best to plant beans at the setting of the Pleiades, but to pick grapes and to make the vintage between the autumnal equinox and the setting of the Pleiades; then begin to prune and set slips of vines and to plant fruit trees. In some areas where severe freezes happen early, these jobs are best done in the spring.

35. (1) In the seventh interval between the setting of the Pleiades and the winter solstice they say the following tasks should be performed: plant lilies and crocus. A rose bush which has already set root is cut at the root into twigs about the length of a palm and then buried in the ground; later, this same shoot is transplanted after it has grown into a living root. It is not economical to set up violet beds on the farm because the beds must be constructed by making a pile of earth which irrigation and storm showers wash away and thin out the top soil. (2) From the onset of the prevailing westerlies to the rising of Arcturus it is advantageous to transplant the thyme (*serpillum*) from the nursery; it derives its name from the idea that it 'creeps' (*serpit*). Dig new channels, clean out the old ones, and prune the orchard and vineyards as long as you do not do it during the fifteen days before and after the winter solstice. But it is proper to plant some trees, like the elm, at that time.

36. In the eighth interval between the winter solstice and the beginning of the west wind you should perform the following tasks: drain any standing water from the crop lands; if there is a drought and the land has a certain soft quality, harrow. Prune vineyards and orchards. When work cannot be done in the fields, then you should undertake projects that can be done indoors on early winter mornings. You should keep the formulas I have outlined on the villa grounds and post them particularly for the foreman to know.

37. (1) The days of the lunar cycle also must be observed, which are bipartite in nature as the moon waxes from the new to the full and then wanes again toward a new until it arrives to the time between months; on that day the moon is said to be last and first; in Athens they call it the *old and new* day,[51] others say the *thirtieth*. Some tasks preferably should be done in the fields during the waxing rather than the ageing of the

---

51: Aristophanes in *Clouds* 1178-1200 has a humorous elaboration of this anomaly of the 'old and new' day.

moon; some crops, conversely, in the other phase should be gathered, such as grain and firewood." (2) "Why, I myself," Agrasius said, "observe that practice which I learned from my father of not only shearing the sheep but of cutting my own hair to prevent myself becoming bald by getting a haircut during the waxing of the moon." Then Agrius asked, "How is it that the moon is divided into four phases? and what impact does that division have on agriculture?" (3) "Haven't you ever heard in the country," Tremelius responded, "about the Jana moon rising on the eighth day and conversely the ageing moon on the eighth day? And that of the operations to be performed when the moon is waxing, some are, nonetheless, better done after this Jana moon on the eighth day rather than before it? And as the tasks to be completed are more properly performed when the moon is ageing, so are they much better done when the heavenly body has less light? I have already outlined the quadripartite division in agriculture."[52]

(4) "But there exists another division of the seasons," Stolo said, "a sixfold one that is related to the sun and the moon in that for almost every product, completion comes in the fifth stage of production and sees the storage jar or bushel on the estate; after that a sixth stage markets the product for use. The first step consists of the preparation; the second the planting, the third the cultivation, the fourth the harvesting, the fifth the storing, and the sixth the marketing. In the preparation of some crops, you must dig ditches, re-dig them, or make furrows, for example, when you want to make a plantation or orchard; (5) in preparation of other crops you must plow or dig, as in starting grain crops; and of some you must more or less deeply spade the earth, because some trees, like the cypress, spread roots less extensively, and others, like the sycamore, more. In one case Theophrastus reports that one sycamore in the Lyceum at Athens, even when it was a young tree, had spread its roots thirty-three cubits. In some instances when you split up the earth by oxen and plow, you must repeat the operation before you sow seeds. Any preparation to be performed with pastures involves keeping grazing off them, which is a practice that they observe at the blossoming of pear trees; and if they are irrigated, it involves watering at the right time.

38. (1) You must note what areas of the farm you have to manure, how to set up the procedure, and what kind is the best to use because there are numerous varieties. Cassius maintains that the best manure comes from birds, except the marsh and sea varieties. Of these the most excellent is the dung of pigeons because it retains the most heat and can best make the ground ferment. It should be spread over the land like seed, not piled up like the dung of herded animals. (2) For my part, I think that the dung from the aviaries of thrushes and blackbirds excels because it is not only beneficial for the soil but also serves as nutritious

---

52: see 5.3 above.

food for cattle and pigs in order to fatten them up. So, those who rent out aviaries and follow the agreement with the owner to let lie the manure on the estate, pay less than those who have access to it. Cassius writes that human excrement is second to pigeon dung, and third best is goat, and sheep, and ass manure; that horse dung is least effective except for field crops; (3) for pastures, however, it is the best, as is the dung of the other working animals which feed on barley, because it produces a lot of grass. The manure-pile should be set up around the farm house so that the manure may be hauled out with the least amount of work. If a hardwood stake is driven down through the middle of it, then, they say, no serpent will breed in it.

39. (1) The second step is planting, which demands some care in regard to the season for planting that suits the nature of each seed. In a field it matters, of course, toward which direction each plot is oriented and in which season each crop grows best. Do we not see that some plants flower in the spring time, others in summer, and that the same ones do not grow in autumn as in winter? (2) Thus some plants are planted and grafted and harvested earlier or later than others. Most are grafted in the spring rather than in autumn; figs, however, are grafted around the solstice and cherries during the winter days. (3) Whereas there are in general four kinds of seeds: those which nature has provided, those which are transplanted from soil to soil via living root-slips, those which are cut from trees and set into the ground, and those which are grafted from tree to tree, in each case you should observe what procedure you should follow at each season and location.

40. (1) First, the seed, which is the origin of generation, consists of two kinds, one which escapes our notice, the other visible. Two examples of the unnoticeable are: one, the seeds that exist in the air, as the physical philosopher Anaxagoras maintains, or, secondly the seeds carried by water which often flows in the field, as Theophrastus writes. Farmers must diligently observe that visible seed. Some seeds, like the cypress, which easily generates, are so small that they are almost indistinct. The nuts, which they produce and that seem like small balls of bark, are not the seeds, but contain them inside. (2) Nature provided the original seeds, whereas farmers discovered the others by experimentation. The first are those seeds that grow unsown by a farmer; the second, derived from the first, do not grow unless sown. One ought to see that the seeds are not dried out from age, nor mixed or adulterated with others of similar appearance. An old seed in some plants is so powerful that it changes its nature. There is a story that an old seed of cabbage was sown and from it grew mustard, and conversely, from old mustard seeds came cabbage. (3) Secondly, you should take precautions not to remove them too early or too late to transplant. The right time according to Theophrastus is in spring and autumn and the rising of the Dog Star, but that time is not the same for all locations and all varieties. In dry ground, and thin, and

in soil with clay spring is the proper time, when it is less humid; in good, rich soil fall is proper because spring is too wet. For the planting some allow about thirty days. (4) The third kind of seeding transfers shoots from the tree to the ground. If the shoot is planted in the ground, you should see to it that it is removed when it should be, and that means before any plant begins to bud or flower. The shoots that you transplant from the tree you should tear from the trunk-root rather than break off from the limb, because the base of a shoot is steadier, and the wider it is, the more easily it sprouts roots. These shoots they quickly set into the ground before the sap dries up. In olive grafts you must see to it that the shoot is cut from a young branch, with each end sharpened equally. Some call these grafts "little stakes" (*clavolae*), others "little sticks" (*taleae*), and each is about a foot long. (5) For the fourth type which has a slip passing from one tree to another, you should observe the variety of the trees involved in the transfer, at what season it is to take place, and the method of binding. A pear, for example, does not graft with an oak, although it may with an apple. Many, who have paid attention to and heeded fortune-telling seers, have followed their pronouncement that in the case of individual trees grafted with several other varieties, the one which lightening strikes in a single stroke bursts into as many bolts corresponding to the number of different grafts. However good the pear slip you graft onto a wild pear, the fruit will not be as sweet as the fruit from the tree grafted onto the tamed variety. (6) If the trees are of the same species in grafting, for example, if both trees are varieties of apple, then you should do the grafting with a view toward the final product, that is, the shoot should be of a better quality and kind than the tree on which it is grafted. There is another process in grafting from tree to tree recently noted in the case of trees planted very close to one another. From the tree you wish to cut the shoot, direct a runner of a small branch onto the tree to which you wish to graft and unite it with a cut and split branch of that tree; the part that is inserted into the branch must be sharpened on both sides with a blade so that the one side, exposed to the sky, will have bark dovetailed with bark. Take care to direct the tip of this inserted slip up toward the sky. Next year, after it has taken hold, cut it off the other tree from which it had generated.

41. (1) You must especially observe the proper season for your grafting: some plants that used to be grafted in the spring now are also grafted during the summer solstice; for instance, the fig, since it is not a hard wood, ideally calls for a hot climate. For that reason fig groves cannot survive cold localities; and water damages the young graft, quickly causing the tender slip to decay. (2) Therefore, it is thought that fig trees are most properly grafted when the Dog Star is in ascendance. For plants, however, which are naturally not so soft, a vessel is tied up above the slip from which water may slowly drip to prevent the shoot from drying out before it bonds with the tree. You must protect the bark

of the shoot without injury and sharpen it, being careful not to expose the pith. To prevent showers from outside and excessive heat from injuring it, you should smear on clay and tie it with bark. (3) Therefore, three days before making the graft they cut off the vine to allow excessive moisture to drain off before it is grafted; or they cut into the part on which the graft is made a little lower than the grafted section in order to permit the flow of any collected water. Conversely, in the case of figs, pomegranates, and other plants that have a drier nature, grafting is performed at once. However, in some processes of grafting, such as of figs, you must see to it that the tip of the graft contains a bud.

(4) Of these four types of generations, it is preferable to use slips for some slow-developing plants. For example, the natural seed of the fig is inside the fruit which we eat and consists of tiny grains; small stems are unable to grow from these small grains. It seems that all seeds which are tiny and dry are slow to grow, while those which are looser are also more productive; just as the female grows faster than the male, so proportionately do slips; therefore, the fig, the pomegranate, and the vine have a penchant for rapid growth because they share a feminine softness, whereas, on the other hand, the palm tree, the cypress, and the olive are slow to grow. (5) Since, then, the more moist seeds grow more quickly than the drier varieties, it is preferable to plant in greenhouses small shoots from the fig tree rather than the grains from the fig fruit, unless you cannot do otherwise, such as when you wish to export the seeds overseas or import them. In that circumstance you run a thread through the figs ripe for eating and wrap them up after they have dried, and ship them off to any place you choose, where they may be planted in a greenhouse and proliferate. (6) In this way several varieties of figs, such as Chian, Chalcidian, Lydian, African, and other overseas kinds were imported into Italy. For a similar reason, in regard to the seed of the olive, since it is a nut, we chose to plant in nurseries the shoots which I have mentioned, because the seedling sprouted more slowly from the olive nut than from others.

42. You should exercise special care not to plunge seed into an earth too dry or too wet on the surface, but into a moderately moist soil. Some writers maintain that a bushel and a half of clover is required for sowing a iugerum, if the ground is naturally moderate. The sowing is done in the same way that seed is scattered when sowing of forage crops and grain.

43. Sweet clover, like cabbage seed, is sown on ground that has been well worked. Then it is separated and planted at foot-and-a-half intervals; or shoots are plucked off from the clover stem that has grown sturdier and is planted in the arrangement outlined above.

44. (1) Beans are sown four bushels to a iugerum, wheat five bushels, barley six, spelt ten, or a little more or less in some places; if the soil is thick and rich, more; if thin, less. So, you should observe that whatever

is customarily sown in a region, that much you should do. The locality and the nature of the soil determine the yield; in one region the same seed may have a return of ten times, in another a yield of fifteen times, as it is in some fields of Etruria. (2) In and around the area of Sybaris in Italy they say that the usual yield is one hundred bushels to one, and similarly in Syria near Gadara, and in Africa near Byzacium.[53] It makes a big difference whether you plant on unworked soil or on land worked every year—called 'renewable land'—or on a field which has 'reposed' for some time." (3) To that Agrius said, "In Olynthia[54] they say land worked every year bears a richer crop every other year." Licinius responded to that statement, "Land ought to be left with a little lighter crops, that is, those crops which less exhaust the soil." Agrius rejoined, "You will now speak about the third stage, that is, about the nurture and nourishment of plants."

(4) Then Stolo began: "Plants spring up and grow in soil; they mature and conceive, gestate, and bear fruit or grain awns, or some such thing. The seed returns whence it came. Therefore, if you pick a bloom or a bitter, that is, an unripe pear, or the like, nothing re-grows in the same place and in the same year because the same plant cannot have two gestations in the same season. Just as women have a set period up to birth, so do trees and plants.

45. (1) For the most part barley makes its appearance from the earth in seven days, wheat not much later; millet and sesame and other similar plants in about an equal number of days except when the region or the climate brings a blight to prevent the sprouting. (2) Shoots, produced in a nursery and by nature tender, if the locale is too cold, should be covered with leaves or straw during the winter season. If rains ensue, you must take care not to let water stand anywhere, because, if frozen, it is like a poison to the tender roots. (3) Plants do not grow equally and at the same rate below and above ground; in autumn or winter roots grow more extensively below ground than above because they are covered and are nourished by the heat of the earth, whereas the growth of those above ground is restrained by the colder air. Wild plants which a planter has not come near prove the validity of this observation. Normally roots grow before the plant which rises from them. Roots go no deeper than the extent that the sun penetrates the earth. There are two causes contributing to the growth of roots: first, nature propels one wood a greater distance than another, and secondly, one kind of soil proves more productive than another.

46. Because of elements of this kind there are several amazing differences indicated by nature; from some leaves, such as the olive, silver

53: a region of the province of Africa (modern Tunisia) whose capital was Hasdrumetum.
54: the area around the city of Olynthus in Thrace, near the border of Macedon.

poplar, and willow, the season of the year can be told by their rotation. When their leaves turn over, it is said that the summer solstice is over. No less remarkable is the action of flowers which they call heliotropes from the fact that in the morning they are oriented toward the rising sun and follow its course to the setting, yet always facing it.

47. In plants such as the olive and fig grown in the nursery from shoots and which have naturally delicate tips, their tops should be protected by two slats tied on the right and left; and weeds should be rooted out and they should be pulled while they are young, because, if they become dried out, they offer resistance and break more quickly than they come out. On the other hand, grass grown in the pastures and expected to be baled into hay must not be pulled in its maturing stage, nor even trampled. For this reason herds must be interdicted from the pasture, as well as humans and every kind of working animal. The foot of man is death to grass and forges the foundation of a path.

48. (1) In grain crops the stalk brings forth grain in the ear. If this is not 'mutilated' as in barley and wheat, it has three components: the grain, the husk, and the beard, and also the sheath when the ear first arises. The solid inner part is called the grain; the husk is its shell, and the beard protrudes from the husk like a long, thin, needle, just as if the very tip of the grain is husk and beard. (2) The terms 'beard' and 'grain' are well known to everybody, but 'husk' only to a few. In fact, as far as I know, it is found only in Ennius' translation of Euhemerus' books. The word (*gluma*)[55] seems to have its derivation from 'stripping' (*glubendo*) because the grain is stripped (*deglubitur*) from this covering of a shell. The same word describes the covering of the edible figs. The beard (*arista*) is so called because it is the first thing to dry (*arescit*). 'Grain' (*granum*) derives from 'bearing' (*gerendo*), that is to say, the grain is planted that the ear may bear (*gerat*) the grain, not the husk or the beard; similarly, the vine is planted not to bear leaves but to produce grapes. (3) The ear (*spica*), however, which farmers, in a practice of long standing, call *speca*, seems to be derived from the word 'hope' (*spe*) because they plant with the hope or expectation (*sperant*) that the ear will form. The ear which is beardless is said to be 'mutilated,' as the beard is, as it were, the 'horns' of the ears. When they are first forming but not yet clearly apparent, they lie under a green blade which they call a sheath, very much like the sheath a sword is stored in. The part on the very top of the ripened ear, which is smaller than the grain, is called *frit*; whereas the section at the bottom of the ear right at the highest point of the stalk, which is also smaller than the grain is called *urru*."[56]

49. (1) Stolo stopped and was silent. When there were no questions, he judged that nothing further about nutrition was required; thus, he

55: in this and the following section Varro again indulges in some spurious etymologies.
56: the derivations of *frit* and *urru*, two very un-Latin words, are unclear.

began again: "Now I will treat the harvesting of the ripened crops. When it has stopped growing and has begun to dry out from the heat, the growth on the pastures should be cut close with sickles, and, as it is drying out, be turned with pitchforks. When it has thoroughly dried, it should be bundled and transported to the barn; then the stubble on the pasture should be raked up and added to a haystack. (2) When this operation is completed, the pasture lands must be recut, that is, hewing with sickles what the mowers have missed, leaving the field with lumps, as it were, of grass. I believe that the word to 'recut' (*sicilare*) derives from this 'cutting' (*sectione*) of the pasture.

50. (1) The word for 'harvest' (*messis*) properly is said of those crops which we 'take measure of' (*metimur*), especially in the case of grain, and is derived from that word. There are three methods in the harvesting of grain: first, as it is done in Umbria, they cut the stalks very close to the ground with a sickle and they lay on the ground each bundle as they have cut it. When they have created many bundles, they make a thorough review, cutting from each bundle the stalk at a point close to the ears. They then toss the ears into a basket and haul them off to the threshing floor, while they leave the straw in the field where they are stacked. (2) In the second method, as in Picenum, they employ a small curved wooden rod having a small iron saw at the tip. When this tool catches a bundle of spikes, it cuts them off and leaves the straw standing in the field to be cut close later. In the third method, as used in the territory near Rome and in many other places, they seize the top of the stalks with their hand and then cut them in the middle. I think that the word for harvest (*messis*) is derived from this 'middle' (*medio*).[57] The section of the stalk below the hand which remains rooted in the earth is cut down later; (3) whereas the other part that is attached to the ear is hauled off in baskets to the threshing floor. The word 'straw' (*palea*) may be so named from the fact that it is separated in an exposed area, openly (*palam*). Some think that the word for 'stalk' (*stramentum*) derives from 'standing' (*stando*), as does the word for 'warp' (*stamen*); others derive it from the word 'spread' (*stratus*) because it is 'spread beneath' (*substernatur*) the cattle. The time for cutting is when the crop is ripe, and in an easy field it is said that about one working day is sufficient to harvest one iugerum. Within that period they must also carry baskets of harvested ears to the threshing floor.

51. (1) The threshing floor[58] should be set up on the grounds of the estate in a slightly elevated spot so that wind can sweep across it; its measurements should be proportionate to the size of the crops, and preferably it should be round, raised slightly at the center so that, if it

---

57: Varro has just stated (quite correctly) that *messis*, the "harvest," derives from the verb *metere*. Now he connects it to the word for "middle."
58: for the threshing floor one should compare Vergil, *Georgics* 1.178-192.

rains, water will not collect but will be able to drain off the floor by the shortest possible way; certainly, the shortest line in a circle extends from the center to the outer circumference. It should be constructed of solid earth, hard packed, especially if it is of clay, to prevent cracking in the heat and granules catching in the chinks, or taking on water and opening doors for mice and ants. For that reason they usually coat it with an oil-lees by-product called *amurca*,[59] which is toxic to weeds, ants, and moles. (2) To make the threshing floor solid, some strengthen it with stone or even pave it, while others, such as the Bagienni,[60] shelter the floors because in their country rain storms often arise at that time of the year. When the floor is left uncovered and the climate of the region is hot, a shed should be built close to the threshing floor to which workers can retreat in the heat of the midday.

52. (1) The fattest and best ears that the crop has produced should be separated and placed apart on the threshing floor to insure the best seed, and the grain should be threshed from the ears on the floor. This operation is done among some people with a team of work animals and a sledge. This equipment is made of a platform studded with rocks or iron which, as it is pulled by yoked animals with a driver seated on top or a heavy weight set on it, separates the grain from the ear; or it is made of toothed axles set on small rollers which they call a Punic cart; on it sits a person who drives the animals pulling it, a device commonly used in Farther Spain and other places. (2) Among other peoples threshing is accomplished by driving teams of work animals onto the floor and goading them with switches, whereby the grain is worked out of the ears by their hooves. After the threshing is completed, the grain should be tossed from the ground, when a gentle wind is blowing, with winnowing fans or forks. This process causes the lightest element of it, called needles and chaff, to be winnowed outside the floor, and the grain proper, because it possesses some weight, comes unadulterated to the collecting basket.

53. After the harvest is finished, you should contract out the gleaning of the field or gather leftover stalks with a domestic staff, or, if the remaining ears are very few and the cost of the work high, you should leave it for pasture. The following point must be particularly observed: that the expense of the operation does not exceed the profit.

54. (1) In the case of vineyards, the vintage should begin as soon as the grapes ripen; at the outset you should see to choosing the variety of grapes and the location. The early grapes and hybrids, called the black, ripen sooner and, therefore, must be gathered sooner; and you ought to strip the vines first from that part of the plantation and vineyard which

---

59: for the production of *amurca* see chapters 61 and 64.
60: these people are unknown, although some suggest a corruption of Vagienni, a people of Liguria.

receives more sun. (2) In the vintage of a diligent owner not only are grapes gathered but also selected; he gathers some for drinking, but selects others for eating. Therefore, those that are gathered are hauled into the vintage-making area, and from there they go into empty jars. On the other hand, the selected grapes are taken to a separate basket, then apportioned into small pots and stuffed into jugs filled with grape skins; others, stored in an amphora sealed with pitch, are placed into a pond, while still others go to take their place in a pantry. Once the grapes have been tromped, they should be put, along with stalks and skins, under a press so that whatever juice they have left may be pressed out into the same vat. (3) When the flow stops under the press, some people cut around the edges of the pressed matter and press again; the liquid of this second pressing is called the 'circumcision' must and kept separated because it tastes of iron. The pressed grape skins and seeds are put into jars to which water is added; this mixture they call *lora*, because the skins are 'washed' (*lota*); and it is distributed to workers in winter instead of wine.

55. (1) About the olive harvest: the olives that you can reach from the ground and by ladders, you ought to pick by hand rather than to shake down from the tree because those that are bruised from the fall dry up and yield less oil. But picking them by hand with bare fingers is better than the use of gloves because the hard texture of gloves not only crushes the berry, (2) but also strips off some bark from the branches and leaves them unprotected against frost. Those which cannot be reached with the hand should be beaten down by using a reed rather than be struck by a pole; the heavier blow requires the attention of a tree surgeon. In any case the striker should not hit the olive head on, (3) because an olive battered in that way often rips the shoot off the branch, which causes the loss of next year's fruit. This action may be the chief reason that they say that olive trees fail to bear fruit every year, or at best they do not produce as large of a yield.[61] (4) The olive arrives to the estate house by the same two avenues as the grape, one for food, the other liquefied to oil the body inside as well as on the outside; and for that reason it follows the master into the bath and to the gymnasium. (5) The selection from which olive oil is made usually is heaped day by day into mounds on a level flooring so that it may mellow somewhat; each pile is diminished by straining the olives through large jars and other vessels to the press, which is an olive mill contraption fitted with hard and jagged stones. (6) Picked olives that remain too long in the piles rot from the heat and become rancid. Thus, if you cannot finish the pressing operation promptly, then you ought to toss them about in the piles in order to be ventilated. (7) The olive produces two products: the oil which is familiar to everybody and *amurca* whose use the major-

---

61: in general olives only produce once every other year.

ity is ignorant of; it is possible to see it flow from the presses onto the fields, blackening the ground as well as making it barren, if applied in huge quantity; on the other hand, in a moderate amount, the liquid has many purposes, particularly important for agriculture; for instance, it is usually poured around the roots, primarily of olive trees, and wherever a growth of weeds damages the field."

56. Agrius then spoke up, "I have been sitting in the villa and waiting with my key for you, Stolo, to bring the goods into the barn." "OK," Stolo replied, "here I am; I am coming now to the threshold, so open up the doors. First, it is better to store the hay under a cover, next in haystacks because in that way it makes better fodder. That herd animals prefer the latter when both types are set before them proves the point.

57. (1) Wheat ought to be stored in granaries elevated off the ground, which are ventilated by wind from the east and north, and upon which no damp breeze from the vicinity breathes. The walls and floor are to be plastered with marble stucco; (2) if not that, then a coating made of clay mixed with chaff and amurca , which blocks mice and vermin and makes the grain firmer and more solid. Some sprinkle the wheat applying about four gallons of amurca for a thousand bushels. Likewise, different owners resort to different substances to crumble and scatter over it, such as Chalcidian or Carian chalk, or wormwood, and other materials of this kind. Some keep granaries in underground caves, which they call *sirus*, as in Cappadocia and Thrace. Other peoples, such as in the territory of Carthage and Osca in Nearer Spain, use wells. They cover the floor of these wells with straw and make sure that no moisture or air touch them, except when they bring up the grain to use, knowing that where air fails to penetrate, no weevil breeds. Wheat stored in this manner keeps for fifty years, and millet stays good for more than one hundred years. (3) Some construct granaries in the field, elevated above the ground, such as in Nearer Spain and in Apulia. Wind is able to cool them from the sides through windows as well as from the ground. Beans and legumes are preserved a very long time in olive jars sealed with ashes.

58. Cato says that the small and large Aminnian grape varieties, and the Apician, are best stored in jars and that the same varieties keep well in boiled and regular must; and the best to hang up to dry are the hard grapes and Aminnian variety.

59. (1) For preserving various varieties of apples, quinces, both large and small, the Scantian, the Scaudian, and the small rounded variety which used to be called a must-apple, but is now commonly referred to as a honey-apple, they think that all of these kinds are well preserved if set in a dry, yet cool, spot and placed on straw. For that reason, those who build storage houses for fruit orient their windows toward the north wind to have ventilation; yet they provide them with shutters to prevent the fruit becoming shriveled after they have lost their juice under a persistent wind. (2) Therefore, they coat vaulted ceilings, walls, and floors,

with mortar-like stucco to keep it cooler. Some even lay out a table for dining there; and, whereas luxury has allowed some to make this set-up in an art gallery in which art provides the scene, why shouldn't they also enjoy what nature has provided in a charming setting of fruit? But you should not practice what some do, that is, buying fruit in Rome, and transporting it to the country to pile it up in a fruit museum all for the sake of a dinner party. (3) Some think that apples keep well enough in a greenhouse placed on planks atop the stucco, but others believe that they are better preserved, if laid out on straw or wool skins; that pomegranates keep well, if their stems are set in a jar of sand, and the varieties of quinces in hanging baskets; on the other hand, keep the Anician variety of pears that ripen at seed time well stored in boiled must; and some maintain that sorbs are preserved by cutting them up and tenderizing them in the sun, like pears; yet sorbs, wherever they are put, easily last as they are, if it is a dry spot; and that turnips, cut up, are preserved in mustard, and walnuts in sand. Pomegranates are also stored in sand that are gathered fresh and ripe, and even unripened ones, still clinging to their branch, if you put them in a pot without a bottom and bury them in the ground after you coat around the branch so that no outside air blows on them; these fruits, they say, are taken out unblemished and even larger than they would have been, if left hanging on the tree.

60. About olives Cato writes that the olives for eating, the orcites and posea, are best preserved either green in brine, or, if bruised, in mastic oil. The black dried orcites, if they are cured with salt for five days and then, after the salt is shaken, are placed in the sun for two days, usually stay sound; those same varieties can safely be preserved in must boiled down without salt.

61. Experienced farmers store their amurca in jars in the same way as they store oil and wine. The process of preserving it is: as soon as it flows out from the pressing, immediately two-thirds of it is cooked down, and after cooling is stored in vessels. There are other processes, such as the addition of must.

62. Since no one stores products except to bring them out later, a few comments on this subject, the sixth stage, must be added. Products are brought out of storage either to be protected, used, or sold. Whereas these purposes are inherently different, the protecting and the consuming occur at varying times.

63. That grain which weevils begin to eat should be brought from storage in order to save it. When it is brought out, bowls of water should be placed by it in the sun, around which, once the weevils gather, they will kill themselves by drowning. Those who store their grain under ground in the so-called *sirus* should bring it out sometime after opening the underground chamber, because entry immediately after the opening is dangerous, as some have suffocated by it. Spelt which you stored

in the ears during harvest and you wish to consume as food should be brought out in winter to grind up in a mill and to roast.

64. Store the watery fluid of amurca and its sediment in an earthenware vessel, after it has been pressed from the olives. Some use the following practice to preserve it: after fifteen days the very light film on top is blown off in order to decant the liquid to other vessels; they repeat this procedure at the same intervals twelve times within six months; the last operation is best performed when the moon is waning. Then, they cook it down in a bronze pot over a gentle fire until they have reduced it to two-thirds. After that it is ready to be drawn off for use.

65. The must stored in jars to produce wine must not be brought out while it is fermenting, not even if the process has proceeded so far as to have made wine. If you wish to drink aged wine, which means that it is not drinkable before it has aged for at least one year, bring it out at one year old. But if the variety of grapes sour quickly, you should consume it or sell it before the next vintage. There are varietals, like Falernian, which become more valuable the longer you store them proportionate to the time before you bring them out of storage.

66. If you bring out the fresh, white olives that you stored away too quickly, the palate will spit them back out because of their bitterness; and likewise, the black olives, unless you steep them first in brine, the mouth will not receive with relish.

67. In the case of the walnut, date, and Sabine fig, the sooner you consume them, the more flavorful they are, because with age the fig turns too pale, the date too putrid, and the nut too dry.

68. Hanging fruits, such as grapes, apples, and sorbs, themselves demonstrate when they should be gathered for consumption by a change in their color and the shrinking of the skin, and if you do not pluck them from the tree to eat, then they give signs of falling just to be thrown away. If you store ripe and soft sorbs, you should use them up rather quickly; sour sorbs that are hung up linger longer because they tend to reach a maturity in the house before they ripen, and one that they cannot gain on the tree.

69 (1) The portion of spelt harvest that you wish to prepare for food you should take out in the winter to roast at the mill; but the portion set aside for seeding should be brought out when the croplands are ripe for receiving it. As far as seeding is concerned, each product should be taken out at its proper time. And for those goods to be sold, you should take care to remove them also at the proper time. For instance, those products which cannot last in storage, you should bring out and sell before they change and spoil; but those which can be preserved, you should sell when the price is dear. Goods stored for a long time often recoup the interest and even double the profit, if you sell at the right time."

(2) As he was speaking, the temple keeper's freedman comes up to us in tears and begs us to forgive him for detaining us; he also asks us to attend a funeral for him the next day. We all jumped up and together shouted, "What? To a funeral? What funeral? What has happened?" Still in tears, he tells us that someone had stabbed his patron with a knife and that he fell to the ground; and that in the crowd he could not make out who the culprit was, but that he had heard a voice say that a wrong had been committed. (3) When he himself had carried his patron home, he sent out slaves to find a doctor and to bring him as soon as possible; he thought it only fair to be pardoned because he had performed that service rather than coming to us. Although he could not keep his patron from expiring a little after that, yet he had acted properly. We were not at all upset with him; we stepped down from the temple and we all left, going our separate ways and complaining more about human misfortune than being in shock that this event had occurred in Rome.[62]

BOOK III

16. (1) "OK," Appius said, "There remains the third act[63] of the cultivation on the villa's grounds: fish ponds." "Why third?" Axius asked. "Or is it because in your scrimping youth you did not drink mead that we will overlook honey?" Appius then reported to us, "He is speaking the truth. (2) Yes, I was left in an impoverished state along with my two brothers and two sisters, one of whom I married off without a dowry to Lucullus, who later bequeathed me a legacy. Because of that, for the first time in my life I began to drink mead at home, although in the meanwhile it was served to everybody almost daily at dinners. (3) In addition, it was my prerogative, not yours, to know those winged creatures to whom nature has endowed with preeminent talent and art.[64] Therefore, so that you may comprehend that I know bees better than you, hear then of the incredible art provided them by nature. Our good historian Merula, as he has done in other cases, will show what procedures beekeepers usually follow. (4) First of all, some bees are born from bees, while others arise from the rotten carcass of a bull.[65] Thus in an epigram Archelaus[66] says that they are: *the wandering offspring of a decayed cow,* and from the same author: *wasps are born from horses, but bees from calves.* Bees are not solitary by nature, like eagles, but are more like humans. But even if grackles act similarly, it is not the same in every

---

62: Varro alludes to the political turmoil of his day.

63: the first category treated was birds and fowls, the second concerned game.

64: Varro punningly alludes that via his name Appius has the right to discourse on bees (*apes*).

65: a reference to the *bougonia* so well described in Vergil, *Georgics* 4.538-558.

66: it is not probable that this Archelaus is the fifth-century Athenian philosopher and follower of Anaxagoras.

respect; in the case of bees here is a shared community of work and building that does not exist in the case of grackles; also, in bees there is reason and skill, and from them humans learn how to work, how to build, and how to store food. (5) Their *raisons d'etre* are three: food, home, and work. The food is not the same as wax, nor honey, nor the home. Doesn't the cell in the honeycomb have six angles that correspond to the number of the bees' feet? Geometricians show that a hexagon set in a circle encompasses the most space. As for bees, they forage outside, but do their work within the hive to create a product which, because it is the sweetest of all, is satisfying to both gods and humans from the fact that the honeycomb arrives at the altars and honey is served at the beginning of a dinner and for dessert.[67] (6) Their society is like the states of men, because among them are king, a chain of command, and community. They pursue all pure things. Thus, no bee lands on a soiled spot or a place that reeks or even one that exudes a sweet perfume. Therefore, one who approaches them, scented in any way, they sting, unlike flies that lick him; and no one ever sees bees, as he does flies, on meat, blood, or fat; instead, they only light on substances which possess a sweet savor. (7) The bee is no pest, sucking up and damaging someone's work; but neither is it so cowardly not to resist anyone attempting to disrupt its own work; nevertheless, it is very cognizant of its own weakness. With good reason bees are called the wings of the muses, because, if ever they have been scattered afar, the rhythmic clash of cymbals and the clapping of hands bring them back to one place. As men have ascribed Helicon and Olympus to the gods, so nature has assigned to the bees the flowers and virgin tracts of the mountains. (8) They follow their own king wherever he goes, lift him up when he is tired, and if he is unable to fly, they carry him on their shoulders in their desire to save him.[68] They are themselves very hard working and despise the lazy; for this reason they attack and drive out drones because they do not help in the work and they eat the honey, and even a few bees chase hordes of drones no matter the intensity of the buzzing. Outside of the entryway of the hive they plug up all crevices, by which air can penetrate between the combs, with matter the Greeks call bee-bread (*erithace*).[69] (9) They all live as if in an army, sleeping and working in regular shifts; and their leaders perform their duties with a buzz sounding like a trumpet. This happens when they pass between themselves signals for peace and war. But, Merula, so that our good friend Axius here does not waste away

---

67: wine sweetened with honey was often served among the *hors d'oeuvres* and with dessert.

68: the ancients believed that the queen bee was male.

69: pollen is collected from the hairs on the bees by brushing it with a set of legs into a mass which is then stored in a receptacle of the third set of legs. This substance provides food for the larvae and young. According to Aristotle it tasted like fig.

listening to this discourse on natural history, during which I have said nothing about profit,[70] I now pass the torch in the race to you."

(10) Merula then began: "About the profit I say the following, which perhaps will be enough for you, Axius, and I have as an authority not only Seius,[71] who contracts his apiaries at an annual rent of 5,000 pounds of honey, but also our friend Varro right here. I have heard him say that he had two soldiers under his command in Spain, wealthy brothers from the territory of Falerii, who were named Veianus. Although their father had left them a small farm house and a small plot of land no larger than a iugerum, they constructed apiaries all about the estate and kept a garden for the bees; the rest of the land they planted with thyme, sweet clover, and balm which some call honey-leaf, some bee-leaf, and others bee-plant. (11) As they calculated it, they never failed to receive less than 10,000 sesterces from their honey, and they said that they preferred waiting to accept a buyer at their own time rather than to sell too quickly at a time disadvantageous to them." "Tell me, then,'" said Axius, "'where and what kind of apiary I should build to bag a huge profit." "You ought," Merula replied, "to construct apiaries that some call 'bee-houses' and others 'honey-houses.' First, they should be located close to the villa where echoes do not rebound (in fact, this sound is thought to lead to their flight); where the air is temperate, not boiling hot in summer nor without sun in winter; that they be oriented to the winter sunrise and have nearby areas that possess an abundant supply of food and clear water. (13) If nature does not provide a source of food, then the owner ought to sow crops which bees particularly enjoy; these crops are: the rose, wild thyme, balm, poppy, bean, lentils, peas, clover, rush, alfalfa, and especially sweet clover, which is most beneficial to bees when they are sick. It begins to flower at the vernal equinox and lasts until the next equinox. (14) But, whereas clover is most appropriate to the health of the bees, thyme is best for making honey. Sicilian honey wins the palm because abundant and excellent thyme is found there. Some crush the thyme in a mortar, then soak it in lukewarm water, and sprinkle all the seed beds planted for bees. (15) Regarding the location for an apiary, one should choose it preferably very close to the villa; some even place the apiary in the colonnade of the villa to keep it safer. Some build hives round in shape and made of osiers for the bees to be in, others out of wood and bark; some use the hollow of a tree, others clay pots, and still others construct them out of fennel stalks, square in shape, about three feet by three feet, and one foot deep, but building them narrower when the number of bees is too few to fill them and lest they become

---

70: throughout the book Axius has been depicted as one particularly interested in the profit-making potential of the various operations of the farm.
71: Marcus Seius, repeatedly referred to in this book, owned a large villa and multifaceted estate.

despondent in such a vast empty space. All of the hives are called 'bel-
lies' (*alvi*) because of the 'nourishment' (*alimonio*) of the honey within; for
that reason beekeepers seem to make them with a very narrow center
to imitate the shape of the bees themselves. (16) They smear those made
of wicker with cow dung inside and out so that the bees will not be
frightened off by any roughness, and they set up these hives on brackets
of the wall where they are arranged in rows. This arrangement prevents
their being shaken and does not allow any contact between them. At a
set interval they construct a second or third row below; they say that
one should subtract a number of rows rather than add a fourth. In the
middle of the hive they make small holes, left and right, for the bees to
enter. (17) At the end beekeepers put covers where they can remove the
comb. The best hives are made of bark, the worst of clay because those
are most affected by the extremes of the cold in winter and of the heat
in summer. In spring and summer time the beekeeper ought to inspect
the hives three times per month, smoking them gently, and to clean the
hive of filth and remove the vermin. (18) In addition, he should take care
not to allow the existence of several kings because they cause trouble by
fomenting revolt. Some maintain that there are three varieties of kings
among bees: the black, the red, and the striped; Menecrates, however,
writes that there are only two types, the black and the striped; and he
is the better authority for the beekeeper to follow. When two kings exist
at the same time, kill the black one because, when he is with the other
king, he is rebellious and ruins the hive, either routing the other king
or being routed with a sizable swarm behind him. (19) The best of the
bees is the small, round striped variety. The one some call a thief, and
others a drone, is dark and has a wide belly. The wasp, although it looks
similar to a bee, does not share in the work, but often injures the bee with
a sting; thus, the bees generally avoid and separate themselves from the
wasps. Bees differ from each other in that some are wild, while others
are cultivated. By wild bees I mean those that feed in forests, and by
'tame' I mean those that feed in cultivated areas. The bees of the forests
are smaller in size, hairy, but are more efficient workers.

In making a purchase of bees, the prospective buyer should note
whether they are healthy or sick. (20) The signs of good health are: that
the swarm is thick, that the individual bees are sleek, and that they make
a uniform and smooth comb. Indications of sick bees are that they are
hairy, shaggy, dusty-looking; unless the season of work pressures them,
then, because of the heavy labor, they become rough and thin in appearance. (21) If they have to be transferred to another place, then you ought
to exercise care in doing it and observe the most suitable time for making the change, and to scout out the most appropriate locations for the
transfer. The best time is in spring rather than winter because in winter
the bees have difficulty in habituating themselves to the new spot, and
most fly away. If you convey them from a good location to one where

there is no suitable source of food, they become fugitives. And if you transfer them from one hive into another hive in the same general area, you must not be careless in the operation. (22) The hive, in any case, into which they are being moved should be smeared with balm, a special lure for the bees; and the comb of rich honey should be placed inside, not far away from the entryway so that they do not notice the lack of food...He says that,[72] when bees become sick because in early spring they have fed on the blossoms of almond and cornel, they contract bouts of diarrhea from which they may be cured by drinking urine. (23) They call *propolis* the substance which the bees produce,[73] especially in summer, as a cover (*protectum*) over the opening of the entrance in front of the hive. This same substance with the same name doctors use for plasters, and for that reason it demands a higher price on the Sacred Way than honey. They call the stuff with which the bees glue together the ends of the combs bee-bread (*erithace*); it is different from honey or propolis and contains a powerful element that attracts the bees. Thus, beekeepers smear this substance mixed with balm all about a branch or some other object, when they want the swarm to settle. (24) The comb is the entity which the bees fashion in many cells of wax; each cell has six sides, which corresponds to the number of feet endowed to the bee by nature. All the materials which they bring in to make the four basic substances, propolis, bee-bread, comb, and honey, they do not gather from the same matter, it is said. A single purpose and material suffice, as in the case of the pomegranate and asparagus, from which they gather only food;[74] from the olive tree they service only wax, from the fig only honey, but of not good quality. (25) A double function is sometimes served, such as when they gather wax and food from the bean, balm, cucumber, and cabbage; similarly a double function exists, when food and honey are gathered from apple and wild pear trees; likewise, another double function is performed when they gather wax and honey from poppy. There is also a triple service, when they gather food, honey, and wax from the walnut and mustard. From other blossoms they garner some materials so that they take for a single substance, and others materials for more than one substance; (26) and they follow another decisive factor in their gathering, or it follows them;[75] take the case of honey: they make liquid honey from the flowers of 'sweet potato,'[76] but in another instance they make thick honey from rosemary, and yet in another case they make a tasteless honey from fig, and a good honey from clover, but the best variety comes from thyme.

72: after the lacuna in the text the "he" referred to is most likely Menecrates
73: often referred to as bee-glue, this resinous substance is made by bees from
    the sticky buds of various trees.
74: he means that the flower of the various plants and trees furnishes the raw
    material(s) for the basic substance.
75: i.e. the bees act instinctively.
76: my translation of *sisera*, supposedly the skirret.

(27) Whereas drink is a component of food and for bees that drink is clear water, they should have a source from which they drink and it should be near, flowing by them, or collecting into a pool, which should not reach the height of two or three fingers; and in this water tiles or small stones should lie that protrude slightly from the water on which the bees can settle and drink. Great care should be shown to keep the water pure because it is extremely beneficial in producing quality honey. (28) Because weather conditions do not always allow bees to go forth very far to feed, the beekeeper must prepare food for them in order to prevent them from forced subsistence on honey alone or from abandoning the exhausted hives. For that reason beekeepers cook down about ten pounds of fat figs in six gallons of water, which, after the concoction is boiled, they roll into little balls and place near the hives. Other keepers take care to mix water with some mead and keep it nearby in vessels; then they immerse a swatch of pure wool through which the bees sip the mixture. In this way they do not overfill themselves with drink and at the same time do not fall into the water. Individual vessels are placed near the hives and kept filled. Others grind raisins and figs together, soak them in must, then make balls out of this concoction, and put them where the bees can come out for food, even in winter.

(29) When the bees are on the point of swarming out, which usually takes place when there are extensive numbers of new born, and they wish to send out the young offspring as a colony, just as the Sabines often did because they had a huge number of children, you can realize it by two signs that often portend the swarming. First, during the preceding days, especially in the evenings, many ball up and hang intertwined like grape clusters; (30) secondly, when they are on the point of flying out or actually have already begun their flight, they make a fierce buzz, as soldiers do when they strike camp. Those who have flown out first flit about in sight, looking back for the rest that have not yet amassed, to swarm. When the beekeeper has noticed what they have done, he arouses fear in them by throwing dust on them and banging on a bronze drum; the spot where he wishes to lead them, not being very far away, he smears with bee-bread, balm, and other substances which attract them. (31) When they have settled, beekeepers bring a hive smeared on the inside with alluring enticements and place it nearby; they then gently smoke around it, forcing the bees to enter. When they have entered into the new colony, they remain willingly, and, even if you place it next to the hive from which they came, they would still be content with their new home.

(32) Since I have outlined what I think on the subject of their forage, I will now treat the theme to which all this attention is directed—profit. They receive the sign for removing the hives[77]...and make an educated

---

77: a corrupt text leads to much uncertainty.

guess, if the bees hum loudly inside and if they dart about as they enter and exit, and if, when you remove the coverings over the hives, the openings of the comb seem to be clothed in membranes because they are replete with honey. (33) Some maintain that in withdrawing the honey you should take out nine-tenths but leave one-tenth; if you remove it all, then the bees will abandon the hive. Others say that the beekeepers should leave more than I have mentioned. Just as in plowed lands, those who alternate planting with fallowing reap more grain from the staggered harvests, so in the case of hives: if you do not remove the honey every year, or not in equal amounts, you will have more active and profitable bees. (34) They think that the first season for removing the combs is at the onset of the Pleiades, the second at the end of the summer before the complete rising of Arcturus, the third after the setting of the Pleiades, in which season, if the hive is teeming, no more than one-third of the honey should be withdrawn, and the remainder should be left for wintering. But if the hive is not prolific, then no honey should be removed. When the withdrawal is sizable, you should not take all of it out in one removal nor do the operation in the open because the bees may become despondent. If some part of the combs that are removed contains no honey or has honey that is soiled, it should be cut out with a knife. (35) You should exercise care that the weaker bees not be overpowered by the stronger ones; in that event the productivity declines; so keepers separate the weaker bees and put them under another king. Those that frequently fight among themselves should be sprinkled with a mixture of honey and mead. They stop fighting when this is done, and even swarm together, lapping the liquid; and they react even more strongly, if they are sprinkled with pure mead, because the odor drives then to join more eagerly and to drink up until they become stupefied. (36) If they exit the hive in smaller crowds and some remain at rest, you should fumigate lightly and place some pleasant-smelling herbs, especially balm and thyme, nearby. (37) Extreme caution should be taken to prevent the bees from dying from heat or cold. If ever they are overwhelmed by a sudden shower during their foraging, or surprised by a sudden frost, before they have foreseen it would occur—it rarely happens that they are caught by surprise—and if they lie prostrate, wounded by thick drops of rain, as if struck dead, you should collect them into a vessel and store it in a covered and warm spot; on the next day under the most favorable weather conditions possible, dust them with ashes formed from fig wood, a little hotter than warm. Then you should lightly shake the vessel, being careful not to touch them with the hand, and then place them in the sun. (38) Bees which have been warmed up by this method recover and revive, as it often happens in the case of flies treated similarly after they were killed by water. You should perform this operation near the hives so that those that have recovered may return to their respective work and home."

VITRUVIUS

ON ARCHITECTURE

Vitruvius' prefaces to his books on a technical subject possess a certain charm and warmth. In this collection two of the prefaces are translated with the first chapter of Book I wherein Vitruvius defends his field and its art. The training and education of an architect that he maintains as necessary for the profession stand as a great testament to the "liberal arts." Although some of the justifications for immersion into a particular area may sound strange and trivial to a modern ear, there is virtually no area of education excluded from the work of an architect. Vitruvius' thoughts on the value of a liberal education are of intrinsic value and are consistent with the research and scholarly interest of the age.

BOOK I, PREFACE

(1) When your divine mind and power, O Emperor[1] Caesar, took possession of the empire of the world, Roman citizens basked in your victory and triumph over all your enemies laid low by your invincible prowess. And now that all the peoples who had been subdued have come to look to your nod of approval, the people and senate of Rome now, too, have been freed from fear and stand governed by your imaginative and illustrious ideas and policy. In such an atmosphere and with you occupied with so many important issues, I did not dare to publish my work on architecture organized on basic principles and treating grand

---

1: translates the Latin *imperator,* a title assumed by a victorious general and one possessing the power of command, i.e. *imperium.*

projects. I feared interrupting at an inconvenient time and causing offense and displeasure.

(2) But I observed that you not only made the lives shared by all peoples and the constitution of our state your deep concern but that also you directed attention to suitable public buildings. As you have expanded the state by annexing provinces, so too your public buildings have created conspicuous proof of the grandeur of empire. Therefore, I thought I could not let pass the golden opportunity of publishing my work on these matters for you, especially since I had been known to your father and was a partisan of his valor. When the council of gods on high, however, had consecrated an immortal spot for him and had transferred your father's empire to your power,[2] that same loyalty that abided in memory of him has transferred its allegiance to you. Accordingly, together with Marcus Aurelius and Publius Mimidius and Gnaeus Cornelius, I was put in charge of the construction and repair of ballistic stone throwers and missile launchers called "scorpions," and other machines of war. We received promotions, and as for me, you granted the office of inspector and on the recommendation of your sister[3] have continued it .

(3) I was indebted to you for such benefits that to the very end of my life I would have no fear of poverty. Therefore, since I have perceived that you have engaged and are now carrying on a vast building program, I undertook to compose this book for you. I am also sure that you will make it your concern in the future that the structures, both public and private, will conform to the grandeur of your accomplishments and be handed down as memorials to posterity. I have written the compleat treatise on the subject; if you refer to it, you may learn to evaluate both the previous treatments and the works yet to come. In the following volumes I have set forth all the systemic principles of the discipline of architecture.

BOOK 1: CHAPTER 1

(1) The expertise of the architect involves his immersion into many disciplines and various studies which are perfected by other arts. His work originates in both practical craft and theory. Craftsmanship is the continued and usual practice which is done manually and uses material of whatever kind necessary for the execution of design. Technological

2: the "father" refers to Gaius Iulius Caesar who adopted Octavius, the future Augustus, in his will. Octavius, however, did not inherit Julius Caesar's powers; those he had to gain on his own.
3: Octavia was the sister of Octavius/Augustus. She was very active in a building program dedicating the Porticus Octavia and its library to her son Marcellus.

theory, on the other hand, entails the presenting and explaining of things produced by technical skill and method.

(2) So architects who try to compete without a liberal arts background and vie to gain manual skill cannot obtain a prestige that corresponds to their efforts; whereas those who rely solely upon theory and scholarly literature seem to pursue a shadow, not reality. But those who have learned both approaches, like men well-equipped in full arms, quickly acquire prestige and reach their goal.

(3) In all matters, but particularly in architecture these two categories are contained: the signified and the signifier.[4] By the "signified" is meant the subject matter proposed; the "signifier," on the other hand, is the presentation demonstrated by systems of precepts. So, the person who professes to become an architect must be experienced in both. He should have natural talent and be ready to learn. Neither natural genius without instruction nor instruction without innate talent can produce the complete professional. He should be educated in literature, a skilled draftsman, a master of geometry, knowledgeable in studies of history, a diligent student of philosophy, familiar with music, not ignorant of medicine, erudite in the judicial opinions of legal scholars; and he should have some knowledge of astrology and the science of astronomy.

(4) There are valid reasons for this: the architect should know literature to enable him to compose an articulate running record in his notebooks; he should have proficiency in drafting to delineate easily in illustrated sketches the effect he desires. Geometry provides multiple resources for an architect; first, it teaches the proper use of ruler and compass, whereby the buildings on their sites are disposed according to the blueprints, and made level, set in squares, and aligned. Optics is beneficial for proper lighting in buildings, which comes from specific celestial configurations. Arithmetic is used in totaling the cost for buildings and to establish quantifiable methods of measurements; and geometrical theorems and methods solve difficult problems of symmetry.

(5) Architects should also know several histories because they often design works embellished and extensively decorated for which they will have to render reasoned accounting to inquirers of their meaning. For example, if instead of columns some one erects marble statues of women in long gowns—called "caryatids"—and sets mutules[5] and cornices in place above them, he will render his account to anyone who asks in this way: the Peloponnesian city of Caryae conspired with the Persian enemy

---

4: these terms, "signified" and "signifier" derive from Epicurean language and thought. Vitruvius adapts the philosophical language. By "signified" he means the objects under consideration, i.e. the buildings, the grounds, and by "signifier" he understands the terminology used in literary treatment.

5: mutules are rectangular panels of the soffit of a Doric cornice

against Greece.[6] After their glorious victory freed them from war, in allied policy the Greeks declared war against the Caryans. They captured the town, killed the men, and declared the state abolished; they then led away the matrons into slavery, not permitting the women to remove their matronly gowns and jewelry. In this apparel they were led in triumph, but not for just one time. Instead they were to be depicted as crushed by grievous insult and enslaved as a constant warning and to be on view paying the penalty on behalf of the state. So architects of that day and age designed their public buildings with figures of women set up carrying burdens to make known and to record for future generations the punishment for the sin of the Caryan women.

(6) Likewise, the Spartans, under the leadership of Pausanias, the son of Agesilas, after they had defeated an incredibly large army of Persians with a small force in a battle near Platea,[7] with the spoils and plunder they gloried in their celebration of a triumph; they constructed the "Persian" colonnade from the booty to indicate the courage and excellence of the citizens and as a trophy of victory to their descendants. In it they placed statues of the prisoners in barbarian dress to support the roof, a sign that their arrogance was being punished with well-deserved insults. The idea was to make their enemies, seeing the result of Spartan bravery, shudder with fear and to arouse their fellow-citizens to prepare themselves to defend their freedom upon viewing that model of manly courage. Therefore, from this example many have set up statues of Persians to support architraves and their decorations. With such a motive they have enriched the outstanding variations of their works. There are other historical accounts of the same kind, the knowledge of which architects should possess.

(7) Philosophy, however, keeps him from being arrogant and makes the architect principled, easy going, fair, loyal, and, most importantly, without greed. In fact, no work can truly be done without good faith and pure morals; let him not be greedy nor have a mind occupied with acquiring bribes, but let him treat with seriousness the protection of his dignity and the keeping of a good reputation. These are precepts of philosophy. Besides, philosophy expounds the nature of things which in Greek is *physiologia*, a subject that requires careful study because it

---

6: Vitruvius means either the destruction of Caryae, a town near Sparta, in 479 BCE because the Caryans had supported the Persians (called "Medizing" by the Greeks), or alludes to the city's destruction in 367 by Sparta after Caryae had sided with the Thebans at the battle of Leuctra in 371. Vitruvius would have been knowledgeable of "caryatids," that is, female figures used in place of columns, firsthand because they adorned the attic of the portico of the Forum of Augustus and the Pantheon of Agrippa.

7: The battle of Platea in 479 BCE decisively ended the second Persian invasion of Greece. Vitruvius, however, mistakes the father of the Spartan commander, Pausanias. He was Cleombrotus, not Agesilas.

contains various kinds of inquiry into natural problems, for example, in the system of aqueducts. Water channels that meet, bend, and flow, or those forced into a passage on a level plain, produce at different points and in different ways natural gaps in pressure that cause obstructions which no one can remedy without knowledge of the principles of natural philosophy.[8] And even he who reads the treatises of Ctesibius or Archimedes, and others who have published works of this kind on water pressure, will not be able to perceive their import unless he has been trained in the discipline by philosophers.

(8) The architect should know music; with an understanding of the theory of harmony and of mathematical relations he will be able to adjust properly the specifications of the machines of war, the ballista, the catapult, and the scorpion. For example, in the cross-beam on the right and left are spring holes of "half-tones" and through them ropes made of twisted straps are stretched and pulled tight by winches and levers. The ropes are not wedged in place and tied up, unless they make distinct and identical sounds to the ears of the craftsman. The arms which maintain the tension, when they are extended, should provide an even and equal force on both sides. But if the tension is not equal, then they will prevent the launching of missiles on a straight course.[9]

(9) In theaters, the bronze vessels—the Greeks call them *echeia*—which are placed in chambers under the rows of seats, correspond in mathematical proportion. The differences of the sounds produced by them blend into symphonic harmonies and chords conforming to the circle divided into *fourths, fifths,* and *octaves.* So, the sound thundering from the stage strikes these devices and affects the senses, then increases in volume until in clearer and sweeter tone it reaches the ears of the spectators. This too: no one lacking in the science of music can make water-organs and similar machines.

(10) The architect ought to know the discipline of medicine as it relates to the climate—the Greeks say *climata*—the atmospheric nature of localities, healthy and unhealthy, and the water supply. Without an accounting of these factors no habitation can be healthy. He must also have familiarity with the laws that are necessarily associated with the buildings having common walls, such as the extent of eaves, drains, and lighting. The water supply and other matters of this kind also should be known by the architect so that, before he initiates construction, he may take precautions to prevent lawsuits lingering among proprietors after work is completed; and in the writing of the contracts prudent care

8: Vitruvius divides "philosophy" into two separate branches: moral and natural. By natural or physical philosophy the ancients included what we recognize as "science."

9: exact calibrations of these armed machines was a necessity for success, and knowledge of their intricate workings was not an easy acquisition.

may be directed to both client and the contractor. For if the contract is skillfully drafted, it will be possible for either party to be released from the terms without injure to the other.[10] By astronomy the architect learns the east, west, the south, north, the structure of the heavens, the equinox, the solstice. If he lacks understanding of these operations, he will fail miserably to understand the proper construction of timepieces.

(11) Since so magnificent a profession as this is embellished with varied arts and abounds in numerous disciplines, I do not think they can justly proclaim themselves architects unless from boyhood they have scaled the steps of these disciplines and have been nourished on the study of the liberal and fine arts, and with this background have arrived atop the lofty temple of architecture.

(12) But perhaps it will seem amazing to the inexperienced that human nature can learn and remember so many, numerous disciplines. When, however, they have discerned that all fields of study are interconnected and share methods, they will believe it can easily occur. The course of study in education is put together much like a body is from its constituent members. So those who from a tender age are instructed in various disciplines recognize the same patterns in all the academic pursuits and the interconnection of all the disciplines, and, thereby, they more easily learn the requirements. On this very point one of the architects of old, Pythius,[11] who designed and constructed the noble temple of Minerva at Priene, says in his notebooks that an architect should be able to perform better in all the arts and sciences that those who by their energetic labor and experience have promoted individual subjects to the highest renown. That, however, is not substantiated in reality.

(13) The architect neither ought nor can be a literary critic like the famous Aristarchus, yet, he should not be illiterate; nor be a musician like Aristoxenus, yet not uneducated in some music; nor be a painter like Apelles, yet not unskilled with his drafting pencil; nor be a sculptor like Myron or Polyclitus, yet not ignorant of the art of sculpture; nor be a doctor like Hippocrates, yet not untrained in medicine; nor be singularly distinguished in the other sciences, yet in these disciplines be unskilled. In fact, in such a variety of subjects no one individual can achieve remarkable refinement in all because it rarely drops into his power to find out and to perceive their methodologies.

(14) Nevertheless, whereas architects are not the only ones who are unable to attain the utmost achievement in all disciplines, yet some artisans who individually specialize in particular qualities of the arts do not succeed in reaching the ultimate pinnacle of distinction. Therefore,

---

10: Vitruvius emphasizes the areas of law most pertinent to architecture: building contracts, zoning, and property contracts.

11: beginning with Pythius and continuing to Hippocrates in section 13, consult the glossary for the names.

if individual artists, not all, but a few, in each profession have scarcely achieved prominence throughout human history, how can an architect who must be skilled in several arts fail to compass a remarkable and grand success since he has no deficiency in any of the areas, and since he surpasses all those artists who with intense energy have devoted their constant attention to a single occupation?

(15) So, in this matter Pythius seems to have made a mistake because he failed to discern that individual arts are composed of two features: practice and theory. Of these the former is appropriate for those who are skilled in particular occupations, that is, the execution of the work; while in the latter, theory is shared with all educated people. For example, doctors and musicians both deal with the rhythm of pulse and foot-movement. If one must heal a wound or save a sick man from a life-threatening danger, he does not summon a musician; the case requires the appropriate expertise of a doctor. Likewise, it will not be the physician but the musician who will tune a musical instrument to delight the ears in sweet song.

(16) The case is similar when a dispute arises among astronomers and musicians about the "harmony of spheres"[12] and the harmonics of music, of quadrants and triangles, of fourths and fifths; geometricians deal with vision which the Greeks call the *science of optics*. In all the other disciplines many subjects, or all of them, are common to scholars as far as the question of theory is concerned; but the undertaking of works which are produced and refined by manual dexterity or by technical means belongs to those men who have been trained to perform in one area of expertise. Yet, he who has even a modicum of knowledge in the individual disciplines of the separate disciplines and methods which are necessary for an architect, is not at sea if he must judge and test any product from those subjects and skills.

(17) On the other hand, those individuals who have been gifted by nature with much ingenuity, acumen, and a good memory to allow them to possess familiarity with geometry, astronomy, music, and other related studies, far surpass the duties of architects and become pure mathematicians. Thus, they can with ease dispute and refute those disciplines because they have been better armed with the weapons of their scholarly arsenal. These individuals, however, are rarely found, as once were Aristarchus of Samos,[13] Philolaus and Archytas of Tarentum, Apollonius of Perga, Eratosthenes of Cyrene, and Archimedes and Scorpius from Syracuse; all of these men have bequeathed to posterity many treatises

12: a reference to Pythagorean ideas on the orbits of planets spaced according to musical intervals in which tone and pitch depended upon rotation, velocity, and the distance from the center of the cosmos.

13: Aristarchus of Samos begins a list of famous philosophers and mathematicians. Consult the glossary.

on machines and sundials which were discovered and explained by the study of mathematical proportion and natural philosophy.

(18) Since it is not granted to all peoples everywhere, but only to a select few individuals to possess such genius endowed by nature, still the architect ought to practice his profession skilled in all the branches of learning. But, because of the vast scope of the proposition, human reason limits the possession of complete understanding and allows only a moderate mastery of the subjects. Therefore, I beg you, Caesar, and you, the readers of these volumes, to pardon my treatment that if it be deficient in rules of literary style. Bear in mind that I have labored to write this discourse not as an erudite scholar of philosophy or as an elegant speaker, or a literary critic practiced and steeped in the methodologies of his field; no, but as an architect imbued with a touch of those studies. As for the significance of my art and the principles contained within it, I promise to dedicate these volumes with no hesitation and to present them, I hope, with confidence and positive authority to builders and to all scholars everywhere.

BOOK VI, PREFACE

(1) The Socratic philosopher Aristippus once was shipwrecked on the coast of Rhodes. When he discovered some geometrical designs sketched on the beach, they say that he exclaimed to his companions: "We have hope! I see the traces of humans." Immediately he headed to the city of Rhodes and made his way directly to the gymnasium. It was there he engaged in philosophical arguments and was rewarded handsomely; he was able to outfit himself and provide his companions with clothing and the other necessities of life. When they decided to return to their fatherland, they asked what sage message that he wanted them to report back home; he bid them to say: people should furnish children with goods and travel items of the sort that can swim away with them and survive a shipwreck.

(2) Yes, those are the protections of life which neither the storm and injustice of fortune, nor political change, nor the ravages of war can harm. Theophrastus supports this opinion and encourages trust in the learning of scholars rather than in money. He posits the following: of all of humanity only the learned man is no stranger in foreign countries, nor lacking in friends even if he has lost kinsmen and intimates; no, on the contrary, he is a citizen in every state and is able to despise without fear the difficult vicissitudes of fortune. But the man who thinks that he is fortified not by the defenses of learning but by success travels upon slippery roads and is harassed by a life unstable and unprotected.

(3) Epicurus, too, says somewhat the same thing: that fortune provides few emoluments to the wise; although they may be few, they are the best and indispensable, namely, being governed by the judgments

of heart and mind. So a majority of philosophers have said, and poets as well, particularly those composers of Greek comedies of the old style who have propounded on stage those views in verse, such as Crates, Chionides, and Aristophanes; but, Alexis[14] earns special mention who says that the Athenians deserve credit because, whereas the laws of all the other Greeks compel children to take care of their parents, in Athens only do those parents who have educated their children in the arts receive the care. All the gifts that fortune bestows it can easily take away. Discipline, however, combined with mental rigor never fails, but remains stable to the final days of life.

(4) And so, I give undying thanks to my parents and have the deepest respect for them because they approved of that law of Athens and saw to it that I was trained with a skill, one which cannot be mastered without the knowledge of literature and the liberal arts in general. When I had expanded the storehouse of my studies under the care of my parents and the instruction of my teachers, I took pleasure in works of literature, technical treatises, and the commentaries written upon them; in this pursuit I gained the intellectual possessions of which this sentiment summarizes the fruit of my labor: that it is not necessary to keep acquiring more and more possessions, for true wealth is properly to want nothing, least of all, riches. But perhaps some regard these possessions as trifles and think that those are wise who possess money in abundance. Therefore, many individuals who have exerted themselves with that aim in mind and have employed a cocky attitude to correspond with their wealth, have won some notice.

(5) But for my part, Caesar, I have not devoted myself to study just to make money from my skill; conversely, I have proven by experience that a narrower existence with a good reputation should be pursued rather than affluence rife with shame. Thus little celebrity has followed me. Nevertheless, I have published these volumes with the hope that I will be known to future generations. There is no great surprise that I am at present unknown to the majority of the public. Other architects beg and bicker for construction jobs; but I observe a practice handed down by my teachers: not to bid to undertake a commission, but to be sought out, since in an honest man natural color blushes from the shame of requesting something of a suspicious nature. For those who provide services, not those who accept them, are courted. What are we to think the man will suspect who is asked to entrust expenditures drawn from his estate to please a petitioner? Except that he will judge it should be done for the profit and gain of the other person?

14: Crates, Chionides, and Aristophanes are all fifth-century comic playwrights of the so-called Old Comedy. Alexis is a fourth-century comic poet of Middle Comedy.

(6) Therefore, our ancestors, first of all, entrusted employment to architects of proven pedigree, and secondly, they asked if they had been brought up and trained honorably, judging that the commission be awarded to those with a sense of decency befitting a free man and not to those who are aggressive and insolent. In fact, the craftsmen themselves trained no one except their children or relatives, or deserving individuals who because of their loyalty were permitted access without hesitation to huge amounts of money for important projects.

When I see, however, that untrained and inexperienced men proudly profess knowledge of such a magnificent art, as do those who have absolutely no knowledge whatsoever of architecture or even of construction, then I cannot keep from praising those patriarchs who, strengthened by their confidence in their literary education, build for themselves and make the following judgment: that if a commission is given to inexperienced men, they themselves are empowered to spend their money as they please rather than to be beholden to anyone else.

(7) And so, no one tries to practice any other skill at home such as cobbling or laundering or any of the many other occupations that are easier, except that of architecture, because individuals who profess it are wrongly called architects since they lack a genuine education. For these reasons I thought that I had to compose a systemized account of architecture and its methods, believing it would not be an unwelcome service for all peoples.

LIVY

THE HISTORY OF ROME

With its poetic coloring and fast-paced narrative, Book I of Livy has always captivated its readers. The lore of the heroes and villains of early Rome seemed to have fit the idea and ideal of what the Roman had of himself and his ancestors. This appeal of the subject matter and lively treatment must have resonated deeply with Augustus and his age. The book points to a simpler yet more righteous time when there was self-sacrifice for the sake of an idea or value, manly courage even among foes soon to be Romans, and a destiny assured by divine approbation and by the human will to succeed.

BOOK I

(Preface) [1] I am not quite sure I would achieve anything worthy of my effort,[2] nor, were I sure, would I dare say so, if I treated in detail the history of the Roman people from the foundation of the city, inasmuch as I perceive that the subject is both old and extensively published, since writer after successive writer believes that he will contribute something more authoritative to the facts or by his skillful writing style surpass the crudities of his antiquated predecessors. However that may be, it will greatly please me none the less to have offered my best effort to

---

1: in his preface Livy details the purpose and scope of his history. He also directs his audience to his own attitude toward history. Livy's sentiments and language should be compared and contrasted with Sallust, *Catiline* 1-4. But, unlike Sallust, Livy seems to have no political scheme.

2: Livy emphasizes the magnitude of his task, a recurrent theme of the preface. Note lines 10-16 below.

the memory of the accomplishments of the greatest people on the earth. And should my reputation be shaded among the throng of writers, I will console myself with the noble renown and splendor of those who eclipse my name.[3] Besides, the subject demands enormous energy, requiring that I trace over 700 years of a story that starting from small beginnings has grown to such an immense stage that it groans beneath its massive size. I also have no doubt that the majority of readers will not find as much pleasure in the origins and early history, as they hurry to reach recent events in which the strength of a long-ruling people is imploding. I, on the contrary, by laborious study shall strive for an additional reward in that I will be distracting myself from the sight of the miseries that our present age has witnessed now over so many years;[4] as long as I recall those ancient times, I shall be free of every anxiety that could torment the mind of a writer, even though it would not veer it from the truth.

It is not my intention either to affirm or to refute the traditions that before and during the foundation of the city have been passed down to us more embellished with poetic fantasies than grounded in history's unadulterated archives. To antiquity is awarded the following license: that the involving of human aspirations with divine affairs in the origins of cities makes them more dignified. And if any people can rightly assert consecrated origins and claim divine connections, then it is the Roman race. Their military glory allows it when they champion Mars, that most powerful figure, as their own parent and as the divine father of their founder. Thus, the peoples of the world acquiesce in the claim as compliantly as they endure Rome's imperial power. But, however these matters and similar cases may be perceived or interpreted, I consider them of no great significance. Instead, I would have each person keenly devote his intellect to these topics: what sort of life they led, what customs they observed, through what men and by what skills in domestic and foreign affairs the empire was engendered and expanded; let him then trace in his mind the collapse of discipline. Gradual at first, it was succeeded by a chasmal, as it were, decline of morals, sliding more and more, until they began to plunge headlong into ruin such that we have reached our modern times when we can neither endure our vices nor suffer the remedies for their cure.[5] In the study of history one particular thing stands out as sound and fruitful: that you see and contemplate records of every experience emblazoned on an illustrious memorial. From them you may choose for yourself and your country what to imitate

3: Livy alludes to the noble background of figures such as Quintus Fabius Pictor, Marcus Porcius Cato, Quintus Tubero, and other predecessors of distinguished rank or families.
4: Livy's escapist attitude is unprecedented.
5: Some see in Livy's reflection of Roman moral decline and of the inability to redirect Roman society a reference to Augustus' failed attempt to reform moral conduct in the decade of the twenties.

and, if shameful in its origin and disgraceful in result, what to avoid. Moreover, unless my love for my scholarly enterprise deceives me, no country has ever been greater, more religious, or richer in outstanding exemplars. In no other community have greed and luxury invaded so late, and nowhere has respect for thrift and frugality run so deeply and for so long a time. For the less acquisition of material things, so less the covetous greed. But in recent times wealth has brought avarice and through sensual excess and sexual desire, self-indulgent pleasures galore have imported a longing for utter ruin and destruction.[6] But, contentious carping, unlikely to be welcomed, although perhaps necessary, begone, away from the undertaking of a massive project. Rather, if it were also the custom of us historians, as it is for poets, we should begin with favorable omens, vows, and prayers to gods and goddesses all to bestow the blessing of success upon the undertaking of so great a task.[7]

(1) It is generally agreed that after the capture of Troy the Greeks continued to vent their rage against all the Trojans except for two, Aeneas and Antenor.[8] Because of their ties of hospitality of long standing and because they had been supporters of peace and the restoring of Helen, the Greeks abstained from exercising the recognized right of war against them. The two men had divergent destinies: Antenor fell in with a large body of Eneti who had been driven out of Paphlagonia because of their rebellious actions and were in search of locales to settle and a leader, for their king, Pylaemenes, had been lost at Troy. He arrived to the uppermost bay of the Adriatic and evicted the Euganei, a people who were living between the sea and the Alps, and whose territory a mixture of Eneti and Trojans then occupied.[9] The spot where they first disembarked is called Troy and the area around it carries the name of the "Trojan district;" the combined peoples were called Venetians.[10]

As for Aeneas, exiled from home because of a similar disaster, his destiny guided him to greater enterprises. First, he came to Macedon, then sailed to Sicily in quest for a settlement and from there steered his fleet to the area of Laurentum.[11] This territory too got the name Troy.

6: again, one should compare Sallust, *Catiline* 7-9.
7: Livy's invocation of the gods, unique for historians, parallels the invocation of numerous poets.
8: Livy begins by linking two Trojan foundations in Italy, Aeneas for Rome and Antenor for the district of Padua, his native city.
9: little is known of the Euganei. It is uncertain whether they are Pre-Indo-European or Italic.
10: the Veneti can be identified as a distinct culture from the tenth century BCE. Although their ethnic background remains a mystery, by the sixth century they are speaking an Italic dialect of close affinity with Latin.
11: it is not clear whether "Laurentum" designated a town or a people of the area so-called. The word later is associated and became synonymous with Lavinium.

Inasmuch as the Trojans had nothing left from the almost endless wandering except some weapons and ships, they began, after they landed, to engage in rustling a few cattle from the farmlands. They met Latinus, the local king, and the natives,[12] who at that time inhabited this territory, all around and running from city and fields to check by force the attack of the invaders. There are two common accounts of this confrontation. Some writers maintain that Latinus was defeated in battle, made peace with Aeneas, and then joined and made an alliance with him through a marriage to his daughter; others say that, after the battle lines were drawn up and stood ready, but before the signals had sounded, Latinus came forward among the officers and summoned the leader of the newcomers to a parley; he inquired who his men were, from where they had come, what chance drove them from their home, what they were seeking in coming to the territory of Laurentum. He listened to the reply and learned that the host of men were Trojans, that their leader was Aeneas, son of Anchises and Venus, that they had been forced into exile after their city had been torched, and finally that they were seeking a home and a locale for founding a city. Admiring both the noble look of the people and the man, and the spirit readied either for war or for peace, Latinus offered his right hand and pledged his good faith for future friendship. A treaty was struck right then and there between the two leaders and the two armies exchanged greetings. Latinus welcomed and entertained Aeneas in his home, and before his household gods gave his daughter's hand in marriage to Aeneas, thereby sanctioning a private bond that paralleled the public pact. This turn of events encouraged the Trojans' hope of ending at long last their wanderings in a permanent and stable home. They founded a town which Aeneas called Lavinium from his wife's name Lavinia, and soon a boy was born of the marriage whom the parents named Ascanius.[13]

(2) Then an assault upon both natives and Trojans erupted into armed conflict; Turnus, the king of the Rutulians, to whom Lavinia had been pledged before Aeneas' arrival and who deeply resented the fact that the stranger had been preferred over him, had declared war on both Aeneas and Latinus. Neither army left the field satisfied; on the one hand, the Rutulians met defeat, but on the other, the victorious natives and the Trojans lost their leader Latinus. Discouraged by the state of affairs, Turnus and the Rutulians fled to the flourishing realms of the Etruscans and in particular to king Mezentius who controlled and governed the then affluent city of Caere. He was displeased from the very beginning at the founding of the new city and believed that the Trojan state was

---

12: the Aboriginals whose fusion with Trojans produced the Latins became a constant element in the legendary founding of Rome.

13: Livy here follows the tradition that Ascanius was the son of Lavinia; later in chapter three he mentions the other tradition that he was Aeneas' son by his Trojan wife Creusa, as Vergil, *Aeneid* 2.651-652 and 665-684 attest.

expanding far more than was safe for its neighbors; therefore, Mezentius was not reluctant to join forces with the Rutulians as their ally. To counter the dread of a massive war and to mitigate the feelings of the natives, Aeneas adopted the name Latins for both people, the locals and his own, believing that they would bond together under the same government and the same name. From that time forward the locals displayed as passionate a loyalty to their king Aeneas as the Trojans did. Because he trusted in the spirit of the two peoples becoming more united day by day, and, although he could have defended against and repelled any attack from the walls, Aeneas himself led his troops out to do open battle, despite the fact that Etruria's resources were vast and its reputation on land and sea echoed the entire length of Italy from the Alps to the strait of Sicily. The Latins won the battle; for Aeneas, however, it was his last mortal engagement. He was buried by the Numicus river; and, however right and proper he may be named, the locals call him Jove Indigenous.[14]

(3) Although Aeneas' son, Ascanius, was not yet mature enough for political power, authority awaited intact for him until he reached manhood. In the meantime a woman's regency—Lavinia had a very strong character—maintained the Latin state and the kingdom of her boy's grandfather and father. Because of the doubt I cannot affirm who this Ascanius was—for who could prove something so ancient—either he was the aforementioned or an elder brother, the son of Creusa, born when Ilium was standing, who accompanied his father in flight, the same boy whom the Julian family calls Iulus and claims as the originator of their name.[15] Wherever he was born and whoever was his mother, there is no doubt whatsoever that he was Aeneas' son. As the city of Lavinium was flourishing and, considering the time, wealthy and heavily populated, he left it to the care of his mother or to his stepmother. He himself founded a new town along the Alban mountain range; because it stretched out along a ridge, the city was called Alba Longa. Between the founding of Lavinium until the planting of the colony at Alba Longa covered a period of thirty years. The resources of the Latins had grown so powerful, particularly after the rout of the Etruscans, that neither Mezentius and the Etruscans nor any other neighboring inhabitants dared to launch an attack, although Aeneas was dead and it was the time of a woman's regency and a boy's learning the rudiments of power. Terms

---

14: a number of sites attests to the worship and cult of Aeneas that includes a dedication to Lar Aineas near modern Tor Tignosa, itself near Lavinium.

15: Livy provides the two separate traditions of Ascanius' birth, 1) the son of Aeneas by Lavinia, or 2) Aeneas' son by the Trojan Creusa. The name Iulus was connected with Ilos, an early progenitor of the Trojans. It was politic, then, that the Julian clan of Alba promoted the connection of Ascanius/Iulus with Alba Longa. Hence, the legendary link of Alba with the history of Rome through its founder Ascanius/Iulus served the interests of the Julians, including their famous adopted member, Augustus.

of peace were drawn up so that the Albula river, now called the Tiber, would serve as the boundary between the Etruscans and Latins.

Silvius, Ascanius' son, succeeded in the rule, so named because he happened to be born in the woods (*silva*), and he fathered Aeneas Silvius, his successor, who in turn produced Latinus Silvius.[16] This king founded several colonies known as the "Old Latins."[17] All the subsequent kings of Alba kept the name Silvius. After Latinus came Alba, from Alba was born Atys, next after Atys Capys ruled, then Capetus, then his son Tiberinus who, when he drowned while crossing the Albula river, gave it his name, prevalent among later generations. Next Agrippa,[18] Tiberinus' son, ruled and after him Romulus Silvius inherited the kingdom from his father. Romulus was struck by lightning and handed down his kingdom to Aventinus, who was buried on the hill which is now part of the city Rome (This hill bears his name, the Aventine.). Then Proca who fathered Numitor and Amulius came to power. Proca bequeathed the ancient realm of the Silvian family to his older son Numitor. Brutal force, however, proved stronger than the will of the father or the respect for primogeniture, for Amulius drove out his brother and seized power. He compounded crime upon crime, murdering the male offspring of his brother and annulling the hope of his niece, Rhea Silvia, of ever giving birth. In a pretense of religiosity he made her a Vestal, binding her to perpetual virginity.

(4)   But it was destined, I think, that the genesis of a mighty city and the dawn of the most powerful empire—next to the gods—arise by fate, for the Vestal was forcibly violated and gave birth to twins. She named Mars as the father of the illegitimate birth, either truly believing it were so, or because a god as the responsible party would be a more honorable sanction of her guilt. Whatever the case, neither the gods nor humans sheltered her or her offspring from the cruelty of the king: the priestess of Vesta was bound and locked up under guard; under the king's order the boys were to be set adrift on the river. But destiny's luck played out: the Tiber's banks overflowed creating stagnant pools that prevented the approach to the course of the regular river; but those executing the orders and actually carrying the children had hope that they could be drowned in the sluggish flood water. Following the order (so to speak) of king Amulius, they exposed the boys at the closest pool of overflow, where the Ruminal fig tree now stands, traditionally called the fig tree of Romulus. In those times the area was uncultivated. The prevailing story goes that the basket in which the infant boys had been exposed

16: the genealogy of the Silvii was contrived to account for the four hundred years from the fall of Troy to the foundation of Rome.
17: Livy uses this term for his contemporaries to distinguish the ethnic designation of Latins from the peoples given "Latin Rights" during the Republic.
18: it would be very difficult not to think of M. Vipsanius Agrippa, Augustus' great general and son-in-law.

was dumped on dry land with the receding of the shallow water and that a thirsty she-wolf, coming down from the nearby hills, wound her way toward the bawling of the babies. She positioned herself and offered her teats so gently for the infants to suck that the king's chief herds-man—tradition ascribes the name Faustulus to him—found her licking the infants with her tongue; he took them to his hut and handed them over to his wife Larentia to nurse. Some believe that Larentia prosti-tuted her body and was called "wolf" by the local shepherds; such then was the reason for the miraculous story of their birth and upbringing. When they reached early manhood, they were active in work among the pens and herds and roamed the groves in hunting. In this pursuit they gained strength, fortifying their bodies and spirits, up to the point that they not only went after wild game but also began to attack bandits weighted down with stolen goods, and then to distribute the booty to other shepherds. For the gang of young men that grew daily occupied themselves sometimes in serious matters, sometimes in horse play.

(5) Even in those days long past they say that the frolicking festival of the Lupercal was celebrated on the Palatine Hill and that the hill was first named Pallantium, deriving from Pallanteum, a city in Arcadia, then called the Palatine; it was there that Evander of Arcadian stock, who for many seasons previously held the area, brought from Arcadia and instituted the ritual whereby naked young men venerated Lycaean Pan—the Romans later called him Inuus[19]—by running about engaging in wanton sport. As the rite was well-known, the robbers, enraged at the loss of their booty, laid a trap for the youths celebrating this festival. Romulus warded them off, but they captured Remus, handed him over to king Amulius, and impudently accused him and Romulus, charging them and their gang of youths specifically with habitually conducting raids upon Numitor's fields and rustling his cattle. For punishment Remus was turned over to Numitor. Right from the first Faustulus had suspected that the boys he was rearing were of royal birth. He was very much aware that the king had ordered the exposure of two infants and that the time frame for that event coincided with his salvation of the two children. But he had been unwilling to disclose the matter unless either the right opportunity arose or necessity compelled him. Circumstances forced the issue and his fear spurred him to disclose the facts to Romulus. And as for Numitor, while he was holding Remus in custody, and when he heard that the brothers were twins, the memory of his grandchildren flashed through his mind as he compared their age and their far from servile demeanor. His inquiries led him to the same conclusion so that he all but acknowledged Remus. On every side a web of chicanery was spun for the king. Romulus attacked the king not with his band of young men, for he was not yet a powerful enough match for a direct assault.

19: sometimes this figure is identified with Faunus rather than Pan.

Instead, he ordered shepherds by different routes to make for the palace at a predetermined time and to launch a strike against him; Remus for reinforcements recruited another band from Numitor's household. So Romulus slaughtered Amulius the king.

(6) During the first rush of the assault Numitor sent word that an enemy had invaded the city and had stormed the palace; next he summoned the Alban youth to secure the citadel under an armed garrison. When he saw the two young men approaching to congratulate him after they had finished off the killing, at once he called a meeting of the people and detailed the crimes of his brother against him, the background of his grandsons' birth, how they were reared and then recognized, and, finally, his own responsibility for the subsequent murder of the tyrant. With their troops Romulus and Remus marched right through the assembly and hailed their grandfather as king, at which a unanimous shout from the crowd ratified the king's title and power.

After the government of Alba was entrusted to Numitor, Romulus and Remus were seized with a desire to found a settlement in that area where they had been exposed and reared. There was at the time an excess population of Albans and Latins and the shepherds added to this problem; it was easy for all of them to engender a hope that Alba and Lavinium would be small in comparison with the new site they would establish. But then the evil that ruined their grandfather intervened to affect their plans: the desire for power. Because of it a disgraceful quarrel arose from an innocent and minor event. As they were twins and the respect emanating from seniority could not be used as a criterion, they decided to let the gods who protected the site proclaim by augury who should give his name to the new settlement and who would govern it after it was founded. So, Romulus occupied the Palatine and Remus took up the Aventine to observe the skies for divine signs.

(7) Tradition has it that Remus was the first to receive an omen: six vultures. And as soon as it was announced, double that number appeared to Romulus. Quickly, each one was hailed king by his respective following: the former group claimed the priority of time, the latter the number of birds as the basis for rule. When they met, an argument ensued that, because of the conflict of passions, turned to violence; in the melee Remus was struck and killed. The more common story, however, is that Remus mocked his brother by leaping over the walls just erected, for which a furious Romulus killed him adding the following insulting words: "*Thus*—to anyone else who leaps over my battlements." In this way Romulus grabbed sole power and consequently the newly founded city was called "Rome" from the founder's name.[20]

20: the civil wars of the first century were often viewed as a legacy of Romulus' crime of fratricide. Romulus is called by some Rhomos or Rhomylos and, conversely, the name "Rome" derives from the city/town, not from the reputed founder.

Romulus first fortified the Palatine, the site of his upbringing. Except for Hercules, he sacrificed to the gods in the Alban practice. For this god he used the Greek ritual as it had been instituted by Evander. The story is that, after he killed Geryon, Hercules drove his cattle into this area; they were exceptional specimens, and close to the Tiber river he had herded them and had swum across. On a grassy spot he lay down to rest his own trek-weary body and to refresh the cattle with rest and restorative food. There, drowsy from food and wine, he fell into a deep slumber during which a local shepherd of the region, Cacus by name,[21] an insolent brute, was captivated by the beauty of the animals. Hankering to steal them, he reasoned that, if he herded and drove the cattle into his cave, their tracks would lead their master there in his search. So, he dragged the choicest and most beautiful of the cattle backwards by the tail into his cave. When Hercules awoke from his sleep at the crack of dawn and scanned the herd, he perceived that some of the number were missing. He proceeded toward the nearest cave to see if perchance the tracks led there, but he noticed that they were turned away and led nowhere. Confused and bewildered, he began to drive off the rest of the herd from the mysterious spot. But some of the cattle being driven off began to low, as it usually happens, missing the others, and from the cave rebounded the lowing of the cattle shut up there. Hercules turned at the sound and walked toward the cave. Cacus tried to stop him, but, as he called in vain upon the loyalty of fellow shepherds, he was struck by Hercules' club and died from the blow.

In those days Evander,[22] an exile from the Peloponnese, ruled that region, more from personal prestige than from raw power. He was venerated for the wondrous invention of the alphabet, an innovation among a people lacking and crude in the arts; but he was even more revered because of the divine connection attributed to his mother Carmenta. The people thereabouts, before the coming of the Sibyl[23] into Italy, honored her as a prophetess. Now this Evander, alarmed by the scurrying of excited shepherds all around the newcomer, caught red-handed in the killing, and then, learning of the crime and the cause of the crime, took a look at the hero's bearing and stature, somewhat grander and more august than a mortal's, and asked who he was. As soon as he heard the name, he shouted, "Hercules, son of Jupiter, welcome. My mother, true diviner of the gods, prophesied that you would increase the number

---

21: the story of Cacus is a fusion of Greek and Roman sources. Compare a similar version in Vergil, *Aeneid* 8.185-275.

22: according to Vergil (*Aeneid* 8.470-519) Evander welcomed Aeneas and formed a military alliance with him.

23: refers to the Sibyl of Cumae, the prophetic priestess of Apollo, who came to Rome bearing the Sibylline Books which she sold to Tarquin the Proud. This collection of prophetic verse was stored and guarded by priests and consulted in time of perplexity.

of gods, and an altar would be dedicated to you here, and the people, destined one day to be the most powerful on earth, would call it the 'Greatest Altar' and worship at it with rites to you." Hercules gave him his right hand and said that he accepted the omen and would fulfill the prophecy by erecting and consecrating an altar. On the spot an excellent specimen was picked out from the herd and for the first time a sacrifice was performed to Hercules; the service and the accompanying feast were administered by the Potitii and Pinarii, two prominent families of the area. It just so happened that the Potitii were present at the right time and were served the sacrificial entrails; on the other hand, the Pinarii arrived for the rest of the feast after the vitals had been eaten. As long as the Pinarii family was around, it remained the custom that none of the Pinarii eat the sacrificial entrails. The Potitii, instructed by Evander, were the priests of this cult for many generations until the ritualistic practice was turned over to public slaves after the demise of the Potitii family. Romulus adopted only this one foreign religious rite; for even then he was the respectful champion of immortality gained through manly valor to which his own destiny was directing him.

(8) After he had duly attended to religious ceremonies, Romulus summoned the great number of citizens to a meeting and gave them a code of law, since only through that and by no other means could he unify his people into a single body. He reckoned that the uncouth country folk would respect the laws only if he himself assumed a more revered posture in the trappings of power; so, in just about every aspect, but particularly in the assumption of the twelve lictors, he presented himself as more august. Some think that he selected the number twelve from the number of birds that portended and heralded his kingdom. For my own part I do not regret sharing the opinions of those who accept that the attendants of this type, and the very number as well, derived from neighboring Etruscans, from whom the chair of state and the bordered toga were also borrowed. They believe too that the Etruscans used the number because each of the twelve tribes who united to elect the king contributed one lictor each.[24]

Meanwhile, the circuit of the city, as it encroached on different areas, kept expanding, and they fortified it with walls thinking of the future population more than of any regard to the existing one. Next, to avoid the city being drained of inhabitants and to increase the population, Romulus initiated a scheme used by founders of cities; they amass a host of lowly and nameless men and falsely claim that these individuals are born of the earth just for them. Romulus opened an asylum, a sanctuary which now as you go up the hill[25] is hedged off between two groves. Here from

24: the Etruscans were said to have formed a league consisting of twelve major cities and their territories.
25: the hill referred to is the Capitoline.

the neighboring people fled a throng, an undistinguishable mix of free and slave, eager for a new start, and they comprised the first elements of a strong state well on its way to greatness. Not at all dissatisfied with his strength, he then instituted a political program to accompany the power. He appointed one hundred senators, either because that number was sufficient or because there were only one hundred who could be designated as fathers. To be sure they were labeled "fathers"[26] from their rank and their descendants were called patricians.

(9)[27] The state of Rome was now strong enough to hold its own in war against any of the neighboring states. Because of a lack of women, however, its greatness seemed destined to last only a single generation inasmuch as there was no hope of progeny at home nor the right of intermarriage with peoples who bordered them. Then, relying on the advice of the fathers, Romulus sent diplomats around to the neighboring nations to negotiate an alliance and the right of intermarriage for the new state. They argued that cities, like all other things, arise from the humblest beginnings; that those which their own merit and the gods assist win great wealth and a splendid reputation. They were sure that the gods had favored Rome's origin and that valor would not be lacking, and that they, as neighbors, should not be reluctant as humans to mingle their race and blood with other humans. Nowhere did the embassy receive a favorable hearing: everywhere the other states despised and at the same time feared for themselves and their progeny a power growing so strong in their midst. As the diplomats were dismissed, sometimes they were asked if they had opened up a sanctuary for women too, since apparently that was the only way they would find suitable wives. The young men of Rome resented this insult and no doubt it foreshadowed hostilities. Romulus, concealing his deep resentment, began readying the time and place for the use of force, targeting the solemn festivities honoring Neptune of the Horse,[28] which he called the Consualia. Under his orders a notice was sent to the neighboring peoples proclaiming the spectacle; for their celebration they produced as much magnificent preparation as was within the scope of their knowledge or ability to advertise the coming glorious event. Many people, very eager to see the new city, especially those inhabitants who lived closest, the people of Caenina, Crustumium, and Antemnae,[29] came to the happening; and

26: the Latin word is *patres*, hence, English derives 'patrician' i.e. 'of or pertaining to the fathers.'

27: with this chapter and continuing through chapter 13 Livy treats the relations of Rome with the Sabines and the external (foreign) affairs between these two peoples. They lead ultimately to a synoecism and fusion of the two ethnic elements: Sabine and Latin.

28: among the Greeks one of Poseidon's (Neptune's) cultic names was *hippios*, i.e. 'of the horse.' At the festival horse races became standard.

29: these three towns close to Rome were all eventually absorbed by an expanding Rome.

the Sabines arrived en masse with their wives and children. They were welcomed and entertained hospitably in house after house and, when they gazed upon the design of the site, the walls, and the city packed with houses, they were surprised to see how the state of Rome had grown so much in such a short time. When the time for the show came, all eyes and thoughts were directed to it; then a signal was given and the prearranged attack was under way. Roman youths scurried to seize the young women; most of the women were taken by whomever they happened to have bumped into; those of remarkable beauty were marked for prominent senators; and special plebeians who were designated for the job carried them off to the houses. One young lady, exceptionally surpassing all the others in beauty and looks, they say was grabbed by the gang of a certain Thalassius. When many were questioned to whom they were conveying her, to stop anyone from violating her they shouted out, "to Thalassius!" over and over; hence, the origin of this shout at weddings.[30]

Panic and turmoil ensued, breaking up the festival. The parents of the young women left in sorrow and hurt, cursing the violation of the treaty of hospitality and invoking the god to whose solemn festival, in a blatant breach of religion and good faith, they had been tricked and deceived into coming. Romulus, however, passed among the women pointing out that the cause of their predicament was the arrogance of their fathers who had refused intermarriage with their neighbors. Nevertheless, they would be married and fully share all the fortunes of the Romans, that is, citizenship and children, the dearest prerogative of the human race. They should, however, temper their anger and entrust their hearts to those men to whom pure chance had given their bodies. He stressed that often a sense of injustice turns to genuine affection, and they would end up with kinder husbands for this reason, that each and every one would strive to perform his proper role to the best of his ability and also to fill the void of the loss of parents and home. The men added their own sweet nothings seeking to excuse their actions, fired by passion and love, pleas which most effectively move a woman's heart.

(10) The feelings of the abducted women had softened a great deal at the time their parents, dressed in mourning clothes, and wailing complaints and weeping, stirred up their cities. And they did not constrain their indignant feelings to their home towns, but from all over they gathered at Titus Tatius', the king of the Sabines. Because of Tatius' eminent reputation in those parts, here too assembled ambassadors; the men of Caenina, Crustumium, and Antemnae shared in the wrong. But in their view Tatius and the Sabines seemed to have acted too slowly. Between them those three peoples together prepared for war. Yet even

---

30: Livy provides this unlikely aetiological account of the shout "Thalassio" at weddings. Some believe that Thalassio is the name of an Etruscan deity.

the Crustuminians and Antemnates did not move energetically enough to satisfy the burning rage of the men of Caenina; so on their own initiative in the name of the people of Caenina, they attacked Roman territory. But as they were dispersing and pillaging, Romulus appeared with his army and in a minor skirmish he taught them that anger without power was useless. He routed and scattered their force and pursued it in flight; he killed their king in battle and stripped him of his armor. With the enemy's king dead, he captured their city with one assault. Romulus then led his army back in victory and was no less eager to parade his achievements as a splendid hero of valorous deeds. Therefore, he fixed the spoils of the enemy's slain commander on a frame specifically designed for that purpose, and carrying it he ascended the Capitol where near an oak tree sacred to shepherds he laid it down, and at the same time as he proffered his gift, he marked out the holy confines for a temple to Jupiter and ascribed to the god an honorific name. "Jupiter Feretrius," he prayed, "These arms of a king I, a king, the victorious Romulus, bring to you[31] and I dedicate a sacred precinct in the confines measured out in my mind, a resting place for the spoils of honor which, following my example, men in the future will bring, stripped from the slain kings and commanders of the enemy." This was the origin of the first temple consecrated in Rome. The gods decreed that the words of the temple's founder should not be in vain, when he affirmed that men of the future would bring the spoils there, but that the honor of the gift should not be prostituted by a large number of claimants. Only twice in the numerous wars over so many years have the spoils of honor been won, so rare has been the good fortune of deserving men to win this honor.

(11) While the Romans were involved with these matters in the city, the army of the citizens of Antemnae, seizing advantage of the opportunity provided by the Romans' absence, made a hostile incursion into Roman territory, but a quick strike by a Roman levy surprised them as they were dispersed in the fields. The enemy was routed by the first charge and attack and their town was captured. As Romulus was celebrating his double victory, his wife Hersilia,[32] harassed by the pleas of the captive young women, implored him to forgive their parents and to bond in harmony; her request was readily granted. Then, he marched out against the Crustuminians who were making war on him. Because their confidence was lagging owing to the defeats suffered by the others, in that confrontation there was even less of a battle than previously. To both locales colonies were sent. Most settlers volunteered their names

---

31: Livy derives "Feretrius" from the verb *ferre*, 'to bring,' although Propertius 4.10.55 maintains that it comes from *ferire*, 'to strike.'

32: although Livy makes Hersilia Romulus' wife, other writers pair her with others or state that she was a widow.

for Crustumium because of the richness of its soil. Yet, quite frequently many moved from there to Rome, especially the parents and relatives of the abducted young women.

The last to make war were the Sabines. It was the fiercest of struggles, for they did not act out of rage or greed. No, they did not manifest signs of war before they pursued it. To their meticulous planning they added intrigue. For Spurius Tarpeius,[33] who commanded the Roman citadel, had a daughter, a virgin. When by chance she had gone outside the walls to fetch water for a sacrifice, she was bribed with gold by Tatius to admit his armed men into the fortress. Once welcomed within the citadel, the men crushed her with their shields and killed her either to give the appearance that they had overrun the citadel or to set an example that no traitor would find safe haven. There is also the tradition that, because the Sabines generally wore heavy gold bracelets on their left arms and rings encrusted with jewels of exquisite beauty, she bargained for what they had on their arms; therefore, instead of gifts of gold, they heaped their shields upon her. Some sources maintain that she stipulated their handing over what they wore on their left arms, directly demanding their shields, and, when it appeared that she was acting treacherously, she paid with her life in the currency of her demand.

(12) The Sabines took possession of the citadel; the next day the Roman army was drawn up and occupied all the level ground between the Palatine and Capitoline hills, but the Sabines would not come down to the plain until rage and passion goaded the Romans to head up against them. A champion from each side, Mettius Curtius on the Sabine, and Hostius Hostilius on the Roman, led the fight. Although the Romans were at a disadvantage because of the terrain, Hostilius advanced the Roman position with reckless abandon in the front ranks. When he fell, the Roman formation at once buckled and retreated to the old gate of the Palatine. Romulus himself, as he was being pushed by the sweep of the fleeing mob, raised his hands to the sky and shouted: "O Jupiter! It was *your*, yes *your*, birds of omen who ordered me to lay the foundation of the city right here on the Palatine. The citadel, already bought by betrayal, lies in the hands of the Sabines; from there in full arms they are heading across the intervening valley against us here; but you, father of gods and men, at least keep the enemy away from this ground; banish this terror from the Romans and stop their disgraceful retreat. On this spot, Jupiter the Stayer,[34] I vow a temple to you, a memorial for posterity that by your present aid you saved the city." After this prayer, as if

33: the Etruscan name "Tarpeius" is linguistically connected with "Tarquinius."

34: some stone blocks discovered near the slope of the Palatine Hill and the south side of the Sacred Way not far from the Arch of Titus may belong to this temple.

he had perceived that the words had been heard, he added, "Romans, Jupiter Best and Greatest[35] ordains us to resist and re-enter the fight right here." The Romans rallied as if they had been ordered by a voice from on high. Romulus rushed forward into the front ranks. Mettius Curtius on the Sabine side led the charge down from the citadel, driving and scattering the Romans all about the space that is now the forum. Just when he had almost reached the Palatine gate, he shouted: "We have beaten the treacherous host, that weak opponent; now they know that it is one thing to rape virgins, but quite another to fight men." With a gang of fearless young men Romulus wheeled in attack against him as he was uttering this boast. Mettius happened to be fighting on horseback at that time, so he was rather easily put to flight. He was on the run, with the Romans in hot pursuit. The daring of their king fired the rest of the Roman troops to scatter the Sabines. Mettius, his horse spooked by the shouting of the pursuers, plunged into a marsh.[36] The situation was dangerous for the stalwart rider and caused the Sabines to cease operations. And with his men beckoning and calling to him he gained courage from the support of so many and made his escape. The Romans and Sabines then renewed the battle in the valley between the two hills; the Romans, however, gained the advantage.

(13) It was at this time that the Sabine women in the face of their misfortune—the wrong done to them was the *raison d'etre* for the conflict—overcame their feminine fear. With their hair disheveled and their clothing torn they courageously intervened, putting themselves in the cross fire of flying missiles; they rushed from the side to separate the warring parties and to allay their rage, begging first their fathers on one side and then their husbands on the other not to disgrace themselves by shedding blood, and as fathers and sons-in-law not to stain with parricide the children, grandsons of the one group, the sons of the other. "If you men are disgusted by the relationship existing between you, if you find repugnant our marriage, turn your anger against us, for we are the cause of the war, the reason for the wounds and casualties of husbands and fathers. Better that we perish than live as widows or orphans without either of you." The scene touched the combatants as well as the captains. A sudden silence and stillness came over them; then the leaders stepped forward to draw up a truce. Not only did they make peace but they forged a single united government from two. Although they shared the title of king, all power of command they transferred to Rome. In this way the town doubled in population and the Romans in a concession of privilege to the Sabines called themselves Quirites after

---

35: in the late sixth century a great temple to Jupiter, Juno, and Minerva was built on the Capitoline, often referred to as Jupiter Best and Greatest.

36: a monument at a cavity in the ground stands in the forum commemorating the event described here by Livy and mentioned in the next chapter.

the Sabine capital Cures.[37] As a memorial of this battle, the area where the horse first emerged from the deep marsh and landed Curtius safe and sound, was called "Curtius' Lake."

The sudden and joyous peace endeared the Sabine women in a stronger bond to their husbands and parents, and above all to Romulus. After he divided the populace into thirty districts, he named these wards from those women.[38] Although doubtlessly the number of women was much greater than that, tradition does not relate the reason why individual women came to lend their names to the wards, whether they were selected by age, by their own social position or by the rank of their husbands, or by lot. At the same time Romulus created three centuries of cavalrymen, the Ramnenses, named after Romulus, the Titienses after Titus Tatius, and the Luceres, the origin of whose name is very obscure.[39] From that time the two kings shared in joint and harmonious power.

(14) Several years later kinsmen of King Tatius assaulted some ambassadors from Laurentum; when the Laurentians initiated action under prevailing law of the peoples, Tatius was influenced by the position and pleas of his own people. As a result he took their punishment upon himself, for at Lavinium, where he had come for an annual sacrifice, a mob formed and killed him. They say that Romulus felt less regret over the event than was proper, either because of the natural disloyalty attendant upon joint rule, or because he actually believed that Tatius' assassination was not unjustified. He therefore abstained from war; yet, in order to atone for the wrong committed against the ambassadors and the killing of the king, he renewed the treaty between Rome and Lavinium.

The peace with the Laurentians was definitely unexpected; but another war erupted, much closer to home, in fact right at the very gates of the city. The citizens of Fidenae, reckoning that a new power, too close to home, was gathering strength, decided in fear to declare war before that power reached its full force. They sent a company of armed young men to ravage the land between the city Rome and Fidenae; from there they veered to the left, since on the right the Tiber blocked the way. Their pillaging produced extreme terror among the country folk who stampeded en masse from the fields into the city bringing news of the surprise attack. Romulus bolted up—for a war so near could brook no delay—and led out the army, pitching camp about a mile from Fidenae, where he left a light garrison. Then setting out with his entire force he

---

37: the etymology of "Quirites" remains obscure; certainly Livy's version is false.

38: these wards (*curiae*) and their assembly constituted the governing body of the state; their formation, however, dates to the Etruscan period of the monarchy, not to Romulus.

39: the names of these tribes/centuries are also Etruscan in background and are not part of the institutions attributable to Romulus.

ordered some soldiers to set up an ambush lying under cover of thick underbrush; advancing with the majority of the troops and all of the cavalry, he achieved his purpose of provoking and drawing out the enemy by feigning an attack and drawing the cavalry right up to the gates. This same cavalry encounter provided a favorable excuse for the pretense of flight. As the cavalry pretended to waver over whether to fight or flee, the infantry yielded; at that moment the enemy poured out, clogging the gates, and smashed through the Roman line, and in their rage to press the attack and pursuit they were sucked into the ambush. Instantly the Romans sprang the trap and attacked the enemy's flank. The movement forward of the standards from the camp of those stationed as guards caused additional alarm for the men of Fidenae who were threatened with multiple terrors. They turned in flight even before Romulus and his mounted fellow riders could wheel their horses about; they headed back to their town in much greater disarray than the fugitives who had a little earlier pretended flight, except theirs was a true flight. But they did not manage to escape their enemy; hot on their backs before the gates could be barred against them, the Romans broke through as if the two armies rushed in as one body.

(15) The spirit for war inflamed the Veientines and spread by a contagion from Fidenae, provoked also by their kinship, for the people of Fidenae were also Etruscans. Their proximity intensified their feeling that Roman arms would be readied against all of Rome's neighbors. They made an incursion—more like a raid than an act of war—into Roman territory. They pitched no camp, but after raiding the fields and carrying off their loot, they returned to Veii without waiting around for the enemy's army to appear. The Romans, on the other hand, not coming upon the enemy in the fields, crossed the Tiber, and stationed their army, ready and eager for a decisive encounter. When the Veientines heard that the Romans were preparing camp and were about to advance on the city, they went out to confront them, thinking it was better to decide the issue on the battle field than to be shut in, under siege, and fighting from the rooftops and walls. King Romulus used no special stratagem, rather he employed force, winning solely by the raw power of his veteran army. After he routed the enemy and pursued them to their walls, he abstained from an attack upon the city because it had been fortified with battlements and was a site especially easy to defend. He, therefore, marched back to lay waste their fields more from revenge rather than from a desire for plunder. This calamity, coupled with their defeat, compelled the Veientines to send diplomats to Rome to sue for peace. They had to pay reparations of part of their cultivated land and they were granted a treaty of one hundred years.[40]

40: the wars with Fidenae and Veii are apocryphal, set in the period of Romulus to account for a much later rivalry.

These, in sum, were the achievements accomplished at home and in military affairs during Romulus' rule. None of them were inconsistent with the belief in his divine origin or the divinity attributed to him after his death, not the heart he showed in recovering his grandfather's kingdom, not his program in founding his city or in strengthening it by war and in time of peace. It was clear that due to him the city's success and energy were to produce an untroubled peace for forty years. But he was better liked by the plebeians than by the patricians, and was dearest and best loved of all in the hearts of the soldiers. He kept as his bodyguard both in time of war and in peace an armed squad of three hundred whom he called the "Swift."[41]

(16) These were the immortal exploits of Romulus. As he was reviewing the troops in an assembly in the Campus Martius near the marsh of Capra, a sudden storm arose amid crackling lightning and clapping thunder and covered him in a cloud so thick that it screened him from the sight of those assembled. At that point Romulus was no longer upon the earth. When the stormy period passed to clear and serene skies, the Roman soldiery soon recovered from their shock. But then they noticed that the king's throne was empty. At first they readily trusted the senators who had been standing next to him when they declared that he had been snatched on high by a whirlwind. Nonetheless, as if thunderstruck by a fear of being orphaned, for some time they lingered in sorrow and silence. Then, after a few individuals began the acclaim, everybody together hailed him as god, born of a god, as king, and as father of the city Rome; they prayed for his continuous favor to be always gracious and to protect his own children. Even at that time, though, there were a few, I believe, who secretly maintained that the senators had ripped him apart with their bare hands; this story too, although it remains very obscure, has become part of the tradition; their intense awe and admiration for the man ennobled the other story. Indeed, the measured action of a single man added credibility to the situation. For, when the citizenry was distracted by the loss of the king and embittered against the senators, Proculus Iulius,[42] a man, so the record says of authority on various weighty matters, addressed the assembly. "Citizens," he exclaimed, "today at the crack of dawn Romulus, the father of his own city, descended from heaven and presented himself in front of me. I stood, shocked and in awe, praying that he permit me to look upon his face; 'Go,' he responded, 'announce to the Romans that the gods ordain that my Rome be capital of the world. Let them cultivate the military ethic, know, and teach to their children that no human power can resist Roman arms.' When he said this, he ascended on high." It is a wonder

---

41: these *celeres* were cavalrymen of Romulus' army.
42: from other authors we learn that this Proculus Iulius was a farmer from Alba Longa.

how much credibility they gave to his account, and to what degree the assurance of immortality comforted the people and army for their loss of Romulus.

(17) A greedy struggle for power inflamed the passion of the senators. Because no single man had distinguished himself in the new state, it had not yet come down to a competition between individuals. Instead, a rivalry of racial strains defined the dispute. Those of Sabine origin wanted a king chosen from their body because there had been no sovereign of their stock after the death of Tatius and they felt they would lose any hold on royal power even though they shared equal rights. The old-timers among the Romans regarded the thought of any foreign king with contempt. Despite the factional divisions, however, they all desired there be a king, inasmuch as they had yet to experience the sweetness of liberty. But then a state of panic came over the senators: the state was without a structure of command, the army was lacking a leader, and many of the neighboring cities felt resentful—just the right conditions for an attack from the outside. Therefore, they decided there should be some head but no one was disposed to yield to anyone else. So the one hundred senators grouped themselves into ten decades and appointed one individual to represent each decade and wield power. These ten governed, but only one at one time had the trappings of power and the escort of lictors. After a period of five days his power ended and passed to each one in rotation. For a year there was a lapse of kingship and that interval was called the *"interregnum,"* a term used even now. The people began to grumble that their servitude had multiplied exponentially, that instead of one master they now had one hundred; it was evident that they would now no longer submit to any power except to that of a king, and only if they elected him. When the senators perceived the movement of events, they thought it best to offer on their own what they most likely would lose. In that way they obtained the favor of the people by granting them the utmost power so as to surrender no more privileges than they reserved for themselves. For they decreed that the people's choice of a king would only be validated if the senate ratified it by their authority. Although its power had been diminished, the same prerogative in the passing of laws and voting for magistrates operates even today: that is, before the people vote, the senators ratify it even when the result of the election is in doubt. On that occasion the *interrex* convened an assembly and addressed it: "May your choice be good, prosperous, and blessed; citizens, choose your king. The city fathers have decided, if you elect a worthy successor of Romulus, the senate will ratify him." The people were very pleased; unwilling to be judged as surpassed in generosity, they resolved and voted that the senate decide who would be king.

(18) In those days Numa Pompilius[43] was a man distinguished by his

---

43: the name "Numa Pompilius" is Etruscan as are the formulae and institutions attributed to him.

sense of justice and religiosity; he lived at Cures, Sabine country, a very
learned man, so far as anyone could be in that period, in both divine
and human law. As the teacher of his learning—because no other name
has come down to us—some claim (falsely) Pythagoras of Samos. For
it is commonly agreed that Servius Tullius was the king of Rome some
one hundred years later when groups of young men thronged around
Pythagoras to study philosophy in the southern most part of Italy near
Metapontum, Heraclea, and Croton.[44] Even if he were contemporary of
Numa, how could his reputation from that area have reached the Sabines?
In what common language did he instruct anyone desiring to learn? Who
protected this single person as he traveled among so many people different in language and customs? I believe, however, that Numa's natural
temperament tempered his virtuous qualities and that he was trained
not so much in foreign skills as in that austere and rigorous discipline
of the old-time Sabines, whom no others rival in incorruptible morals.
When the Roman senators learned that the name of Numa had been put
forward, they thought that, if he assumed the throne, then power would
shift to the Sabines. Nevertheless, no one ventured to present himself,
or any member of his faction, or any colleague, or, indeed, any citizen to
contest against that man. Therefore, unanimously they voted to proffer
the kingship to Numa. He was summoned to the city, whereupon he
ordered that the gods be consulted on his behalf just as Romulus took
the auspices in the founding of the city and in assuming royal power.
So, an augur, who from then on as a sign of respect retained that priesthood from the state in perpetuity, led Numa to the citadel and sat him
on a stone facing south. This augur then covered his head and took a
seat to his left holding in his right hand a knot-free crooked staff, called
the *lituus*. Then looking out over the city and countryside, he prayed to
the gods and marked out the celestial regions from east to west and
declared the section to the south the "right" and to the north the "left."
In his mind he fixed a point opposite to him as far as the eyes could
carry; then he transferred the staff to his left hand, put his right hand
on Numa's head, and made the following prayer: "Father Jupiter, if it is
ordained that this man, Numa Pompilius, whose head I am touching, be
king of Rome, make it clear to us by a sure sign within the parameters I
have traced." He explicitly detailed the omens he wanted to be sent, and
when they were duly sent, Numa was declared king, and afterwards he
descended from the sanctified area.

(19) As soon as he gained royal power, Numa at once prepared
to endow the new city, founded by the violence of arms, with justice,
fresh laws, and religious ceremonies, for he perceived that the people
could not accustom themselves to these institutions in the face of war

44: Pythagoras lived and practiced at both Croton and Metapontum. His influence remained strong in the Greek South.

nor tame their spirit by warfare. And thinking that their fierce passion
had to be assuaged by the disuse of their military weapons, he built a
temple to Janus at the foot of the Argiletum[45] as an indicator of peace
and war. If opened, it indicated that the city was in a state of war; if
closed, it meant that all the peoples about accepted terms of peace. Only
twice since the rule of Numa has it been closed, once in the consulship of Titus Manlius at the end of the First Punic war,[46] and secondly,
which the gods have granted our generation to see, after the campaign
at Actium when the emperor Caesar Augustus brought peace on land
and sea. Numa closed the temple after first winning over the minds
and hearts of the neighboring peoples with treaties of alliances. Worries
about dangers from abroad were mitigated, but, to prevent luxury and
leisure dulling their minds that had been occupied in constant fear of
the enemy and in military training, he thought to instill in them a fear
of the gods as the most effective measure for the populace, uncivilized
and crude in those days of yore. Whereas it was impossible to penetrate
their minds without inventing a miracle, he pretended to have nightly
visitations with the goddess Egeria; it was her advice which prompted
him to establish the holy rites most agreeable to the gods and to install
the priests proper to each deity. First he divided the year into twelve
months in accordance with the revolutions of the moon.[47] But, since each
lunar month does not quite give thirty days and some days are lacking
in the completion of the circuit of a year, he inserted intercalary months
and structured it so that in the twentieth year the cycle of all the years
would be terminated and the days would correspond to that set position
of the sun from which they had started. Next, he established unpropi-
tious and propitious days on which occasionally it would be useful that
no public business be conducted.

   (20) He then directed his attention to the appointing of priests, although he himself performed most of the sacred rites, especially those
which now belong to the High Priest of Jupiter.[48] Yet, since he thought
that in a warlike society more kings would turn out to be like Romulus
than Numa, and that they would personally be leading the campaigns,
to prevent the neglect of the sacrificial duties of the king's office he appointed a high priest to Jupiter, a permanent priesthood. He honored
him with distinguished robes and a kingly curule chair. In addition, he
designated two more high priests, one to Mars, the second to Quirinus;
for Vesta he chose virgin priestesses, a cult deriving from Alba and not

---

45: the main approach from the northeast into the forum.
46: Titus Manlius Torquatus was consul in 235; Aulus Manlius Torquatus may be
    meant because he was consul at the conclusion of the First Punic War in 241.
47: the introduction of a twelve-month calendar was brought about by the
    Etruscans.
48: the High Priest is called a *flamen*; that of Jupiter, *flamen dialis*.

at all foreign to the progenitors of the founder. In order to maintain a constant number of priestesses for the holy shrine, he paid them a stipend from public funds, and endowed them with the sanctity and reverence of virginity and other religious prerogatives. He also enlisted twelve Salii, priests to Mars Gradivus, and invested them with a distinctive embroidered tunic and over it a bronze breastplate. He accorded to them the right to carry the divine shields, called *ancilia*, and to move through the city chanting their hymns to the triple time of their ritual dance. Then he chose one of the senators, Numa Marcius,[49] the son of Marcus, to be head priest, and ascribed to him the regulations, written out and fully annotated, for all the rituals, such as the species of sacrificial victims, the days proper for observances, the temples designated for sacrifices, the source of the money to pay for all expenses incurred. All other rituals, public and private, he subjected to the decisions of the Head Priest[50] so that the common people could have someone to consult and in order to prevent muddling of divine law through the neglect of ancestral rites and the adoption of foreign practices. The same priest was to teach the ceremonies of the gods on high as well as the correct funeral rites, the appeasing of dead spirits, and also the portents heralded by lightning or some other sighted omen which were to be accepted as such and performed. To elicit the will of the gods he dedicated an altar to Jupiter Elicius on the Aventine and consulted the god by augury as to what omens he should recognize and adopt.[51]

(21) Thinking about and attending to these matters diverted the entire population from violence and arms; their minds were occupied both with something to ponder and with the constant attention to the gods. It seemed to them that the divinity of the gods on high participated in human affairs and had imbued all their hearts with such religious piety that good faith and the sanctity of oaths governed the state more than laws and punishments. While Romans themselves emulated the king as the unique example of good character, the bordering peoples, who previously believed that Rome was not a city positioned in their midst, but an armed camp stationed to threaten the peace, were induced to such reverence that they considered it a sacrilege to do violence against a state so totally involved in the worship of the gods.

There was a grove where in its center a constant spring, arising out of a shaded grotto, trickled and watered. Here Numa often traversed without witnesses to meet, as it were, his goddess. So, he made this grove

49: the praenomen (first name) is attributed to the fact that the father, Marcus, claimed kinship with Numa. The son named here married Numa's daughter Pompilia and was the father of Ancus Marcius.

50: the priest here is the Pontifex Maximus.

51: the cult of Jupiter Elicius (the Elicitor) was set up on the Aventine Hill to procure rain via a ceremony of a "rain-stone."

sacred to the Camenae, Italic muses, because, as he said, meetings took place there with his partner Egeria.[52] He instituted an annual worship to Good Faith[53] and he ordered that flamens, high priests, be transported to her shrine in a covered carriage drawn by two horses, where they would perform the divine rites with their hands wrapped up to their fingers, a sign that Good Faith must be religiously observed and that she made her sacred home in the right hands of men. He initiated many other rites and places for performing sacrifices which the priests called the Argei.[54] But of all his accomplishments the greatest was that throughout his entire reign he safeguarded the peace as strongly as his kingdom. Thus, the two successive kings each expanded and promoted the state, each in his own way, the first by war, the second by peace. Romulus ruled for thirty-seven years and Numa for forty-three. The city not only was strong but also disciplined in the arts both of war and of peace.

(22) At Numa's death the Roman state reverted to an *interregnum*; then the people voted and senators ratified as king Tullus Hostilius, grandson of that Hostilius who had been prominent in the battle against the Sabines at the foot of the citadel; he was very different from the late king and even more warlike than Romulus. His age, his strength, and his grandfather's glory fired his mind; he believed that the state was becoming senile because of the peace, and he looked everywhere for a pretext to stir up war. It just so happened that some Roman country people rustled cattle from Alban territory (at that time Gaius Cluilius held power in Alba), and some Albans reciprocated with a raid on Roman fields. Each side almost simultaneously sent diplomats to seek redress. Tullus had instructed his team that they negotiate nothing until they had executed his orders; he was convinced that the Alban ruler would refuse his demands, and, thus, he could righteously declare war. The Albans handled the diplomacy carelessly; welcomed and entertained graciously and kindly by Tullus, they celebrated the king's dinner too freely. Meanwhile, the Romans had already sought redress, then, after the Alban leader refused restitution, declared war, to commence in thirty days. The Roman envoys returned to make their report to Tullus who at that point empowered the Alban ambassadors to declare the purpose of their diplomacy. Unaware of all the events, at first they spent their time in making apologies, then stated that they were loathe to say anything disagreeable to Tullus, but were compelled by orders to speak out: their mission was to seek restitution, and if they were denied it, they were under orders to declare war. To this Tullus replied, "Tell your king that the Roman king calls the gods to witness which of the two peoples first

52: the Camenae and Egeria were divinities of springs reputedly from Aricia.
53: the cult to Good Faith (*Fides*) was not inaugurated until the third century BCE.
54: not much is known of this religious priesthood.

spurned the other's appeal for redress and dismissed the ambassadors, and to inflict upon that people all the disasters of this war."

(23) The Alban diplomats repeated these words in Alba. Both sides began preparing for war with all possible resource, a conflict that was the closest thing to civil war, one almost between fathers and sons, for both were of Trojan stock, since Lavinium derived from Troy and Alba in turn from Lavinium, and the Romans came from the line of Alban kings. The issues of the war, however, made the conflict pitiable because there was no pitched battle and only the buildings of one city toppled; in the end the two peoples fused into one. The Albans with a huge army made the first foray into Roman territory, pitching and entrenching their camp not more than five miles from the city. For many centuries this trench carried the name "Cluilius' moat," from the name of the Alban leader, until trench and name vanished over time. Cluilius, the Alban king, died in this camp, upon which the Albans designated Mettius Fufetius dictator.[55] Meanwhile, Tullus, particularly invigorated by the death of the king, kept asserting that the mighty power of the gods would take vengeance upon everyone bearing the name of Alban, and it was already begun in the case of their chief, for their sacrilegious war. After by-passing the enemy's camp at night, he proceeded straight into Alban country with a force ready to attack. This turn of events aroused Mettius from his headquarters. After leading his troops as close as possible to his enemy, he ordered a legate sent ahead to report to Tullus that he thought they ought to have a parley before active combat, and that, if Tullus agreed to meet with him, he was very confident that he would offer something important to both the Roman and Alban interests. Tullus did not reject the request out of hand, but in the event the discussions came to nothing, he led out his men and drew them up in ranks. The Albans also grouped into formation. As both sides stood drawn up in battle array, the two leaders, with a few officers, marched forward in between the two forces. The Alban Mettius began: "The wrongs and the refusal to make restitution of property as detailed in our treaty I seem to recall, having heard our king Cluilius say were the cause of this conflict; and I have no doubt, Tullus, that you, too, assert the same. But if the truth be spoken and not glib arguments, it is the lust for power that incites two related neighboring peoples to war. I make no interpretation whether rightly or wrongly: that was the consideration of him who undertook the war. As for me, the Albans have chosen me to conduct the campaign and I'd like to make a little friendly suggestion: as you are acutely aware, the Etruscan state encircles us, and particularly you, who are so much nearer. Their power on land is extensive and on sea even more so. Keep in mind that, as soon as you give the signal for battle, the Etruscans will

---

55: the name "Mettius" is a Latinization of an Oscan designation of the chief magistrate (*meddix*).

be watching our two armies, poised to attack us, who are weary and exhausted from fighting, victor and loser alike. Therefore, for heaven's sake, since we are not content with genuine liberty and are heading to the uncertain roll of the dice to determine control or slavery, let us find some way by which we can decide the issue of which people will rule the other without much slaughter, without much blood on both groups." Tullus was not at all displeased with the idea, although he was much more warlike by nature and confident of victory. As both sides were searching for a plan, mere chance provided the solution.

(24) It just so happened that in each of the armies were triplets, not unlike each other in age and physical strength. It is generally agreed that they had the names Horatii and Curiatii, and their history is one of the most noble of ancient times. Yet, despite a story so illustrious, there persists the question of their names: to which people belong the Horatii and to which the Curiatii. Historians make claims for both sides; however, I find that the majority of sources say that the Horatii were Roman and I am inclined to follow them. To these triplets the king proposed that each set fight for their own country and that rule would go to the surviving victor.[56] There was no objection. The time and the place were agreed upon. But before the engagement the Romans and Albans ratified a treaty with the following provisions: that the citizens whose champions won this contest would master the other nation in the peace settled by the fight. Different treaties are drafted with different stipulations, but the method always remains the same. In the oldest treaty that we have in our archives, we learn of the following procedure: the *fetial* priest asked king Tullus, "Do you bid me, my king, to fashion a treaty with the plenipotentiary of the Alban people?" When Tullus so ordered, he continued: "Then I demand from you, my king, the clump of pure grass." The king responded: "Gather it pure." The *fetial* priest then brought from the citadel an undefiled, fresh clump of grass and next asked the king: "My king, do you empower me, the king's ambassador, and sanction my sacred emblems and my companions to be spokesman for the Roman people of the Quirites?" The king replied: "I hereby grant it without prejudice to me and to the Roman people of the Quirites." The *fetial* priest was one Marcus Valerius who made Spurius Fusius the plenipotentiary priest by touching his head and hair with the grass. The empowered representative was bound to vow the oath, that is, to sanctify the treaty, and he performed it in a long litany, whose complete metrical form it is not worthwhile here to repeat. But then he recited the stipulations and chanted: "Hear me, O Jupiter; hear me, spokesman of the Alban people; and *you*, hear me, Alban people. As the conditions of

---

56: the battle of champions for power is paralleled in numerous legends throughout the world. Livy structures his story with the embedded account of the legalistic making of a treaty by *fetial* priests.

the compact, first to last, have been openly read from these wax tablets without malice aforethought, and they have been most clearly understood here today, the Roman people will not be the first to veer from these terms. But if it will be the first to swerve by public consent or with malice aforethought, then on that very day, O Jupiter, strike the Roman people as I now on this day strike this pig and do so with much greater force, as it is in your strength and power." As soon as Spurius uttered this, he struck the pig with a flint. Through their leader and their own priests the Albans in a similar manner performed their own litany and administered their own oath.

(25) Just after the treaty was ratified, as it was agreed, the six young men took up arms. The fellow soldiers of each side were cheering them on, reminding them that their ancestral gods, their fatherland, their parents, all their fellow citizens at home, and all their comrades in the army would be watching their swords and their courage. Thus, they proceeded to the area between the two drawn up lines, fired up by their natural temperament and inspired by the encouraging shouts. The two armies were stationed in front of their respective camps. They were free of immediate danger, yet very tense since supremacy was at stake, dependent upon the courageous valor or the luck of so few. Excited and on tenterhooks, they directed their attention to the unpleasing spectacle. The signal was given, weapons were drawn, the sets of the three young men, like battle lines in action, charged with the passions of mighty armies. It was not the danger planted in their minds, but the thought of national supremacy or slavery and the future fate of their country they would be settling. The instant they met, shields clanged, blazing swords flashed; a hair-raising tremor gripped the spectators, and as neither side's hopes were dashed, they could hardly speak or breathe. They engaged in hand-to-hand combat; visible to all were the movements of the bodies, the swishes of swords, the flash of shields, and gory wounds. Then two of the Romans collapsed, expiring one atop the other; the three Albans were wounded. The Alban army raised shouts of joy at the death of the Romans; on the other hand, the Roman troops had abandoned all hope, but not their anxiety, for they were almost without life themselves anticipating the dilemma of their one fighter surrounded by the three Curiatii. But he was uninjured. Although alone no match for the three, one on one he was most eager for the battle. Therefore, to divide their attack he took to his heels, believing that each one would pursue him as the wounded body of each would allow. He had run quite a distance from the spot where the earlier combat took place; looking back, he saw them strung out with one hot on his back. He wheeled and rushed him in a direct assault; the Alban army shouted to the other Curiatii to help their brother, but Horatius had already killed his enemy and triumphantly was speeding on to face his second opponent. Then with a roar such as partisans shout at an unhoped-for swing in momentum,

the Romans cheered on their man, and he eagerly advanced to finish off the battle. He killed the second of the Curiatii before the other, who was not too far away, could catch up. Now the competition was equal, one fighter per side left, yet in confidence and energy not at all evenly matched. Horatius was unscathed and flushed by his double success; he rushed into the third encounter. But the other youth, exhausted by the wound and his running, was dragging a weary body. His spirit was broken as well because before his eyes had been the slaughter of his brothers and now he had to face a triumphant enemy. It was not much of a fight. The exultant Roman shouted out: "Two I have already dedicated to the shades of my brothers; I am about to offer the third to the cause of this war, that Roman may rule Alban." Into the throat of his foe who could barely hold up his shield he plunged his sword and stripped him where he lay. The Romans cheered and jubilantly welcomed Horatius with a joy all the greater, as the fight had produced so much despair. Both sides turned to the burial of their champions, but with different feelings, inasmuch as one side was exalted to rule, while the other was brought under foreign domination. The graves are still existent where each one fell, the two Romans in one spot, nearer Alba, the three Albans toward Rome, but separated just as they had done battle.

(26) Before they left the field, Mettius asked Tullus, in accordance with the treaty, what were his orders; Tullus responded that he should keep the fighting men in arms and that he himself would be employing them, if war with the people of Veii were to erupt. So then the armies marched home. Horatius led the procession carrying his triple spoils; he was met in front of the Capena gate by his virgin sister who had been engaged to one of the Curiatii. When she recognized on the shoulders of her brother her fiance's cloak which she herself had made, she undid her hair and, crying, she called out the name of her dead fiancé. His sister's outburst of grief during his triumph and amid so much public rejoicing enraged the volatile young man. He drew his sword and, at the same time that he was rebuking the girl, he stabbed her through. "Take your untimely love to your lover, as you have forgotten your dead brothers and the one who still lives, and have forgotten your fatherland! So perish every Roman woman who laments for an enemy!" It was an horrendous sight that the senators and people witnessed, but his recent service mitigated the deed. Nevertheless, he was hailed before the king for trial, but the king did not want to be perceived as the sponsor of a severe and unpopular decision and subsequent punishment. So he called an assembly of the people and made the following announcement: "In accordance with the law I hereby appoint duumvirs[57] to decide upon the

---

57: a panel of two men who served as state-prosecutors of high treason. They conducted the case. Livy is again projecting back to monarchial times an early Republican institution.

case of treason against Horatius." The language of the law was very stern; it read: "Let the *duumvirs* judge treason; if he appeals to the people the *duumvirs'* decision, let the appeal be tried; if the decision of the *duumvirs* is upheld, let the bailiff veil the defendant's head, rope him to a fruitless tree, then whip him either within or outside the sacred precinct of the city." The *duumvirs* were appointed in accordance with this law, and thinking that they could not acquit even an innocent person by those provisions of the law, they convicted Horatius, whereupon, one of them intoned: "Publius Horatius, I convict you of treason. Bailiff, go, tie his hands." The bailiff had already come forward and was on the point of tying the knot when Horatius, prompted by Tullus, who was a liberal interpreter of the law, said, "I appeal." Therefore, the people took up the case of appeal. In that trial many were deeply influenced by Publius Horatius, the father, asserting that he judged his daughter had been justly killed, and if it had been otherwise, he would have punished his son by the right of the father. He then pleaded with them not to render him childless when just a little before they had seen him a father of an outstanding family. In the meantime, embracing the young man and pointing to the spoils of the Curiatii, fixed in that spot which now carries the name of "Horatius' Spears," he said, "This man, citizens, you saw just recently arrayed, striding triumphantly to cheers, can you bear seeing him bound beneath a fork, whipped and tortured? Even the eyes of the Albans themselves could scarcely endure such a foul sight. You, go ahead, bailiff, tie up the hands which moments ago wielded weapons and brought empire to the Roman people. Yes, go ahead, veil the head of this city's liberator, bind him to a barren tree, whip him inside the sacred precinct, right here with the spears and spoils of the enemy, or outside of the sacred precinct by the graves of the Curiatii. For where can you take him without the honors he has won, vindicating him from so shameful a punishment?" The people could not withstand either the tears of the father or the courage of Horatius, unmatched in every danger; they acquitted him more out of admiration for his valor than for the justice of his cause. Yet, in order to cleanse the flagrant killing with some sort of expiation, they ordered the father to pay a fine to purge his son. So, he made some sacrifices of atonement which from that day on were handed down through the family of Horatii, and erecting a small beam across the street, he sent his young son under the yoke, as it were, with his head covered. The beam, often restored at public expense, is extant today. They call it "Sister's Beam" after Horatia whose tomb was constructed out of squared stone at the very spot where she was struck and fell.

(27) Peace with Alba did not last long.[58] The resentment of the masses over the fact that Mettius had entrusted the fate of the state to three

---

58: this begins the account of war, the treachery and gruesome death of Mettius Fufetius, and the destruction of Alba Longa.

young soldiers punctured the leader's weak character. And since honorable policy had not been successful, he turned to evil to regain popularity with the people. Therefore, just as earlier he had pursued peace in time of war, so now in time of peace he sought war. As he observed that his citizenry had more courage than military power, he stirred up the other nearby peoples to declare and wage war openly, while under the guise of being an ally, he harbored betrayal in his heart. The men of Fidenae, a Roman colony, and of Veii, who were co-conspirators of his design, were incited to take up arms and go to war on the understanding that the Albans would desert to their side. Fidenae openly revolted; thereupon, Tullus summoned Mettius and his army from Alba and led out his own forces against the enemy. When he crossed the Anio river and pitched camp at the confluence of Anio and Tiber, he learned that between that spot and Fidenae the Veientine army had crossed the Tiber. These troops, in formation along the river, formed the right wing; on the left nearer the mountains the men of Fidenae were stationed. Tullus posted his men against the Veientines, and arranged the Albans opposite the ranks of the Fidenates. The Alban leader had no more courage than he had loyalty. Not daring either to make his stand or openly to desert, he gradually and cautiously withdrew toward the mountains. Then when he reckoned that he had gotten close enough to them, he led up his entire force, and, as he wavered, he deployed his men in ranks in order to temporize. For it was his plan to pivot his force to the side that fortune was favoring. At first the Romans, who were stationed next to the Albans and perceived their own flank exposed by the withdrawal of their allies, were dumbfounded. Then a cavalryman quickly rode off to announce the Alban retreat to the king. In this critical situation Tullus vowed to appoint twelve Salii priests and to dedicate shrines to Pallor and Panic.[59] So that the enemy could overhear, he rebuked the rider in a loud voice, ordering him to re-enter the fray and exclaiming that there was no need for alarm; it was by his command that the Alban army was circling around to attack the exposed rear of the troops of Fidenae. He also ordered the cavalry to raise their spears. This stratagem screened a large part of the Roman infantry from viewing the withdrawal of the Alban army; but for those who did see it, believing what they had heard the king say encouraged them to fight even more fiercely. Terror now gripped the enemy. The Fidenates had heard the king's distinct voice and a majority of them understood Latin because Romans had long settled among them. And so, they retreated to prevent being cut off from their town by a sudden charge of Albans from the hills. Tullus pressed the attack, first routing the wing of the soldiers of Fidenae, then remounting a fiercer assault against the Veientine army unnerved by the panic of

---

59: some locate these shrines on the Quirinal Hill where there were the headquarters of the Salii Collini near the Temple of Quirinus.

their allies. Unable to withstand the attack, they scattered, their flight checked only by the barrier of the river at their backs. There, where they fell back in flight, some shamefully threw away their arms and jumped blindly into the river, while others, who wavered on the banks deliberating whether to flee or fight, were surprised and captured. Never before had there been a bloodier battle for the Romans.

(28) The Alban army, reduced to being a spectator of the battle, at last marched down into the plain. Mettius congratulated Tullus on his decisive defeat of the enemy; to Mettius Tullus gave a kind response. After a prayer of success he ordered the Albans to link up their camp to the Roman one, for he was in the process of readying a purificatory sacrifice on the morrow. At first light, when everything was prepared according to custom, he summoned each army to a joint assembly. Heralds, starting from the outermost tents summoned the Albans first. Intrigued by the new experience, they stood close by the king to hear the Roman leader deliver his address. The Roman troops by prearranged order were armed and arrayed around them, and the captains had been given the mission of executing orders without delay. Tullus then began: "Romans, if ever before in war you had cause to give thanks first to the immortal gods and secondly to your valor, it was yesterday's battle. For not only did you do battle with the enemy, but also, in a fight much more serious and dangerous, with the betrayal and treachery of allies. I don't want you to have a false impression: I did *not* order the Albans to retreat to the mountains, no, that was not my command, but a stratagem and pretence on my part ordered so that you would not discern you were being deserted. I wanted you to keep your mind on the battle, and to make you think that the enemy, believing they were being surrounded from the rear, would submit to panic and would flee. My accusation of guilt does not belong to all Albans: they simply followed their general, just as you would have done, if I had ordered the formation to swing around anywhere I wanted. Yon Mettius is the perpetrator of this march, yes, Mettius, the contriver of this war, Mettius, the breaker of the treaty between Roman and Alban. No one will dare to do such things again, if I exact now a penalty upon this man which will serve as a distinctive example to all mankind." When the armed captains surrounded Mettius, the king continued what he had begun: "My intention, men of Alba,—and may it be positive, propitious, and prosperous to the Roman people, to me, and to you—is to transfer the entire Alban population to Rome, to extend citizenship to the people, to choose a senate from the nobles, to make a single city, a single government. As once from one people the Alban state was divided into two, so now may it be reunited." Hearing this, the Alban youth, unarmed and hemmed in by armed soldiers, notwithstanding their differing sentiments, and compelled by a shared fear, kept silent. At that point Tullus continued: "Mettius Fufetius, if you could learn loyalty and abide by the words of a treaty,

I'd let you live for me to provide you instruction. But since your moral character is incurable, then by your punishment you will teach the human race to hold the very things you violated as sacred. Whereas just a short while ago you had a mind divided between the cause of Fidenae and of Rome, so now you will suffer your body to be divided into two parts." He then had two four-horse chariots wheeled in and tied Mettius spread-eagled to the chariots; then he slapped the horses, driving them in opposite directions; the limbs of the ripped apart body clung to the ropes. Everyone turned his eyes from such a disgusting sight. That was the first and last time that that punishment, a type that ignores the laws of humanity, was executed among the Romans. In other cases we may boast that no other people chose milder forms of punishment.[60]

(29) In the meantime, horsemen had been sent on ahead to transfer the Alban population to Rome. Then the infantry was brought in to raze the city. As they entered the city's gates, it was not at all like the tumult or panic that usually accompanies the capture of cities, when gates are breached, or walls smashed with battering-ram, or citadel stormed by force, when the yells of the enemy and the running of armed men, bringing fire and sword, through the city create confusion everywhere. Instead, there was a grim silence and an unspoken sadness that numbed the sensibilities of all there. Because of the shock they lost any power of decision and were unable to collect their thoughts as to what to leave behind, what to carry with them; they kept asking each other's advice, sometimes standing at their doorways, sometimes wandering about, crisscrossing the homes they were to see for the last time. So, when the horsemen began their insistent shouting, bidding them to leave, when they heard the crash of buildings being leveled on the outskirts of town, and when dust, rising from separate regions, like a hovering cloud darkened everything, individuals grabbed what they could and left, abandoning their gods of hearth and home and the very rooms in which they were born and reared. A continuous line of refugees filled the streets, and the sight of so many others sharing their misery brought fresh tears to their eyes; pitiable cries of women were heard, especially when they passed by august temples under armed siege and when they had to abandon their captive gods. After the Albans left the city, the Romans everywhere leveled to the ground all buildings, public and private ones, and in a single hour brought to destruction and ruins the work of the four hundred years of Alba's existence.[61] Under the edict of King Tullus only the temples of the gods were spared.

60: the annals of Roman criminal law and punishment show no other example of this form of punishment.

61: Livy's chronological reckoning of the supposed life of Alba Longa is confused, disagreeing with his own chronology developed in chapter three.

(30) Rome grew with the collapse of Alba and doubled its population and citizens. The Caelian Hill was added to the city; to encourage its habitation Tullus chose this location for his palace and took up residence there from that day forward. The leading men of the Albans he made senators in order to expand the state in that class also, ennobling the following families: the Iulii, Servilii, Quinctii, Geganii, Curiatii, and Cloelii.[62] For this order, which he himself had increased, he built a sanctified structure, a senate house, that down to our fathers' time bore his name: the *curia Hostilia*. In order to strengthen all the orders by some addition from the new people, he then enrolled from the Albans ten squadrons of cavalrymen, replenished the veteran ranks with Alban personnel, and recruited new ones.

With confidence in his fighting strength Tullus declared war against the Sabines, the wealthiest people after the Etruscans at that time and most powerful in men and weapons. Each side had suffered wrongs, and negotiations for restitution proved fruitless. These were said to be the cause of the hostilities. Tullus complained that some Roman businessmen had been arrested at a crowded market near the shrine of Feronia, while the Sabines argued that the Romans earlier had taken and were detaining in Rome refugees who had fled to the sanctuary in the grove. The Sabines had long memories, recalling that Tatius had relocated a portion of their force in Rome, and that the Roman state through the addition of Alban people had recently been expanded. They also began to look around for outside support. Etruria was near by and the closest of the Etruscans were the Veientines. Among them deep resentments left over from the wars attracted volunteers and incited their minds to revolt (money to some vagabonds and poor people also contributed). But no official help was offered and the Veientines—for in others it would be less surprising—honored the sanctity of the treaty agreed on with Romulus.[63] Both sides prepared for war with all their might; the issue seemed to turn on this: which side would attack first. Tullus anticipated everyone by crossing into Sabine territory. A gruesome battle was fought near the "Rogue's Wood" where the Roman forces prevailed, partly because of the strength of the infantry, but chiefly because the cavalry, reinforced by the new recruits, charged against the Sabine ranks and threw them into such confusion that they could not without great loss stand to fight nor extricate themselves by flight.

(31) The Sabines were defeated; Tullus' reign and, in fact, the entire Roman state were basking in glory and wealth when it was reported to

62: these names are of Latin origin but the patrician status of these families cannot go back to the original patrician families instituted by Romulus (cf. chapter 8). Thus, the families are provided an aristocratic Alban background. The prominent listing of the Iulii is a direct compliment to Augustus.
63: refers to the peace outlined in chapter 15.

the king and senate that on mount Alba it had rained stones. Because the story could hardly be believed, a few investigators were sent to look into the prodigy. While they watched, stones, thick from the sky, fell just as balls of hail sweep onto the lands, driven by winds. They also believed that they had also heard a loud voice from the grove on the summit of the mountain intoning Albans to perform sacrifices in the ancestral manner, rites which they had consigned to oblivion as if they had abandoned their gods along with their fatherland. For they either had taken up Roman cults or, enraged at their lot in life, had forsaken, as it usually happens, the worship of the gods. The Romans also, as a result of the same portent, undertook a public festival lasting for nine days; they either obeyed the divine voice from Mount Alba—for that story, too, is part of the tradition—or acted upon the advice of diviners. For sure there remained a yearly rite that, whenever the same portent was proclaimed, the Romans held celebrations for nine days.[64]

Not long afterwards a plague afflicted Rome. In spite of the fact that it caused a reluctance for military service, the bellicose king brooked no respite from armed conflict. He truly believed that young men maintained healthier bodies in military service than in civilian life. But he contracted an illness, slow and lingering, that broke his body as well as that spirit of his, so fierce and proud. Yet he who had thought that nothing was less regal than to condemn the mind to religion, suddenly was spending his life a slave to superstitions great and small, and was imbuing the people with the power of religion. Now people generally were seeking to regain the status of things that had been prevalent under king Numa and believed that their only resource left for their debilitated bodies was to acquire peace and pardon from the gods. Tradition has it that the king, in reading the commentaries of Numa, came upon certain occult sacrifices offered to Jove Elicius, and, hidden from everyone, devoted himself to the sacrifices.[65] But, he did not initiate or perform the rite properly, and, therefore, failed to obtain any divine manifestation; instead, in anger by his incorrect religious methodology, Jupiter thunderbolted him and he was consumed with fire in his house. Tullus, renowned in war, reigned for thirty-two years.

(32) At Tullus' death the government, as was the custom from the very beginnings, reverted to the control of the senators who named an interim king. He chaired the election at which the people chose Ancus Marcius as king, and which was ratified by the senate. This man, Ancus Marcius, was the grandson of Numa Pompilius, born of his daughter. He began his rule very mindful of the grandfather's glorious success and believing that the last administration, outstanding in other mat-

64: the reference is to the "Latin Festival" which the Latin communities celebrated with a sacrifice to Jupiter on Mount Alba.
65: see chapter 20 and note # 51.

ters, but in one respect had not prospered because of the neglect of religious observances and the improper conduct of rituals. He thought that to perform the public rites as Numa had established them was the most reverential thing to do; consequently, he appointed a pontiff to copy all the rituals recorded in the commentaries of the king and to post them in public on a white tablet. Citizens desirous of peace and neighboring city-states had a hope that the new king would imitate the character and institutions of his grandfather. Therefore, the Latins, who had ratified a treaty with Rome when Tullus was in power, were emboldened: they made a raid into Roman territory. When the Romans sought restitution, they returned an arrogant reply, believing that the Roman king would sit idly by and act the role of king at shrines and altars. Ancus had a two-sided nature, reminiscent of both Numa and Romulus. Besides, he believed that in his grandfather's reign peace among a young and belligerent people had been more necessary, and that he would not have an easy time attaining unimpaired the peaceful conditions that Numa had achieved. His patience was being tested, and all he received for the test was contempt; the times, too, were more fit for a king Tullus than a Numa. As Numa had instituted religious cults in peace, so Ancus wanted to produce ceremonies for war, feeling that wars should not only be conducted, but that there should also be a ritual by which they were declared. So, he copied from the ancient Aequiculi people[66] the formula (which the *fetials* now possess) by which redress was demanded.[67] A diplomat goes to the borders of those from whom redress is demanded. He covers his head with a cap—it must be wool[68]—and says: "Hear, O Jupiter; hear O boundaries of (naming the people involved). Hear O righteousness. I am the official spokesman of the Roman people; I come commissioned with justice and sanctity. Trust my words." He then proceeds through the litany of demands after which he calls Jove to witness: "If my demand that those men and that property be consigned to me be unjust and impious, let me never be a member of my father's city." He repeats these words, when he crosses the boundary, and the same to whomever he first meets, likewise upon passing through the city gates, and the same, when he has entered the forum, with only a few changes in the wording of the litany and in the form of the oath. If they do not turn over those whom he demands, after thirty-three days—that is the traditional wait—he declares war with the following formula: "Hear, O Jupiter, and you, O Janus Quirinus,

66: another term for the Aequi.
67: this antiquarian ritual had to be drastically changed after Rome expanded beyond its Latin borders. But, Octavian revived it when he declared war on Cleopatra in 32.
68: the *fetials* were forbidden to wear linen. Wool had magical associations because it was the representation of the sacrificial victim.

and all you celestial gods, you gods of the earth, and you gods of the underworld, hear! I call you to witness that this people (here he names whichever it is) is unjust and does not pay just reparation; concerning these matters we will consult the elders in our country, as to how we may obtain justice." This spokesman then returns to Rome for consultation. Immediately the king would begin deliberations with the senators in approximately these words: "As regards the matters, lawsuits, and causes which the plenipotentiary of the Roman people of the Quirites has demanded from the representative of the Ancient Latins and from the people of the Ancient Latins, tell what they have not given back, fulfilled, and redressed, all of which ought to have been given back, fulfilled, and redressed, speak," and addressing whom he would ask for his opinion first, "What do you think?" Then the other man would reply, "I think those things should be sought by a righteous and holy war, and so I consent and vote." The others would be asked by rank; if the majority of the quorum concurred with that opinion, then war was agreed on. It was usual for the fetial to take a spear, tipped with iron or tempered by fire and stained with blood, to the borders of the offending people and in the presence of no fewer than three men of military age to say: "Whereas the peoples of the Ancient Latins and the men of the Ancient Latins have acted against and offended the Roman people of the Quirites, whereas the Roman people of the Quirites have commanded that a state of war now exist with the Ancient Latins, and whereas the senate of the Roman people of the Quirites has voted, consented, and concurred that war be made with the Ancient Latins, therefore, I and the Roman people hereby declare and make war with the peoples of the Ancient Latins and with the men of the Ancient Latins." When he has said this, he would hurl the spear into their territory. In this way satisfaction was demanded from the Latins and war was declared, and later generations have adopted this custom.

(33) Ancus handed over the supervision of the cults to the head priests and other pontiffs. He recruited a new army and set out for Politorium, a Latin city that he captured by force.[69] Following the policy of the previous kings, who enlarged the Roman state by converting enemies to citizens, he transferred the entire population to Rome. The early Romans had settled the Palatine and thereabouts, while the Sabines had occupied the Capitoline and citadel and the Albans dwelt on the Caelian Hill; the Aventine was reserved for the new arrivals. Not much later, new citizens from the captured cities of Tellenae and Ficana[70] were combined with this population. When the Ancient Latins occupied an empty Politorium, a second war was undertaken which offered a convenient excuse for the Romans to destroy the city to prevent it becoming

69: the city of Politorium was located somewhere between Rome and Ostia.
70: these two cities were south of Rome on the way to Ardea.

a constant refuge for enemies. Finally, all the Latin element in the war was forced back to Medullia[71] where a battle raged for some time, and in indecisive fighting victory alternated between the opposing forces. For the city was fortified by battlements and protected by a formidable garrison, and the Latin army from their camp, set upon the open plain, now and again came face to face with the Romans. In the end, exerting all of his troops, Ancus won the battle; then laden with immense spoils, he returned in triumph to Rome. Many thousands of Latins received citizenship and were granted a community near Murcia's Altar,[72] thus joining the Aventine to the Palatine. The Janiculum,[73] too, was annexed, not because there was a lack of space, but so that it would never become a stronghold of the enemy. It was decided not only to fortify it with a wall but also to link it to the city. He eased the traffic between the two areas by constructing the first bridge over the Tiber, the so-called Sublician Bridge. Another project of king Ancus was the Quirites' Trench, a major defense work at places easily accessible. In an already increasing population there was a huge expansion; in such an overpopulated mass of people the distinction between right and wrong became blurred and clandestine crimes were being committed. So, as a terrible deterrent to the growing problem of criminal enterprises, he constructed a prison overlooking the middle of the forum. Under this king the city not only grew but Roman territory and boundaries also expanded. The Maesian Forest[74] was wrested from the Veientines, which extended Roman power all the way to the sea, and at the mouth of the Tiber the city of Ostia was founded and the salt-flats there were worked. In view of the splendid success of military operations, the temple of Jupiter Feretrius was enlarged.

(34) During Ancus' reign Lucumo,[75] an active and very rich man, immigrated to Rome. He was extremely ambitious and had the hope of acquiring an eminent status, the opportunity for which he was denied in Tarquinii, because he was born from foreign stock. He was the son of Demaratus from Corinth, who had been exiled from his home because of political agitation, and who happened to have taken up residence in Tarquinii. There he married and had two sons whose names were Lucumo and Arruns. Lucumo survived his father and inherited all his property, but Arruns died before his father leaving a pregnant wife. The father did not long survive his son. Because Demaratus was unaware that his daughter-in-law was carrying a child, he died leav-

71: the city is usually located north of Rome, near Nomentum.
72: the altar was located in the depression between the Aventine and the Palatine hills.
73: the hill on the right bank of the Tiber overlooking the city.
74: it is unclear where this stretch of woods along the coast lay.
75: from various Etruscan inscriptions we learn that Lucumo means something like 'chief magistrate.'

ing out his grandson in his will. A boy was born after the death of his grandfather, but bequeathed no share of the estate; thus, he was given the name Egerius (i.e. Needy) because of his poverty. Lucumo, on the other hand, the heir of all the property, took pride in his wealth and the marriage with Tanaquil puffed him up even more. For she was an aristocrat by birth and one who—whatever her married life—would not easily endure a humbler life style than that to which she was born. The Etruscans disdained Lucumo as a son of an exile and newcomer, and Tanaquil could not suffer this indignity. Forgetting any native devotion to her fatherland, she fashioned a plan for emigrating from Tarquinii in order to see her husband exalted; to her Rome seemed perfect. Among a new people where all nobility sprang up quickly and depended upon merit there would be a spot for a brave and vigorous man; king Tatius, after all, had been a Sabine; the city summoned Numa to the throne from Cures; Ancus was the offspring of a Sabine mother, and had only one bust of pedigree—that of Numa. She easily convinced her husband, who was desirous of high status and who regarded Tarquinii merely the birthplace of his mother. Therefore, they gathered their belongings and left for Rome. As it happened, they had come to the Janiculum where husband and wife were sitting in their carriage when an eagle spread its wings and gently swooped down and snatched off his cap. Then, with a loud roar he flew off again circling above the carriage, and, as if divinely sent for this purpose, neatly replaced the cap on his head and soared on high. They say that Tanaquil was quite happy; she took this as an omen, as she was a woman skilled in celestial phenomena, like most Etruscans. She embraced her husband and bid him to aspire to a lofty and sublime destiny, prophesying that such a bird came from such a quarter of the sky bringing a message from that god; that the very crown of a man's head meant an omen; that the bird lifted the adornment worn on a human head only to replace it by command of the gods upon the same head. They brought these hopes and thoughts with them as they entered the city. There they bought a house and Lucumo assumed the name of Lucius Tarquinius Priscus. The fact that there was a wealthy newcomer in town attracted the attention of the Romans. His kind words, his courteous hospitality, his generosity, and favors to whomever promoted his position until his reputation reached even the palace. In a brief time, by performing services for the king with liberality and skill, he had parlayed his acquaintance into privileges associated with a close friendship and had participated in deliberations of public and private affairs, of domestic and foreign policy. Passing every test, in the end he was appointed the guardian of the children in the king's will.

(35) Ancus reigned twenty-four years. In the arts of war and peace his fame was unmatched by any previous ruler. His sons had almost reached the age of majority, which spurred Tarquinius to insist ever more vehemently that elections be held as soon as possible to choose a king.

About the time announced, he sent the boys off on a hunting trip. He was the first man to have campaigned for the rule and is said to have delivered a speech expressly composed to curry favor with the populace: in it he argued that he was not setting a precedent in that he was not the first outsider—a situation which could have evoked indignation or shock—but the third to aspire to power; Tatius not only was a foreigner, but an enemy who became king, and Numa, although he knew nothing of the city and was not actively seeking rule, was actually requested to take control; whereas he, as soon as he became a master of his own destiny, had moved to Rome with his wife and all his belongings, and had lived a greater portion of that period of life in which men generally devote themselves to public service in Rome rather than in their own fatherland; nor was he ashamed to have had king Ancus himself as his mentor in domestic and foreign affairs and under whom he had also learned Roman law and Roman religion; and that in deference and duty toward the king he had competed with everybody else, but in generosity toward others the king himself was his only competitor. The things he mentioned were not false; by an overwhelming consensus the Roman people elected him to rule. He was a person otherwise noble, but once in power he finagled his agenda, conducting himself as he had while aspiring to power; and being no less attentive to securing his own rule than to expanding the state, he appointed one hundred men to the senate who were subsequently called the "Fathers of the Lesser Families;" they comprised a faction loyal and supportive of the king who had promoted them to the senate.[76]

His first war he waged against the Latins; he stormed and captured their city of Apiolae.[77] From the booty brought back, more extensive than reports about the war led one to believe, he put on games more opulent and magnificent than any of his predecessors. On that occasion he first marked out the track which now is known as the Circus Maximus.[78] Places were divided and assigned to senators and equestrians where they would each have private seating for themselves; these were called "stands." From seats propped from the ground twelve feet high they watched the events. Horses and boxers, especially imported from Etruria, comprised the entertainment. From then on the games continued to be celebrated annually and were called the Roman or Great Games. The same king also allotted building sites around the forum to private individuals and he built arcades and shops.

76: the "Lesser Families" comprised a large number of Etruscan immigrants to Rome, perhaps to fill the religious priesthoods introduced and expanded by the Etruscans.

77: the site of this Latium town is unknown.

78: the Circus Maximus was constructed in the depression between the Palatine and Aventine Hills.

(36) He was in the process of erecting a stone wall around the city when war with the Sabines interrupted the project. So sudden was the flare-up that the enemy had crossed the Anio before a Roman army could deploy to stop them. At Rome there was panic and the first battle produced no clear victor, with heavy casualties on both sides. When the enemy withdrew their troops to camp, the Romans were provided a respite to renew the war effort. Tarquinius, believing that his forces lacked an adequate cavalry, decided to add to the Ramnes, Titienses, and Luceres,[79] the centuries which Romulus had enlisted, units that were to bear the honor of his name. Romulus had held auspices before he took this action; therefore, a certain Attus Navius,[80] a very distinguished augur at that time, asserted that nothing could be changed nor any innovation instituted before the birds had shown their consent. The king was infuriated by this; tradition has it that in mockery of the art he exclaimed, "Well, OK, you interpreter of the divine, by your augury predict if what I am now thinking can come true." He took the auspices and said that it would surely happen; "OK," the king rejoined, "In my mind I had pondered that you would split a whetstone with a razor. Take the items and perform what your birds portend can happen." The story goes that without a moment's hesitation Navius split the whetstone. A statue of Attus with his head covered was set up at the very spot where this action took place, in the comitium on the steps to the left of the senate house.[81] Tradition also has it that a whetstone was placed in that same spot to serve as a memorial to posterity of the miracle. Auguries and the priesthood dealing with auguries definitely gained so much respect and honor that nothing after that, absolutely nothing, either in foreign or domestic affairs was undertaken without the taking of auspices; assemblies of the people, recruitment of the army, the most vital of public affairs were cancelled, if the birds denied their assent. Tarquinius at that time made no changes in the equestrian centuries, but doubled their number so that the three centuries ended with 1,800 cavalrymen.[82] The recruits enrolled under the original named tribes were called the "secondary" equestrians; because of doubling the number the centuries are now called the "six centuries."

(37) When this branch of the armed forces had been expanded, conflict with the Sabines resumed. Although the Roman army had increased its strength, it was strategic subterfuge that contributed the most to success. Men were sent in secret to gather a huge quantity of wood lying on the banks of the Anio, set it afire, and throw it into the

---

79: see chapter 13 and note # 39.
80: the name is Etruscan.
81: the *comitium*, a large meeting area, was shaped like a theater; seating was arranged in tiers.
82: see chapters 13 and 15 and note # 41.

river. A favoring wind fanned the flames and set the wood ablaze, most of which smashed into boats, clung to piles, and set the bridge on fire. This situation also brought terror to the Sabines during the fighting, and in their rout prevented their escape. Many men escaped the Romans, their enemy, only to perish in the river. Their shields floated down the Tiber to the city where they were recognized, and their recognition made clear the victory almost sooner than the news of it could be reported. Particularly glorious in this battle was the cavalry; stationed on the flanks, and, when the center ranks of the infantry were being driven back, they attacked from both flanks, as the story goes, so vigorously that they stopped the Sabine legions that were pressing hard upon the Roman infantry as they were giving ground, and suddenly put them into flight. Scattered and routed, the Sabines headed for the mountains, but few reached them. The majority, as I mentioned previously, were driven into the river by the cavalry. Thinking to press his success during their panic, Tarquinius sent the loot and prisoners to Rome, and the spoils of the enemy—he had vowed them to Vulcan—he set afire in a huge heap, and then set out leading the army into Sabine territory. Although the Sabines had failed and could not hope to gain better results, nevertheless, because the situation did not allow time for deliberation, they hastily levied soldiers to face the enemy. They were routed again and, with their cause and means practically lost already, they sued for peace.

(38) Collatia and the territory around it, belonging to the Sabines, were taken from them. Egerius, the son of the king's brother, was left in Collatia with a garrison. As I have it, the surrender of the city and its citizens followed a set formula, as follows: the king asked, "Are you the ambassadors and spokesman sent by the people of Collatia to surrender yourselves and the people of Collatia?" "We are." "Do the people of Collatia act under their own authority?" "Yes." "Do you surrender yourselves, the people of Collatia, the city, the lands, water, boundaries, shrines, utensils, all instruments, human and divine, into my power and into the authority of the Roman people?" "We so surrender." "I hereby accept it." When the Sabine War ended, Tarquinius returned to Rome in triumph. He then made war against the Ancient Latins. Nowhere did they come to fight a decisive engagement, instead Tarquinius brought up his armed forces to one town after another and conquered every Latin community, namely: Corniculum, Old Ficulea, Cameria, Crustumerium, Ameriola, Medullia, Nomentum[83] were captured, all towns either of the Ancient Latins or tribes who had defected to the Latins.

From then on Tarquinius undertook operations for peace with a greater intensity and with a more vigorous effort than he had exerted in his military campaigns. As a result, the people lived less restful lives

---

83: all of these towns as well as Collatia lay along the Anio.

at home than they did in military service. He began construction of a stone wall to encircle the city in that section where it was unfortified—a job which had to be postponed because of the Sabine War. The low-lying areas of the city, both around the forum and the other valleys situated between the hills which could not easily carry off the overflow of surface water, he drained by digging sewers on a slope leading to the Tiber. Envisioning the future grandeur of the place, he laid foundations for a temple to Jove on the Capitoline, which he had vowed during the war with the Latins.

(39) In the king's palace at that time there occurred an omen, a wondrous sight and of extraordinary outcome. Tradition notes that the head of young boy, named Servius Tullius, caught fire while he was sleeping, and many people witnessed it. The loud shrieking, produced by so great a wonder, aroused the king and queen. A servant of the household brought water to extinguish the blaze, but he was stopped by the queen, who calmed the uproar and ordered that the boy not be disturbed until he woke up naturally on his own. Soon afterwards, the flame disappeared as he stirred from sleep. At that point Tanaquil led her husband aside and in strict confidence said, "Do you see this boy whom we are bringing up and educating in such a humble way? You can count on it that this child will one day be a light to our varied crises and a shield for the palace in time of distress. Accordingly, let us nourish with all our care the essence of the bringer of great distinction to public affairs and to our own family." From that moment they began to treat the boy as their own son and to educate him in the skills which inspire men to cultivate greatness. It went as heaven willed it. The boy turned out to be of genuine royal character and when Tarquinius was looking for a son-in-law, the king promised his daughter to him because no Roman youth could compare with him in any trait. The conferring upon him of this distinguished honor, no matter the grounds, prevents us from believing that he was born of a slave woman or in his childhood was ever a slave. I am more inclined to follow the opinion of those who maintain that, after Corniculum was captured, Servius Tullius, the leading citizen in that city at that time, was killed, but that his pregnant wife was recognized among the other prisoners and the Roman queen, out of respect for her noble status, rescued her from slavery, and she gave birth in Rome at Tarquinius Priscus' house. Consequently, this act of kindness fostered an intimate bond between the women, and the boy, reared from childhood in the royal household, was well-liked and respected. Yet the fate of his mother, to have fallen into the hands of the enemy after the capture of her native city, encouraged the belief that he was born of a slave.

(40) Almost thirty-eight years had passed since Tarquinius took up the reins of power, and not only the king but also the senators and the people regarded Servius Tullius with the greatest respect. But the two

sons of Ancus had always felt an outrage that they had been cheated and driven out of their father's kingdom by the fraud of their guardian Tarquinius. They considered that Rome was being governed by a complete newcomer, not even from a nearby tribe, and one un-Italian in blood at that.[84] Their indignation grew even more intense thinking that rule would not revert to them after Tarquinius, but would plunge headlong, straight into the power of slaves, and that Servius, a slave born of a slave, would come to possess power in the very city which Romulus, a god born of a god, as long as he was on this earth, had ruled almost one hundred years before. To them it would be a shared disgrace, not only an insult to the name Roman but also to their house, if, while the male line of king Ancus lived, the kingdom of Rome would be open to newcomers as well as slaves. Therefore, they decided to resort to the sword to correct this insult. But, the pain from a perceived wrong stirred them to direct their attack against Tarquinius rather than Servius, because, they reasoned, the king was likely to be a more powerful avenger of murder than a private citizen; then, too, if Servius were eliminated, it seemed to them most likely that the king would designate him the heir to the throne whomever he chose as son-in-law. For these reasons they conspired and plotted against the king. They chose two shepherds for the crime. These ruffians, who were both armed with the farm tools they were accustomed to carry, pretended to be having a brawl at the threshold of the palace, raising as boisterous racket as possible, and thereby attracting all the royal attendants. They both appealed to the king, their shouting reaching deep inside the royal quarters. They were summoned to approach the king. At first they started screaming, each striving to shout down the other until one of the bodyguards restrained them and ordered them to speak in turn, one at a time; finally, they stopped interrupting. As planned, one began to put forward his argument. The king became engrossed and totally absorbed in the case; when he turned all the way around, the other shepherd wielded his ax and split open the king's head. They left the weapon in the wound and together rushed out the door.

(41) About the time his attendants had lifted up the dying Tarquinius, the lictors caught the fugitives. There was a scurrying of people and an uproar from those wondering what was happening. Amid the tumult Tanaquil ordered the palace locked up and any witnesses booted out. She busily prepared balms necessary for healing the wound, as though there was still hope, and took protective measures in case her hope would fail. She quickly summoned Servius to show him her husband's almost lifeless form, and taking him by his right hand, she implored him not to allow his father-in-law's death to go unavenged and his mother-in-law to be the object of mockery at the hands of enemies. "Yours, yes,

---

84: Tarquin was half Greek and half Etruscan.

Servius, it is yours," she said, "the kingdom, not theirs who committed this most heinous crime by hired hands. Arouse yourself, and follow and make as your guides the gods who once portended that this head, when they encircled it with divine fire, would be illustrious. Now, yes, now let that celestial flame provoke you; wake up, right now. We, too, though foreigners, ruled; think, think of who you are, not of where you were born. If your resolve dulls in a sudden crisis, then follow my plans." Since Tanaquil could not have withstood the clamor and rush of the crowd, from an upper story of the house where the king was living near the temple of Jupiter the Stayer through windows overlooking New Street,[85] she addressed the people. She bid them to be calm, that the king had been stunned by a sudden blow but the blade had not penetrated deep into the body; that he had regained consciousness, his wound examined and cleaned of the gore, and he had a clean bill of health; that she was confident that they would soon see him. But she commanded that in the meantime the people heed Servius Tullius who would render justice and perform the other duties of the king. Servius then publicly appeared with the broad-striped robe of state,[86] proceeding accompanied by the lictors, and decided some issues while seated upon the royal throne, but adjourning others he pretended that he would consult the king. So, for several days after Tarquinius had expired, he kept the death concealed, feigning to perform another's office, while he strengthened his own position. At long last the matter became an open record when loud lamentation filling the palace revealed it. Servius protected himself by a strong guard; he was the first king to rule without the sanction of the people, but he had the consent of the senators. After the arrest of the perpetrators of the crime, the sons of Ancus had received the report that the king was still alive and that Servius was ensconced in secure power. They chose to go into exile in Suessa Pometia.[87]

(42) Now Servius turned to consolidating his position by personal as well as by public measures, and to prevent any ill will from Tarquinius' children aimed at him as had been directed from Ancus' sons toward Tarquinius, he married his two daughters to the young royal pair, Lucius and Arruns Tarquinius. But he failed by human design to break the tide of destiny; envy of his power affected even household members to engage in all kinds of treachery and intrigue.

A very opportune war, undertaken against Veii after the one hundred-year old treaty had expired, preserved the peaceful state of affairs. In this war Tullius' manliness and good luck sparkled. When he routed

---

85: New Street (*Via Nova*) was, in fact, a very old street that ran along the base of the north side of the Palatine Hill.

86: Livy refers to a short purple cloak of Etruscan origin that became the ritual dress first of the kings and then the wear of magistrates.

87: a town south of Rome near the borders of the Volscians.

the huge army of his enemies, he returned to Rome; there was no doubt now that he was king and no need for him to test the feelings of the city fathers and the people. He then entered upon by far the most significant work of peace: as Numa had originated and sponsored religious law, so posterity would acclaim Servius as the originator of every distinction in society and of the socio-political ranks that emit radiant degrees of status and fortune. He initiated the census, an institution most propitious for an empire destined for greatness, since the duties in war and peace could be performed not indiscriminately, as before, but in proportion to an individual's wealth. He divided the population into classes and centuries according to a scale based on the census, suitable either for peace or for war.

(43) From those whose property was assessed 100,000 *asses* or higher he formed eighty centuries, forty of "seniors" and forty of "juniors." All of these centuries were called the "first class." The seniors were for defending the city proper, the juniors were for fighting wars abroad; they were required to have the following armor: helmet, round shield, greaves, and breast-plate, all made of bronze and for protecting the body; the weapons to be used offensively against the enemy were spear and sword. He added to this class two centuries of engineers who were to perform their military service unarmed; their assigned duty was to provide the siege-engines in war. The second class consisted of those assessed between 100,000 and 75,000 in property value. From these he conscripted twenty centuries of seniors and juniors; their required armor was the same as the first class except that they had a long shield in place of a round shield and no breast-plate. For the third class he set the assessment of fifty thousand, having the same number of centuries and the same distinction of ages; in armed equipment there was no change except that greaves were subtracted. In the fourth class the property was assessed at twenty-five thousand, having the same number of centuries, but in armor there was a change: nothing was provided except a spear and javelin. The fifth class was enlarged, comprising thirty centuries. For equipment the men of this class carried slings and stones as missiles. Assessed with them and enrolled in three centuries were buglers and trumpeters. The rate for this class was set at eleven thousand. Any assessment below this included the rest of the population who comprised one century; they were exempt from military service. When the infantry was equipped and distributed into these classes, Servius enrolled twelve centuries of equestrians, comprised of the foremost men of the state; six other centuries—Romulus had instituted three—under the same names as they had been inaugurated, he formed. To buy horses the public treasury provided ten thousand *asses* to them and widows, designated to support and feed the horses, had to pay two thousand *asses* each per year. All these burdens were shifted from the poor to the wealthy, who received a special privilege. Individual voting with equal power and

equal rights, an institution established by Romulus and observed by the other kings, was no longer indiscriminately extended to all, but a graded scale was introduced; although no one seemed to be excluded from the voting, yet all the power of the state resided in the hands of prominent citizens. The equestrians were called to vote first, then the eighty centuries of the first class of infantry voted. If there were a disagreement—a very rare occurrence—then the second class would be called to the vote. They hardly ever descended so far down on the scale to reach the lowest orders. It should not be surprising that this system which now exists after the empowering of the thirty-five tribes, their number doubling the centuries of junior and senior members does not agree with the total established by Servius Tullius. He divided the city into four parts comprising the inhabited regions and hills; these four communities he called 'tribes,' a word I think is derived from 'tribute.' For he also planned the method of contribution of each person based equally on the census. These tribes had nothing to do with the distribution and number of centuries.

(44) To facilitate the completion of the census he introduced a law that threatened those unassessed with fear of imprisonment and death. He sent out a proclamation that all Roman citizens, equestrians and infantry, to be present at first light, each in his respective century, in the Field of Mars. There he drew up the entire army and purified it by a sacrifice of a pig, sheep, and bull; the ceremony was called the "closing of the *lustrum*," because it brought an end to the census. In this lustral census eighty thousand citizens are said to have been enrolled. Fabius Pictor,[88] the oldest of our historians, adds that that number comprised all those capable of bearing arms. It became evident to all that the city also had expanded to accommodate this new population. So, he added two hills, the Quirinal and the Viminal, and enlarged the quarters on the Esquiline where he himself took up residence to impart a dignity to the area. He fortified and encircled the city with a rampart of earthwork, trenches, and a wall, thereby extending the *pomerium*.[89] Those who study the derivation of the word interpret the meaning to be 'the area behind the wall;' more likely, however, is the meaning 'the area on both sides of the wall,' the place where the Etruscans of old, whenever they founded new cities, would fix boundaries, hold auspices, and consecrate where they intended to lay their wall. In this way they kept the buildings on the inner side from encroaching upon the wall, which are in our own day commonly joined with them, and on the outer side of the walls they maintained some ground restricted from human use. This space, which it

---

88: the historian Quintus Fabius Pictor was a senator. After a stint as ambassador to Delphi in 216, he wrote a history of Rome in Greek.

89: the line made by a plow pulled by a bull and cow. It marked out the city constituted by augury.

was impious to inhabit or cultivate, the Romans called the "pomerium," not so much because it was behind the wall, but because the wall stood behind it. As the city expanded, these consecrated boundaries spread out as far as the scope of the walls was to be extended.

(45) The population of the city had increased, and he had settled issues to provide for the contingency of war and of peace. To prevent always resorting to the force of arms Tullius attempted to expand power by statesmanship and at the same time to add splendor to the city. Even then the temple of Diana at Ephesus was famous; the story was spreading that it had been built in a cooperative effort by Asian communities. Servius praised this cooperative agreement and the unity of divine worship before the Latin elders with whom both publicly and privately he assiduously cultivated ties of hospitality and friendship. Repeating and repeating the same point, he drove home his plan to have the Latin people cooperate with the Romans in constructing a temple to Diana in Rome. This was an open admission that Rome was the capital, an issue over which an armed struggle had often occurred. Although all the Latins seemed to have abandoned attention to this controversy because they had so often failed so miserably in war, however, there was one person, a Sabine, who believed that he had a plan to recover power that mere chance was offering. The story was that on Sabine land belonging to a head of a household a heifer was born, a specimen astonishing in size and looks—its horns fixed for many generations in the vestibule of Diana's temple attested to the miracle of this animal. The heifer was held to be a prodigy, and, indeed it was. Seers prophesied that the city whose citizen sacrificed the animal to Diana would hold supremacy. The news of the prophecy reached the priest of Diana's shrine. As soon as the first day seemed most suitable for the sacrifice, the Sabine drove the cow to Rome and brought it to the temple of Diana, and stationed it in front of the altar. There the Roman priest admired the size of the sacrificial victim already celebrated and heralded, and remembering the prophecy, he addressed the Sabine: "What are you devising, stranger?" he asked; "Are you about to make an unpurified sacrifice to Diana? You should first bathe in a living stream. The Tiber flows low there in the valley." The stranger was moved by religious scruple. Inasmuch as he wanted all the rituals of the ceremony strictly observed in order to make the event correspond to the prophecy, he at once went down to the Tiber. Meantime, the Roman sacrificed the heifer to Diana, which delighted king and country.[90]

(46) By this time Servius undoubtedly held a prescriptive right to the royal throne. Yet, he kept hearing reports that the young Tarquinius was tossing out criticisms that he was ruling without the consent of

90: other accounts emphasize the direct involvement of Servius in the sacrifice of the heifer.

the people. First, he won over the goodwill of the people by dividing up land captured from enemies and allotting it individually, and then dared to bring before the people the motion to approve and to vote upon his rulership. He was declared king with an unprecedented unanimity. But this state of affairs did not deter one whit Tarquinius' ambition of obtaining royal power, no, not at all, for he thought that the king's act of distributing captured land to the people ran counter to the sentiment of the city fathers, and afforded him the opportunity to censure Servius and promote his own standing among the senators. He himself was a young man of fiery temperament and his wife Tullia goaded on his restless ambition. Like others, Roman royalty produced an example of tragic criminality.[91] The disgust for kings quickened the arrival of liberty, and that rule, gained by crime, was to be the last of royal power in Rome. This Lucius Tarquinius—it is not clear if he was the son or grandson of Tarquinius Priscus; I follow the majority of the sources who claim he was the son—had a brother, Arruns Tarquinius, a young man of gentle temperament. As I mentioned earlier, these two youths married the two daughters of the king, both named Tullia, but very different in character. It was just pure luck that the two of a violent nature did not marry; yes, I believe the luck of the people won out, allowing the rule of Servius to continue for a little longer and the character of the state to develop. The high-strung younger Tullia felt humiliated and pained that her husband lacked the stuff of ambition and daring. Turning completely away from him to the other Tarquinius, she admired the brother, called him a hero and one truly sprung from royal blood; she despised her sister because to complement him, although she had gotten a real man for a husband, she lacked a woman's daring. Soon like attracted like, as it usually happens, and evil appealed to evil. But in this case the woman initiated all the trouble and turmoil. After numerous conversations held in secret with the other's husband, she spared no insults, complaining of her husband to his brother and of her sister to her husband. She contended it would have been better for her to have remained unmarried and for him to have been a bachelor rather than for them to be joined in marriage to an inferior and to languish away their lives controlled by the cowardice of others; if the gods had granted to her a husband such as she deserved, she would have soon seen in her home the royal power which she was witnessing in her father's. Very quickly she inspired the youth with the fire of her own daring; soon two deaths followed, one hard upon the other, that emptied two homes and prepared them for a new marriage, whereupon Lucius Tarquinius and the younger Tullia wed, a union that Servius tolerated without giving his blessing.

91: in fact, Livy treats this section on the death and murder of Servius as a parallel to Greek tragedy. For example, Tullia and Tarquinius are characterized similar to Electra and Orestes.

(47) Day by day the aging Tullius lived in increasing danger, and his rule also began to suffer. For that woman was looking from one crime to another; night and day she did not allow her husband to rest in peace, unwilling to let the past murders be accounted in vain. She had not lacked a man to marry nor would she stand by in silence to be a slave with him; but she did lack a man to believe that he deserved rule, to remember that he was the son of Tarquinius Priscus, and to prefer having power rather than the hope for it. "If you are the person I think I married, I call you both a man and a king; if not, then the situation has changed for the worse in that you have combined criminality with cowardice. Why don't you stir yourself to action? You are not just arriving from Corinth or Tarquinii, as did your father, compelled to toil for a foreign throne. The gods, those of your household and your ancestral ones, and the bust of your father, the royal palace, the kingly throne in his palace, and the name Tarquinius create and declare you king. But if you have too little courage for this, why do you cheat the citizenry? Return to Tarquinii or Corinth; sink back to the level of your roots, more like your brother than your father." With these and other insults she berated her young husband; and she could not rest with the thought that Tanaquil, a foreigner and a woman, had been able to accomplish so much by her strong will, endowing two consecutive kingdoms, first for her husband and then to her son-in-law, yet she, born from royalty, exerted no influence either in the bestowing or the unmaking of a kingdom. Tarquinius was goaded by the stinging fury of the woman; he cultivated and solicited the support of senators of the "Lesser Families."[92] He reminded them of his father's generosity and asked for repayment in kind; and he attracted the young by bribes. His promising of huge rewards and his slandering of the king increased his position everywhere. Finally, it seemed the right time for him to initiate action; with a gang of armed thugs he burst into the forum. During the panic and general turmoil, he took his seat on the royal throne in front of the senate house and ordered a herald to have the city fathers come to the senate house to meet king Tarquinius. They assembled immediately; some were already prepared for it in advance, while others were afraid that by not coming, they would suffer harm. The novelty of the situation and the wonder astonished them and they thought that it was all over for Servius. Beginning with Servius' most distant ancestors, Tarquinius cursed the king, castigating him as a slave born of a slave after the disgraceful death of his own father; moreover, he added that the customary interval between kings had not been observed, no elections held, no vote of the people taken, no ratification made by the senators, but instead he had usurped the throne by the gift of a woman. He listed Servius' birth, his appointment as king, his favoritism of the

---

92: see chapter 35, note # 76.

lowest class of humanity of which he was a member, his dislike of the nobility of others, the land seized from prominent men and allotted to the riff-raff of society; all the burdens which once were shared equally, he tilted towards the most distinguished citizens; he had instituted a census to mark the prosperity of the wealthier citizens in order to induce envy and to provide access for him to make lavish grants, whenever he wanted, to the neediest.

(48) Aroused by the alarming report, Servius hurried to the scene of Tarquinius' harangue and immediately from the vestibule of the senate house he cried out in a loud voice: "What is this business, Tarquinius? What reckless daring has driven you to summon the city fathers, while I am still alive, and to consult them, seated upon my very throne?" Tarquinius answered in an insolent way: that he was occupying his father's seat, that the son of a king was a preferable heir of power to a slave; that he, Servius, for too long had mocked and presumptuously insulted his betters. Partisan shouting arose from the supporters of each and many people rushed into the senate house. It was obvious that the kingdom would go to the winner. Tarquinius was being compelled by necessity to carry his undertaking to the end; his youth and vigor gave him an advantage over Servius; consequently, he grabbed Servius around the waist, lifted him, bearing him out of the senate house, and hurled him down the stairs to the lowest step. The king's attendants and servants fled. The king himself, half dead and gasping for breath, was on his way home without his retinue, when he was killed by those sent by Tarquinius to pursue and catch the fugitive. Many believe that Tullia suggested the crime, since she had not hesitated from other criminality. It is generally agreed that she drove her carriage into the forum and, without any respect for the all-male meeting, she hailed her husband out of the senate house and was the first to address him as king. He ordered her to leave such a tumultuous scene. On her way home she came to the top of Cyprius Avenue, where the shrine of Diana was recently located, and as she was turning her carriage to the right onto Umbrius Slope that carries one to the Esquiline Hill,[93] the driver of her team pulled in the reins and in shock halted; he pointed out to his mistress the murdered body of Servius lying in the street. Foul and inhuman was the crime that tradition relates happened, and the place they now call the 'Avenue of Crime' commemorates it. Here, Tullia, crazed and goaded to madness by the avenging furies of her sister and her husband, drove the carriage over her father's body. And some of her father's blood and gore from his murder stained and defiled her as she wheeled her bloody vehicle to her household gods and those of her husband, gods who became angered at the evil start of their reign and soon brought retribution in kind.

93: these important streets were the main avenues from the northeast forum leading to the Esquiline.

Servius Tullius ruled for forty-four years. It would have been difficult for even a good and moderate successor to match his record: that just and lawful rule perished with him added to his glory. However mild and moderate his rule was, some authors state that he nevertheless intended to abdicate because power was in the hands of a single man. The crime within his family, however, interrupted his plans to liberate the fatherland.

(49) Then Lucius Tarquinius began his reign. His actions earned him the name "the Proud," because as son-in-law he denied the rites of burial to his father-in-law, stating that Romulus, too, died without being buried, and he executed some prominent senators who he believed had favored the political cause of Servius. Very much aware that the bad precedent he himself had set in unlawfully gaining rule could be turned against him, he surrounded his person with an armed bodyguard. He had no rightful claim to the throne at all since he was ruling without the consent of the people and without the authority of the city fathers. In addition, as he put no stock in the favor of the citizens, he had to protect his power by intimidation. To strike terror into many he resorted to conducting by himself and without counsel investigations involving capital charges; under this pretext he could execute, send into exile, or confiscate property of those not only suspected or despised, but those men from whom he could hope for nothing else than plunder. The senators were especially affected by this practice; their numbers were reduced, and he decided to appoint no others to the senatorial ranks, thinking that the order would be held in greater contempt because of their small number, and they would feel less indignant if they transacted no state business. This Tarquinius was the first of the kings to break the tradition, established by his predecessors, of consulting the senate on all issues; he governed the state on the advice of his household; war, peace, treaties, alliances, with whomever he wanted, on his own authority without the consent of the people or the senate, he made and unmade. He tried hard to win the favor of the Latin people, hoping that by securing foreign resources he might be more secure at home. He also cultivated ties of hospitality and of marriage with their prominent aristocrats. To Octavius Mamilius of Tusculum, by far the most eminent prince of the Latin name—and if we can believe the story, descendant of Ulysses and the goddess Circe—he gave his daughter in marriage; through this marriage he won over Mamilius' relatives and his friends.[94]

94: Mamilius is a Latin name, but Octavius is probably Etruscan in background. There were two Mamilii who were consuls in the third century. Tusculum, near modern Frascati in the Alban Hills, was a member of the Latin League and identified itself with Latin interests after the expulsion of the monarchy.

(50) Tarquinius' prestige was already high among the prominent Latin citizens when he declared and fixed a date for them to meet at the grove of Ferentina.[95] He had some common and shared concerns that he wanted to discuss with them. They assembled en masse at daybreak; Tarquinius himself kept the appointment but arrived just before sunset. During the whole day the meeting covered many topics in various speeches. Turnus Herdonius of Aricia[96] violently denounced Tarquinius and his absence, protesting that it was no surprise that the Romans attached the name of "the Proud" to him—already the gossip and whispers murmured in secret were calling him that name—what could be more arrogant than to insult all the Latin country in this way? Leaders had been summoned from distant homes, yet he had not bothered to be present at the council he himself called. It was obvious that he was testing their patience so that, if they submitted now to the yoke, then he would squash them once they were in his power, for anyone could see that he was aiming at control of the Latins. But if his own citizens had acted properly by entrusting this power to him—if indeed it was entrusted and not stolen by parricide—then the Latins, too, ought to entrust it; yet, not even then would he, Turnus, do it, since he was of foreign birth. If his own subjects had become disgusted with him (he argued), since one after another they have been executed, forced into exile, or suffered confiscations, what prospects would be portended for Latins? If they heeded him, they would all go to their respective homes and would no more observe the date of the meeting than did the one who called it. Just at the moment this trouble-making dissenter was making this harangue in those words and others of the same import, characteristic of the skills by which he gained influence in his own city, Tarquinius' arrival interrupted and brought an end to the speech. Everyone turned to greet Tarquinius. There was dead silence, and, advised by his retainers to provide an excuse for his tardy arrival, Tarquinius claimed that he had been called upon to be an arbiter in a dispute between a father and son, and that he was delayed by his attention to reconcile them. Accordingly, as this matter had taken up that day, on the morrow he would deal with the agenda that he had drawn up. They say that Turnus did not suffer this excuse in silence; instead, he countered that no dispute was more quickly settled than one between a father and son, as it could be dispatched in just a few words: if he failed to obey his father, then the son would find trouble.

95: most identify this site near Nemi where there was the sacred grove of Diana.

96: Herdonius is a Sabine name. Because the name Turnus is Etruscan, it seems unlikely that the leader of Latin resistance would be Etruscan in background.

(51) The man from Aricia[97] made these denunciations against the king and left the conference. Tarquinius was much more upset at the episode than he let on, and at once began scheming the death of Turnus in order to induce the same terror among the Latins by which he crushed the spirit of his own citizens at Rome. Since he could not exercise his raw power and have the man killed, he brought a false charge against the innocent man and destroyed him. Employing some political opponents from Aricia, he corrupted one of Turnus' slaves with gold to permit a large quantity of swords to be sneaked into his apartment. This was completed in a single night; a little before daybreak Tarquinius summoned the leading men of the Latins where he pretended to be alarmed by a new matter. He explained that his delay on the previous day, as if by some divine providence, had saved himself and them as well. He was told that Turnus was plotting to murder him and the prominent citizens and was out to grab sole power over the Latins; that on the day before he would have attacked them at the conference, but had to postpone the assault because the person he particularly targeted, the initiator of the meeting, was absent; that provoked the denunciation of himself in his absence, for his tardiness frustrated Turnus' expectations; he had no doubt, if the reports were true, then at dawn, when everyone had convened for the conference, he would have come armed and supported by a gang of conspirators. He was also told that a great number of swords had been conveyed to him, and it could immediately be known if that was true or false. He then invited them to accompany him to Turnus. Turnus' arrogant character, his speech of the day before, and Tarquinius' delay encouraged the suspicion that the accusation was true and it seemed a plausible reason to have postponed the massacre. They left, their minds inclined to believe the story, yet, they were ready to judge all else false, if the swords were not seized. When they arrived at the place, guards surrounded and awoke him from his sleep; his servants, who were on the point of resisting because of their devotion to their master, were also arrested. When the swords were produced from the various hiding-spots in the apartment, Turnus' guilt seemed an open-and-shut case. He was thrown into chains. A conference of Latins was called at once amid an uproar. When the swords were displayed in their midst, such unrelenting odium arose that the accused was convicted without a hearing and was subjected to a new form of execution. At the source of the Ferentine waters he was plunged, bound underneath a crate upon which stones were piled, and drowned.[98]

(52) Then Tarquinius called another meeting of Latins and praised them for meting out a well-deserved punishment to the revolutionary

97: Aricia was located on a spur of the Alban Hills near Nemi. The city passed to the control of the Romans in the early fifth century.
98: the form of punishment seems peculiar to Carthage.

Turnus for his flagrant treason. He then addressed the gathering: he could act in accordance with an ancient right, whereby, since all the Latins sprung from Alba, they were bound by the treaty by which in the time of Tullus the entire Alban state and its colonies had passed into the power of Rome; he was of the opinion that it would be more advantageous to everyone to renew that treaty and for the Latins to share in and enjoy the good luck of the Roman people than for them always to expect and to suffer through the destruction of their cities and the devastation of their fields which they endured first during the reign of Ancus and then of his own father. It was not difficult to convince the Latins, although this treaty favored Roman interests. As for the rest, they saw that the chief men under the Latin name stood and voted with the king, and in the case of Turnus each man had recent proof of the risk, if he offered any opposition. So the treaty was renewed and the juniors of military age from the Latins were directed to present themselves, fully armed and en masse, at the grove of Ferentina on a set day as the treaty prescribed. In accordance with the edict of the Roman king men from all the tribes assembled, and, to prevent them from having their own leader or separate command or standards of their own, he combined the Roman and Latin companies to make single companies from two and two from single ones. In this way he doubled the companies and placed centurions in charge of them.

(53) Although he was an unjust king, he was not a poor general in war. In fact, he would have equaled the previous kings in this art, if his degeneracy in other areas had not eclipsed his distinction in that one. He was the first to wage war against the Volscians, continued for over two hundred years after his time, and he took from them by force their city of Suessa Pometia[99] where the sale of the booty netted forty talents of silver. From these proceeds he conceived constructing a temple to Jove so grandiose as to be worthy of the king of gods and men, of the power of Rome, and of the majesty of the site itself. He set aside the money from the booty to build this temple.

He then undertook a war, more tedious than he expected, that frustrated him; he unsuccessfully attacked Gabii, a city nearby.[100] When he was driven back at the walls in his hopeful attempt to besiege it, as a last resort he turned to a very un-Roman stratagem, the use of trickery and deceit. He pretended to have abandoned the war and to have focused himself intently with laying the foundations of the temple and with other urban projects. As planned, he had Sextus, the youngest of his three sons, desert to Gabii; and there to complain bitterly of the intolerable savagery of his father against him. Sextus claimed that the king's

99: this city was a member of the League of Diana at Aricia, captured by the Volscians.
100: an ancient site some twelve miles east of Rome.

arrogance had turned, directed from foreigners to his own family; that
also he had grown sick of the large number of children and, as he had
effectively already done in the senate house, he was bringing about a
solitude at home in order to leave no descendant, no heir to his throne;
that he himself had escaped, eluding the spears and swords of his father, and believed no place anywhere was safe for him except with the
enemies of Lucius Tarquinius. They should not be mistaken: war was
waiting for them, a war only pretended to have been abandoned, and
that he would soon be attacking them unawares (when the opportunity
came). If , however, they had no room for suppliants, he would traverse
all of Latium to seek out the Volscians, then the Aequians, and then
the Hernicans, until he could reach a people who knew how to protect
children from the savage and impious punishments inflicted by fathers.
Perhaps he would find some spark of eagerness for war and arms against
the most arrogant of kings and the most savage of peoples. When it
seemed to them that any hesitation on their part would cause him to
leave in a rage, the Gabinians kindly welcomed him. They bid him not
to be surprised that the king indulged in the same treatment against
his citizens, his allies, and ultimately against his children; that in the
end, when he ran out of others, he would turn his rage and brutality
against himself. They welcomed his coming and for their part believed
that with his help in a very brief time the war would shift from the gates
of Gabii to the walls of Rome.

(54) Sextus soon gained admission to councils of public policy where
he deferred to the opinions of the elder Gabinians in those areas of concern of which they were more knowledgeable, but repeatedly he took
the lead in promoting war; he assumed a special expertise in it because
he was acquainted with the strengths of both peoples and knew first
hand the king's arrogance, hateful to his citizens, and insufferable to his
own children. So, little by little, he goaded the leading men of Gabii to
renew the war, while he himself led a most enthusiastic group of young
men on raids amd looting expeditions. All his words and actions were
calculated to deceive. Their blind trust in him kept growing until he
was chosen to lead the war effort. No one in the population had a clue
to what was going on, as skirmishes between Romans and Gabinians
erupted in which the Gabinian cause more often than not prevailed. In
this atmosphere, the Gabinians, the highest and lowest of citizens, vied
with one another in voicing their belief that the gods had sent to them
the gift of Sextus Tarquinius as their commander-in-chief. His sharing
and undertaking risks and hard work and his abundant largess of the
booty endeared him to the soldiers so much that not even his father
Tarquinius was as powerful in Rome as his son was at Gabii. So, when
Sextus perceived that he had amassed enough strength to embark upon
any enterprise, he then sent one of his intimates to Rome to inquire of
his father what he wanted him to do next, since the gods had granted

that he alone had power in every department of state at Gabii. To this messenger (I suspect because the king did not believe that he could be trusted), he said not a single word in response.[101] Instead, in pensive mood he crossed into the garden of the house as his son's messenger followed; and there, pacing to and fro and in silence, he is said to have lopped off with a stick the heads of the tallest poppies. The messenger grew weary of asking his questions and of waiting for an answer. He returned to Gabii feeling that he had failed in his mission. He reported what he himself had said and what he observed: whether from anger, hatred, or some innate arrogance, the king uttered not one word. It was patently clear to Sextus what his father intended and what he meant by the silent hints. He got rid of the leaders of the Gabinian state, accusing some before the people, and charging others who were susceptible because of the personal dislike against them. Many were openly executed; some were killed in secret because their indictment would have seemed less plausible. To some voluntary exile was permitted, or they were forced to leave, and their property was confiscated and made available for distribution just as in the case of those executed.

These measures led to lavish living and excess, and in the sweetness of private gain sensitivity to public wrongs stole away until the Gabinian state, robbed of public planning and assistance, was handed over into the hands of the Roman king without a single struggle.

(55) Tarquinius took possession of Gabii, and made peace with the people of Aequi, and renewed the treaty with the Etruscans. Then, he turned his attention to urban affairs, foremost to bequeath the temple of Jupiter on Mount Tarpeius[102] as a monument of his reign and name: that of two Tarquinii, both kings, what the father had vowed, the son fulfilled. To free the area of other religious cults and to have it entirely committed to Jupiter and his temple which was under construction, he decided to deconsecrate the shrines and chapels, several of which, first vowed by king Tatius in the critical moment of the battle against Romulus, had later been consecrated and inaugurated with proper auspices. Tradition has it that during the early stages of this work the gods prompted a divine sign to indicate the power of a mighty empire; for the birds of augury consented to the deconsecration of all other shrines, but refused assent in the case of the shrine of Terminus.[103] This omen and augury were understood in this way: the fact that the seat of Terminus had not been moved and he alone of the gods had not been called from the grounds consecrated to him portended strength and stability. When this augury of perpetual rule was received, a second omen portending the grandeur

101: a similar story of the messenger is found in Herodotus.
102: Mount Tarpeius refers to the Capitolium.
103: Terminus was a god of boundary-stones; his cult was moved to the main cella of the Temple of Jupiter Best and Greatest where a shrine was placed.

of Roman rule followed: a human head with features intact, so we hear, was found by men laying the foundations of the temple. There was no ambiguity to this vision: it portended this was to be the citadel of an empire, the capital of the world. In their chants seers interpreted it that way, both those who lived in the city and those whom they summoned from Etruria to consult over this matter.

The king then directed his attention to increasing expenditures; the money from the spoils of Pometia which had been destined to pay for the work up to the roof, scarcely sufficed for the foundations. I am inclined to believe Fabius—he is, after all, the oldest authority—that the money was only forty talents, over Piso[104] who writes that forty thousand pounds of silver were set aside for the project, a sum of money that one could not expect from the plunder of a single city of those days, and no contemporary structure, however splendid the foundation, would exhaust that expenditure.

(56) Tarquinius was intent on finishing the temple; he summoned engineers from all over Etruria[105] and used not only public funds but labor from the pool of the common people for it. This work was not easy in itself and was added to their military service. Yet, the building of temples of the gods with their own hands distressed the plebeians less than their transfer to other projects, although less pretentious, yet involving harder labor: the construction of seating in the circus, and the digging of an underground sewer, known as the "Greatest," to receive the waste of the city. Scarcely any new magnificent edifice of today could equal these two works. The people were exploited in these jobs; Tarquinius believed that a populace unemployed and unused was a burden to the city, and by dispatching settlers he wanted the frontiers of his rule extended. Therefore, he sent colonists to Signia and Circeii[106] to serve as protectors of the city by land and sea.

A terrible omen appeared to him while he was engaged in these projects: a snake slithered out of a wooden pillar and caused panic and flight into the palace. The event did not so much strike sudden terror in the king's heart as filled it with anxiety and foreboding. Although by tradition only Etruscan seers were employed for public prodigies, this domestic portent, so to speak, frightened him and spurred him to send a delegation to Delphi,[107] the most famous oracle in the world. Not daring to entrust the answers of the oracle to anyone else, he sent Titus and

104: Livy cites two of his sources. First, Quintus Fabius Pictor (see note # 88), a Roman senator who wrote the earliest history of Rome in Greek ca. 200, and, secondly, Lucius Calpurnius Piso Frugi, a consul of 133.
105: the craftsman responsible for the cult image and the architectural decoration was Vulca of Veii.
106: these two towns border on Volscian territory.
107: the story of the embassy to Delphi confirms the early contact of Etruria with Greek Delphi where Caere had erected a treasury.

Arruns, two of his sons, across uncharted territory in those days and across even stranger seas. They set out taking along a companion, Lucius Iunius Brutus, the son of Tarquinia, the king's sister; he was a young man of very different character from the mask he assumed and wore. For after he had heard that some leading men of the state, including his brother, had been killed by his uncle, he decided to leave nothing for the king either to fear in his person or to covet in his fortune and resolved to secure his safety by being the object of contempt, since he had little protection from the law. Therefore, he assumed the look of stupidity on purpose, allowing himself and his belongings to be seized and subject of the king. He made no effort to reject the surname "Brutus,"[108] that under the cover of this name that spirit, destined to be the liberator of the Roman people, would bide its time unnoticed. This was the young man whom the Tarquinii took to Delphi to be more of an amusement than a companion. They say that he carried a golden staff inserted into a rod of cornel-wood as a gift to Apollo, a clever symbol of his own nature. When they arrived and had completed their father's instructions, a desire seized the hearts of the young princes to ascertain to which of them would come the rule of Rome. From the depths of the crevice a voice echoed: "He will have the highest power in Rome who will be the first of you, O young men, to kiss his mother." To keep Sextus, who had been left in Rome, ignorant of this oracular response and without a share of power, the Tarquinii brothers ordered the strictest silence on the matter be observed and for themselves they left it to the drawing of lots to choose which of them, when he arrived in Rome, would be the first to give his mother a kiss. But Brutus thought the voice of the Pythia meant something else. So, he pretended to slip; he fell forward and touched the earth with his lips reasoning that *it* was the mother common to all mortals. They then returned to Rome where war against the Rutulians was being prepared with the utmost energy.

(57) The Rutulians held Ardea, a very wealthy and powerful people for that region and that time. Their prosperity was the main cause of the war because the Roman king, exhausted by the high outlays on public works, was eager to enrich himself and to soothe with the booty the feelings of the populace. In addition to his arrogance, they were hostile to his regime because they deeply resented being used for so long in engineering jobs and being forced by the king to perform the work of slaves. An attempt was made first to capture Ardea by a direct assault, but that met with little success. So, the Romans began to blockade and pressure the enemy with siege-works. In their permanent camp, as it usually happens in a long war of attrition rather than in a campaign of fierce battles, frequent and generous furloughs were made available, especially to the officers over the enlisted soldiers. The young men of

---

108: 'Brutus' means 'stupid.'

the royal court often passed their leisure time among themselves in eating and drinking parties. They happened to be drinking in Sextus Tarquinius' quarters, where Tarquinius Collatinus, the son of Egerius,[109] was also dining, when someone made a chance mention of wives. Each man praised his own wife in extravagant terms. When the rivalry and contention heated up, Collatinus said there was no need for talk, for in a few hours they could know for sure the extent of his own Lucretia's supremacy over the rest. "Say, since we have the vigor of youth in us, why not mount our horses and observe first hand the nature of our wives? Let the decisive test for each wife be the unexpected arrival of her husband and what he sees with his eyes." They were already hot with wine. Everyone agreed with him: "Yes, let's go." Spurring their horses at full gallop, they flew off to Rome where they arrived just as early darkness was descending. Then they headed off to Collatia.[110] There they found Lucretia, not at all acting like the royal daughter-in-laws, which they had often seen, whiling away their time in dinner parties with their friends. But Lucretia, although it was late at night, was seated in the middle of the house surrounded by maids hard at work by the light of lamps, and totally absorbed in working wool. The honor in this contest of wives was won by Lucretia. As her husband and the Tarquinii arrived, she kindly welcomed them. The victorious husband graciously invited the royal princes in. At that point a depraved lust overwhelmed Sextus Tarquinius to seduce and dishonor Lucretia; her beauty and her proven chastity fired him on. For now, their juvenile prank over, they rode back to camp.

(58) A few days passed; without the knowledge of Collatinus, Sextus Tarquinius came to Collatia with a single slave as companion. He received a courteous welcome by the staff who were totally ignorant of his intention, and after dinner they escorted him to the bedroom of the guest's quarters. When he thought everything was secure and safe and all were in deep slumber, burning with love, he drew his sword and approached Lucretia who was fast asleep. With his left hand clasped around and clutching her breast, he said, "Keep quiet, Lucretia. I am Sextus Tarquinius. In my hand is a sword; if you utter a sound, you die." Awakened from sleep and in terror, she saw there was no ready assistance and death was an imminent possibility. Tarquinius professed his love, pleaded with her, interspersed some threats, and resorted to every ploy to influence her woman's mind. But when he saw that she was inflexible and not even the threat of death swayed her, he added disgrace to the threat: he told her that after he killed her, he would cut his slave's throat and lay him naked by her dead body; then everyone would say that she was put to death, caught in sordid adultery. This threat terrified

---

109: for Egerius see chapter 38.
110: Collatia was located on the Anio, modern Lungezza. See chapter 38 and
    note # 83.

her, and victorious lust, as it were, overpowered her resolute chastity. Tarquinius left, proud of his successful conquest of a lady's honor. Lucretia was depressed; she sent the same message to her father in Rome and to her husband at Ardea that each should come with a trustworthy friend; speed and action were absolutely necessary; an atrocious thing had happened. Spurius Lucretius arrived with Publius Valerius,[111] son of Volesus, and Collatinus came with Lucius Iunius Brutus with whom he was traveling on his way to Rome, when he was met by his wife's messenger. The arrival of her family members brought on tears; and to her husband's question: "Are you well?" she replied: "No, not at all. How can a woman be well when she has lost her honor? Traces of another man, Collatinus, are on your bed. It is only my body that has been violated; my heart remains innocent, and death will be my witness. But give me your right hands and promise that the violator will not escape punishment. Sextus Tarquinius is he who last night, an enemy in the guise of a guest, armed, and with violence took his pleasure with me—a deadly matter to me and to him, if you are men." One at a time they all made their promise; they comforted her, sick at heart, by deflecting the guilt from her who was forced to submit upon the perpetrator of the crime, and saying that it was the mind that sinned, not the body, and if intent was lacking, so then was guilt. "You," she said, "will see to it that he gets what he deserves; as for me, I absolve myself of guilt, but I do not release myself from punishment; hereafter, no woman will live unchaste through the example of Lucretia." A knife which she had kept hidden under her clothes she plunged into her heart, and, falling forward over the wound, she lay dead. Both husband and father began to wail.

(59) While they were absorbed in their grief, Brutus extracted the knife from Lucretia's wound, and holding it, still dripping with gore, in front of him, he vowed, "By this blood most pure before the prince wronged it, I swear and I call upon you gods to witness that I will pursue Lucius Tarquinius the Proud, his criminal of a wife, and every offspring of his children with sword, with fire, and with whatever violent means I can, nor will I ever endure them or anyone else to be king in Rome." He handed the knife to Collatinus, next to Lucretius, and finally to Valerius, who were to a man dumbfounded at the miracle of the situation, wondering from where the new character in Brutus' heart had come. They swore an oath as he instructed them. As their grief quickly turned to anger, Brutus seized the moment to summon them to declare war from that time forward against monarchy and to follow his lead.

They carried out Lucretia's corpse from the house and brought it to the forum; there they attracted a crowd because of the wonder, as it happened, of the strange event and because of resentment. Each person

---

111: both Spurius Lucretius and Publius Valerius became consuls in the first year of the Republic (509).

independently complained of the prince's crime and violence. Not only the pitiable grief of the father moved them but Brutus as well who took the role of critic, berating them for their tears and bootless complaints, and urging them to act like proper men and Romans and to take up arms against those who dared to treat them as enemies. The most spirited young men stepped forward with weapons and volunteered their services; the rest of the youths followed. A garrison was left at Collatia and guards were posted at the gates to prevent any messenger reporting the news of the uprising to the court. The others were armed and under the command of Brutus they set out for Rome. When they arrived there, wherever the armed mob advanced caused terror and panic; but when the people saw the leaders of the state marching in the front ranks, they believed whatever was the reason, it had to be a valid one. Moreover, the atrocious incident with Lucretia caused as much resentment in Rome as it had in Collatia. So from every community of the city men came running into the forum. As soon as they got there, a herald summoned the people before the tribune of the "Swift" equestrians, an office which at that time Brutus happened to be holding.[112] There he delivered a speech quite inconsistent with the mind and disposition which he had counterfeited up to that very day. He detailed the violence and lust of Sextus Tarquinius, the unspeakable rape of Lucretia, her horrible death, the bereavement of Tricipitinus[113] for whom the cause of his daughter's death was even more shameful and deplorable than the death itself. He also mentioned the arrogance of the king, the wretched condition and forced labor of the plebeians who were plunged into trenches and sewers to clear them out; that they were men—Romans, the victors over all the peoples thereabout—made into craftsmen and stonecutters instead of warriors. He related the story of the despicable murder of king Servius Tullius and his daughter's indecent driving of her carriage over the body of her father; he then invoked the gods who avenge parents. He mentioned these events and others, I believe, even more atrocious which his sense of outrage of the moment suggested but extremely difficult for writers to record, whereby he inflamed the populace and aroused them to annul the king's power and to order the exile of Lucius Tarquinius, his wife, and his children. Brutus himself enlisted and armed the junior infantry who voluntarily had turned in their names, and with them he set out for the camp near Ardea to provoke the army to turn against the king. He left the command of the city in the hands of Lucretius, sometime before installed as the prefect of the city by the king.[114] During

112: this office did not exist; but in the tradition Brutus is given an office from which he could convene an assembly.
113: Tricipitinus is Spurius Lucretius.
114: this old office of the prefect of the city was revived during the Augustan period. Originally, the holder of the office served as a temporary deputy of the king absent from the city.

the commotion Tullia fled the palace; wherever she passed, both men and women cursed her and invoked the avenging spirits of wronged parents upon her.

(60) When reports of this crisis reached camp, the king, somewhat alarmed by the strange turn of events, proceeded to Rome to crush the uprising. Brutus, on the other hand, sensed his arrival and detoured to avoid meeting him; though by different routes, Brutus came to Ardea at about the same time Tarquinius arrived at Rome. Tarquinius found the gates closed and exile decreed against him. The liberator of the city, however, was welcomed enthusiastically in the camp from where the king's children were expelled. Two of them followed their father and went into exile at Caere in Etruria. Sextus Tarquinius departed for Gabii, as if it were his own kingdom, and there avengers of old feuds, which he had provoked upon himself by his murders and robbery, killed him.

Lucius Tarquinius the Proud reigned for twenty-five years. Monarchy in Rome lasted from the foundation of the city to its liberation, a period of two hundred forty-four years. At the assembly by centuries two consuls[115] were chosen in elections presided over by the prefect of the city in accordance with the commentaries of Servius Tullius.[116] They were Lucius Iunius Brutus and Lucius Tarquinius Collatinus.

BOOK II

(1) From here on I shall treat the history of a free Roman people, their annually elected magistrates, and the authority of their laws superior to that of men. The arrogance of the last king made this freedom all the sweeter. For the earlier kings may be accorded, and not without merit, to have been founders of parts of the city because they added new communities for an expanding population; nor can one doubt that the same Brutus who earned such a distinguished reputation by expelling the haughty king would have done the greatest harm to the state, if his passion for liberty had forced him too soon to wrest monarchial power from any of the previous kings. For what would have happened, if that gang of shepherds and vagrants, runaways from their tribes, under the protection of an inviolable sanctuary had gained either freedom or at least impunity from authority? And, if freed from the threat of a king, they had begun to be buffeted by the storms of political agitations led by tribunes, and to foment contentious quarrels with the fathers of a city not belonging to them, before the pledges of wives and children and the love of the very soil—which they had gotten used to after a long period of time—had united their patriotic spirits? The state would have been

---

115: originally, these officers of state were called praetors.
116: most understand that a manual of priestly observances comprised the so-called commentaries attributed to Servius Tullius.

ripped apart by dissension before reaching maturity. But benign moderation of power favored it, nurtured, and sustained its growth until it could bear the good fruit of liberty once its strength had matured.

You may regard that political liberty originated more in the power of the consul being limited to one year than in any loss of kingly power. All the rights, all the trappings of power the early consuls kept. Only one cautionary measure was taken: both consuls together did not possess the *fasces* to prevent doubling the terror of the symbol. Brutus was the first to have the *fasces* (when his colleague deferred to him), and he was as fierce in protecting liberty as he had been a champion of it. First of all, he pressed the people, enthusiastic for their new freedom, in order to keep them from being swayed otherwise by the entreaties and bribes of the king, to swear an oath that they would allow no man to become king in Rome. Next, to strengthen and to augment the senatorial order, he chose prominent members of the equestrian class to fill out to a total of three hundred the number of senators diminished by the murders of the king. It is said that the tradition of summoning to the senate the fathers and the "conscript fathers"[117] derived from this measure. The name "conscript" designated those enrolled. This process in a wonderful way produced harmony in the state and unified plebeian political interests with those of senators.

117: "conscript fathers" became an honorific title and address of senators.

GLOSSARY

ACTIUM: a promontory of the Ambracian Gulf of western Greece. It gave its name to a naval battle in which Octavius and Agrippa defeated the combined forces of Antony and Cleopatra on 2 September, 31. The victory made Octavius the undisputed dynast of the Roman world and paved the way for his principate, the beginning of the Roman Empire.

AEDILE: an elected Roman official responsible for city administration, the holding of most public games and the grain supply.

AEGATES: a group of three islands west of Sicily off the promontory of Lilybaeum.

AEQUI: an Italic tribe occupying the Apennine range east of Rome. They were fierce fighters and a formidable enemy of Rome.

AENEAS: a Trojan hero, son of Anchises and Venus. Aeneas escaped the sack of Troy with his father and son, Ascanius. He traveled to Italy where he founded Lavinium and became the progenitor of the Roman race. Via the Julian house he was seen as the ancestor of Augustus himself.

AGRIPPA, MARCUS VIPSANIUS: close friend, confidant, advisor, and very successful general of Octavius/Augustus. Until his death in 12 he was the second most powerful man in Rome after Augustus. He married first Attica, a daughter of Pomponius Atticus, and then Julia, Augustus' daughter by whom he had five children. He assisted Augustus in his vast building program and was personally responsible for the Pantheon and a portico nearby.

ALBA LONGA: a town in the Alban Hills about twelve or thirteen miles southeast of Rome. In legend it was founded by Ascanius/Iulus, the son of Aeneas, whereas, in fact it was not much older than Rome itself.

ALEXIS: (ca.375-275), poet of New Comedy, born at Thurii in Italy. He reputedly wrote 245 plays, some of which were adapted by Roman playwrights.

ALLOBROGES: a Gallic tribe in the Rhone area who were enticed by Catiline to join his conspiracy in 63.

ANAGNIA: a city about forty miles southeast of Rome where Cicero maintained a home.

ANIO: a tributary of the Tiber flowing from the Apennines east and northeast of Rome through Tibur.

ANTENOR: wise, old counselor and friend of Priam, the king of Troy. He proposed returning Helen to the Greeks in order to stop the war, for which he was branded a traitor to the Trojan cause. Like Aeneas, he survived the sack of Troy to travel to Italy and to found a settlement.

ANTIOCHUS III: ruler of the Seleucid Empire (242-187). His two defeats at the hands of the Romans at Thermopylae in Greece and at Magnesia checked his imperialism.

APELLES: a famous painter from Colophon who was known for his portraiture and realism. He was commissioned by Philip II and Alexander the Great of Macedon.

APOLLONIUS: of Perge (fl.200), a mathematician who wrote on conics.

APOLLO ON THE PALATINE: the temple of Apollo on the Palatine Hill was formally dedicated on 9 October, 28 BCE. It had two libraries and an L-shaped portico.

APULIA: large region of southeast Italy on the Adriatic Sea.

ARCHILOCHUS: seventh-century poet of Paros, known best for his savage lampoons and satirical abuse.

ARCHIMEDES: (287-212) the great mathematician and inventor of Syracuse. He wrote numerous scientific works touching on various fields including statics. He was killed in the sack of the city under Marcus Claudius Marcellus (212).

ARCHYTAS: a Pythagorean philosopher and mathematician from Tarentum (ca.400) who created a type of sundial.

ARCTURUS: the brightest star in the constellation of Bootes.

AREZZO: ancient Arretium, a city in Etruria, southeast of modern Florence.

ARICIA: ancient town of Latium, south of Rome near Lake Albanus.

ARISTARCHUS: 1) the third-century astronomer of Samos, best known for his theory of the heliocentric nature of the solar system; he was also recognized for his work in clocks and timepieces. 2) of Samothrace (ca. 215-144). He became the head of the library at Alexandria and was the founder of analytical grammar; he is known for the rigor and severity of his literary criticism, particularly of Homer.

ARISTIPPUS: a contemporary and associate of Socrates from Cyrene. He was the founder of the Cyrenaic school of philosophy that argued for a sensationalist theory of knowledge and stressed pleasure as the primary goal of life.

ARISTOPHANES: 1) [ca.257-180] famous grammarian of Byzantium who headed the great library of Alexandria. 2) [ca.455-377] the premier comic playwright of Old Comedy, eleven of whose comedies survive.

ARISTOXENUS: a fourth-century intellectual from Tarentum who joined the Lyceum in Athens under Aristotle. He was particularly interested in music.

ARRUNTIUS, LUCIUS: a commander at Actium, consul in 22 whose son, Lucius Arruntius served as consul in 6 CE. He also wrote a history of the Punic Wars.

ARPI: a city in Apulia.

ASSEMBLY: the convening of the voting population in groups (centuries or tribes) for electoral, legislative, and political purposes.

ATHENODORUS CALVUS: AKA Athenodorus the Bald, stoic philosopher from Tarsus and friend of Cicero.

ATTICUS, TITUS POMPONIUS: (110-32) friend and advisor of Cicero, and editor of Cicero's works; he was a very wealthy and distinguished equestrian who refused a political career in favor of business. His neutrality insured his survival during the many civil wars of his time. His daughter married Marcus Vipsanius Agrippa.

AUGUR: member of a priestly college of official diviners; before major public acts they interpreted signs usually connected with the sky. This college was generally filled by nobles.

AUSPICES: types of divination practiced at elections, inauguration of offices, conduct of wars, and other major public acts.

AVENTINE: one of the seven traditional hills of Rome opposite the Palatine to the south.

AXIUS, QUINTUS: a wealthy senator, acquaintance of Varro; he corresponded with Cicero.

BALBUS, LUCIUS CORNELIUS: a Roman Spaniard and financial supporter of Octavius. In 40 BCE he became the first foreign-born consul.

BITHYNIA: large territory in northwest Asia Minor that became a possession of Rome in 74 after which it was organized into a province.

BRUNDISIUM: modern Brindisi, a prominent Italian port at the "heel" on the Adriatic from which ships most conveniently departed to Greece and points eastward.

BRUTUS, MARCUS IUNIUS: after Pharsalus in 48 he was pardoned by Caesar, made governor of Cisalpine Gaul in 46, and was praetor in 44. He joined with Cassius and a distant kinsman, Decimus Brutus, in the assassination of Julius Caesar. Brutus operated in Greece and took possession of it and recruited in the East. He perished at Philippi in 42.

BRUTUS: Decimus Iunius Brutus Albinus had served under Julius Caesar during the civil war and governed Cisalpine Gaul in 48-46. Although he was designated consul for 42 by Caesar, he was a leading conspirator against him. In 44 and 43 he led Republican forces against Antony in Cisalpine Gaul; when he followed Antony into Transalpine Gaul in June of 43, he was deserted by his troops, captured by a Gallic chief, and executed on Antony's orders.

BUTHROTUM: a city in Epirus whose lands were confiscated and distributed to veterans of Caesar's army. Atticus paid money to Caesar on behalf of the people of Buthrotum. An agreement was in progress regarding the case of Buthrotum when Caesar was killed. Some time passed before Antony and Dolabella, the consuls of 44, carried out the arrangement.

CAECINA: an agent of Octavius.

CAERE: modern Cerveteri; an Etruscan city about thirty miles north of Rome. The enormous size of its surviving tombs, dating as early as 700, attests to its prosperity and importance. The city had connections with the Tarquin family.

CAESAR, LUCIUS IULIUS: a distant relative of Julius Caesar. He served as consul in 64; he remained neutral in the Pompey-Caesar civil war. His opposition to Antony brought about his proscription, but he was saved by the intercession of his sister Iulia, Antony's mother.

CALATIA: a town six miles southeast of Capua on the Appian Way.

CALENUS, QUINTUS FUFIUS: a political supporter of Julius Caesar, consul in 47; he became a strong partisan of Antony.

CALES: a city in northern Campania known for its wines.

CALVENA: a nickname for Gaius Matius.

CAMPUS MARTIUS: 'The Field of Mars,' the plain adjoining the Tiber where the assembly of the centuries and elections took place.

CANUSIUM: a city in Apulia.

CAPITOL: always refers to the Capitoline Hill and specifically to the Temple of Jupiter Best and Greatest.

CAPPADOCIA: large area of east-central Asia Minor.

CAPUA: capital of Campania that developed from an Etruscan colony.

CARYAE: a city in Laconia in the Peloponnesus from which the term 'caryatid' derived, i.e. the shaft of a column carved in the form of a draped woman.

CASALINUM: modern Capua in Campania about three miles northwest of ancient Capua.

CASSIUS: Gaius Cassius Longinus. As tribune in 49 he joined Pompey against Caesar. Pardoned afterwards by Caesar, he was praetor in 44 and was one of the leading conspirators in Caesar's assassination. He organized forces in the East, first against Antony and his supporters, then against the triumvirs. He died at Philippi in 42. At the time of his death he was married to Iunia Tertulla, half-sister of Brutus.

CASSIUS DIONYSIUS: of Utica. In 88 he published a Greek translation of the work on agriculture of Mago the Carthaginian.

CATANIA: city on the eastern coast of Sicily.

CATILINE, LUCIUS SERGIUS: a bankrupt patrician best known for the conspiracy that bears his name. After he failed to win the consulship for 62, he organized a conspiracy which Cicero suppressed in late 63. Forced to leave Rome, he was defeated and killed near Pistoria in Etruria in January 62.

CATO, MARCUS PORCIUS: 1) [234-149], known for his integrity and austere life style, as censor he attempted to reform Roman morals. He wrote (among others) a treatise on agriculture. 2) [95-46] fought with Pompey against Julius Caesar and helped lead the Republican forces after Pompey's death. He committed suicide at Utica in North Africa in 46.

CATULLUS, GAIUS VALERIUS: (84-54) poet of lyric, erotic poetry and epigrams; he is most famous for his love poems addressed to Lesbia, usually identified with Clodia, sister of Publius Clodius Pulcher, the arch-enemy of Cicero.

CATULUS, GAIUS LUTATIUS: consul of 242 whose victory over the Carthaginians off the Aegates Islands west of Sicily forced a conclusion of the First Punic War.

CENSORS: two officials elected every five years to serve for eighteen months. They revised the roll of citizens, assessed property, and reviewed the qualifications of both equestrians and senators; they also controlled public contracts and were guardians of public morality.

CENSORINUS, LUCIUS MARCIUS: partisan of Julius Caesar, then of Antony. After Cicero's death he took possession of Cicero's house on the Palatine.

CENTURIES: one of the voting assemblies originally organized and conducted by blocks of 100; this assembly elected consuls and praetors.

CENTURION: the principal professional officer in the Roman army; there were sixty selected to a legion.

CHALCIDICUM: a generic term for a porch or annex to a building, with its own decoration. It is usually used to denote the porch in front of the Curia Iulia, the Senate House in the forum.

CHIEF PRIEST: see PONTIFEX MAXIMUS.

CICERO, MARCUS TULLIUS: son of the famous orator; he was a competent officer in the republican army; pardoned after Pharsalus, he spent some time in Athens, joined Brutus, and then Sextus Pompeius; he took advantage of the amnesty of 39. Under Octavian/Augustus he enjoyed a successful political career, serving as consul in 30 BCE, and later as governor of Syria.

CICERO, QUINTUS TULLIUS: 1) brother of the orator Marcus who married Pomponia, the sister of Atticus; and 2) the son of # 1 above; he favored Julius Caesar after Pharsalus.

CINNA, LUCIUS CORNELIUS: a supporter of Marius who governed Rome as consul from 86-84. Organizing troops to oppose Sulla, he was killed in a mutiny.

CLATERNA: a town on the Aemilian Way between Bologna and Forum Cornelii.

CLODIUS: Publius Clodius Pulcher: 1) Cicero's bitter enemy who as tribune in 58 drove Cicero into exile. He used mob violence to bring about political agenda. He was killed in a fight in 52 for which Titus Annius Milo was held responsible. 2) son of # 1 of the same name; he was Antony's stepson after his marriage to Fulvia, the boy's mother.

CLOELIUS, SEXTUS: a client and dependent of Publius Clodius; his recall was the subject of an exchange between Antony and Cicero.

COHORT: military unit of the Roman legion. In a legion of full strength there were ten cohorts.

COMITIUM: an area in the northwest sector of the forum between the senate-house and rostra where assemblies were held.

CONSENTES: twelve native Italic gods particularly important to agricultural life.

CONSENTIA: the chief city of the Brutii, inhabitants of Calabria in southern Italy.

CONSUALIA: a festival to Consus, a god of the granary, held on 21 August and 15 December.

CONSUL: the highest political and military officer of the Roman Republic; there were two in number elected to office for one year. The elected consuls gave their names to the year.

CREUSA: the Trojan wife of Aeneas, lost at Troy during the sack of the city.

CROTON: a Greek city on the East coast of modern Calabria that revolted against Rome during the war with Hannibal.

CRUSTUMERIA (CRUSTUMIUM): a town a few miles northeast of Rome in Sabine territory.

CTESIBUS: an Alexandrian inventor and scientist of the third century BCE who was most interested in pneumatics.

CULARO: modern Grenoble on the Isere River.

CURES: the capital of the Sabines, Italic people who occupied an extended area northeast of Rome to the Apennine uplands.

CURULE: referring to the official "chair" of an official invested with *imperium*, from which power was exercised.

DEMOCRITUS: fifth-century philosopher from Abdera in Thrace, adopter and proponent of the atomic theory of Leucippus.

DENARIUS: (pl. *denarii*), normally a silver coin worth four sesterces.

DICAEARCHUS: (fl. 320-300), a scholar from Messina whose prolific writings influenced many subsequent writers including Eratosthenes and Varro.

DICTATOR: a supreme magistrate appointed in emergencies for a period of six months; his second in command, selected by the dictator, was the "Master of the Horse." Sulla held the office for two years and Julius Caesar was declared "dictator for life."

DIOPHANES: of Bithynia, a writer who abridged the agricultural treatise of Cassius Dionysius who in turn had translated Mago of Carthage.

DIVINE JULIUS, TEMPLE: begun in 42, it was opened in 29 BCE. Located in the forum, it commemorated the spot where the corpse of Julius Caesar was cremated.

DOLABELLA, PUBLIUS CORNELIUS: son-in-law of Cicero who was divorced from Cicero's daughter Tullia in 46. A partisan of Caesar, he was appointed consul after the assassination of Julius Caesar. He obtained a five-year governorship of Syria in 43. After crossing over to Asia, he killed Gaius Trebonius, but then committed suicide after being besieged by Cassius.

DUUMVIRS: two officials or an official board of two men.

EGERIA: a nymph of Latium who was the consort and advisor of King Numa.

ELEPHANTINE: capital of upper Egypt, modern Gesiret Assuan near Aswan.

ENNIUS, QUINTUS: (239-169) one of the earliest poets of Rome who became known as the father of Latin Literature. He is particularly famous for his *Annales* that records in eighteen books the history of Rome.

EPICURUS: (342-270), famous Greek philosopher, founder of the philosophy that bears his name. His school was set up in the garden of his house in Athens.

EPIRUS: district of northwestern Greece, opposite of Corcyra (modern Corfu).

EPOREDIA: modern Ivrea, a town in the foothills of the Alps.

EQUESTRIAN: non-senatorial order of citizens possessing an annual evaluation of 400,000 sesterces. Members had special privileges and could control and manage large business enterprises.

ERATOSTHENES: of Cyrene (285-194), a student of Callimachus at Alexandria, who headed the library. A very versatile writer and scholar, he was active in literary criticism, philosophy, mathematics, and especially geography.

ERYX: a site in western Sicily famous for its temple to Venus; it was occupied by Carthaginians in the First Punic War.

EUMENES II: (197-158) king of Pergamum, an ally of Rome against Antiochus III. He waged war against Prusias I of Bithynia who was aided by Hannibal.

EUTRAPELUS, PUBLIUS VOLUMNIUS: a celebrated wit who joined with Antony and became his prefect of engineers.

EVANDER: an Arcadian Greek migrant to the future site of Rome who founded Pallanteum on the Palatine Hill.

EX-CONSULS: consulars who made up a corps of elder statesmen and provided leadership of the Senate.

FABIUS: Quintus Fabius Maximus Verrucosus, called the "Delayer," Roman general in the Second Punic War who fought a campaign of attrition against Hannibal in Italy

FADIUS, GAIUS: a freedman whose daughter, Fadia, had an affair with Antony.

FASCES: a bundle of rods normally surrounding an ax, carried by a bodyguard (lictors) before an official invested with *imperium*. They became a symbol of magisterial power.

FETIAL: member of the priestly college in charge of diplomacy and the procedures for declaring wars and making treaties.

FIDENAE: a town along the Salt Road that frequently opposed Rome.

FLAMEN (FLAMINES pl.): priest(s) in charge of the cult of a particular deity, usually fifteen in number; the *flamines* of the cult of Jupiter, Mars, and Quirinus were considered superior to the others.

FLAMININUS, TITUS QUINCTIUS: he defeated Philip V at Cynocephalae (197), known as the liberator of Greece. He was involved in many Greek affairs of the 190s and 180s, including his demand from Prusias for the surrender of Hannibal.

FLAMINIUS, GAIUS: consul of 217 who died at the Battle of Lake Trasimene against Hannibal.

FLAMMA, TITUS FLAMINIUS: a friend of Montanus who was most likely a client of Cicero or his son. He, like Montanus, had incurred a debt which Cicero "took care of."

FLAVIUS, GAIUS: financier and friend of Marcus Iunius Brutus. He served as the prefect of engineers under Brutus; he died at Philippi in 42.

FORMIAE: town on the coast south of Rome, near the border of Campania; Cicero had a villa there.

FORUM CORNELII: a town about twenty miles east of Bologna on the Aemilian Way.

FORUM GALLORUM: a town near Mutina.

FRAGELLAE: a Latin colony south of Rome.

FULVIA: wife of Mark Antony who supported her husband's interests in Rome during his absence. She died in 40 leaving two sons by Antony.

FURNIUS, GAIUS: a friend of Cicero who supported Julius Caesar. He served first Plancus, then Antony; he was pardoned by Octavian after Actium.

GAIUS IULIUS CAESAR: eldest son of Agrippa and Julia, Augustus' daughter; he was adopted by Augustus in 17 BCE. He died in 4 CE from a wound suffered in war.

GORTYNA: city in central Crete, made the capital of the Roman province of Crete-Cyrene.

GRACCHUS, TIBERIUS SEMPRONIUS: a general in the Second Punic War who served as Master of the Horse and consul. He was successful in relieving Cumae in 215, but died in an ambush in 212.

HAMILCAR BARCA: father of Hannibal, who took command of the Carthaginian fleet during the last years of the First Punic War (264-241). He negotiated the peace treaty of 241 with Rome and managed Carthaginian interests in Spain until his death in 229.

HASDRUBAL: son-in-law of Hamilcar Barca, who headed Carthaginian operations in Spain after the death of Hamilcar (229).

HELICON: a mountain in Boeotia, reputed dwelling of the muses.

HERNICI: Italic people occupying an area in southeast Latium between the Aequi and Volsci.

HESIOD: late eight-century poet from Ascra near Thebes who wrote the didactic pastoral-like *Works and Days* that includes much agricultural lore.

HIPPOCRATES: (ca. 460-377) the putative founder of Greek rational medicine from Cos. He was famous for the corpus that bears his name and that outlines and treats numerous areas in the field of medicine.

HIRTIUS, AULUS: served under Julius Caesar, designated consul in 43; he died fighting against Antony at the siege of Mutina. He is credited with writing some of Caesar's accounts and volumes of letters to Cicero.

HORTENSIUS: Quintus Hortensius Hortalus, consul of 69 and preeminent orator. He was a close friend of Atticus.

IMPERATOR: a title for a Roman general possessing *imperium*, and a title of honor for a triumphing general.

IMPERIUM: the technical term for the executive and military authority and power of high public officials and provincial governors.

ISARA: the modern Isere river, tributary of the Rhone.

JANA: a variant of the name 'Diana' or the feminine counterpart of the god Janus.

JANICULUM: the ridge on the west bank of the Tiber whose name is connected to Janus, the god of beginnings and doorways.

JANUS QUIRINUS: Janus was god of doors and gates whose honorific gateway near the Palatine was closed only in times of universal peace. Quirinus, the local spirit of the Quirinal Hill somehow merged with this figure of Janus.

IUGERUM (iugera, pl.): an area approximately 2/3 of an acre.

JUGURTHA: king of Numidia (118-104), captured by Marius in 104 and executed after being led in Marius' triumph.

LATERENSIS, MARCUS IUVENTIUS: served as a legate under Lepidus (44-43). When he despaired of the perceived treason of his general, he committed suicide.

LAVINIUM: the supposed site in Latium south of Rome settled by Aeneas.

LEGATE: a senator on the staff of a provincial governor or general; he commanded a legion or cohort.

LEGATE, FREE or VOTIVE: a person appointed by the senate to a special position with official status or as an envoy, usually allowing for travel abroad.

LEGION: the Roman army unit divided into ten cohorts each of which had six centurions and its own standard.

LEPIDUS, MARCUS AEMILIUS: consul of 46 and partisan of Julius Caesar. After Caesar's death he became Pontifex Maximus; in 44-43 he was governor of Narbonese Gaul and Farther Spain; he joined Antony and became Triumvir. In 36 he was forced to retire from politics by Octavian.

LIBERALIA: the festival of Liber Pater, commonly identified with Bacchus, that was the usual occasion for a coming of age ceremony.

LICTOR: official attendant and bodyguard of those possessing the authority and power of office (*imperium*). The number varied with the rank of the official, but each lictor carried a bundle of rods with an ax in the center (*fascis*).

LIGURIA: major region of Northwest Italy

LITUUS: a staff or scepter used by religious and political VIPs as a symbol of authority.

LUCIUS IULIUS CAESAR: second son of Agrippa and Julia, the daughter of Augustus; he was adopted by Augustus in 17 BCE. He died in 2 CE in Marseilles.

LUCRETIUS: Titus Lucretius Carus, early first-century Latin poet who wrote *On the Nature of Things*, an Epicurean look at scientific realism.

LUCULLUS, LUCIUS LICINIUS: (ca.117-56), consul in 74, he had an Eastern command against Mithradates of Pontus which he was forced to relinquish to Pompey the Great. After his return to Rome he lived a life of refined luxury.

LUPERCAL: a grotto in the Palatine where sacrifices were offered to commemorate the suckling of Romulus and Remus by the she-wolf.

LUSTRUM: a purification ceremony traditionally performed by the censors after each census.

LYCAEAN: referring to a mountain in Arcadia, a haunt of Pan and the site of his cult.

LYCEUM: a gymnasium on the outskirts of Athens where Aristotle taught, hence, his school.

MAGO: youngest brother of Hannibal, who assisted his brother in military action and political affairs in Spain, Italy, and North Africa.

MANLIUS, AULUS: legate of Marius in the war against Jugurtha.

MARCELLUS: Marcus Claudius Marcellus. 1) distinguished general in the Second Punic War who served as Master of the Horse and consul. He is most known for his capture and reduction of Syracuse in 212 BCE; 2) Augustus' nephew and son-in-law who died prematurely in 23. The theater built in his name was opened in 11 BCE. 3) consul of 51, a bitter opponent of Julius Caesar. He joined Pompey, but after Pharsalus he was pardoned.

MARCELLUS, MARCUS: Marcus Claudius Marcellus Asserninus, a partisan of Julius Caesar who served as consul in 22.

MASTER OF THE HORSE: see DICTATOR.

MATIUS, GAIUS: long-time friend and loyal agent of Julius Caesar who financially helped Octavius in 44.

MENECRATES: of Ephesus, fourth-century poet who composed a work on agriculture, particularly the cultivation of bees.

MESSALLA: Marcus Valerius Messalla Corvinus (64 BCE – 8 CE), a republican noble who after Philippi turned his allegiance first to Antony and then to Octavian. He had a reputable political and military career and headed a literary circle that included Tibullus, the young Ovid, and his niece Sulpicia.

METELLUS: Quintus Caecilius Metellus Numidicus, consul (109) and general in the war against Jugurtha. He was recalled and replaced by Marius (107).

MEZENTIUS: an Etruscan from Caere who allied with Turnus to oppose Aeneas' settlement in Latium

MINUCIUS RUFUS, MARCUS: elected Master of the Horse to the Dictator Quintus Fabius Maximus Verrucosus in the war against Hannibal. For a brief period he held power equal to that of the dictator; he died valiantly at the Battle of Cannae (216).

MONTANUS, LUCIUS TULLIUS: a friend and client of the younger Cicero whose debts Cicero and Atticus paid.

MUTINA: a city west of Bologna (modern Modena) besieged by Antony in 43, relieved by the consuls of that year, Hirtius and Pansa, who were assisted by Octavius. Hirtius and Pansa were killed in the operation and Antony fled, leaving Octavius the victorious survivor.

MYRON: an Athenian sculptor of the fifth century, most famous for his naturalistic treatment of animals and the *Discus Thrower*.

NOMENTUM: Latin town, modern Mentana, about 15 miles northeast of Rome.

NUMICUS: a stream near Lavinium south of Rome.

NUMIDIA: North African area west of Carthage, kingdom of Jugurtha.

OLYMPUS: highest mountain in Greece in Thessaly that was the reputed home of the mythical Greek gods.

OLYNTHIA: the area around Olynthus, a city in Thrace.

OPTIMATES: the "best" or leading citizens, conservatives in the senate who supported the senate as the ultimate determiner of political action.

OVATION: a victory celebration which was a lesser form of triumph.

PACUVIUS, MARCUS: (220-130), famous writer of tragedies from southern Italy.

PALATINE: the large hill south of the forum where, according to tradition, Rome began.

PAMPHYLIAN SEA: the general area of the Mediterranean Sea off the coast of southern Asia Minor, bordering Lycia and Cilicia.

PANAETIUS: stoic philosopher (185-109) who was a friend of Scipio Aemilianus; he influenced Cicero's *On Duties*.

PANSA: Gaius Vibius Pansa Caetronianus, served under Julius Caesar and protected Caesar's interest as tribune in 51; he governed Bithynia (47-46) and Cisalpine Gaul; designated by Caesar as consul in 43, he died from wounds received in the Battle of Forum Gallorum near Mutina.

PAPHLAGONIA: a territory of northern Asia Minor between Bithynia and Pontus, extending inland as far as Galatia.

PARMA: a city in Cisalpine Gaul west of Bologna.

PATRON-CLIENT: a client was a free man who attached himself to a patron (usually wealthy and socially and politically well-connected) in exchange for money and protection. For services rendered the patron commanded votes. The custom of this institution was extended to whole communities in Italy and in the provinces.

PAULLUS FABIUS MAXIMUS: consul of 11, a good friend of Augustus; he married Augustus' niece Marcia.

PAUSANIAS: a king of Sparta; he led the Greek forces at Platea in 479 against the Persians who had invaded under the order of Xerxes.

PHILIP V: (238-179) king of Macedon whose defeat by the Romans at Cynocephalae in Thessaly (197) limited his power in the Greek World. His treaty with Hannibal (215) offered him little help.

PHILIPPUS, LUCIUS MARCIUS: a consul of 56, he married Octavius' mother Atia. He was a moderate in the power struggles between Antony and the senate, and Antony and Octavius.

PHILOLAUS: (ca. 470-390) a Pythagorean philosopher from Italy, either Croton or Tarentum. He was an influence upon both Plato and Aristotle.

PHRYGIA: rather large area of northwestern Asia Minor. Ancient Troy was located in this region.

PICENUM: a large geographical region on the Adriatic coast in east-central Italy that bounds Cisalpine Gaul and the Apennines..

PILIA: wife of Atticus.

PISIDIA: a region of southern Asia Minor eventually included in the province of Galatia.

PISO: Lucius Calpurnius Piso Caesoninus, consul in 58. He was bitterly attacked by Cicero in 55; he remained neutral in the civil war of Pompey and Caesar. For the most part he opposed Antony, but eventually tried to promote a compromise with him. He was the father of Calpurnia, Julius Caesar's last wife.

PLANCUS, LUCIUS MUNATIUS: served under Julius Caesar; as governor of Transalpine Gaul he joined Antony in 43 after asserting loyalty to the republican cause. Before Actium he switched his allegiance to Octavian. He enjoyed a successful career, serving as consul in 42 and censor in 22.

PLEIADS: a constellation whose ascendance in the spring portends rain and stormy weather. The name derives from seven daughters of Atlas and Pleione.

POLYCLITUS: fifth-century sculptor from Argos who worked primarily in bronze. Most known for his *Spear Bearer*, he wrote the influential *Canon* which explained the principles of sculptural proportion.

POMERIUM: the city's religious boundary within which all auspices were taken.

POMPEII: town on the Bay of Naples where Cicero had a villa; it was destroyed by the eruption of Vesuvius in 79 CE.

POMPEIUS, SEXTUS: son of Pompey the Great who revived the war in Spain after Caesar's death. His control of Sicily and the Tyrrhenian Sea proved to be a danger to Italy and Octavian's power. He was defeated in 36 in Sicily, then fled to the East where he was executed by Antony's orders.

POMPEY: Gnaeus Pompeius Magnus (106-48), famous general and statesman, member of the so-called First Triumvirate with Gaius Iulius

Caesar and Marcus Licinius Crassus. He was defeated by Julius Caesar in 48 at the Battle of Pharsalus and murdered as he landed in Egypt. He built a famous theater and portico in the Campus Martius.

PONTIFEX MAXIMUS: the chief pontiff who headed the priestly "colleges" of the various Roman cults.

PONTUS: the region of northern Asia Minor encompassing most of the south coast of the Black Sea. By the end of the Augustan Principate the territory had become a Roman province.

POSIDONIUS: (135-51) Stoic philosopher who headed the school in Rhodes. He traveled extensively and was in Rome several times.

POSTUMUS, GAIUS RABIRIUS: an equestrian financier who was an ardent supporter of Julius Caesar; he helped Octavius particularly in financial support of the games of July 44.

PRAETOR: second highest ranking official, elected annually with *imperium*; his primary duty was judicial. After his year in office he normally governed a province as propraetor.

PRAETORIAN GUARD: a special military unit serving as a general's bodyguard.

PREFECT: an officer appointed by a magistrate or governor for military or civil duties. The appointment conferred official status; in the army prefects usually commanded cavalry squadrons.

PRINCEPS: meaning "the first citizen," became the favored term that Augustus used to describe himself. He characterized his rule as a "principate."

PROCONSUL: "acting consul" who exercised the authority and power outside of the city of Rome, usually as a commander and governor of a province. Cf. the case of the propraetor.

PROPRAETOR: "acting praetor," appointed by the senate; one who exercised the power of praetor outside of the city of Rome, usually in the field or a province.

PRUSIAS I (ca.230-182): king of Bithynia. He lost his war with Eumenes II of Pergamum, after which he was forced to cede Phrygia and surrender Hannibal.

PULVINAR: a box-seating arrangement from which to watch races in the circuses.

PULVINARIA: refers to the practice of bringing statues of gods from their shrines and temples to share in a public, sacred banquet; theses statues were laid out on special couches (*pulvinaria*).

PUTEOLI: modern Pozzuoli, a city west of Naples across the bay from Baiae.

PYRRHUS: a Greek king of Epirus who responded to cries of assistance from Greeks in Italy, particularly of Tarentum, against the burgeoning power and encroachment of Rome. He invaded Italy; after two costly victories and a defeat at Beneventum, he returned to Epirus.

PYTHIUS: famous fourth-century architect of Priene who designed the Mausoleum of Halicarnassus and the Temple of Athena Polias at Priene.

QUAESTOR: the lowest and first office of state in a senator's career. Twenty in number (after Sulla) quaestors served consuls or governors, largely concerned with finance and pay.

QUINCTILIUS VARUS, PUBLIUS: the famous general whose legions were lost in the Teutoburgerwald in 9 CE; he had also served as consul in 13 BCE.

QUIRINAL: one of the canonical seven hills of Rome, north of the forum.

QUIRINUS: a god of Sabine origin whose cult perhaps centered on the Quirinal Hill, identified with Mars and assimilated to Romulus.

QUIRITES: a term derived from "Quirinus" that designates Roman citizens, literally "offspring of Quirinus," i.e. of Romulus.

REATE: modern Rieti, a town in Sabine territory about 55 miles northeast of Rome, birthplace of Varro.

RHEA SILVIA: daughter of Numitor, mother of Romulus and Remus by Mars, often called Ilia, i.e. descendant of Ilion, Troy.

RHEGIUM: modern Reggio Calabria, on the Italian side of the Straits of Messina.

RHEGIUM LEPIDUM: modern Reggio (Emilia), seventeen miles northwest of Bologna on the Aemilian Way.

ROSTRA: the speaker's platform in the *comitium* (assembly area) so designated from the beaks of captured ships that decorated it.

RUMINAL: relating to an obscure goddess Rumina who was connected with suckling (*ruma* = 'breast'). For this reason the term refers to Romulus' and Remus' being suckled by a she-wolf.

RUTULIANS: the Rutuli, the traditional name given to the people in central Italy south of Rome. Their capital was Ardea.

SABINE: the Italic people who occupied an extended area northeast of Rome. The Sabines competed and warred with the early Romans for control of the hills in and around the city.

SACRED WAY: the main avenue in the Roman forum that leads eastwardly to a small hill called the Velia.

SAGUNTUM: a Spanish city near the Ebro, whose siege and capture by Hannibal in 219 initiated the Second Punic War.

SALII: priests of Mars (originally Quirinus) whose ritual include an elaborate dance and a yearly sacred banquet of sumptuous proportions.

SAMNIUM: region of central Italy; the area of the Samnites, an Italic people who spoke Oscan.

SASERNA: 1) Sr. and 2) Jr. authors in the early first century of a lost work on agriculture often referred to by Varro.

SCIPIO: 1) Publius Cornelius Scipio Africanus Maior, the conqueror of Hannibal. Scipio assumed command of Roman forces near the close of the Second Punic War and led an invasion into North Africa. He met and defeated Hannibal and the Carthaginians at Zama in 202. 2) Publius Cornelius Scipio Africanus Minor, often called Aemilianus to distinguish him from his namesake # 1. Adopted from the Aemilian family Aemilianus was the supreme commander in the Third Punic War (149-146). He defeated Carthage in that war and razed the city. 3) Publius Cornelius Scipio, father of # 1 who defeated Hannibal at Zama in 202. He was consul of 218 and lost two battles against Hannibal in northwest Italy, the first at Ticino, and the second at the Trebia.

SCOPINUS: of Syracuse, invented a type of sundial.

SCROFA, GNAEUS TREMELIUS: colleague and friend of Varro; after a solid political career, he wrote a treatise on agriculture.

SEMENTIVAE: a country festival celebrated shortly after the sowing of seed; it was set up and arranged by Roman priests.

SEPTIMIUS: a friend of Cicero and Atticus whose daughter Septimia had an affair with Antony.

SESTERCES: unit of currency whose modern equivalent is difficult to assess. The following may be used as a guideline: a Roman legionnaire received 900 sesterces per year; an equestrian had to have a property evaluation worth 400,000 sesterces, and a senator had to meet an evaluation of 1,000,000 sesterces.

SEXTUS PEDUCAEUS: an associate of Atticus who was a friendly critic of Cicero's literary work.

SICCA: a friend of Cicero whose wife, Septimia, had an affair with Antony.

SILENUS: of Sicily, like Sosylus, a historian of Hannibal's campaigns.

SMYRNA: famous Ionian city on the western coast of Asia Minor, modern Izmir.

SOSYLUS: a Greek historian who wrote a history of Hannibal's campaigns. He had accompanied the general as *de facto* official historian.

STOLO, GAIUS LICINIUS: friend of Varro, who was an expert on the practice and theory of agriculture.

SULLA, LUCIUS CORNELIUS: ruthless winning general of the Civil War (83-81) against the Marians. Although Sulla instituted some positive political reforms, his proscriptions and confiscations during his dictatorship (81-80) earned him opprobrium. Writers of the Augustan age often decried the horror of the civil war between Marians and Sulla and its subsequent massacres.

SULPICIUS: Publius Sulpicius Rufus, Tribune of the People in 88. In exchange for Marius' support of his political program, he had the command against Mithradates VI transferred from Sulla to Marius. After Sulla marched on Rome, Sulpicius was captured and executed.

SULPICIUS: Servius Sulpicius Galba, supporter of Julius Caesar who joined in the conspiracy against him; he fought under Pansa at the Battle of Mutina.

SULPICIUS: Servius Sulpicius Rufus, friend and contemporary of Cicero, consul in 51. He joined Pompey but was pardoned after Pharsalus. He was a distinguished jurist.

SYBARIS: a wealthy Greek city in southern Italy destroyed in 510 but refounded as an Athenian colony in 444/3.

SYRACUSE: the great coastal city of southeastern Sicily.

TARENTUM: modern Taranto, wealthy city on the inner "heel" of Italy.

TARQUINII: preeminent Etruscan city about 55 miles north of Rome. According to legend it was the home of the Tarquin immigrants who ruled Rome, beginning with Lucius Tarquinius Priscus, the fifth king of Rome.

TAUROMINIUM: city on the eastern coast of Sicily, south of Messana (Messina).

TEANUM: a town in Campania near Cales.

THEOPHRASTUS: (ca. 371-287), student of Aristotle who directed the Lyceum after Aristotle's death. He was a prolific writer on philosophy, politics, and natural science, particularly botany.

TIBERIUS CLAUDIUS NERO: the son of Livia, wife of Augustus, consul in 13; adopted by Augustus in 4 CE, he became emperor upon Augustus' death in 14 CE.

TIBERIUS SEMPRONIUS LONGUS: consular colleague of Publius Cornelius Scipio (#3 above) who lost the battle with Hannibal at the river Trebia (218).

TIBUR: modern Tivoli about twenty miles northeast of Rome in Sabine territory.

TORQUATUS, AULUS MANLIUS: a supporter of Pompey who lived in exile in Athens after Pharsalus; he was allowed to return to Italy.

TORQUATUS, LUCIUS MANLIUS: a friend of both Cicero and Atticus who died in Africa (46) during the Alexandrine War of Julius Caesar. He was also a poet of erotic verse.

TRASIMENE: a lake in Umbria, site of a major Roman defeat dealt by Hannibal on 21 June, 217. Gaius Flaminius, the consul, died in the battle.

TREBONIUS, GAIUS: although a partisan of Julius Caesar and consul in 45, he joined the conspiracy against Caesar. As proconsul of Asia in 43 he was captured and executed by Dolabella.

TREBATIUS: Gaius Trebatius Testa, friend and correspondent of Cicero who supported Julius Caesar. He was a prominent jurist and befriended Horace.

TREBIA: a river flowing into the Po near modern Piacenza, the site of a battle with Hannibal in 218.

TRIBE: a political and geographical division of the Roman voting body. All Romans registered into one of the thirty-five tribes, four of which were located in the city proper, the others in rural areas. They elected some magistrates and could pass legislation proposed by tribunes.

TRIBUNES OF THE PEOPLE: a group of ten men originally appointed to protect plebeians from the capricious power of patricians. Tribunes had the power to initiate legislation and to veto any measure of public transaction, including senatorial laws.

TRIBUNES OF THE MILITARY: six senior officers of the legion who had at least five years military experience. They were generally young, the sons of either equestrians or senators.

TRIBUNES OF THE TREASURY: a class of citizens with a property qualification lower than the equestrians. By a law of 70 they served on juries with an equal number of senators and equestrians.

TRIBUNICIAN POWER: the term denoting the power of the tribune exercised by Augustus without serving the office. Both the power and title were instituted in 23 BCE and were extended yearly.

TRIUMVIR: a member of the "three man" rule; the term refers to the coalition of Octavian, Antony, and Lepidus, formally recognized and constituted by law in November 43 giving dictatorial powers to the members. The power of this triumvirate expired on 1 January, 32.

TURNUS: Rutulian king who led the Italic opposition against Aeneas and the Trojan immigrants.

TUSCULUM: a town south of Rome near modern Frascati, where Cicero had a villa.

VALERIUS, PUBLIUS: an equestrian who collected state taxes.

VARRO, MARCUS TERENTIUS: (116-27) after a distinguished military and political career under Pompey the Great, he devoted himself to literary and scholarly pursuits after Pharsalus. He was the foremost scholar of his time, writing many works of which, however, only a few survive; they include three books on *The Latin Language* and three books *On Agriculture*.

VEII: important Etruscan city ten miles north of Rome, a rival of Rome for the control of the lower Tiber and its lands.

VELIA: ancient Elea, a Greek city south of Naples that was a center of philosophy associated with Xenophanes and Parmenides.

VESTAL VIRGIN: one of six priestesses in service to the goddess Vesta. Their main duty was to keep the eternal flame burning in the shrine of the goddess. They had to maintain strict celibacy.

VESTINUS, GAIUS CATIUS: a military tribune of Antony.

VESUVIUS: the famous volcanic mountain peak in the Bay of Naples in Campania.

VINICIUS, MARCUS: consul of 19 who had a distinguished and long military career.

VOCONTII: a people of southern Gaul between the Rhone and the Alps.

VOLSCIANS: Volsci, a people of ancient Italy who occupied southern Latium.

VULSO, GNAEUS MANLIUS: consular general who defeated the Galatians in 189. In the following year he concluded peace with the defeated Antiochus III at Apamea.

XENOPHON: prolific Athenian historian of the fifth and fourth century. In his *Hellanika* he continued Thucydides' work on the Peloponnesian War.

ZAMA: site near Carthage where Publius Cornelius Scipio defeated Hannibal in 202, effectively bringing the Second Punic War to an end.

Suggested Further Reading

GENERAL

Chisholm, Kitty, and Ferguson, John. *Rome: The Augustan Age* (New York: Oxford University Press) 1991

Galinsky, Karl. *Augustan Culture: An Interpretive Introduction* (Princeton: Princeton University Press) 1996

Gurval, Robert Alan. *Actium and Augustus: The Politics and Emotions of Civil War* (Ann Arbor: University of Michigan Press) 1995

Raaflaub, Kurt A., and Toher, Mark. *Between Republic and Empire: Interpretations of Augustus and His Principate* (Berkeley: University of California Press) 1990

Southern, Pat. *Augustus* (New York: Routledge) 1998

Syme, Ronald. *The Roman Revolution* (New York: Oxford University Press) 1960

Wallace-Hadrill, Andrew. *Augustan Rome* (London: Bristol Classical Press) 1993

Zanker, Paul. *The Power of Images in the Age of Augustus*, trans. by Alan Shapiro (Ann Arbor: University of Michigan Press) 1988

RES GESTAE

Brunt, P. A., and Moore, J. M. *Res Gestae Divi Augustus: The Achievements of the Divine Augustus* (New York: Oxford University Press) 1967

CICERO

Fuhrmann, Manfred. *Cicero and the Roman Republic*, trans. by W. E. Yuill (Oxford: Blackwell) 1992

Habicht, Christian. *Cicero the Politician* (Baltimore: John Hopkins University Press) 1990

Lacey, Walter K. *Cicero and the End of the Roman Republic* (London: Hodder & Stoughton) 1978

Shackleton Bailey, D. R. *Cicero* (London: Duckworth) 1971

Shackelton Bailey, D. R. *Cicero's Letters to Atticus*, 7 vols. (Cambridge: Cambridge University Press) 1965-1970

Shackelton Bailey, D. R. *Cicero: Epistulae ad Familiares*, 2 vols. (Cambridge: Cambridge University Press) 1977

Stockton, David L. *Cicero: A Political Biography* (Oxford: Oxford University Press) 1971

SALLUST

Earl, Donald C. *The Political Thought of Sallust* (Cambridge: Cambridge University Press) 1961

Syme, Ronald. *Sallust* (Berkeley: University of California Press) 1964

Wistrand, Erik. *Sallust on Judicial Murders in Rome: A Philological and Historical Study* (Goteborg: Goteborg University Press) 1968

CORNELIUS NEPOS

Horsfall, Nicholas. *Cornelius Nepos: A Selection, including the lives of CATO and ATTICUS* (Oxford: Oxford University Press) 1989

VITRUVIUS

McEwen, Indra Kagis. *Vitruvius: Writing the Body of Architecture* (Cambridge, Massachusetts: MIT Press) 2003

Rowland, Ingrid D., and Howe, Thomas Noble. *Vitruvius: Ten Books on Architecture* (Cambridge: Cambridge University Press) 1999

LIVY

Dorey, T[homas] A. *Livy* (Toronto: Toronto University Press) 1971

Felderr, Andrew. *Spectacle and Society in Livy's History* (Berkeley: University of California Press) 1998

Luce, T[orrey] James. *Livy: The Composition of His History* (Princeton: Princeton University Press) 1977

Miles, Gary B. *Livy: Reconstructing Early Rome* (Ithaca, N.Y.: Cornell University Press) 1995

Walsh, P[atrick] G[erard]. *Livy: His Historical Aims and Methods* (Cambridge: Cambridge University Press) 1961